I0769130

The *Trouble: Girl Detective* mystery series

My Name is Trouble

Trouble Always Finds Me

Trouble Takes a Holiday

Game On, Trouble

Trouble to the Last Drop

Trouble to the
Last Drop

JAMES TAYLOR

story by JAMES TAYLOR & MARCO SPARKS

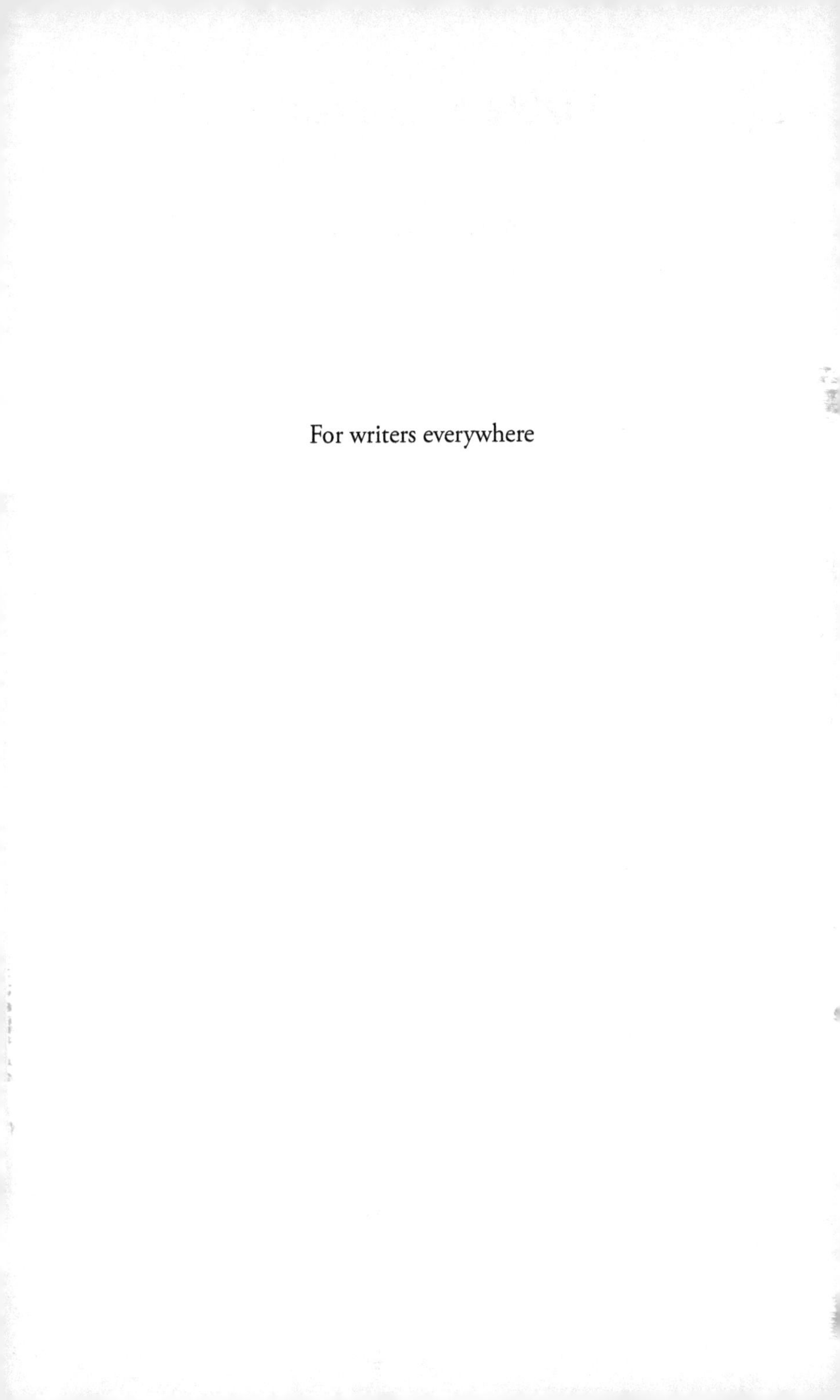
For writers everywhere

Table of Contents

Chapter One
A Movie Script Ending
1

Chapter Two
Hunted
13

Chapter Three
Ms. Bolívar
23

Chapter Four
Tierce and Steele
36

Chapter Five
Duck Amuck (Eliza's Tale)
48

Chapter Six
Silence Is Golden
58

Chapter Seven
Secret
69

Chapter Eight
The Troublemakers
81

Chapter Nine
Hospital Blues
95

Chapter Ten
Three's a Crowd
108

Chapter Eleven
And Introducing...
119

Chapter Twelve
One Surprise After Another
132

Chapter Thirteen
Tunes for Mister Valentine
142

Chapter Fourteen
Safari West
155

Chapter Fifteen
Jumping to Conclusions
166

Chapter Sixteen
Fan Fiction
178

Chapter Seventeen
Vital Signs
189

Chapter Eighteen
Déjà Vu
198

Chapter Nineteen
An Honest Woman
210

Chapter Twenty
Calistoga College
222

Chapter Twenty-One
Serendipity
236

Chapter Twenty-Two
Minutemen Mail
247

Chapter Twenty-Three
Blown
261

Chapter Twenty-Four
Parallel Construction
270

Chapter Twenty-Five
Deadly Force Authorized
281

Chapter Twenty-Six
This Thing Might Go All the Way to the Top!
289

Chapter Twenty-Seven
The Wine Train
301

Chapter Twenty-Eight
You Come in Bruised
313

Chapter Twenty-Nine
Teacher's Pet
328

Chapter Thirty
Paintball
344

Chapter Thirty-One
A Wolf in Sheep's Clothing
355

Chapter Thirty-Two
The Rake's Song
368

Chapter Thirty-Three
Killroy Is Here
379

Chapter Thirty-Four
Goodbye Stranger
388

Epilogue
404

Dramatis Personae

The Decedent

RJ Valentine ....Mystery Novelist

The Heirs

Jennifer Trouble Valentine .... Girl Detective
Alicia Aaron .... High School Senior, Author (deceased?)
Blake Lockhart .... Blackbird Springs Sheriff
Declan Dillion ....Entrepreneur (deceased)
Jack Valentine .... Trouble's Half-brother
Valerie Valentine .... RJ's Widow
Yvonne Griffin ....Editor in Chief of the Blackbird Times

The Rest

Elizabeth Danger Valentine ....Trouble's Secret Twin
Shelly Onishi .... Trouble's Aunt
Drew Porter .... Trouble's Sidekick
Penny Griffin ....Valedictorian
Dinah Black...Trouble's Girlfriend
Victoria "Tori" Valentine .... Val's Daughter
Jimmy Figg ....Nerd
David Tierce .... FBI Special Agent
Bic Steele... FBI Special Agent

Zoey Cartright.....................................FBI Special Agent (undercover)
Dalton Doyle .... Paramedic
Mirai Bolívar .... Drew's Mother
Richard Carter..Vice Principal
Jeffrey Jordan .... Housing Activist
Asha Chowdhury.................................. Former Pixeldrome Employee
Rob Haines.....................................Pixeldrome Proprietor (deceased)
Tony Kobayashi .... Lawyer
Hector Villanova... Mayor
Lambert ....Private Detective

The Stranger ....A Tall, Dark, and Strangesome Menace (Beware!)

TROUBLE AWAITS...

Chapter One
A Movie Script Ending

RJ Valentine's final manuscript, bequeathed to the one who solved his murder, opened with a surprising wrinkle: Trouble, the pint-sized Girl Detective with a penchant for mischief, had finally grown up.

I Dream of Trouble

Chapter 1

The Poison Pen is dead. I just spent an hour rearranging the Staff Favorites shelf by color, without a single customer asking for help. Finally, Mrs. Carnegie relents and says we can close early, which is how I find myself unexpectedly free on a Friday evening. The weather is unseasonably warm for Blackbird Springs in April, warm enough to ditch my purple hoodie and let the humid air from the hot springs tickle my bare arms. I head across the park lawn in Town Square to see if the girlies at the Basque want to hang. Gusts of wind keep blowing out my matches before I can light a cigarette.

"Ya know, those things will kill you, Trouble," says Jack.

My half-brother appears at my side with a Zippo lighter.

"So I hear," I say, letting him light me up.

I've only known Jack a year—since Dad remarried an old flame. Kinda weird to learn at sixteen that you've got a sibling you never knew about, but Jack is all right. Bit of a fancy boy. Annoyingly tall. His mother has money. His mother hates me.

"Off early?" he asks.

"Was thinking about going to the movies."

"What movie?"

I shrug and take a drag. He nods and turns his face into the wind, letting it ripple his chestnut hair. We share a smoke. We share the same cheekbones, too, but his eyes are a deep, melancholy blue.

"Something dumb," I say. "Something with kissing and explosions and dinosaurs. And no murder."

"It's been six years, Jenny."

Six years since the Stranger, my arch-nemesis, threatened to end my sleuthing career for good—and then disappeared without a trace. Sometimes, it feels like a dream. Did it really happen? Was it all in my head?

I used to be a human lie detector. Now I can't even tell if a girl likes me.

I let him kill the last of the dart, and he flings the stub into the bushes.

"I'll handle the girls. Why don't you find Mason and the boys and meet us at the Ryalto," I say.

Somehow, I get stuck in the worst seat, even though this movie was my idea. I'm at the end of the row, one seat from the aisle. Penny's on my left, sharing her Mike and Ikes and laughing at jokes a half-second before the others. She's sharp like that. I already can't concentrate on the plot, and then, fifteen minutes into the movie, some weird guy takes the last seat on my right.

I try not to turn and gawk. He's got his hood up, I think. He smells like gin and turpentine. Every breath he takes comes with a wheeze that only I can hear. At some point, out of the corner of my vision, I sense his head rotating my way. I refuse to look, my eyes locked on the screen.

Forty-five minutes later, the man gets up and leaves. My intuition says he won't return. Penny offers me the last Mike and Ike. The oafish protagonist shares a kiss with the ingenue. She can do better. The climactic third-act chase is kicking into gear when the man surprises me by returning.

Except it's not the same guy.

I never saw the first man's face. I didn't mark what he was wearing. But I *know*—I'd know even blindfolded—that this isn't him. He doesn't smell the same, he doesn't breathe the same. He doesn't *feel* the same.

I steal a glance. Nothing but a black silhouette—his hood is up, too. There's something familiar, though… My whole body shivers, and I'm not sure why. Is my Girl Detective intuition coming back?

I sit in rapt silence through the rest of the movie. Anyone watching might think I was captivated by the story. I'm actually easing the box cutter from my back pocket a centimeter at a time.

A satisfying explosion annihilates the bad guy, and the hero throws his arm around the girl. They've saved the world and have a pet dinosaur now. One last sight gag with the comic relief sidekick, then a hopeful shot of the horizon. Her head on his shoulder, a movie script ending.

The patrons are leaving, but the man on my right sits silent and still.

I don't want to get up. I want to wait the man out.

"Wait, I heard there's a post-credits scene," I say.

Penny passes it down the line as my classmates rise and pick out their wedgies. We all wait for the bonus scene.

The credits end. There is no final stinger. The production company logo comes up, and the lights turn on.

"Bad intel, sis," says Jack.

The man stays seated. One by one, everyone files out of the theater until it's my turn to leave. I steal a glance as I pass, and this time, I get a glimpse of his chin—*her* chin. It's a girl! I'm sure of it. But then I'm past her, at the auditorium doors, exiting to the lobby.

My classmates have gathered by the arcade. Mason and Meghan want to hit the taqueria. I stall, keeping the conversation on the movie, one eye on the auditorium doors. The girl will have to leave sooner or later, and then I can get a better look at her.

Dinah Black says something, and my ears are burning. I look back, realizing I've been asked a question.

"I said, quit deflecting and tell us what you think," Dinah says.

That's a loaded question, Miss Black! Sometimes, it feels like she hates me. But she's always talking to me.

It's been five minutes. Surely, the cleaning staff would have kicked the girl out by now—wait! She might have left through the back exit! Damnit! I need to know.

"In a second, I have to check on something," I say.

My gait is casual but determined. Dinah follows me, her longer strides outpacing mine as I return to the auditorium.

"What's up?" she asks.

"I don't know."

A lone member of the cleaning staff is sweeping the back row. Closer to the front, the hooded figure remains seated where I left her—no, *him*! It's not the girl anymore, it's the man from before! I can tell from the smell. He waits, motionless, his eyes hidden under his protruding hood. He's too patient. Too still. I walk over and push the hood back.

Dinah shrieks.

The man's eyes have been carved out, leaving bloody sockets behind. Two red maws, peering into my soul. I check his pulse. He's dead. The blood, like tears streaking his cheeks, is already dry.

There's a commotion around me. My classmates rush in. The theater employee is panicking. I tune them out. There's something in the dead man's mouth. A paper card clenched between his teeth.

I'm not prepared. Trouble would have a latex glove in her pocket for a situation like this. I have to settle for covering my fingers in a shirttail and worrying the card free of the dead man's bite. But it's a formality at this point. I almost don't even need to look.

I MISSED YOU TOO

And then a little drawing of a man in a hat, peeking over a fence. I could almost cry. I knew I didn't dream it. He was real. It did happen. Welcome back, Stranger.

THE STORY STOPPED THERE, WITH NOTHING MORE TO READ—EXCEPT a postscript in blocky handwriting:

WANT TO READ MORE? START TAKING THE GAME A LITTLE MORE SERIOUSLY. YOU'RE RUNNING OUT OF TIME.

Jenny Valentine was short on more than just time. She didn't have a dollar to her name, and the police would arrest her if she went home. The Pixeldrome VIP room, in the basement of the arcade, had seemed like a safe place to hide—until Jenny found the owner, Rob Haines, dead on the couch. Choked on his own golden game tokens, courtesy of her arch-nemesis: the Stranger.

An endless stream of '80s pop music played on the sound system of Pixeldrome's VIP room. Jenny slumped into the leather recliner opposite Rob's corpse, too exhausted to contemplate how she could be taking her father RJ Valentine's dangerous game any more seriously. Solve the famous author's murder using one of the seven heirloom clues he left in his will and win his fortune. Sure, how hard could it be? Dad neglected to mention that his killer—performing the villain role from his *Trouble* books—would be playing a game of their own. One which frequently involved attacking the people in Jenny's orbit, friends and enemies alike.

With a distant pop, the air conditioner switched back on. She shivered. There'd never been time to zip up the back of the cocktail dress she'd thrown on. Her shoes were who knew where. Probably discarded in the carnage at Valentine Manor. The sedative she'd taken still had her woozy and lethargic. Her face was smeared with dried blood—Alicia Aaron's blood—to obscure her identity.

Today was her 18th birthday.

She wasn't supposed to be Jenny Valentine at the moment. She was posing as Kazumi Onishi, Jenny's mercurial, distant cousin from Okinawa. The one who the police handcuffed to a stretcher after finding her unconscious at the scene of a triple murder. It was a role her secret twin Eliza Valentine normally filled, but a role Jenny had insisted on taking over, sending Eliza fleeing to safety in her place.

Why did I? For all Jenny knew, Eliza *was* the Stranger. If they hadn't already, the police would soon link the little kunai dagger Kazumi/ Eliza was known to carry to the one plunged into poor Mason Lockhart's chest, after it slit Meghan May's throat.

Eliza, whom Jenny had found in Dad's study, surrounded by the bodies of their friends. Eliza, who'd somehow secretly met with Dad before his death—and never mentioned it to Jenny in a year and a half...

Or could the Stranger be Jenny's ex, Dinah Black? An ex who'd been so eager to rekindle their spark earlier tonight but was conveniently absent when the murders occurred. Dinah's initials **DEB** had been entered as the new top score on the nearby *Mystery Girl* video game after Rob was killed: as clear a calling card from the Stranger as the manuscript pages of *I Dream of Trouble* in Rob's lifeless lap. But was the high score Dinah's way of telling on herself? Or was it a setup from someone who wanted to frame her?

Eliza never much liked Dinah; she would have gladly set up the girl whom she derisively referred to as "Blondie."

Jenny's half-brother Jack used to date Dinah. He was debatably a sociopath. Could he still bear Dinah ill will?

Dinah had always been rivals with Penny Griffin for Valedictorian. Were the **DEB** initials a final "fuck you" from the brilliant Penny, having orchestrated a double identity as the Stranger so expertly that she never even came up on any suspects lists?

Was Jenny's trusty sidekick Drew jealous of losing Jenny's attention to her old flame?

Could Dinah have been working with a partner, throwing off everyone's alibi—even more than Tori Valentine's revelation about Dad's secret plan to fake his death had already done?

These angles and more were what Jenny *should* have been contemplating in that hellish arcade basement. Instead, the thing that stuck in her craw, the detail she couldn't get out of her head, had nothing to do with tonight's grisly killings. It was Dad's manuscript for the final, unpublished *Trouble* book.

How did he know I was gay?

North of the city, on a bumpy gravel road running into the forest, Eliza Valentine had more important things on her mind. Like trying to guide Sheriff Blake Lockhart to the granddaughter he never knew he had without getting her head blown off.

"You can put that away, you know," she said, leaning away from the pistol he kept aimed at her. "Driving's easier with both hands, and it's not like you're gonna shoot me."

"Jury's still out on that if you're lying, Jenny," said Blake.

He didn't know she was Eliza. He didn't know there *was* an Eliza. She and Jenny were identical twins, able to seamlessly switch places with each other whenever the situation called for it. With Jenny—disguised as Eliza's alter ego, Kazumi—in custody for murder, who knew when they might be able to switch back?

"I'm not lying, Mr. Lockhart," said Eliza. "I promise."

Blake grimaced, wiping his eyes. An hour ago, he'd burst into the study of Valentine Manor to find Mason, his only child, slain at the hands of the Stranger, whom they now assumed to be Kazumi Onishi. Blake lost his wife to cancer a few years back. If Eliza hadn't found him and told him that Mason and Meghan had a child they'd been hiding away, he might not have lived through the night.

The police SUV pulled up to the cabin in the woods and parked.

"They just leave the baby here alone?" Blake asked.

"There's a nanny," said Eliza.

Blake hopped out of the cab, keeping his pistol trained on Eliza as he came around to her side and let her out.

"How could they afford that?" he asked.

"I paid for it," said Eliza.

Out of my stash—fuck! Eliza's Kazumi identity had a good chunk of cash in her bank account. That was probably going to be frozen any minute now. They walked to the cabin door in near pitch black, the waning crescent moon providing scant illumination amidst the passing storm clouds above.

"You'll scare the nanny if you keep that thing out," she said.

Blake tucked the gun behind him. With Eliza's hands manacled behind her back, it fell to him to rap his knuckles on the door. It took the nanny a couple of minutes to answer; she'd been sleeping and didn't immediately react to Blake's presence in her drowsy state.

"Hi Gabi, something's happened to Meghan and Mason," Eliza told her. "Something bad. This is Mason's father."

A shadow fell over the nanny's face.

"Are they…" the nanny asked.

One look at Blake was all the confirmation she needed.

"He needs to see the baby," said Eliza.

The nanny nodded grimly and signaled for them to wait. Beside her, Blake tensed.

I suppose if I were lying, this is where I'd spring the trap.

But it wasn't a lie or a trick. The nanny returned with Lilah Lockhart, not yet two years old, her little head crowned with her late grandmother's red tresses. Blake inhaled sharply, swallowing half a sob, and reached out, pleading to hold her. Eliza nodded, and Gabi cautiously handed Lilah over.

It was the look on Blake's face that finally broke her. Hope and grief and love all mixed up in those hooded eyes. Eliza wept. The nanny retreated inside, giving them some privacy.

"Why didn't Mason...?" Blake asked when he'd pulled himself together enough to speak again.

"It wasn't you, I don't think," said Eliza. "It was Meghan's parents. She never said, but there was some kind of abuse there, I got the feeling. They were waiting until Meghan graduated and could move out."

The radio in Blake's pocket crackled to life.

"Boss, we got a problem," came Deputy Calderon's voice.

The spell between grandfather and granddaughter was broken. Blake shifted Lilah into the crook of his arm and pulled out his radio with his spare hand.

"Go ahead?"

"The Kazumi girl never made it to the hospital," said Calderon. "The paramedic claims she got free and overpowered him. Made him drop her off on the south side. She's in the wind."

Eliza inhaled sharply. By Kazumi, they could only mean Jenny. She must have faked an injury, then somehow escaped. And if she was on the south side...

The cabin door reopened, and the nanny stepped out with a suitcase in tow. She reached out and dropped a key into Blake's hand.

"What are you...?" Eliza asked.

"I read the *Blackbird Times*," said the nanny. "I know all about the Stranger. If he came for Mason and Meghan, I want nothing to do with this. I'm sorry."

She hurried off, dragging her suitcase over the rough gravel. Blake's radio crackled again.

"Boss?"

Blake blinked and pressed **TALK** on the radio.

"Right. South side?" he asked. "No, I know where she's going. Get the squad to the Pixeldrome arcade. That's where she'll be hiding."

"Got it," said Calderon. "What's your ETA? Should we wait for you?"

Jenny, you'd better not be there! Don't be foolish!

Damn! There was no way to warn her sister. Jenny's phone was in Eliza's pocket, but she'd destroyed "Kazumi's" when they swapped, in case the cops searched it. Could the nanny deliver a message? Not with Blake watching her like a hawk. Eliza could only watch in frustration as the nanny's little hatchback pulled out of the small concrete driveway and drove away down the wet gravel road. She had to stall.

"You know what Mason would want," Eliza said. She nodded to Lilah. "You can't let George and Sandra May have her. You don't have a car seat, and you won't leave me here with her."

Seconds ticked away.

"Come again, boss? Do we wait?"

"Her name is Lilah, by the way," Eliza said, nodding to the baby. Mason and Meghan named her after Mason's late mother, the love of Blake's life.

The name cut him to the bone, as Eliza knew it would. Blake wiped his nose on his sleeve and pressed **TALK**.

"Don't wait," he said. "Try to take her alive. But if you can't, I'll understand."

Blake opened the cabin door and shoved Eliza inside.

Jenny, if you're at the arcade, you'd better get out now!

A PANG OF URGENCY BROKE THROUGH JENNY'S REVERIE, BRINGING with it an epiphany: the mystery would have to wait. RJ's bizarrely prescient *I Dream of Trouble*, Eliza's deceit, Dinah's high score initials, and the many Stranger suspects: they would all have to chill for a sec. Jenny's hierarchy of needs had narrowed to a single objective: don't get arrested. At a minimum, she needed to stay free until she could find Eliza, resume her identity, and question her sister about what else she'd been hiding. And to do that, Trouble needed resources.

Rob didn't carry any cash in his wallet, but he had a hypebeast credit card made out of chromium. She took that and his phone, too, though the battery was dead. Unfortunately, Rob's feet were too big for her to steal the dead man's boat shoes.

Leaving him to the maggots, Jenny returned upstairs and ransacked Rob's office. First, she plugged his phone into a charger. Next, she found a stash of Pixeldrome T-shirts, throwing on a Men's Extra Small over her cocktail dress. (Of course, Rob didn't stock any in girls' sizes. Dickhead.) There was a set of keys in his desk drawer. Jenny used the little circular one to open up the token machine in the main arcade and score a few hundred bucks, mostly in small bills.

Returning to the office, she stuffed the cash into a Pixeldrome-branded fanny pack, cinched it tight around her waist, and checked on the phone—still not enough juice to boot up. Jenny's eyes danced around the office, searching for anything she could use. Her gaze passed over the police scanner, Rob's computer, the little server for the security cameras…

The cameras! Maybe the Stranger finally screwed up, and she'd have him on tape!

Jenny tapped the trackpad to wake the computer up. *Asha used an app called Alfred…* Once launched, the video monitoring app displayed a grid of black screens—all the cameras had been switched off. In the server archive folder for March 10th, there wasn't a single file. She went back one day: again, empty. Back another day: March 8th had a folder full of video files.

"Must have killed Rob sometime yesterday," Jenny muttered to herself. "Turned off the cameras and deleted the whole day's footage so I couldn't pin down a precise time for the attack. Damn."

Her attention turned to the police scanner.

"What are you saying about me?"

She flipped it on and listened.

"—to secure Pixeldrome. Ready to breach on your signal," came an all-business voice over the scanner.

"Oh fuck!" said Jenny.

She lunged for the trackpad, frantically clicking on each camera. The monitor grid flickered to life, one rectangle after another filling in as the cameras came online. It was even worse than she feared. There had to be a dozen cops gathered at the front and back exits. Jenny was trapped like a rat in a cage. She grabbed Rob's phone and fled from the office.

"Go! Go! Go!" she heard over the scanner, followed swiftly by tremendous pounding at the front and back of the building.

The cops battered the doors down and rushed into the arcade.

Chapter Two

Hunted

J ENNY VALENTINE'S CONTINUED AUTONOMY WAS RELYING AN awful lot on Rob Haines. First, stealing his shit. Then, using his police scanner. And now, Jenny was counting on him to have built his stupid VIP clubhouse in the arcade basement to fire code.

Rob! You fuck! It's my birthday!

Jenny's luck held. At the end of the Club Pixeldrome bar, half hidden by a *Robocop* poster, was the familiar green **EXIT** light. Even more fortuitously, she'd reached the VIP room before the cops forced their way in upstairs. They didn't know she was down here and might not think to check the basement for precious minutes yet.

The emergency exit had one of those **PUSH TO OPEN — ALARM WILL SOUND** bars to open the door. A hindrance to most, but Jenny wasn't the greatest Girl Detective in the world for no reason. This model was defeated by a simple credit card, or, in this case, Alicia Aaron's Pixeldrome membership card. She slid it between the doorjamb and door, depressing the latch without needing to press on the **PUSH TO OPEN** bar. Jenny held her breath and pushed on the door itself.

It swung open without a sound.

Beyond, a dank stairwell climbed to a narrow alley on the north side of the arcade. There wasn't a cop in sight; they must all be at the front entrance. Jenny ran the other way, scampering away on bare feet into the dark alley. On First Street, she stopped short and pressed herself against the brick wall. Just in time: a police SUV rolled by moments later. Jenny held her breath as they passed, then dared to lean out and watch as they drove two blocks down and turned their car perpendicular to block traffic.

"Roadblocks. Shit."

The cops would find Rob Haines's body any second now—if they hadn't already. If they set up their net before Jenny could slip beyond it, she was well and truly fucked. She needed a distraction. Or a ride.

As if answering her call, a dull rumble grew louder on her left. A street cleaner! The bulky vehicle hugged the sidewalk and rolled right past the police SUV, dutifully sweeping the gutter as it went. It would drive right past Jenny's alley; all she needed to do was hop on. This was more Eliza's department, but how hard could it be?

Pretty hard, it turned out. Jenny stepped out and trailed behind as the sweeper passed, intending to leap up and climb aboard in the back where the driver wouldn't see. It took three tries, and her bare legs were pelted with a million tiny pieces of gravel and debris kicked up by the whirling sweeper wheels before she got a solid handhold. Summoning core strength she didn't know she possessed, she pulled herself up onto the roof of the vehicle and lay flat, wincing in pain.

Surely, someone had seen. Surely, the driver had felt a passenger come aboard. Jenny clenched up, waiting for the sign that she'd been found out. The street sweeper slowed but didn't stop. Jenny chanced a peek over the driver's side. They were passing by another police SUV. A cop stood beside his patrol vehicle and waved the sweeper on, too bored to glance up and examine the top of the sweeper.

That's what you get for underestimating me!

Jenny couldn't wait to tell Lizzy about this—just as soon as she finished interrogating her. She rode atop the street cleaner for another four blocks until she was sure she was beyond any perimeter the cops set up to contain her. When the driver stopped at a light, she dropped down from the back (Ouch! Her poor feet!) and made for the nearest alley.

Okay, she'd made her great escape—for the second time tonight. Now what? Her mind returned to Dad's manuscript. Trouble Valentine, a teenager at last. Already, Jenny could feel the pull of her fictional counterpart. Was her brain trying to rewire itself to match Book Trouble's emotional state, or was she forcing the character to fit into a Jenny-shaped box?

She'd seemed so sad, just like me…

Jenny couldn't explain it rationally, but it felt important— *essential!*—that she read on. The Stranger was promising more manuscript pages if she played the game to his liking. Like any paperback mystery villain, he (she?) wanted to be caught. They were dying to get to the best part of the story: the big reveal. They wanted to gloat about their genius.

So be it. Jenny was happy to oblige, but she needed her clues and research and supplies. The cops might already be raiding her bedroom, and the Stranger had stolen her heirloom photo. But there was one other stash of mystery files that might still be unspoiled.

From the south side of Blackbird Springs, it was a hike. She'd have to stick to alleys, back roads, and shadows to get there undetected, making a long journey even longer. Jenny rubbed her sore feet, the soles black from running barefoot on asphalt, and peeked out from the alley. The coast was clear. With renewed vigor, she sprinted across the street, melted back into the shadows, and headed for Drew's house.

BLAKE LOCKHART SAT IN THE CABIN'S OLD OAK ROCKING CHAIR, cooing to his granddaughter, lazily rocking back and forth. It was adorable and heartbreaking. Eliza wanted nothing more than to hug him. She could use one herself. Instead, she was tied to a dining chair, her hands cuffed behind her back.

"Explain it again," Lockhart said. "How did you get into the study? The door was locked."

Eliza grimaced. She and her sister had both been running around the mansion as Jenny tonight, and they hadn't had time to get their stories straight. She didn't know which lie to tell.

"I-I came in through the secret passage, from the conservatory," Eliza said.

"And this was after you split up from Drew?"

"Yes. And, uh, after I ran into Dinah. I heard screams inside the study, and the door was locked, so I went around."

"And that's when you saw the victims? And someone in a black mask?"

In truth, she'd gotten into the study via a heretofore undiscovered secret passage that started in the staff kitchen pantry and ended behind the study fireplace. In the room, there were only bodies—and Jenny. But in the official version of Jenny's story, Eliza didn't exist, so Jenny needed a reason to flee.

"Yes."

"Describe him."

"It was dark, but he was big. Imposing. Like a shadow, but darker," Eliza said. "Black shoes, black jeans, black shirt, black latex gloves, and a big black coat. He had a black mask over his face. Not something hard like plastic; more like a black nylon, but thicker. And a black fedora. I saw him, and I ran back into the passage."

She'd certainly seen the Stranger before, enough to know what he looked like.

"And you don't think it's possible that this person was your cousin Kazumi?" he asked.

"No," said Eliza. "I—I thought she was dead too, until you got that radio call."

"Only injured," said Blake. He narrowed his eyes. "But she seems to have made a miraculous recovery. What happened after you ran?"

"I got back to the conservatory and kept going. All the way to the woods," said Eliza. "I was trying to circle back when I ran into you."

Blake's lip quivered as if suddenly remembering the grief that prompted this interrogation.

"I'm so sorry," she said.

"SHUT UP!" he yelled.

In his arms, Lilah began to cry. Eliza glowered through the pain.

"Don't shout in her ear, you ass!" she hissed at him. "And uncuff me, my shoulders are burning."

The sheriff grumbled and set the baby down on the couch. He came around and unlocked her handcuffs—only to cuff them again in her lap. At least her poor joints had some relief.

"I'm sorry, little buddy, grandpap shouldn't have shouted," Blake said, shifting to simpering baby talk for Lilah. "No, he shouldn't have. He didn't mean to. It's just that your Aunt Trouble has a lot to answer for." He sniffled and wrinkled his nose. "But first, you need a change."

He carried Lilah to the back room to change her diaper. Eliza waited till he was out of sight before pulling Jenny's phone from her front pocket to message Dinah. Explaining everything would take too long; she'd just have to be her sister for a moment.

> **Jenny:** If anyone asks, you went to lie down after we got booze from the study, and I ran into you later, after I split up with Drew.

Blake's radio beeped. Eliza tensed, but there was no sound from the back room. The phone vibrated with Dinah's reply.

> **Dinah:** Jesus Christ, Jenny! Where are you??
>
> **Jenny:** With Blake, can't talk long.
>
> **Dinah:** They're saying Kazumi did it. I don't want to believe it, but after what Tori told us about Eliza…

Eliza hissed, the message hitting her like a physical blow. Tori told you *what??* Her fingers shook as she texted back.

> **Jenny:** I need to know exactly what you told the cops.
>
> **Dinah:** Just that we found Tori in the Archive Room and that someone had attacked her.
>
> **Dinah:** I went for help, and you went back inside.

Eliza bit her lip, afraid to hope. Okay. Okay. This might still be salvageable.

"What's going on out there?" Blake called from down the hall. "It's too quiet."

"Suck a dick, Lockhart!"

That seemed like something Jenny would say. She messaged Dinah back.

> **Jenny**: Got it. Just remember, you went to lie down after getting drinks, and I ran into you later in the hall.
> **Jenny**: On the second floor. Gotta go! Delete this!
> **Dinah**: I'm okay, btw

Whatever, Blondie. Just stick to the damned story.

Eliza deleted the message thread, shoved the phone back into her pocket, and flung herself into the rocking chair just as Blake returned with a freshly changed Lilah.

"Your radio beeped," she said.

He eyed her warily before digging in his pocket for his keys.

"Hands," he ordered.

Eliza was expecting him to cuff her behind her back again, but instead, he freed both her hands—so she could hold Lilah. Only then did he reach for his radio and hit **TALK**.

"Go ahead?" he said.

Oof! Lilah was getting so big! Eliza struggled to properly secure the baby in her left arm. With her right hand, she slapped Blake across the face.

"How dare you interrogate me like that in front of a child!" Eliza screamed at him. "Your own granddaughter!"

Blake was too shocked to retaliate. He tried to glare back, but his face collapsed. That sent Eliza spiraling, too. She flung her arm around his shoulder and buried her face in his broad chest.

"I'm sorry, Blake!" she said between sobs.

She could feel his whole body trembling. Then, pressure on her back as he pulled her and Lilah close. They embraced for a minute or ten. Somewhere in the back of her mind, where Danger loved to disassociate, Eliza finally got it.

Was this what you wanted from RJ, Jenny? He never gave it to me, but maybe for you, he would have.

"Boss, you there?" came Calderon's voice over the speaker. "We got a problem."

Blake grunted, patted Eliza on the back, and pulled away to wipe his damp cheeks.

"What's up?" asked Blake into the receiver.

"We got another 187 at Pixeldrome," said Calderon. "The owner, Rob Haines."

Jenny, you wouldn't! Would you?

"And the girl?" Blake asked.

"We're pretty sure Kazumi was here, but it's weird," said Calderon on the radio. "From the look of it, Rob's been dead for hours. The mayor wants us to put the squeeze on Kazumi's aunt and her school friends. One of 'em might be hiding her."

"Tell the mayor I'll visit her aunt's house and send Darcy and Mack to track down Drew Porter," said Blake. "Last I heard, he and Kazumi were dating."

They were! Eliza couldn't believe they'd slept together earlier that night. That brief bout of passion felt like it happened ten years ago, in a different life.

"Got it," said Calderon. "Uh, Blake, you should know, the mayor is on the warpath. He was pissed you weren't at Pixeldrome. Not that it would have made a difference."

"Understood. You worry about working those crime scenes. I'll worry about Hector," said Blake.

He ended the transmission.

"Home?" Eliza asked.

She could see it in his eyes: he didn't want to. He wanted to be doing something, anything else. Working on the case. Chasing down leads. Writing traffic tickets. Anything that would help him avoid facing his new reality. Eliza did, too.

"We could go back to the mansion," she suggested. "Maybe there's something the police missed."

"No," Blake said. "No, I told Miggy I'd go check on your aunt. Maybe your cousin will turn up there. Go pack the diaper bag for her.

I'll look for a birth certificate."

"Right," said Eliza. She walked to the hallway and paused. "Um. What do I pack in the diaper bag?"

He sighed. "I'll do it. Mason should have her paperwork here somewhere. He's—" His voice caught in his throat. "He was good about stuff like that."

THE JOURNEY TO DREW'S HOUSE TOOK TWO HOURS. EVEN THOUGH the rain had stopped, Jenny was soaked and shivering. A shoeless girl, wearing a T-shirt over a black cocktail dress and toting a neon orange fanny pack, was sure to be memorable to any passing cars. Which meant she'd had to dive into the bushes a dozen times on the trek over, just to be safe. Her feet were killing her.

The lights were off in the main house, and Drew's truck was parked in the driveway. He hadn't driven to the mansion last night; he'd rented them a limo, with Dinah as a surprise addition to the party...

Focus, Trouble!

Jenny hurried over to the detached garage, which Drew had taken over and tricked out with couches, video games, and other boy accessories. She called it his Masturbatorium, a sobriquet he protested. At the door, she realized she'd dropped her lockpick tools somewhere along the way. *Fuck!*

The lock was one of those fancy smart locks with a keypad, so she tried **555789**, Drew's iPhone passcode. It didn't work. *Fuck again!*

Something brushed against her scratched-up leg and meowed. It was Mirai's cat, Trudy. She nudged her head against the door and meowed again.

"I know, I want in too," she told her. "Hold on."

She lifted Trudy and tucked her under one arm. With the other, she hefted a small river rock from a nearby planter and smashed it down onto the smart lock, knocking it right off the door. Drew had tons of her money; he could afford another. Jenny pushed inside and let the cat down. Leaving the lights off, she said, "Hey Siri, Big Board."

A big projector screen began to unroll from the ceiling. *Good job, sidekick!* Taped to the screen's white surface was all of their research. Photos, documents, maps, and red string connecting various suspects, locations, clues, and murders, all tied to the dangerous game Jenny's father RJ Valentine kicked off in his last will and testament.

Seven heirs and seven heirlooms. One, or many, or possibly none of the heirlooms were clues that would lead to Dad's killer. RJ hadn't known for sure—he only knew someone wanted him dead, and the heirloom clues were his best chance at finding the culprit. Well, his second best. Jenny had learned earlier that night from Tori Valentine that RJ's whole heirloom gambit was plan B. He'd meant to fake an attack and a coma, so he could do the investigating himself when everyone thought he was incapacitated. Except something had gone wrong. The killer had gotten to RJ after the ambulance took him to the hospital and attacked him in earnest. The coma was real, and Dad spent three weeks dying, never regaining consciousness.

Jenny stared at the board, noting a Pixeldrome game token taped to a photo of the arcade. A token just like it was a secret eighth heirloom, bequeathed to the Stranger himself (herself?) last autumn. Jenny had only learned from Tori a few hours ago that the whole thing was a trick, an attempt to lure Dad's killer to the arcade. Somehow, the Stranger had seen through it—maybe because RJ blabbed about it to the mysterious new friend he'd been messaging in the weeks before his death. This new friend was likely the Stranger, but they'd been using the Signal app to text, meaning their correspondence was encrypted and untraceable. Tori thought he was texting Jenny, but what if it was Eliza? What if Eliza and Dinah's animosity had been a ruse, and they'd secretly been working together…?

Not now. First things first. She found a charger and plugged in Rob's phone, then set about pulling down all the photos and papers from the Big Board. She stacked each item in order on the couch next to the cat, who was busy bathing herself, unbothered by Jenny's desperate state.

After a few minutes of searching around the Masturbatorium, she found one of Drew's old duffel bags with the extended pouch for a baseball bat, and stuffed the Big Board materials into the main pouch.

She debated taking one of Drew's bats—she could use some kind of weapon for protection, and he had a whole rack of them—but even the lightest Easton ceramic one was too long for a short lady like herself.

She checked Rob's phone. Only 2 percent charged.

The late Arty Porter's workbench and tools were still shoved behind Drew's fancy electronic batting tee gizmo. She surveyed the tools, with a mind for self-defense. A hammer could work, though this one was pretty heavy. She picked up Drew's spring-loaded center punch, recalling the window-breaking rampage she'd committed with it. It was pretty small for a weapon, though. Jenny twirled the little tool in her fingers, considering a socket wrench, when she heard a metallic *chck-chck!* behind her. From watching plenty of movies, she knew what it was: a pump-action shotgun chambering a shell.

"Freeze! Hands up!" a woman's voice shouted. "Turn around."

Jenny did as instructed, the center punch falling from her hand and landing right on her big toe. *Ouch!* She stifled a whimper and slowly turned, dreading to even look. She knew that voice. It wasn't the cops. It was even worse.

"You!" said Drew's mother, Mirai Porter, standing in the doorway.

"Mrs. Porter, I can explain," said Jenny.

Chapter Three

Ms. Bolívar

Mirai Porter wore a simple boatneck dress in forest green, with her face done up in elegant, understated makeup. She was a sommelier by trade and spent most nights classing up the fanciest local restaurants with her boundless knowledge of wine. She must have worked a shift last night and hadn't had a chance to change. Some insane corner of Jenny's mind couldn't help but note that Mirai even made a shotgun seem sophisticated.

"It's Bolívar now," said Mirai, slapping the light switch. "The police are looking for you. What happened to your accent?"

Jenny blinked.

"Oh! I'm not her, sorry," she said. "It's me, Jenny."

Not that it would earn her much leeway. Mirai surely despised Jenny for getting her husband mixed up in Trouble business and killed. She gestured to her hair, and when Mirai didn't shoot her, Jenny pulled off the Kazumi wig. Mirai raised a cultured, European eyebrow, and lowered the shotgun half a centimeter. Jenny considered telling Mrs. Porter that nobody except the sheriff used guns in the *Trouble* books, but thought better of it.

"What happened to your face?" Mirai asked.

Jenny frowned. Mirai walked closer, grabbed one of Drew's PlayStation 5 game discs, and held it bottom-side up to Jenny.

"Jeez!" said Jenny. In the little round mirror, her face was still covered in dried blood from her hasty disguise work at the mansion. "The blood's not mine, it's Alicia Aaron's. RIP."

"She's not dead," said Mirai.

"Oh my god! Really?!"

Jenny's heart soared at the news.

"She's at the hospital, in surgery," said Mirai.

"Meghan and Mason?" Jenny asked, daring to hope.

Mirai gave a sad shake of her head. Damn.

"I just came from there," said Mirai. "That's where Drew and your brother are, praying for Alicia to pull through. They've all been worried sick about you. I only came home because the alarm went off. What happened?"

"I...I don't know," said Jenny. "Everyone was split up, doing a scavenger hunt thing. I knew there was something wrong. Somebody had attacked Tori Valentine in the basement. I told Alicia to hide in the study. I never would have— I didn't—" Every excuse that popped into her head was even more pathetic than the last. This poor woman's husband was dead in no small part to Jenny's existence. "Jesus, I'm so sorry, Mrs. Porter. I've brought so much pain to your family. You have every reason to hate me. Just, please, don't shoot me. Drew wouldn't want that."

Mirai laughed.

"I'm not going to shoot you, niñita," she said, lowering the shotgun. "Eres la hostia! You've got it backward, Jenny Valentine. You didn't inflict yourself on my family, RJ inflicted himself on you. He inflicted himself on Arty, too. And Arty was too proud, too foolish to ask for help. We are both suffering because of them, and it is not on you or me to pay for their sins."

It was a nice thought, and Jenny couldn't appreciate Mirai enough for saying so. She was pretty much the coolest adult Jenny had ever known, and basically who she wanted to be when she grew up. But she was wrong about this. Jenny was Trouble. Which meant it *was* on her. Because it would take a girl named Trouble to catch the Stranger.

"Thank you," said Jenny. "It's very kind of you to say. I um, I came here to collect some case files that Drew was holding for me. I promise I won't involve him any further."

"Bah, Drewboo will do whatever he wants to do, and neither you nor I will talk him out of it, once he sets his mind," said Mirai.

"Does that mean he's going to Arizona State?" Jenny asked, risking a smile.

"He insists it's for the baseball program," Mirai said. She made a gesture to indicate Drew's real attraction to the place (curvy babes) and picked up Trudy from the couch. "What are *you* doing in here?"

"Sorry, she wanted in," said Jenny.

"I got her after Arty passed," said Mirai. "Not nearly as good a cook, but a much better cuddler."

She stroked the cat's silky black fur. Over her shoulder, Jenny saw faint blue light spilling in through the door. It would be dawn soon. She glanced at Rob's phone: 12 percent. That would have to do.

"I should be going," Jenny said. "Um, it would probably be better for both of us if you forgot I was ever here."

"Off to solve the mystery?"

Jenny sighed. "That's the idea. Did Mr. Porter ever say anything at all about RJ? Or leave any hints about the Stranger?"

Mirai bit her lip, thinking.

"Not really, no," she said. "He was never much a fan of your father. Preferred to stay out of his way."

"Before he left for the class trip, did he do anything... weird?" Jenny asked.

"Hmm." Mirai's eyes brightened. "There was one thing."

"What?"

"It's probably nothing," said Mirai. "Last fall, after his death, I received a parking ticket in the mail. It was for Arty's Kawasaki. He'd parked in a loading zone in Downtown Guerneville. The ticket was dated a few days before the trip. I don't know why he would have been there."

Jenny could feel her pulse in her neck. This wasn't nothing. This might be something.

"Do you remember anything about him from that day?" she asked.

"I think it was the day I went to the City to visit a friend," Mirai said. "He could have simply gone for a ride. He liked taking the bike out on the highway now and then, and it gave me a heart attack every time. I might still have the ticket. I try to keep everything for taxes. Would you like to come inside while I look?"

In other circumstances, Jenny would have been suspicious of this sudden benevolence. But she'd be a poor detective if she couldn't read a witness. Mirai was sincere, and Jenny had been wrong to ever think the woman hated her. It was an easy assumption to make, and she'd believed it because she thought she deserved it. There was a lesson there, maybe.

"That would be great," said Jenny.

She hefted the duffel bag and followed the cat, who followed Mirai. The sun would be cresting over the eastern hills any moment now. Alicia Aaron was miraculously still alive. And Jenny might be getting a new clue. All was not yet lost.

"FOUND IT!" ELIZA CALLED FROM THE BACK ROOM. SHE PULLED A folder from the dresser and fanned it open. There, right at the front, was the pink-and-blue birth certificate for Lilah Madeline Lockhart. "It was in the sock drawer."

Blake joined her, loaded down with a jumbo-sized diaper bag and Lilah strapped to his chest in a baby bjorn. He squinted at the document and grunted.

"Who's Madeline?" Eliza asked.

"Dunno." Blake grunted again and cleared his throat. "Look, uh, I'm sorry about earlier—giving you the full Bad Cop routine like that. You've every right to tell Shelly. I'm a mess, kiddo. Maybe I shouldn't be around her right now. Or anyone."

Eliza opened her mouth to perish his thought—and hesitated. She needed to say this in a way Jenny would. But with some Eliza wisdom.

"Why are you so stupid sometimes?" asked Eliza. "No way in hell I'm letting you be alone right now. And if you think I'm gonna talk Shelly into dumping you so you can go sulk, then think again, jackass.

Now, I would never use the word blackmail, so let's just say we've both done some shit that wouldn't make Shelly's life any better if she found out. And someday, probably soon at this rate, I'm gonna need a favor. And you're gonna give it to me."

That last bit came off more like a double entendre than intended. She turned away to hide her glowing cheeks.

"Jesus, Valentine, you might actually be getting smarter," said Blake. "God help us all."

"Don't worry, I'm sure I'll do something monumentally stupid any minute now," said Eliza, thinking of her twin. "Come on, let's go."

Jenny was being very smart right now, thank you very much! Utilizing her scant resources and cultivating allies! Also, Rob's phone still needed to charge.

It'd been over a year since she'd been inside Drew's main house. Arty Porter had made them the most delicious carne asada tacos then. The house was as she remembered it: cozy, earthy, Mediterranean—except Mr. Porter had been replaced by Trudy the cat in many of the picture frames.

"Why don't you clean up while I look," said Mirai.

She set a bottle of rubbing alcohol on the counter and retreated to the den. Jenny sloshed a little antiseptic on a rag and dabbed her raw shin.

"Ahhhh!" she cried out.

"Are you ok?"

"Fine!" Jenny said through tears. "Stings a little."

She rubbed her shins and the soles of her feet, the rubbing alcohol seeping into a thousand microscopic scratches, and told herself she was savoring the pain like a fine glass of *Ressort Rouge*. Trouble was rarely in serious pain in the books. She broke her wrist once in *Trouble Brewing*, but that was mostly an opportunity for her to accessorize with a purple fiberglass cast. Maybe Dad would have Teen Trouble get a little more hardcore in *I Dream of Trouble*…

Once clean, her shins wept tiny beads of blood from a constellation of nicks and cuts. Trudy inched forward to investigate and flicked her tongue out to help.

"Kitty, nooooo!" said Jenny, her body trembling somewhere between laughter and sobs.

Sweet gesture, but Trudy's tongue was like sandpaper on her raw skin. She tore some paper towels off the rack and pressed them against her legs to soak up the blood, then set about washing the blood off her face.

"All right, then?" Mirai asked, returning from the den.

"Pain," said Jenny.

Mirai winced and held up a piece of paper and a pair of flip-flop sandals.

"These are the only shoes I have that will fit you," said Mirai, handing her the sandals. "You're too tiny."

They were big for her feet, but Jenny graciously accepted the sandals and slipped them on.

"It feels like I just shaved my legs with a rusty Bic from 2010," Jenny said.

"A good year, for wine," said Mirai. She put on her reading glasses and held up the paper. "Here we are: near the corner of Third and Mill Street. From July 25th last year."

She handed the ticket over to Jenny. A black-and-white photo was printed on the page, showing a Kawasaki Ninja motorcycle parked at a painted curb.

"Huh. I'll check it out," said Jenny. "I should really be going now, but I can't thank you enough, Mrs. Porter."

"I told you, Bolívar," she said. "I'm back to being Ms. Bolívar again, my maiden name. But you must call me Mirai, Jennifer. Don't make me feel any older."

"Right. Of course," said Jenny. *Bolívar... B...* A stray thought prickled the inside of her skull as she stared at the parking ticket. "Mirai, what's Drew's middle name?"

"That is his middle name," said Mirai. "He didn't tell you? Arturo Andrew Porter. Arturo for Arty, obviously, and Andrew after my favorite uncle. But he always liked 'Drew.' Wanted to be his own man,

I think."

"That sounds like him," said Jenny. Rob's phone was up to 38 percent. More than enough. She unplugged the phone and stood up. "Tell him I said hi, and I'm okay—but also, you never saw me."

"I shall. Perhaps you can do *me* a favor," said Mirai, rising with her. "Let me show you something."

Mirai grabbed a set of keys from the rack by the front door and led Jenny outside. They returned to the detached garage and walked around to the back, where a blue tarp was draped over something stored against the wall. She yanked the tarp away to reveal Arty Porter's pristine and well-maintained Kawasaki Ninja motorcycle.

"Oh, I couldn't!"

"Jenny, I never want to see that damned thing again," said Mirai. "And by the look of your feet, I'm thinking you'd rather not be walking."

From a cabinet next to the motorcycle, she withdrew a full-face motorcycle helmet, murdered out in matte black, just like the Ninja.

"But you must promise me to always wear this when you ride," said Mirai. "And no doing wheelies or anything crazy."

She plopped the Ninja's keys in Jenny's hands, along with the helmet.

"I don't know what to say," said Jenny, blinking back tears.

They embraced, and Jenny was sorry to let go.

"Don't let it be said that Blackbird Springs does not support our favorite daughter," Mirai said with a wink. "Go get 'em, Trouble."

THE MORNING SUN WAS PEEKING THROUGH THE KITCHEN WINDOW at Casa Onishi. Eliza's grandparents would normally be up by now. Jiji with his tea and newspaper, and Baba with her furikake eggs and sudoku. Eliza suspected they were staying in their bedroom this morning to give Shelly and Blake some space. They were both a mess. Blake for obvious reasons, and Shelly on his behalf, and also because Jenny was missing and hiding under an identity wanted for murder, and because suddenly there was a whole-ass *baby* in the middle of her formerly carefree romance.

They huddled on the loveseat in the living room, the baby sleeping symbolically between them. Shelly stroked Blake's hair, occasionally whispering in his ear, trying to get him to eat some Greek yogurt. The grief had finally caught up with him, and tears flowed freely down his stubbled cheeks. Eliza figured they would either get married now or break up within six weeks. She helped herself to some of Jenny's birthday cereal and sat at the kitchen table. Even overcome with grief, she wasn't allowed out of Blake's sight. But with Baba's lavender velvet upholstered couch standing between them, neither he nor Shelly could tell that Eliza had just received a text message from an unknown number.

> **Unknown**:   Switch to Signal. My username is
> sallydraper2003

Eliza felt her pulse race. This could only be her Kiernan Shipka-obsessed sister, right? She shot a furtive glance over at Blake. He and Shelly had their heads together, speaking softly. Eliza was the furthest thing from their minds. Leaving her phone lying flat on the table, she casually used her pinky to navigate to Signal in the App Store and downloaded the special messaging app known for extreme privacy. After creating her username (**dangergranger**), she sent **sallydraper2003** a message.

> **dangergranger**:   How do I know it's you?
> **sallydraper2003**:   You bought me takeout from
> Brick and Flour after I got my
> matching tattoo. Your turn.
> **dangergranger**:   You got mad because I said their
> carne asada fries were just all
> right and too salty.
> **sallydraper2003**:   It's called flavor.
> **dangergranger**:   Don't come home. Blake is here,
> and there's a cop car down the
> street, watching the house.

<pre>
sallydraper2003: Figured so. I need to be Jenny
                  again.
  dangergranger: Not now. Too many eyes on me.
                  I'm skipping class today, but we
                  can do it tomorrow. The usual
                  place.
sallydraper2003: sigh
sallydraper2003: What am I supposed to do until
                  then? I'm outdoors here, and it's
                  supposed to rain tonight.
  dangergranger: You could crash at Charlie's. She
                  left me a key. I could take out
                  the trash and accidentally drop
                  it or something.
sallydraper2003: Nah, people knew about Charlie
                  and Kazu. The cops might think to
                  look there.
</pre>

Eliza bit her lip, thinking. Charlie's condo was out. The treehouse was out because Jenny's delinquent ass burned it down. It was too risky to use Blake's cabin; he might go back there…

<pre>
sallydraper2003: I should have paid more
                  attention to that Fugitive movie
                  Blake made us watch last month.
</pre>

The movies! That was it! Back when Jenny was on house arrest for the first time, before they'd won RJ's game, Eliza had found an empty storeroom above the local movie theater that no one seemed to use. She'd crashed there a few times when the treehouse blew a fuse and the heater stopped working.

<pre>
  dangergranger: Oh! I just remembered. There's
                  an empty storeroom above the
                  Ryalto. It's been a while since
                  I used it, but it might still be
                  free.
</pre>

She texted Jenny instructions on how to get to it. It would require climbing a ladder up the back of the theater, to the roof. Probably fifty feet up. Her sister wasn't great with heights, but this was all Eliza could offer.

sallydraper2003: Ok thanks. If I die it's on your head.

dangergranger: Good luck.

sallydraper2003: Why didn't you tell me you met Dad?

Eliza inhaled sharply. *How did she know?* Something happened to Jenny last night. When she was with Dinah. Was there something in the files they were trying to search?

dangergranger: Not now.

"Jenny?" Shelly called softly from the living room.

dangergranger: Gotta go, will explain later.

sallydraper2003: Fine.

sallydraper2003: I'm destroying this phone. Will see you tomorrow at the place where we met Mason. RIP :(:(:(:(:(:(

With a smooth gesture, Eliza stood up and swiped the phone off the table, tucking it into her back pocket just as Shelly came over to speak with her.

"Hey," Shelly said.

Eliza looked past her aunt to the loveseat. Blake was asleep, with Lilah napping in his lap.

"Good, he needs that," said Eliza.

"I crushed a Valium in his yogurt," said Shelly. She regarded Eliza sternly, one hand on her hip. "I know you're not Jenny. You're being too nice to him."

Eliza blanched. "Jenny has a heart, too, Shells. She's devastated. We both are."

"Where is she?

"I don't know."

"Don't lie to me, Elizabeth," said Shelly.

"She's crashing at Charlie's place," Eliza lied. "Just until we can figure things out. She didn't do it, Shelly. Obviously!"

"That's all the more reason to turn herself in," said Shelly. "Running makes her look guilty."

"The minute the Stranger knows there's a twin, I'm fucked."

"So you girls keep saying. Multiple people are dead, Lizzy. This has gone so far beyond a game."

Eliza rubbed her temples. "Exactly. You've seen what the Stranger will do when he's in a mood. I'm not lying about the danger."

"Isn't Danger your middle name?"

"Right now, it's Trouble, so don't go snitching, Shells, I swear to god!"

Shelly held up her hands in surrender. "I just want you both safe," she said.

"I know," Eliza said. She embraced her aunt in a much-needed hug. "So do I."

What would she tell Jenny, once they were both safe? Eliza would have to burn that bridge when she came to it.

THE RYALTO CINEDOME WAS A RELIC OF A BYGONE ERA. NOT ONLY for being a movie theater, but one borne out of the early '80s, before the multiplex format with a million screens had gained popularity. There were only four screens at the Ryalto, each encased in mauve and tan geodesic dome structures, that looked for all the world like two giant sets of tits. A huge blocky building in the middle housed the lobby and refreshments area, with offices above, and the four domes rising over each corner. It took up a whole city block, not far from Town Square, and was officially the second tallest structure in Blackbird Springs, if you didn't count the high nets at GolfMax.

Jenny tried not to think about this fact while climbing the ladder, some fifty feet up, nearing the roof of the central building. Her mouth was already sour with the threat of nausea.

Don't look down!

The ride here had been almost as terrifying. Even going as slowly as possible, she'd nearly fallen off twice. Motorcycles were decidedly not for Trouble. She'd parked the Ninja behind a dumpster and then used said dumpster to leap up from and grab the last rung of the ladder that led to the roof. Hopefully no one would notice the Ninja—

I told you not to look down, Trouble! Think about anything else!

It turned out that having four massive screens that allowed them to charge premium format prices was pretty advantageous in the current theatrical landscape, which was how this place stayed in business. Maybe someday they'd be showing a *Trouble* movie here...

"Fuck me!" Jenny said, pulling herself onto the theater roof. She had to sit there for a few minutes to master her acrophobia. Some enterprising builder had thought to put in a roof access door up here so employees could dip out for a smoke break. Jenny didn't even have to pick the lock; it was propped open with a brick.

Once inside, she found herself in the middle of a long hallway. To her right: some offices and a staircase that went down to the floor below. Jenny went left, following Eliza's directions to a storeroom at the end of the hall. It was full of old costumes and equipment for theater productions in the park. A thin layer of dust lay atop the boxes and clothing racks. Good. No one had been in here in a while. It was stuffy, though. Jenny cracked one of the small windows set into the far wall and looked out, breathing in the damp air.

It was well into the morning of her birthday. Her classmates would be showing up at school and learning, if they hadn't already, that Meghan May and her boyfriend Mason were murdered at Jack Valentine's party last night. And that Kazumi, the pretty but quirky foreign exchange student cousin who'd been staying with Jenny Valentine, was the prime suspect. And that Kazumi was on the run.

She yawned and tried to focus. This place was a bitch to get to, with no easy way out. If the cops found out she was here, she'd be boned. And it smelled like mothballs. But it was better than sleeping in the woods, and there was a restroom down the hall. She only needed to hide here until tomorrow.

Her eyes drooped closed on their own. She was exhausted. Physically, mentally, and emotionally. Pulling some dusty gowns off a clothing rack, she made herself a little nest, but before she allowed herself to sleep, she pulled out a notepad she'd borrowed from Mirai and made a list.

Leads

- DEB high score = Dinah Eve Black??
- Yvonne's heirloom, *The Stranger of Sausalito* book
- Arty's Parking Ticket
- The Hospital: site of the actual murder?
- The P.I. who worked for Stratford Photography ("Too hot!")

She yawned again, fading fast. She didn't want to do it, but there was one more name she had to add. Until she explained herself.

- Eliza

Chapter Four

Tierce and Steele

T*HE NIGHTMARES WERE WAITING FOR HER, AS SHE KNEW THEY WOULD BE. Images of carnage played in her mind on a loop, forcing her to relive the murders that were all her fault.*

The Stranger was Dinah. The coltish blonde stalked across the study, holding out a caring hand to comfort Alicia, and then punching her in the gut with a dagger. She pushed Alicia aside and ducked down, rifling through the backpack Jenny had given Alicia to hold. Behind her, Meghan and Mason strolled in laughing, heedless to the danger, following their treasure map. Dinah spun and slashed Meghan's throat before she could even react. Mason had time to shout in alarm before Dinah buried the knife in his chest. Meghan collapsed onto the desk, clutching helplessly at her neck as her life drained out...

Or was it her handsome brother, Jack Valentine? The Big Man on Campus and everyone's favorite sociopath. Alicia trusted Jack, the boy of her dreams and fantasies. He asked her for the backpack, dumping it out to reveal Jenny's heirloom photo inside. Alicia looked on, puzzled, as Jack picked it up and tucked it away. Only then did he stick the dagger into her stomach. When Meghan and Mason arrived, he called them over, asking for their help, and stabbed Mason in the front like a true friend—except Jack had no friends, right? He sat Mason down in Dad's chair and took his time with Meghan, bending her back over the desk before dragging a knife across her trachea…

But where was Eliza the whole time? Not with Drew, apparently. She dispatched Alicia without twitching an eye and hid in the shadows until Mason and Meghan rushed in to find the body. When she struck, it was a mortal blow to Mason first, followed by the brutal slash at Meghan's throat, half-decapitating her. Eliza wiped the blood off her knife and returned to the shadows, waiting for Jenny to arrive and witness the carnage.

"It wasn't me," she'd whispered. Why would she say that?

The nightmare shifted. She was in a darkened hallway somewhere— no, an alleyway downtown. Out of the shadows, a large figure stumbled into a sliver of moonlight. It was Drew, wearing his baseball uniform shirt. One of Eliza's knives was sticking out of his back.

"Have you seen Kazumi?" he asked, confused.

Before she could answer, he dropped to his knees and planted his face on the filthy concrete…

All went dark again until Jenny found herself on another nighttime street. Someone was firing a weapon at her, over and over again. She was too numb to feel the impacts. Sirens wailed around her, but they would be far too late to save her—

Jenny shot up with a start, momentarily panicked to find herself in strange surroundings. Why was it so dusty here? She coughed and lunged for the window to get some air. Right, she was in the storeroom above the Ryalto. The sirens from her dreams hadn't stopped. They were still wailing outside. She rubbed her eyes and peered out the window. A half-dozen cop cars had converged on the building across the street. Police were rushing inside.

It was the condo building that Charlie used to live in, Jenny realized. If the cops were swarming, it could only mean they expected to find Kazumi hiding inside. She exhaled a nervous breath. Good thing she'd thought better of crashing there. And if no one was raiding the theater, that meant Eliza hadn't sold her out, at least, right? She got her notebook out and drew a question mark next to her sister's name.

Jiji and Baba had finally come downstairs. They should have stayed in bed.

"You lied to me!" Shelly shouted at Eliza.

"So did you!" said Eliza. "I told you that in confidence! It was a test, and you failed!"

"Would you like me to fail *another* test?" Shelly said, glaring at her. *Okay, chill, Shells!*

"If you know where your cousin is, and you won't tell, I can book you for obstruction," said Blake.

"Well, I don't know, so book yourself!" said Eliza. "You need to be calling off Calderon and your dogs, and searching for the real killer. Kazu just got mixed up in the middle of this shit and ran away terrified. If she hasn't left already, she's probably trying to book a flight back to Okinawa this second."

"I'm sure her parents are quite concerned," said her grandfather, without amusement.

"Let her try, we're watching the airports," said Blake. "We're watching Drew, Jack, Penny Griffin, and anyone else who she might go running to, including you!"

He jabbed a finger at Eliza.

"She—" He gulped, struggling to say the words. "They think she killed a cop's kid. Trust me, it's so much better for her if she turns herself in."

Shelly placed a hand on his shoulder. He covered it with his own and looked back at her.

"I need to get back out there before the mayor throws a shit fit," he said.

"Okay, what about…?" Shelly nodded to Baby Lilah, eating some apple sauce at the kitchen table. Blake raised his eyebrows, a pleading expression. "Oh no! You're not dumping her with me, mister! I am not your nanny."

"Just for a day, please?" said Blake.

"What am I supposed to do if George May shows up?" Shelly asked.

While they argued, Eliza surreptitiously eased her phone out of her back pocket. Jenny wouldn't get this message until she got another phone, but just in case…

> **dangergranger:** Don't trust Shelly. She'll turn
> you in. And don't try to contact
> Drew, Jack, or Penny either.
> They're all being watched.
>
> **dangergranger:** I told them I thought Kazumi
> would have been scared, and
> gone to the airport to go home to
> Okinawa.

There. Wherever Jenny was now, at least she had some warning.

UP IN THE RYALTO'S ATTIC STOREROOM, JENNY HAD ONLY HER wits to rely on. Rob's phone was lying in pieces at the bottom of Nathanson Creek. She'd barely slept an hour and a half, but the police raid across the street had her too wired to go back to bed now. Instead, she watched, waiting until the cops wrapped up shop. Then she got to work.

The theater was open now for early matinees. Not trusting herself on the ladder, Jenny returned to terra firma by way of the stairs. What was it Lambert had told her?

You would be amazed how far you can get by pretending you belong.

There were some black slacks in the costume clothing rack that fit well enough not to fall off. On the second floor, she found an office with spare uniforms and changed into a polyester **Ryalto Cinedome** polo shirt. Then, she simply acted like she belonged and walked out the front door. Her heart leaped into her throat when a cop car rolled by on Broadway, but they were looking for Kazumi Onishi, a taller girl with shoulder-length black hair. Theater employees blended into the landscape, invisible.

The Ninja motorcycle, thankfully, was where she'd left it. She didn't trust herself on the highway, so she rode to a strip mall using side streets. At the Coffee Bean, she shoulder-surfed a brittle blonde woman to get her passcode, and when the woman set her phone down to fix her drink, Jenny quickly lifted it.

She got out of there in a hurry, moving across the parking lot to a Jamba Juice. There, she used the lady's passcode to reset her phone and signed in with a new account. Eliza's message was waiting for her when she logged into Signal.

dangergranger: Don't trust Shelly. She'll turn you in. And don't try to contact Drew, Jack, or Penny either. They're all being watched.

Can't trust anyone, got it.

dangergranger: I told them I thought Kazumi would have been scared, and gone to the airport to go home to Okinawa.

Jenny could work with that, maybe.

sallydraper2003: She was, and she did. RIP Kazumi.

Using Rob's credit card, she ordered some supplies from DoorDash—a red wig, utilitarian coveralls, and black Doc Martens—and had them delivered to a Starbucks in Petaluma. While that order shipped, she went inside Target and purchased two of everything: jeans, Trouble T-shirts, cheap tennis shoes, sunglasses, underwear, makeup, and a new mini backpack. Sadly, not Coach. She threw in some fruit cups, high-protein energy bars, Pocky sticks, bleach, latex gloves, purple hair dye, a box cutter, and heavy-duty zip ties for good measure.

To avoid interacting with anyone, she went to a self-checkout machine, using the cash she'd taken from the arcade to pay for it all. There was a moment of panic when, by force of habit, she punched in a phone number for Target's rewards thing.

Oh fuck! Wait! 707-555-3739? Phew, that's not my number.

It was Asha's, or maybe Drew's. Jenny always used theirs at stores to stymie the algorithm. There was no way the cops were watching their rewards number, right? Still, best not to linger, just in case.

That meant another harrowing motorcycle ride back to the Ryalto. Before she climbed up to her safehouse, she used the stolen phone to book a flight to Tokyo in Kazumi's name from SFO, then she tossed the phone into the bed of a passing fruit truck. That ought to keep the cops busy for a while. Enough for her to focus on the mystery. But first, a costume change.

On the British TV shows Eliza watched, this was what they called a *row*. Shelly and Blake had been at it for ten minutes. Her grandparents gave them both an earful and left for their aquatic fitness class early. But Eliza was stuck holding Baby Lilah, as all her aunt's hopes and anxieties spilled out onto the kitchen table.

"It's not like we never talked about this!" said Blake.

"We talk about a lot of things!" said Shelly. She held up her left hand, displaying her ringless ring finger. "Remember?"

Oh my!

"I'd be a pig if I did that now," said Blake.

"I'm not saying right now!"

"I can't— Michelle, I can't… mentally I can't—"

"I'm sorry, Blake, but you don't have any choice," said Shelly. "I will help you, but you can't treat me like some au pair to pawn your granddaughter off on so you can go self-destruct. I know how bad you were last time. You told me."

"I WAS WORSE!!" Blake thundered.

Eliza tensed. A charged frisson passed between the two. Their relationship stood on the edge of a knife. What happened next would alter it for good or ill.

The doorbell rang.

"I'll get it!" Eliza said, springing up to answer the door.

She sensed the quarreling lovers following behind as she opened the front door to find four grim men waiting on the stoop. The first was Deputy Calderon, Blake's right-hand man. The slick bastard in the expensive suit and greasy hair must be the mayor she'd heard so much about. Behind him were two bland men in government-issue black suits. The bulge under their left arms gave them away as law enforcement.

The mayor frowned at the sight of her.

"Shouldn't she be locked up?" he asked.

"She's clean," said Blake, not too gently pulling Eliza to the side. "It's all in my report. I was just about to head back to the scene. What's up?"

The mayor flashed a bright smile that didn't reach his eyes.

"About that," he said. "I'm sorry, Blake, but you're off the case. Now don't take it personally, you've got your own shit to deal with, and the feds are taking over anyway. Miguel will act as liaison during your *extended* bereavement leave."

"Sorry, boss," said Calderon.

"Well, that settles it!" said Eliza.

One look at Blake's reddening face told her nothing was settled.

"Are you fucking shitting me, Hector?"

"It's not like you haven't had plenty of chances to nip this problem in the bud!" the mayor said.

His eyes flicked over to Eliza for half a second.

What the hell is he implying?

"You're compromised, and I can't have that," said the mayor. "One murder is too many in my quiet little wine hamlet, and I've lost count of what we're up to now. Three in one night!? And no suspect in custody?? You're lucky I don't shitcan your ass on the spot. Rest assured, your stink is not getting on my shoes."

"Just two," said Calderon. "Alicia Aaron pulled through. The doctors say she'll make it."

Eliza clapped her hand over her mouth, stifling a sob. *Thank god.*

"She's a tough kid," said Blake.

"Fucking fabulous," said the mayor. "You're not off the hook!"

"Betty put you up to this, didn't she?" said Shelly. She pushed past Blake to get in the mayor's face. "You've just been waiting for an excuse! His son isn't even in the ground, you son of a—"

"Michelle!" Blake warned.

"I have every excuse! I've had it since last fall, when *this one*"—the mayor jabbed a manicured finger at Eliza—"came back from Austria with two body bags in the luggage. You let Hamilton Webb die right in front of your eyes!"

"That wasn't Blake's fault!" said Eliza.

"Pipe down, you wretched little girl!" said the mayor. "In fact, Agent Tierce, would you mind bringing her in?"

"In due time," said one of the stooges behind the mayor. "We have a process all our own. Booking her now would only slow us down."

The mayor bristled but tried to play it off with another phony smile. "Agents Tierce and Steele here are on loan from Sacramento. They'll be running the show from now on, and I expect your full cooperation while you're on leave."

"Ah, look at that," said Agent Tierce, checking his phone. "Kazumi Onishi just booked a flight to Tokyo on Air Japan. Deputy Calderon, do you mind?"

Calderon gave a sympathetic back-pat to Blake and turned to go.

The mayor grinned. "See, making progress already," he said, gesturing to his new favorites.

The one called Tierce had a wrestler's body with a ruddy complexion and sandy blond hair. His partner Steele was a rangy Black man with a salt-and-pepper push-broom mustache. Both were hiding behind dark sunglasses and placidly smug expressions.

Eliza snorted.

"*Sacramento?* What do these guys know about the Stranger?"

"Is that what you're calling him?" Agent Steele asked, in an unexpectedly high and raspy voice. He grinned tightly. "We try not to fetishize our perps with flashy names. Only encourages them."

The mayor raised his eyebrows like he'd scored a point.

"You can blame my father for that," said Eliza. The spirit of her twin moved within her. "And in case you didn't guess, my name is Trouble. I'll be the one solving the case while you bozos are tripping over your dicks chasing my air-headed cousin to Japan."

Tierce smiled. "My daughter's a huge fan," he said.

"Not mine," said Steele. "She reads those fantasy books where everybody's a fairy or some shit."

"Oh, she'd like Alicia's book. It's coming out soon—"

Shelly covered Eliza's mouth with her hand. "Thanks for nothing, gentlemen. If you'll excuse us, Blake has a granddaughter to care for and a son to grieve." She glared at the mayor. "Say hi to Betty for me."

"We're not done yet," said Tierce. He held out a folded document to Shelly. "We gotta search the place."

"Let's start with your phone," Steele said, holding out his hand.

Fuck.

"Which way to the air-headed cousin's room?" Tierce asked.

Eliza pressed the side and volume buttons on the phone as she handed it over, disabling Face ID. The mayor flashed his perfect smile again.

"Don't say I didn't warn you, Blake," he said. "Oh, and we'll be doing your house next."

Up in the Ryalto attic, Jenny gritted her teeth as the bleach burned into her scalp. She propped open the window to vent the noxious fumes.

Strictly speaking, the dye job wasn't necessary, but the wigs at Target sucked, and Jenny needed to do something more substantial. The world had changed the day she turned eighteen, and she wanted to change with it, to feel the grief burn into her skull. To burn away the bratty child who'd let her depression stall her investigation at that stupid arcade until the Stranger got impatient and killed her friend.

Her eyes watered. What was the message he'd left her?

START TAKING THE GAME A LITTLE MORE SERIOUSLY.

Jenny regarded her transparent reflection in the window. Her brown eyes were black as coals in this light. Grim confidence welled in her breast.

Be careful what you wish for, Killroy.

The FBI turned the Onishi house upside down, moving like a tornado from room to room, taking special delight in emptying every drawer, cabinet, and shelf onto the floor. Already, they'd broken two of Baba's little frog figurines, and Mom's collection of *Ellery Queen* issues was strewn all over Jiji's study. Eliza could only watch helplessly from the kitchen table.

"Still think it's a good idea to trust the cops?" she asked Aunt Shelly.

"Your grandmother is going to hit the roof when she sees what they did to her little Mr. Toad," said Shelly.

"You can file a complaint," said Blake, bouncing Lilah on his knee.

"Will that do anything?" Shelly asked.

"No," he admitted.

A large crash sounded upstairs. Shelly winced. A man shouted. Tierce, Eliza was pretty sure.

"It's okay, that was J—" Eliza caught herself. "Just something I set up in my closet, for exactly this sort of occasion."

Steele stalked in from the front of the house.

"Miss Valentine, I need your face," he said, holding Jenny's phone up to Eliza.

"It's not gonna work," Eliza said.

Sure enough, the phone was demanding a passcode.

"Okay then, I need your code."

"Hm, that's tough," said Eliza. "See, I'm always changing it, and I truly can't remember what I set it to last."

Steele narrowed his eyes.

"I can try a few, but I think it only gives you so many tries before it locks you out permanently," said Eliza. "But you guys have stuff that can crack it in Sacramento, don't you?"

"Cute," said Steele, and pocketed the phone. "You ready to give your statement?"

"I already gave it to him," Eliza said, gesturing to Blake.

"We're gonna need it again," said Steele.

"You're going to have to wait, then," said her grandfather, entering from the hall. He glanced around at the mess—it looked like a bomb had gone off—and locked his crinkly eyes on Steele. "No questioning without a lawyer, you know that. I suggest you observe protocol unless you want my entire law firm slowing you down."

She could see the wheels turning in Steele's head, debating how much he could push Jiji around.

Not much, trust me, dude.

"All the students who were at the party will be interviewed tomorrow at school," said Steele. "Lawyer or no, if they don't talk, the mayor says they'll be expelled."

"She will have a lawyer tomorrow," said Jiji. Baba shrieked from the foyer. "If you'll excuse me, I must prevent a homicide."

The cops carted off boxes of Jenny and "Kazumi's" stuff. None of it would prove useful, Eliza didn't think. They'd find her Kazumi Onishi passport, and would probably figure out it was a fake, but what good would that do them?

After they finished with the Onishi house, it was Blake's turn. Shelly agreed this time to watch Lilah while Blake accompanied the feds. Some sort of understanding had passed between the two lovers since their fight earlier. For Eliza, the rest of the day was spent cleaning up after the feds and documenting every single item they broke. Baba would be sending them a detailed complaint and an invoice.

In the early afternoon, her body remembered it had been up all night and promptly crashed. Shelly let her go lie down, and when she woke up, it was 4:00 AM the following day. She snuck downstairs and used her grandparents' computer to remotely wipe Jenny's phone, then stared out the window, watching the cop car that was watching her, until it was time to get ready for school.

There would be no stopping at the Basque for coffee this morning. Hundreds of flowers and notes had been left in front of the tall sycamores on each side of the main entrance. One tree for Mason and one for Meghan.

"Do you mind?" Eliza asked.

Shelly frowned and pointed across the parking lot to the nondescript car that had followed them here.

"Don't even try leaving," she said. "All they need is an excuse."

Eliza paid her respects to Meghan and Mason before making for a certain ladies' room near the quad. Inside, it appeared empty, so she locked the door.

"Jenny?"

Two feet stepped down from the last stall, and the door swung open. Her sister had dyed her hair bright neon purple and gone heavy on the raccoon eye makeup.

"Come here," said Jenny.

Eliza joined her in the stall and shut the door. Jenny embraced her in a fierce hug. Eliza squeezed back with all her strength, relieved.

Something brushed her wrist and suddenly tightened with a sharp *zzzzip!*

Jenny had zip-tied the two of them together.

"Sorry, but you're not going anywhere until you start talking about Dad," Jenny said.

Chapter Five

Duck Amuck (Eliza's Tale)

T*HE TRAFFIC ON W LOS FELIZ ROAD WAS A CEASELESS CACOPHONY OF squealing brakes, honking horns, and tires grinding on hot asphalt. The busy street was cracked and pitted, desperately in need of repairs. Waves of heat shimmered over the pavement, ready to cook the proverbial egg. People were always talking about LA's great weather, but Glendale, California, in early August was a special kind of hell.*

Glendale Memorial Hospital, on the other hand, stuck out like a glowing white thumb, all bleached concrete and glass in a sea of dirty asphalt and strip malls. Watching from a poorly air-conditioned Burger King across the street, Eliza Valentine wiped a bead of sweat from her forehead and tried to focus on getting inside the Health Center.

"Can I get you anything else?"

The voice belonged to the morning shift lead at the burger joint. He of the greasy blond hair, pock-marked complexion, and deformed left arm, who'd shown a propensity for bossing his co-workers around, and trying to look down Eliza's top every time she placed an order. At the moment, he was taking a break from his one-handed mopping to leer in her direction.

"No, thank you," said Eliza.

"I seen you in here a few times," said the guy. "You new to the area? Need someone to show you around?"

"No, thank you," said Eliza. "I'm meeting someone. My sister."

At least, she was trying to.

"Is she late?"

"No, I am."

Eliza peeled her thighs off the Formica seat and got to her feet. She tossed the detritus from her Croissan'wich into the garbage and braced herself for the heat.

"You didn't tell me your name," said the guy.

"It's Danger," she said, and walked out into an oven.

To be more precise, getting inside Glendale Hospital was easy enough—Eliza had spent almost an hour in the gift shop before they hinted that she should leave—it was getting into the psych ward to meet her sister that had so far flummoxed her. She had a fear, stupid though it may be, that if they caught her, they'd institutionalize her, too, and no amount of "No wait, I'm not Jenny Valentine, I'm her secret twin!" protestations would get her out.

She'd spent nearly a week staking out the hospital, moving between Burger King, a gas station, and a shaded bus stop bench, watching the front entrance, waiting to see if Jenny would get out before she found a way in. Information was sparse, but from cyberstalking students in the area on Facebook, Eliza gathered that Jenny had flipped out and tried to burn down her high school or something.

A few hundred feet down W Los Feliz, across from the hospital parking garage, there was a mini-mall with a car insurance office, a massage place, and a tattoo parlor. It was an L-shaped building, and in the morning hours, the tattoo parlor at the end was shaded from the sun. Eliza had taken to lingering outside it, keeping one eye on the hospital and the other on all the designs in the window. She wanted to get a tattoo, but she couldn't decide on which one.

She had almost worked up the nerve to go inside and talk to the tattoo artist when she heard an odd noise around the corner. It was an electronic ringtone coming out of tinny cell phone speakers. Someone must have been lurking in the alley behind the tattoo parlor.

Except the ringer kept going. No one was answering it.

Curiosity got the better of Eliza. She walked around the side of the mini-mall building and peeked into the alley. It was empty, dead-ending into a chain-link fence.

On the ground, not far from the fence, was the ringing cell phone.

"Someone drop their phone?" she called out.

There was no one around to answer. She walked to the end of the alley and picked up the phone. Someone was calling from a 707 number. Wasn't that the Blackbird Springs area code?

The thought barely registered before a strong hand pressed over her mouth, and she felt a sharp sting in the side of her neck. A cold sensation blossomed at the point of the sting, and she fell into a dreamless sleep.

WHEN ELIZA CAME TO, SHE WAS LYING FACE DOWN ON THE ASPHALT. Consciousness slowly returned, her brain rebooting after a hard reset. The first thought to pierce through her brain fog was that this asphalt was surprisingly pleasant. It wasn't the cracked and baking pavement of W Los Feliz Road, reeking of petrol and exhaust. The blacktop was smooth and warm against her cheek, and her nose filled with the sweet aromas of verdant vegetation. She raised a heavy eyelid and took in her surroundings.

A blur of black and green and blue coalesced into a pristine driveway, a lush garden lawn, and a picturesque azure sky dappled with fluffy white clouds. It was like waking up in a fairy tale.

Did I get my owl?

Eliza pushed herself to her feet. A brief pat down confirmed that her body was intact and undisturbed. She was on a roundabout driveway that circled a quaint (probably fake) wishing well. To her left, the driveway curved back into rows of grapevines. To her right, the pavement ended at the steps of an ostentatious portico entrance to a Mediterranean-style mansion.

Eliza's heart sank. "Oh. Him."

She was pretty sure she knew where she was, though she'd only seen this mansion from a bird's eye view on her Maps app. Valentine Manor, home of the mercurial and mysterious author behind the world-renowned

Trouble: Girl Detective *mystery series, RJ Valentine. Her father. His prodigal daughter had been brought home—400 miles north in the blink of an eye—but, for some reason, deposited on the driveway?? What the hell was going on?*

Only one way to find out. She crossed the roundabout and walked up the coral flagstone steps. The plaque next to the door left no doubt.

Valentine Manor
310 Cellar Drive

She reached out with a jittery hand and rang the doorbell. The door swung open before the ring chime finished sounding. There was no one behind it to greet her.

"Hello?"

Her voice echoed in the huge foyer. Across the wide hall, a double staircase rose to a grand balustrade lining the second floor. Everywhere she looked, wealth sparkled.

"Please, come in," said a male voice.

It had come out of an intercom panel next to the doorbell. Eliza cautiously stepped inside and shut the door behind her. She waited inside for an escort that didn't arrive.

"Now what?" she asked.

"I'm in the study, Elizabeth," said the man. His voice was high and clipped, and not without warmth, but when he said her name, Eliza shivered. "Make a left under the stairs, then it's the second door on your right."

Scowling, she followed his directions to another closed door and knocked. As she waited, she glanced at a peculiar onyx statue of a bird sitting on a short marble plinth. Was it… watching her?

No! Get ahold of yourself, Danger. This isn't one of your fantasy books.

"Come on in," said the voice.

The door opened, revealing a luxurious study. Bookshelves climbed to twice her height, with one of those rolling ladders nearby to reach the upper shelves. Reading chairs and couches clustered around a great marble fireplace. There was a wet bar, a liquor cabinet, and giant bay windows covered by 16-foot velvet drapes. And right across from her was a giant mahogany desk and a high-backed chair. In the chair sat a thin man with dirty blond hair and sharp cheekbones. Eliza's cheekbones.

Despite her best intentions, her lip quivered.

"There you are," said RJ Valentine. "Please, close the door and have a seat."

Eliza pressed the door closed, but she didn't take a seat. She noted that the door was designed to look like part of the wall.

"What the hell is going on?!"

"I'm deeply sorry for the theatrics, Elizabeth," RJ said. "Very few people know you exist, and I'd like to keep it that way—for your sake, not mine. After your mother was killed..."

He trailed off, a shadow passing over his features.

"Right," said Eliza. "So to protect me, you kidnapped me and brought me all the way up here..." She checked her watch, it was the afternoon of the same day she'd gotten breakfast at Burger King. "In the span of a few hours. I'm suitably impressed-slash-intimidated. What do you want?"

"To have a chat," said RJ, gesturing to the chair in front of his desk again. "Please, my intention was not to intimidate. But I do need to ask. I know you've been staking out that hospital all week. The one your sister is currently an unwilling guest of. What are your intentions?"

He had an odd way of speaking. After each pause, his lips would keep moving, silently repeating himself. It was like watching a Japanese film badly dubbed in English. Eliza sighed and plopped down in the offered chair. The adrenaline was wearing off, and whatever she'd been drugged with earlier left her light-headed.

"I'm going to break her out," said Eliza.

"When?"

"Soon."

"Why haven't you done it already?" he asked.

"My plan requires precise timing," Eliza lied.

"And what happens when you do? What will you do next?" he asked. Eliza shrugged.

"Do you need anything? Is there something I can do to help?"

His hand reached for his desk drawer, probably eager to get out the *checkbook.*

"Look, man, I don't need your charity," said Eliza. "I've been doing just fine without you for sixteen years."

"I thought you were dead," he said. "I only learned recently—"

"Whatever, it doesn't matter," said Eliza.

"It does!"

"What? Are you bummed you didn't write a book about me, too? Left some merchandise money on the table?!"

She hadn't expected to be this hostile, but it felt good. RJ closed his eyes, and his lips silently counted to ten.

"Why do you keep talking to yourself under your breath?" she asked.

A genuine smile parted his lips.

"Sorry, I'm writing." He looked up, holding her in his gaze. "I'm sorry, Elizabeth. We're off on the wrong foot. My fault."

"I prefer Eliza, actually," she said.

"Oh? Interesting." He furrowed his brow in consternation.

"Is it?"

"Eliza," he repeated slowly, like he was turning it this way and that with tweezers. His hand shot to that desk drawer again, producing a Montblanc pen and a sheet of Valentine stationery. "Could you write it down for me, please? Your name?"

Eliza hesitated.

"I'm not trying to steal your signature or something, Eliza," he said. "I just want to see how you write it normally. In print."

She couldn't think of a good reason not to, other than being a brat, and a childhood spent striving to please Nurse Bennett was a hard habit to break. She took the pen and wrote out her name. It might be the first time she'd written it like this.

Eliza Valentine

RJ took the paper and studied it for a moment. Then he smiled and seemed to finally relax from whatever had him so tightly wound. He produced a Zippo lighter from his pocket and lit the paper on fire, right there on his desk.

"Right, secrets," said Eliza.

RJ nodded and rolled the lighter between his fingers.

"I understand you're a smoker," he said. "Filthy habit."

He slid the lighter across the desk. Eliza accepted it, still dubious. It was a really nice lighter.

"Well, Dad, I've told you my intentions, vis-à-vis your other abandoned daughter. Now what?"

"I wanted to see you," he said. "See you both, but she's in that hospital. I thought I should, just in case…"

He didn't elaborate further, instead looking over his shoulder.

"In case of what?" Eliza asked.

RJ rose from his chair and adjusted the tall curtains behind him to block even a slim ray of light from passing through. He walked to the bookshelf in the corner and gripped the top of a large tome—then suddenly changed his mind and returned to the desk.

"Sorry," he said again. A pang of loneliness touched Eliza's heart. Nurse Bennett always used to say not to trust guys who never apologized—or apologized too easily. But the smile RJ gave her then was kind, and sad, and matched her own grief. "You're not what I expected at all."

"Somehow, you're exactly what I expected," said Eliza.

"No doubt, and well earned," said RJ. "If you won't accept my help, can I insult you with some advice? It's as I said: you're supposed to be dead. Nobody knows about you. Danger could be a real asset to Trouble. An ace up her sleeve."

He reached out and touched her softly on the wrist. Warm fingers that sent a little jolt up her arm. He held them there like he was taking her pulse.

"How so?" she whispered.

Several heartbeats passed between them. Withdrawing his hand, he got up again, this time to visit his minibar.

"You look just like her," he called over his shoulder. "Use your imagination. Can I get you something?"

Now that she considered it, her throat was parched. "Sure," she said.

"Tell me something about yourself," he said. "I've seen the paperwork, but have no sense of the person."

"Can't say I'm in a sharing mood, RJ," said Eliza. She tried to let the

silence hang, but her emotions got the better of her. "How could you stay here? How could you keep living with that monster? Valerie Valentine had my mother killed! You understand that, don't you?!"

He turned away from the minibar, grimacing.

"Understanding isn't the same as proving. Believe me, I've tried. They don't call it 'Till death do us part' for nothing, kid," he said. "I'm so, so sorry. I know how this must look. I know how unfair it is to grow up without a mother." His voice wavered. "My mother died young, when I was four. I would never wish that on anyone, let alone my own daughters."

He returned to the desk with a tumbler in each hand. Something brown with a big ice cube in it for him, and a glass of dark red wine for her. Good girl that she was, Eliza had never tasted alcohol before—Nurse Bennett didn't drink. But today was a day for new experiences, wasn't it? When in Blackbird Springs…

She took a sip and made a face. It was like drinking extremely sour grape juice. And the aftertaste somehow made her more thirsty, not less, so she took another.

"Breast cancer," RJ said. "That's what took my mom. They say it could be genetic—usually on the mother's side, but make sure you and Jenny get regular mammograms."

"Yeah, thanks."

He was doing that thing again where he was repeating himself under his breath. He sipped his drink and looked up, eyes brightening again.

"Are you right- or left-handed?"

"Right."

He frowned.

"Is that bad?"

"Oh! It's fine," he said. Then, under his breath, "The sinister side would have been so very…"

"Is she right-handed?" Eliza asked.

"Trouble? Yes," said RJ. "I made her ambidextrous in the first book and forgot about it when I wrote Trouble Always Finds Me. Changed it in the second edition. It felt a bit twee, don't you think? How are you planning to break your sister out of that psych ward?"

Eliza yawned, still feeling light-headed, and took another sip of wine.

It loosened her tongue and she began to unfold her plan. She would hide out in the parking garage until the laundry service arrived. Then she'd smuggle herself inside the psych ward in a hamper. She'd have to wait for a shift change to enter the patient dormitory and find Jenny's room…

RJ shook his head and made a face. Eliza's plan was not up to his high standards. She wanted to say something nasty, but his lack of approval was irritatingly disappointing.

"Ambitious. A good trope. But it's too complicated," he said. "Here's what you do: wear some scrubs and grab a clipboard. Walk in like you're slightly annoyed and have shit to do. No one will stop you."

She yawned again, feeling a bit woozy. You weren't supposed to drink on an empty stomach, right? Oops.

"I'll try that," she said, distracted.

"Feeling all right?" RJ asked.

"I don't know," said Eliza. She pointed to her glass. "What is this?"

"That," RJ said, "is a 2003 Campion Pinot Noir. Bottled the year you were born. And some barbiturates."

Her mind was fogging up again, vision getting blurry at the edges.

"Wait, for real?"

"For real," said RJ. "That was a good year, for wine."

Eliza slumped forward onto the desk, happy to leave this dark fairy tale behind.

*W*HEN *E*LIZA CAME TO, SHE WAS BACK IN THAT ALLEY NEXT TO THE MINI-*mall in Glendale. Someone had been conscientious enough to sweep a little patch of asphalt clear of debris before depositing her on the ground. Part of her wanted it all to be a bad dream, but according to her watch, it was early in the morning on August 10th now—a day later.*

Her right wrist was sore. She tried to rub it and got a shock: she had a new tattoo! It was an Ace of Clubs, covered in some kind of shiny protective coating. An ace up her sleeve… In her pocket, she found the Zippo lighter RJ gave her, a travel-size bottle of antibacterial soap, and a little card with a note on it.

Don't scratch it! Leave the Saniderm on for five days, then wash it with soap so it doesn't get infected.
Now get your sister the fuck out of that hospital!
    — Dad

Chapter Six

Silence Is Golden

DEEP INSIDE JENNY'S MANGLED SOUL, SHE SPRANG A LEAK. ALL the anger she'd been so prepared to level at Eliza for keeping her RJ encounter a secret was draining away. In its place, a hollow void formed.

What were you hoping for? A way to blame it all on Lizzy? Would that fix anything? Would that make you feel better?

Maybe…

Using her box cutter, Jenny cut through the zip tie binding her and Eliza together. Her hand lingered on her sister's wrist, and the tattoo there. She would never have guessed…

"Why didn't you tell me?" Jenny asked.

"I mean, I don't know if you were picking up the context clues there, but he was kind of a total asshole!" said Eliza.

"Yeah, for sure," said Jenny. "I mean, he was probably pretty paranoid then, but that's no excuse."

"You hadn't met him yet, and I wanted to wait for you to form your own opinion, you know?" said Eliza. "That seemed fair. But then he fucking died, and I didn't want to sully it. He treated me like a fucking spare, Jenny. It sucked, and I tried to forget it. I'm sorry I never told you, but I didn't think you'd want to hear it, and there wasn't anything about it that would have helped us with the case."

Jenny closed her eyes, forcing herself to hear her sister. She believed her, of course. Absolutely. Maybe it was time to accept that their father wasn't always the greatest guy. Too prone to distraction, too often thinking of himself… And yet, if Dad hadn't intervened, would Eliza have waited longer before sneaking into the psych ward? Without his advice, would she have made it to the roof in time to stop Jenny from jumping? Jenny shivered.

"You can always tell me anything, Lizzy," she said. "I can take it. Thank you. I'm glad I can cross you off the list."

She got out her list of leads and showed Eliza as she crossed off her sister's name.

"Dinah?" Eliza asked. "What's that about?"

Jenny gave her a brief recap of what happened in the mansion basement, finding Rob Haines dead at Pixeldrome with Dinah's initials on the *Mystery Girl* high score, and running into Mirai at Drew's Masturbatorium.

"Can't say I didn't tell you so with Blondie," said Eliza.

"It's not for certain, yet," said Jenny. "It could just be the Stranger fucking with me. Okay, your turn. What the hell happened when I was in the archive room?"

Eliza filled in her side of that night, from Alicia's heirloom key treasure hunt to finding Lockhart and getting Lilah. Eliza had already given him something of a statement, so Jenny would have to go with it and hope no one noticed the timeline was fuzzy.

"I need to be me again, Lizzy," Jenny said. "I need to talk to everyone who was at the party. No offense, but I'll know if they're lying. You might not."

"That's why you're the Girl Detective, and I'm the ace up your sleeve," said Eliza. "RJ wasn't wrong about that."

"You're much more than that," said Jenny. "And we've never needed to be in two places at once more. Those leads I showed you… the Stranger is in there somewhere, I can feel it. But everyone's gonna be watching me now. You're gonna have to be the one to chase them down. Not as me, not as Kazumi. Maybe you can wear a surgical mask and say you have a cold…"

"I can do better than that," said Eliza. "Boost me up."

Jenny helped boost Eliza high enough to reach the bathroom's drop ceiling. She pushed an acoustic tile aside to retrieve a bulky envelope she'd hidden up there.

"We've still got Harmony Valentina, remember her?" said Eliza. She pulled a fake driver's license out of the envelope. It was the first fake identity they'd bought off the dark web and used only once, to get into Bottle Shock a year ago. "The cops will have frozen all of Kazu's bank accounts, but I put this away, just in case."

There was a thin brick of cash along with the ID. About $10 thousand, from the look of it. Eliza counted out twenty $100 bills for Jenny and kept the rest.

"We both need new phones, but I need the rest of this more if I'm gonna be out on my own again, so make it last," she said.

"Agreed," said Jenny. "No phone calls or texts, only use Signal. And stay away from the house. If we need to switch, we do it here. Oh! You'll like this." Jenny retrieved the keys to the Kawasaki Ninja from her pocket and handed them over. "Arty Porter's old rice rocket, courtesy of Mirai. She goes by Bolívar now. It's parked two blocks away at that Presbyterian church. Better get it ASAP, because those bastards will tow it."

As predicted, the keys ignited a little glint in Eliza's eye.

"There's an assembly in the cafeteria this morning, and then the FBI guys are taking statements from everyone at the party after," Eliza said. "Jiji said he'd send a lawyer. Where should I start?"

"Bike, then parking ticket," said Jenny.

Eliza nodded. They stared at each other for a moment.

"I'm glad you're okay," said Jenny. "I—I was scared."

"So was I," said Eliza. "Can you, um… I don't know. Say something to Drew for me. For Kazu, that is. He's going to be confused."

"I'll think of something. Good luck."

They embraced again. Jenny squeezed extra hard, not wanting to part. She had been dreading what Eliza's story would mean for the two of them. Would she ever be able to trust her sister again? Surprisingly, the answer was: *Of course. Absolutely. We've never been closer.*

But RJ, on the other hand… There was a growing hole in her soul where the implicit faith in her maker used to be. What had he been aiming for, bringing Eliza up here? He told her he'd been writing. Writing *I Dream of Trouble*? Was that why it felt so… personal? She needed to get her hands on more pages of that manuscript.

Jenny released Lizzy and walked to the bathroom door. It was time, once again, to play herself. Most of the school already hated Jenny forty-eight hours ago. Who knew what they'd think of her now?

THE QUAD WAS EERILY EMPTY AS JENNY HURRIED TO THE CAFETERIA. Once she threw open the door, she knew why: the whole school was already inside. The bleachers, normally retracted to leave room for lunch tables, had been pulled out to accommodate the entire student body, all of whom were currently staring at her.

"Christ, what an asshole," she heard Mr. Schlafer mutter under his breath.

Jenny tried to ignore the glares, scanning for an empty seat.

"Jenny!" yelled Drew.

He was in the back row, sitting with Penny, Jack, and Dinah. They waved for her to come over. Jenny grimaced and picked her way through the judgy crowd. Her friends wore grim expressions, and their shoulders rode high and tense. They each sat a foot apart, arms crossed, stealing furtive glances at the others.

"Nice hair," said Dinah.

Her eyes were kind, but Jenny didn't know who to trust anymore. She smiled back and remained standing.

"How's Alicia?" she asked.

"In recovery," said Jack. "The knife nicked her small intestine, so they need her to stay there for a while until it heals."

"That's great news," Jenny said. Jack's bloodshot eyes widened. "I mean—when I saw her in the study, I thought she was dead."

"You saw her?" Jack asked, perking up.

"I tripped over her—"

Penny cleared her throat. "We're not supposed to talk about it," she said. "They don't want us coordinating our stories."

"Fuck 'em. How would they know?" asked Jenny.

Penny nodded down at the line of chairs behind the podium, where a blond man in a black suit aimed a directional microphone at them, not even trying to hide it.

Jenny blew a raspberry. "Realistically, what can he do?"

"Charge us with obstruction of a federal investigation," said Penny. "It's a third-degree felony, punishable by two to ten years in prison."

"Oh," Jenny said, frowning.

"What do they think we'd be coordinating?" asked Jack.

"Alibis," said Drew. "They don't believe in the Stranger, and unless we can prove he exists, then someone at the party must be the killer."

"Drew," Penny said in a warning tone.

"That's not obstruction, that's just stating facts," he replied.

Everyone scowled, avoiding eye contact.

"The other option, Drew, is that the Stranger does exist—and someone at the party *is* the killer." Jack let his statement hang in the air while they processed the implication. When he spoke again, his voice was made out of gravel. "Has anyone seen Kazumi?"

"She wouldn't…" said Drew.

"Guys," said Penny.

Jenny followed her gaze to see the other G-man, a tall Black man, rising from his chair behind the podium to walk their way.

"Scoot over," he said to them as he approached. Jenny tried to take a seat between Jack and Drew. "Ah ah, you sit on my right," said the agent.

He sat between Jenny and the others, forcing her to suffer through the assembly in silence. She needed to talk to her friends, dammit! Dinah, most of all. In private. She needed answers.

After the assembly, which was brutal—Meghan's parents bawled their eyes out and glared hatefully at Jenny the whole time—it was time for the feds' inquisition. Drew went first, followed by Penny, JeRay, Lai, and then Thanh. If there was a pattern to the order, Jenny couldn't detect it. Maybe only that the feds wanted everyone else on the record before Jenny gave her statement. They were probably hoping to find some inconsistency they could nail her with.

The FBI agents had commandeered Vice Principal Carter's office for the interviews. Jenny was forced to wait her turn on a folding chair down the hallway, sequestered from the others.

After Thanh, they called for Jack. When he passed her on his way to the office, he winked and leaned down to whisper in her ear. "Don't worry. I got this."

"Break a leg, Junior," she replied.

"Quiet, you two," said a man walking up behind Jack. "Little Miss Columbo here has caused enough trouble already."

"Well, it is my—"

"Zip it!"

He was part-Japanese, like Jenny. Handsome, probably, if you were into dudes. Starched shirt and tie, rolled-up sleeves, and a military-grade crew cut. He carried a slim, black leather briefcase.

"Who the fuck are you?" Jenny asked.

"Your lawyer," said the man. "Tony Kobayashi, but you will call me 'sir.' I'd have thought Ken Onishi's grandkid would know better than to run her mouth during an open murder investigation. Zip!" he repeated when Jenny tried to get a word in and popped the clasps on his briefcase. "You're in the big leagues now. No more skating circles around overworked local cops. Feds are like cockroaches. If you see one, you've got a problem. You see two? You've got an infestation. Your statement is already prepared. Read it. Know it. Don't deviate from it." He pulled a small stack of papers out, held together with a paperclip. "If it's not in here, you *do not recall*. Understand?"

He fanned the pages in front of her. It was Eliza's words, printed in Courier New, double-spaced and official. Jenny would have to hope her sister didn't miss anything important. And that the feds didn't look too hard at the timeline when Jenny went to the garage…

"Hold on, this isn't part of it," said her lawyer. "Where did this come from?"

The text had shifted from big chunks of legalese to shorter

paragraphs and dialogue, like a manuscript…

"Yes, it is!" Jenny said, yanking the pages out of Tony's hands. "It's for me."

He frowned at his briefcase and checked the clasps.

"It's okay, I need to study this too," said Jenny. "Gimme some space, *sir*. Your Axe body spray is making me nauseous."

"It's Dior Sauvage."

"Whatever, I can't read with you hovering," said Jenny.

Her lawyer was dubious but retreated down the hall to a padded chair where he could keep an eye on her. Jenny skipped past her statement to the manuscript pages that the Stranger had somehow snuck into Tony's briefcase. When she last left her counterpart, Trouble had discovered a body courtesy of the long-absent Stranger. Where would that murder take her? And who was the mysterious girl in the theater?

Chapter 2

Stepping into Interview Room No. 2 at the Blackbird Springs Police Station is like stepping back in time. I'm eleven years old again, getting harangued by Sheriff Lockhart for breaking Mrs. Galloway's car window when I tried to throw a rock at an escaping burglar. The smell of the place makes my knees shake. Old body odor, a hint of urine, the stench of fear soaked into the walls like the smoke from a fine Cuban cigar, and the faint trace of dough and sugar on the sheriff's breath.

I can't stop smiling. This is the wrong attitude for these circumstances.

"I'd wipe that grin off your smug face, Trouble," says Lockhart. "I've got an eyewitness who claims they saw you leaving the theater by the back door, minutes before the body was discovered. Care to explain yourself?"

"I was with my friends in the lobby the whole time," I say. "Ask Jack, ask Dinah, ask Mason, ask any of them. Why are you trying to blame this on me? What are you covering up?"

"I'm not—don't try to go confusing the situation!" Lockhart growls at me. "I don't need to ask Mason, I've got enough to arrest you right now. Maybe you'll start telling the truth after a night in a cell."

"You'll do no such thing, Blake," says a voice from the door. It's Daddy! He strolls into the interrogation room and shoves an important-looking document in the sheriff's face. "Section 5, paragraph 3 of the California Civil Code for private investigators clearly states that the police are forbidden from arresting a P.I. involved in an active investigation without a warrant signed by the judge. Are you sure you want to tangle with the Right Honorable Justice Mallett on this? He's just a phone call away."

Dad yanks the document away and holds up his phone. I can see on the screen that he's placing a call to **Judge Mallett**, waiting for the other end to pick up. Lockhart goes cross-eyed as he tries to understand what Dad just said.

"I didn't—Judge Mallett isn't—" Lockhart stammers and tries to bat Dad's phone away. "Let's just settle down a minute."

Dad ends the call and turns to me as if Lockhart isn't even there.

"You okay, sweetheart?" Dad asks. "I'm sorry this is happening again. I'd hoped we'd heard the last of that bastard, the Stranger, but it seems you're fated to dance with him yet again."

"I'm fine, Daddy. I just want to know who that man was. During the movie, I had the strangest sense that he wanted to speak with me. And also—" I hesitate. I want to tell him about the girl in the theater, but it doesn't make any sense. I worry they'll think my imagination is getting away from me again, the way my old therapist always used to accuse me of doing. "What if the Stranger strikes again?" I ask instead.

Dad bites his lip. He knows something and doesn't want to tell me.

"That's a dangerous line of thought, Trouble," Dad says. He glances back at Lockhart. "Is it true, about the ID?"

"How would you even know about that?" the sheriff asks.

"I have my sources," says Dad.

"If someone doesn't tell me what's going on, I'll scream!" I say.

Lockhart rolls his eyes and jerks his finger at Dad to get me out of here.

So I scream.

Wow! That was more refreshing than I was expecting! Nothing like a good scream to flex the old pipes and clear my head. The door to the interview room bursts open again and one of the sheriff's flunkies barges in with a hand on his service pistol.

"Everything all right in here?!" he shouts.

"We're fine, Anthony," Daddy says. "Do us a favor and bring in some more donuts, my daughter has experienced quite the fright."

I glare at him. Come on, Dad! I'm not eleven anymore!

"Damnit, Trouble!" Lockhart roars, plugging a finger in his right ear. "You know I've got that tinnitus!"

"You should hear her when Jack is hogging the bathroom," says Dad.

"If there's a body, there's a motive!" I say. "Who is it!?"

The deputy returns with a pink box of donuts. The sheriff helps himself. I decline. A girl's gotta watch her dainty figure, ya know?

"Yes, it's true about the ID," Lockhart says, his

mustache now dusted with powdered sugar. "Eugene Hodgson, after all these years."

"Who's that?" I ask.

"No one special," says Lockhart. He yanks open his desk drawer to pull out a metal flask. Jameson whiskey, if he's kept up old habits. "Just a bad cop who retired a decade ago."

"The rub of it is," says Dad, "when he was on the force, he was Hector Villanova's partner."

"The mayor??"

"The same," says Dad. "You were too young then. Back before he ran for DA, Villanova was a vice detective for the city."

He shoots me a warning glare. The kind that always used to mean "Don't ask!" The kind I always used to ignore back when nothing could hurt me.

"Got any idea why Hodgson would want to speak with your daughter, RJ?" the sheriff asks.

"You see, I think there was someone else—"

"I haven't the faintest idea," Dad says, cutting me off. "Last I heard, Hodgson was a sad old drunk living up in the hills, scaring the local kids. Perhaps he was confused, and thought my Trouble could help him with a vandal or a missing dog."

Lockhart mutters a curse under his breath and takes a swig from his flask. "Perhaps."

"We'll leave that to you to determine," Dad says. He holds out a hand to lift me out of the metal folding chair. "If there's nothing else?"

The sheriff waves us away with his half-eaten powdered sugar donut. Dad pulls me to my feet and ushers me out of the room. From old practice, I know not to say anything until we've left the station and climbed into his trusty K-car.

"Section 5, paragraph 3 of the civil code, eh?" I say.

"Who do you have in your contacts under Judge Mallett's name?"

Dad chuckles. "My chiropractor. That idiot Lockhart is still falling for it after all these years."

"So what's our move?" I ask. "Check out this Hodgson guy? Maybe the mayor was trying to pass me a message? Through a back channel, ya know?"

"Our move is to get you home," Dad says. "It's past your bedtime."

"Daddy, I don't have a bedtime anymore!"

"I'm serious about this, Jenny. Mayor Villanova isn't the kind of guy you want to mess around with. Promise me you'll leave the shoe leather to me this time."

"But—"

"I'll fill you in as soon as I know more," Dad says. I pout. He grimaces. "You're not a little girl anymore, sweetie. There are people out there who might have thought twice about hurting you before. But they won't this time; you're practically a young woman. Let your old man do his thing and we'll compare notes in a couple of days, capisce?"

"Fine."

"Uh-uh, I need you to promise."

Oh geez, if you insist, Dad! I hold up my left hand, three fingers up with my thumb and pinky together.

"I promise," I say. "Trouble's honor."

But behind my back, I'm not crossing my fingers. And you know what that means.

Chapter Seven

Secret

THE MOTORCYCLE AND PARKING TICKET THING COULD WAIT. FIRST, Eliza needed to return to the scene of the crime. Or, rather, to the woods a quarter-mile away where she'd hidden her backpack before running into Blake.

She swiped Jimmy Figg's mountain bike from the rack and rode north toward the mansion, taking side streets. The feds might be watching Cellar Drive, so she off-roaded it to the woods from a neighboring property using fire trails, walking the bike the last hundred yards to a manzanita shrub near the burnt treehouse.

Thank god, her pack was still there. Even a total dunce of an FBI agent would have started piecing things together if they had found Kazumi's backpack full of Jenny's clothes, a box of condoms, and her bottle of chloroform.

After she backtracked through the fire trails, she hit a GameStop to buy a used iPhone and prepaid service. Then she went straight to the Motorcycle Pro Shop on Fourth Street and dropped a sizable chunk of their limited funds on a full set of gear: riding boots, leather pants, fingerless gloves, and a matte black, form-fitting, ArmorGel-reinforced jacket.

Properly attired and feeling like a total badass, she ditched Jimmy's bike and picked up Arty Porter's Kawasaki Ninja from behind the Ryalto. It was sick! All matte black with chrome accents and a matching helmet. Say what you will about Mr. Porter, the man had taste.

Eliza took it slow until she reached an abandoned strip mall on the south side. There, she did several laps in the parking lot until she felt comfortable on two wheels. Despite her dire predicament, feeling the Ninja's power between her leather-clad hips put the first smile on her face since the mansion party.

She hit the throttle and exploded onto the highway. Cars fell behind her like they were parked on the asphalt. This was a job for Danger, all right. Next stop: Guerneville. According to her Maps app, it was an hour's drive, with no traffic. Eliza got there in forty-two minutes.

The address on Mirai Bolívar's parking ticket was a side street a block away from the main drag. Guerneville was even smaller than Blackbird Springs, hardly more than a strip of businesses and B&Bs, with campsites by the Russian River. There were homes, too, but most of them were tucked back into the forest, away from prying eyes.

Something about the place set Eliza's teeth on edge. It uncomfortably reminded her of those bad years in the foothills, when Nurse Bennett's mind betrayed her, and a too-young Eliza was left to her own devices. Sometimes, these rural towns were charming. And sometimes they were filled with the sort of people who didn't want to be found by the world.

She climbed off the Ninja, flexed her legs, and pulled off her helmet. It smelled nice here, at least. Like old redwoods and cedar.

Eliza glanced around. Up the street was a community center, a beauty shop, and an antique store. And right behind her was a secondhand surplus store. This would also be a good place to park if you wanted to walk down Main Street.

"What were you doing here, Arty?" she asked out loud.

Eliza didn't have her sister's finely tuned detective instincts, but something was pulling her toward the surplus store. She pulled off her riding gloves and walked inside.

This was one of those places that sold old military gear. Fake uniforms. Ammunition boxes. Real grenades with the cores drilled out. Paradise for a certain kind of aging dude who watched too much History Channel. It wasn't all militia gear, though. There was an aisle of secondhand sporting goods equipment, some random heirloom furniture, and a whole wall by the register devoted to old comic books and nerdy figurines.

She fought the urge to ogle the *Harry Potter* merch and instead walked to the far end of the store to peruse every aisle. Looking at the old catcher's gear and baseball bats, it was impossible not to think of Drew. What did he think of her right now? Had Jenny found a way to put him at ease? Would a short message of love from Kazumi hurt?

No, stop it! Eyes on the prize, Danger!

She was just rounding the endcap to the next aisle when her brain caught up to her browsing. She paused before looking back. The baseball equipment had given way to various inflatable balls, some dumbells, and then a rack of weights. Big plates, like the kind you put on a bench press.

Under the ArmorGel jacket, the hair on the back of her neck stood up. According to Jenny, a 45-pound plate had killed Mr. Webb.

Using her new phone, she snapped a picture of the plate weights and moved on. Nothing jumped out at her until she reached the glass cabinets by the register. Next to the expensive figurines and collectibles was a section of knives and swords. Some were highly stylized and impractical, like out of an anime. But others were simple, practical, and lethal. A row of Bowie knives, in particular, made her look twice. Could this be the same kind that the Stranger used? She snapped another photo.

"See something you like?" asked the man behind the counter.

Eliza would have expected some old dude with an unkempt white beard, but the clerk couldn't have been older than twenty-five, with a neatly trimmed chestnut brown goatee and a buzzed scalp.

"Do you sell a lot of these?" Eliza replied, pointing to the edged weapons.

To be honest, that little ninjatō is calling my name...

"Here and there," said the guy.

"I saw those weights back there," Eliza said, pointing to the sporting goods aisle. "You know those big ones for a bench press?"

"Yeah?"

"You wouldn't happen to recall anyone buying some of them last year?" Eliza asked. "Like, early August?"

The man shrugged. "I don't know. People buy those now and then. Or they come in to sell them. Are you looking for weights?"

"No, sorry, more like looking for information," she said. She pulled her phone out and googled Arty Porter's name. "Do you happen to remember this guy ever coming in here?"

She showed him a photo of Arty. He squinted and shook his head.

"A lot of people come in here," he said. "He might have, but the face isn't ringing a bell."

"Okay, how about her?" Eliza asked.

She showed him a photo of Dinah Black, but that only rendered a "Damn! I wish!" Blake's photo struck out, too.

"After a while, it's a blur, you know?" he said. Eliza was about to show him a photo of Mayor Villanova when he said, "Sorry, are you gonna buy anything?"

Eliza put her phone away and heaved a great sigh. Her eyes drifted again to the compact ninjatō under the glass. She could certainly use some self-defense.

"You know what? Sure," she said and pointed to the sword. "How much for her?"

The guy eyed the ninja sword, then Eliza, and bit his cheek.

"How old are you?" he asked.

Honestly, Eliza couldn't remember how old her newest identity was supposed to be, so instead of replying, she got her ID out and handed it over.

"Harmony," the guy said to himself, examining it.

"I prefer Harm," said Eliza.

The guy smirked and handed her ID back, then pulled out the ninjatō from the glass case. The hilt was bound in tight braids of black cord. It was short, for one-handed use. He unsheathed it from the carbon fiber scabbard to reveal a 20-inch blade, painted all black except for the shining steel serrated edge.

"Two hundred bucks," said the guy.

"One hundred," said Eliza.

He smirked and nodded. She slid him over a crisp Benjamin Franklin and took possession of the ninjatō. The scabbard fit perfectly under her ArmorGel jacket, between her shoulder blades, with the hilt sticking out to the right side of her neck, ready for a quick draw.

"Every good sword needs a name, Harm," he said.

That was true. But what an important question! What kind of girl was Harmony Valentina? What kind of girl was Eliza Valentine?

Eliza pulled the sword from its sheath and performed a tight moulinet. "This one's a Secret," she said.

Something from Dad's latest chapter of *I Dream of Trouble* nagged at Jenny. Two somethings. There was the sudden appearance of Mayor Villanova—another real person named in the books! What did it mean? Then there was Trouble herself. Jenny couldn't help it, but her kneejerk reaction when her fictional counterpart screamed to get her way was: *I wouldn't do that.*

She needed to take a long walk in the Haunted Vineyard to sort this out. But instead, she had her stupid interview with the feds.

Agents Tierce and Steele weren't messing around. They grilled her on every word of her prepared statement and had a whole bunch of unexpected questions about Meghan and Mason and their secret child. With her grandfather's bitchy lawyer at her side, Jenny tried to be as non-committal as possible in her answers, and even so, the agents got disturbingly close to the truth of why she'd been secretly supporting the late lovers.

"So you just decided to do a little charity?" asked Steele. "Helping out a girl in Meghan May whom everyone says you weren't friends with?"

"Mason and I got on all right," said Jenny.

"My client has a clear and documented record of charitable acts," said her lawyer, Tony.

"Who else have you been doing charity for, Miss Valentine?" asked

Tierce. "Any tax records to back this up?"

"When it's from the heart, you don't keep track," said Jenny.

"Oh, I'm sure," said Steele.

"Jenny took her whole class trip to a castle in Austria for a week," said Tony. "All expenses paid."

"I'm not sure I'd be citing that one as a character reference," said Tierce. "A dozen people died."

"More," said Jenny.

Tony Kobayashi kicked her under the table.

"What time was it?" asked Agent Steele. "When you went downstairs with Dinah Black?"

"Excuse me?"

"You were with your friend Drew, and then you split up," said Steele. "And then you ran into your friend Dinah, and you both went down to the basement, for reasons I'm not totally clear on."

"To check the generator," said Jenny.

"Of course. So what time was that?" asked Steele.

Jenny did her best to sell confusion and earnest effort, forcing her eyes not to look away in the classic liar's tell.

"I'm not sure," she said.

"See, because I noticed you're wearing one of those fancy smartwatches," said Steele. He held up his wrist to reveal his own Apple Watch. "I've got one too. Every year, on my birthday, it reminds me that I'm a year older the second the clock hits midnight. Wish I could turn it off. You get to be my age, you don't wanna know. But you were wearing your watch that night, weren't you? So when did your birthday alert go off? And where were you when it did? And was that before or after you went downstairs?"

"Sorry man, I know that would be super useful to know, but my battery died," Jenny said. "I remember I checked it later when I went back into the mansion, after Dinah went to call the cops, but it was dead."

Tony kicked her leg again, just for good measure.

"Damn, that's too bad," said Tierce. "And you didn't check your phone instead?"

Jenny shook her head. "It's like a reflex, you know?" she said, mimicking looking at her wrist.

"Will that be all then?" asked Tony.

"Not quite," said Agent Steele. "Your friend JeRay: his watch didn't run out of juice. And he says it was around midnight when he went off to follow one of those treasure maps you gave everyone. And we know 9-1-1 got a call from Miss Black at 12:15 AM."

"Oh, well there you go," said Jenny.

She faked a smile, but her stomach clenched tighter. She and Dinah had split at midnight. Was fifteen minutes enough time to sneak into the mansion, kill Meghan and Mason, and get back to Cellar Drive to call the police?

Tierce leaned closer, licking his lips. "So you're saying that in the time between midnight and 12:15 AM, you went off with Drew Porter upstairs, decided to split up, ran into Dinah Black, went down to the basement, discovered Tori Valentine unconscious, woke her up, left the garage with Dinah, and split up outside with her going to call for help?"

Jenny shivered. *Fuck! Tori!* She'd forgotten all about her. If Tori told the feds about everything that went down in the archive room, the timeline would be fucked and her alibi blown.

"My client—"

"It's crazy how fast it all went to hell," Jenny said, cutting her lawyer off. "One second, it's a dumb treasure map, and then… poor Mason and Meghan."

"Indeed, this has all been very emotional for Miss Valentine," said Tony, glaring at her. "I'm sure you've already spoken to Dinah Black and Tori Valentine to confirm all this."

Jenny tried not to let on that she was holding her breath, bracing for the worst.

"Tori's memory is hazy from the chloroform," said Tierce. "But Dinah's tale lines up. Almost too well, really."

Phew! Tori must still want to keep their conversation about RJ's "Plan A" a secret. Jenny sent her stepsister a mental nudge of grudging respect.

"It lines up because it's true," said Jenny. "The cops met Dinah at the turnoff to Cellar Drive, didn't they?"

The two agents exchanged glances, and Steele nodded. Well, that was a point toward Dinah's innocence, at least. Maybe.

"Maybe you can explain this for us," Tierce said.

He reached down behind Vice Principal Carter's desk to retrieve something, and his hand returned with a thin metal case. It was RJ's medical case, the one that had contained a powerful sedative, part of his "Plan A" to fake a coma. Agent Tierce flipped the lid open to reveal the syringe and vial of barbiturates.

"My fingerprints are on that," Jenny said, smiling to herself as she felt Tony clench his ass next to her.

"Correct!" said Tierce. He elbowed Agent Steele. "And you thought she'd lie."

Steele grunted and passed Tierce a $10 bill.

"We found it in the garage," said Jenny. "When I ran into Alicia in the conservatory, I gave her my bag with my taser in it. I took the syringe, just in case. It was the best weapon I could think of."

"Did you know what was in the vial?" asked Steele.

"My client is not a pharmacist," said Tony.

Jenny shrugged.

"It was a cocktail of barbiturates," said Tierce. "We think your cousin used it. But how would she have gotten it?"

"I—I must have dropped it when I saw the Stranger in the study," said Jenny. "He probably grabbed it and used it on Kazu."

"You say that you saw Meghan and Mason in the study? And that you tripped over Alicia?" asked Steele.

"Yeah."

"What about Kazumi?" Steele replied. "You didn't see her on the carpet, too?"

"It—it was dark," said Jenny. "I don't recall. Once I saw the Stranger, it was like fight or flight took over, ya know?"

"And you flew," said Tierce.

"Fuck yeah, I flew," said Jenny.

"Gentlemen, we're going in circles," said Tony. "This is all in the statement."

The agents exchanged smug smiles and said nothing, only staring placidly at Jenny. They were letting the silence hang. Tempting her to say more than she should. Trouble knew all about this move, but she had moves of her own, too. She reached out under the desk and gripped her lawyer's forearm, signaling for him to keep quiet.

"I know what you're thinking," Jenny said. "I see the Stranger, get scared, and run. Then the Stranger takes the coat and mask off, and it's Kazu underneath. She tranqs herself and plays dead till the EMTs show up. But if that were the case, then where did the Stranger's outfit go?"

"Maybe her cousin carried it off for her," said Tierce.

"You talked to Lockhart," said Jenny. "Did I have it on me when I ran into him?"

"You could have hidden it in the woods," said Steele.

"But you searched the woods," said Jenny. "Didn't you?"

The agents exchanged neutral glances, but Jenny read the annoyance underneath. They hadn't. Not yet.

"We will. Of course, you might have planned for that," said Steele. "Maybe Sheriff Lockhart helped you dispose of the outfit. Strange for the sheriff to leave the crime scene to drive to a cabin outside of town in the middle of the night. To see a baby no one knew existed."

"Be serious," said Jenny, narrowing her eyes. "His kid died."

Neither agent replied, studying her again.

After a while, Steele said, "Don't leave town."

"Wouldn't dream of it," said Jenny. "I go where the mystery is, and the mystery is here."

"Word of advice," said Tierce, "drop the Girl Detective act. We can haul you in for obstruction any time we like."

Jenny bit her lip. "Look, you two don't seem like total assholes, so here's my word of advice: watch your backs. You're in more danger than you realize."

"Threatening a federal agent?" said Agent Steele.

"No, dude, I'm warning you," Jenny said. "The feds never show up in the books. It's always Lockhart and the local cops. Or Interpol, when she travels. You're not canon. And the Stranger doesn't like it when people who aren't canon stick their noses into the mystery. Look what happened to Nilay."

Agent Tierce laughed, and Agent Steele grinned at him.

"We're touched, really," said Tierce. "But I wouldn't worry about that, Miss Valentine. We can handle ourselves."

"Famous last words," said Jenny.

"Use your head," said Steele. "If anyone's in more danger than she realizes, it's the girl who thinks she's untouchable."

It wasn't quite true. Jenny wasn't. Lizzy was.

ELIZA WALKED OUT OF THE SURPLUS STORE A HUNDRED BUCKS lighter, debatably wiser, and grateful to be carrying protection. Though it was a crisp, sunny afternoon in Guerneville, the hint of moisture on the cool breeze chilled her right through her jacket. Everywhere she turned, dark shadows clung to the alleys and wooded forest roads at the edge of her vision. She flexed her back, feeling the reassuring pressure of Secret on her spine.

Her phone vibrated in her pocket. It was **sallydraper2003** calling via Signal. She accepted the call and said, "Hey."

"Can't talk long, the feds might be watching," said Jenny.

"How'd it go?"

"Well, they didn't arrest me. Dinah sort of has an alibi, but who knows... she's a fast sprinter. The others, I have no idea. I wasn't able to talk to anyone without the FBI breathing down my neck and threatening obstruction charges."

"What about Tori?" Eliza asked. "I know you said you found her unconscious, but..."

"Tori could have blown up my alibi, and she didn't," said Jenny. "I think I can trust her."

"Maybe she didn't nuke your alibi because it would have nuked hers, too."

Silence on the other end.

"No, you're right," Jenny said after a beat. "She's on the list. Even

Alicia has to be. We can't assume, right? How'd the parking ticket go? Anything?"

"I don't know," said Eliza. She glanced at the other shops near the place where Arty was ticketed, and her intuition told her that none of them mattered. She told Jenny about the weights and knives at the surplus store. "It's not proof, but there's something about this place. It's… unfriendly. I have the oddest sensation that the Stranger was here. Like, I can feel it, somehow. Do I sound crazy?"

"No, Lizzy. Nurture that," said Jenny. "That's what it feels like."

Eliza smiled to herself. Twins!

"So maybe he was here, meeting Arty," Eliza said. "Getting Arty to buy the weight plates and weapons for him. That means he'll go far out of town for supplies, and still use a proxy. He's very careful. Very disciplined."

"Three can play that game," said Jenny. "I was thinking, you know that Little League photo? If we can't find the Stratford Photography business records for who took it, maybe we just need to ask more of the people in it if they remember."

"Most of those guys are on the high school team," said Eliza. "Drew already asked them last month. They don't remember. They were only eleven."

"Okay, but there's more than one team in Little League, right?" said Jenny. "That can't be the only team photo this guy took."

"How would we even find the other team photos?"

"The same way you found that fortune teller," said Jenny. "War-driving to every pizza parlor, bowling alley, and arcade in Calistoga County."

Eliza cursed under her breath.

"Sorry, but you needed to lie low anyway, right? Might as well stay out of town," said Jenny.

"True. But try to lie low yourself, just in case."

Jenny agreed, and they said their goodbyes. Eliza crossed the street and swung her leg over the Kawasaki's seat. She revved the engine and hit the throttle, fishtailing the rear wheel in a half-circle before shooting off back the way she came. She'd be glad to put Guerneville and its bad vibes in her rearview. But the visit hadn't been entirely fruitless. If she was going war-driving, at least she had a weapon now.

Jenny ended the call and stepped out of the bathroom stall just as the final lunch bell was ringing. They were supposed to be studying the Fourth Amendment in Civics class, but Jenny's mind was far afield, back at the mansion the night of the party. How could the Stranger have done it and gotten away? If not Dinah, then who? Was the mayor involved? Why was he suddenly popping up in Dad's book?

After the last bell, Shelly made her walk straight home. It was like being on house arrest again. Dinah was walking too, not far ahead. Their paths would run together for two more blocks. Jenny quickened her stride when her phone buzzed.

Dinah: I'd love to hang, but you've got a tail.

Jenny's ears burned. Sure enough, a woman she didn't know, dressed like a teenager, was casually trailing her fifty feet behind.

Jenny: Cheaters. Trouble did it solo.
Dinah: RJ always stacked the deck in her favor.
Jenny: Damn. I wanted to talk.
Dinah: I know, but now is not the time. Give it a week.
Jenny: I haven't forgotten about the other night. I mean, before we found Tori.
Dinah: Neither have I.

Up ahead, Dinah turned right at the cross street. When Jenny came to the intersection, she went left. Fine. She'd wait a week. And then she'd ask her girlfriend why her initials turned up as the high score in Mom's *Trouble* video game—exactly where Dad and Tori had expected the Stranger's initials to appear.

Chapter Eight

The Troublemakers

While Eliza crisscrossed Calistoga County searching for old photos, Jenny returned, at last, to her own life. Somehow, Shelly could tell immediately. Quite annoying. She demanded to know how they did it, but after trying to rat Jenny out to the cops, Jenny informed her aunt that she could want in one hand and shit in the other, etc.

Then there was Lockhart. Jenny knew it was coming, but she still wasn't ready to confront the sheriff's staggering grief. Two days of stubble marred his well-groomed face, and his eyes never seemed to focus, always looking off into the mid-distance, hollowed out with despair. Shelly was beside herself. It was more than she'd signed up for, but she couldn't bail now.

"It reminds me of when I got you," she told Jenny one night. They were over at Blake's house, watching Lilah while Blake slept. He slept a lot now, it seemed. "I don't know if I can do this again."

"Was I that bad?" Jenny asked.

"Yes, but it was more about missing Lala," said Shelly. "You were all that was left… her remainder. But sometimes, when I'd see you, I'd lose it. The pain was so raw." She caressed Lilah's red tresses. "I'm sorry for that. If it ever seemed like I didn't love you. I did, it was just hard to look at you sometimes."

"I never felt that way," Jenny lied. All this time, she'd just assumed her aunt didn't like her much. "But that's kind of you to say."

"He's gonna do the same thing every time he looks at her," Shelly said, indicating Lilah. "And if I'm filling in as mom, he'll be putting me in that same mental bucket. Loving me and resenting me."

"Maybe," said Jenny. "Or maybe there's no one better to help him through this than someone who's been there before."

Shelly cocked her head, peering closer at Jenny.

"What?"

"That is Jenny, isn't it?" Shelly asked. "You sure you're not your sister in there?"

"What can I say, Shells?" said Jenny. "Despite my best efforts, I grew up."

THEY HELD THE FUNERAL FOR MASON THAT SATURDAY AT BLACK Rock Cemetery. Blake managed to stuff himself into a black suit, and Jenny used some makeup tips she'd picked up from Charlie Zaleska to hide the bags under his eyes.

"I'd like you to say something for him," Blake said as she dusted his cheeks with a little color.

"Oh, jeez, Lockhart. I don't know how that will go over," Jenny said.

"Who gives a shit?" said Blake. "He was my kid, and I say it's fine."

A cold front had them all in coats, but the sky was clear and crisp above the graveyard. It felt like the whole town was here. Even more than RJ's funeral. There was the mayor, Calderon, Vice Principal Carter, a bunch of teachers, and even some of Mason's teammates from his college baseball team.

The only notable absence was Meghan May's family. In retaliation for Blake taking custody of Lilah, they had refused to let Meghan be buried with Mason and had her cremated instead. Assholes to the end, those miserable fucks.

Blake white-knuckled his way through some opening remarks without breaking down. Jenny was already bawling. Jack said some nice words about the time he and Mason found a Playboy magazine in the woods behind what was now GolfMax. It was just the right amount of transgressive humor to lighten things up. Mason's college teammates placed his baseball jersey on his coffin. Drew kept leaning toward the mic after each speaker like he wanted to go next, but he never pulled the trigger.

"It just feels like anything I could say would be so inadequate," he whispered, sniffling.

Jenny knew the feeling, but Blake had asked her to. When it was her turn to speak, she couldn't bring herself to look at any of them, so her wet eyes found Dad's tomb on the far hill.

"Meghan and Mason were good people," Jenny said. "Better people, I think, than me. They deserved better. They deserved to raise their daughter. Lilah deserved to grow up with her parents. But she won't. She'll be like me now. Because one of you out there is a coward."

Disgruntled murmurs rippled through the crowd. Jenny ignored them.

"Mason kept my secrets, and I kept his. He used to send me baby photos—I think he just wanted to send them to somebody, anybody." Jenny paused, considering. "No, that's not true. He sent them to me because we were friends, even though I was too stupid to realize it. I owe you, Mace. I owe you so much I can't repay."

She held the microphone away to sniffle and wipe her nose.

"There's one thing I can do," Jenny said. "One promise I can keep." She let her eyes fall away from Dad's tomb and scanned the crowd. "Killroy? I know you're here. I know you couldn't resist. This only ends one way. Stop screwing with the canon. Leave the Masons and Meghans of the world alone and come dance with me."

She lowered the microphone and walked away from the coffin. When she'd retaken her place by Jack and Drew, she leaned over and whispered to Drew. "Anything?"

"He didn't seem pleased," Drew said. "But that's kinda expected, isn't it?" *He,* being Mayor Villanova, whom she'd asked Drew to keep an eye on during her speech. "Nothing stood out, I guess, is what I mean," Drew went on. "He seemed annoyed but not malevolent. Not nervous either, though."

"We probably couldn't expect any less from the real Stranger," Jenny said. "Thanks."

So, the jury was still out on the mayor. Why had Dad written him into his final *Trouble* manuscript? She'd just have to get more pages of it to find out.

After a few more speakers, Blake thanked everyone for coming to send his boy off. Then he finally lost it and crumpled into Shelly's arms. Calderon stepped up to the mic to wrap things up and invite anyone who wanted to come by Lockhart's house for food at the repast.

Since Shelly was dealing with Blake, Jenny was put on baby duty. She strapped Lilah to her chest in a baby carrier—*goddamn she's gotten big!*—and lingered by the gravesite as the guests departed. It felt eerily similar to RJ's funeral. Except Eliza wasn't watching from a distance this time; she was somewhere in Petaluma, chasing down a lead on a Little League team photo.

Drew lingered as well. As the crowd thinned out, Jenny noticed that Jack and Penny were standing by, too. So was Dinah. Soon, the only people left in Black Rock Cemetery were the four of them, along with a young girl dawdling by another grave; Tyrone the city worker and his assistant, chilling by the entrance with the backhoe; and those federal agents, Tierce and Steele.

"You really want to stop doing that," said Tierce.

He and Steele strolled up to face Jenny.

"Keep calling this guy out, and sooner or later, he's going to take you up on the offer," said Steele.

"Mama!" Lilah said, from just below Jenny's chin. "Want Mama!"

Jenny's heart broke for the fourth or fifth time that afternoon. She glared hatefully at the agents and caressed the top of the baby's head.

"She'll be here soon," Jenny lied.

"Your concern is duly noted," said Jack. "We'd like to pay our final respects now. You have our statements. You're not entitled to our grief. So if you don't mind… you know… fuck off."

"Don't forget what I told you, Valentine," said Tierce. "You're not the hero. Don't try to be."

Except he said it to Jack, not Jenny.

As the fed walked away, Jenny frowned at her brother.

"What's that about?" she asked.

"It's nothing," said Jack, clearly lying.

"I can't believe he's gone," said Dinah, staring at the coffin. "It all seems so unreal."

"I felt the same way, after Nilay," Penny said. She swallowed a sob. "It's like there's a hole in the world where they're supposed to be."

"This can't happen to anyone else," said Jack. He set his jaw, his hands gripped into fists. "I won't let it."

"It's not up to you, Jack, it's on me," said Jenny.

"Yeah, about that," said Penny.

But before she could go on, they were interrupted by a little girl clearing her throat.

"Excuse me, are you Trouble?" asked the girl who had been standing by another grave a minute ago.

"Guilty as charged," said Jenny.

She was ten or eleven years old, at a guess. Pale, with long dark hair, wearing a black Sunday school dress with a lace collar. There was something familiar about her that Jenny couldn't place.

"Maddy, are you sure you should be here?" asked Dinah.

"It's okay, my parents think I'm at a friend's house," said the girl, who must be Maddy. She turned to look hopefully at Jenny. "Meghan told me I could trust you."

A fresh wave of grief washed over Jenny. Of course. That's why Maddy looked familiar. She was Meghan May's little sister.

"Is everything all right? Are your parents doing anything they shouldn't?" Jenny asked her.

"It's okay, I'm the good one," said Maddy. "They leave me alone. But I thought I should give this to you."

Maddy unslung the backpack she was wearing and produced a sealed hydro flask.

"What is it?" Jenny asked.

"It's—it's Meghan," said Maddy. "I stole her and replaced her with some ashes from the fireplace. Mom and Dad wanted to spread her at the beach, but I know she'd rather be here. With Mason."

The heartbreaks would never cease. Jenny smiled at Maddy, willing herself to keep it together for the poor girl.

"That's very thoughtful of you, Madeline," said Jack. "I think you're right."

He put a hand on Maddy's shoulder and nodded to Jenny that she should take the makeshift urn. Some primal part of Jenny's psyche vehemently rebelled against the idea of handling human remains, but the superego she usually ignored demanded obedience.

You're an adult now, Jenny Valentine. Fucking act like it!

"Thank you, Madeline," Jenny said, taking the hydro flask. "See, Lilah, Mama's here now."

She held the cup close to Lilah's cheek, and maybe she was imagining it, but the baby seemed to calm.

"Can I hold her?" Maddy asked.

Jenny unstrapped the baby and gently handed Lilah over to her. She helped Maddy properly support Lilah's head, trying not to wince as Maddy struggled under the weight.

"She's so big!" said Maddy.

"Her middle name is Madeline, you know," said Jenny.

"Oh wow," said Maddy, and her eyes blinked away tears.

"Give it a year or two, and I think we'll have found Blake and Shelly a babysitter," said Dinah.

"As long as you keep it a secret from your parents," said Jenny.

"I will! I promise," said Maddy. "I—"

"Holy shit," said Drew, pointing behind Jenny.

Dinah let out an involuntary scream and covered her mouth. Jenny spun on her heel, reaching into her bag for her expandable baton. A hundred yards away, at the entrance to Black Rock Cemetery, a lone silhouette stood silent in the gap, watching them. With the sun setting behind them, it was impossible to make out any features. But Jenny knew there wouldn't be any. He'd be wearing a mask.

Tall. Dark. Strangesome. A menace who haunted her every move.

"Fuck it! We ball!!" said Drew, and took off sprinting at the figure. Jack followed a few steps behind.

"Wait! Stop!!!" Penny called out.

Lilah began to wail in Maddy's arms.

The tall figure immediately ducked behind the fence that surrounded the graveyard. Before Jack and Drew made it halfway there, tires squealed, and a brown sedan sped away from the scene. Jenny was ready for it—barely. She had her phone out, shooting video as the Stranger made his escape.

"Anything?" Dinah asked, leaning over.

Jenny played the recording back and grimaced. It was rough. She'd zoomed in so much that every slight movement produced massive shaking. Even going frame by frame, the license plate was a blur of white, totally indecipherable.

"Hmm. It looks like the rear bumper is a lighter shade of brown, right?" she asked, squinting at the best frame she could find. "Like maybe from a cheap repair."

"Huh." Penny pressed a thumb to her chin. "I feel like I've seen a car like that in town before."

"Yeah, maybe," Dinah said.

"Why did you say stop?" Jack asked, panting as he returned. "We could've had that pussy!"

"Earmuffs, Maddy," said Dinah, covering the little girl's ears. "Don't be crass, Jonathan!"

"What were you going to do, fight him bare-handed!?" said Penny. "Nilay tried that! And now he's dead."

"We could take him together!" Drew insisted.

"No, I don't think you could," said Jenny. "But it doesn't matter. He wasn't here to fight. He just wanted to scare us."

"I guess we know the Stranger isn't any of us, at least," said Dinah.

Alarm bells!

"Nah, no we don't," said Drew. "If I was the Stranger, I would 100 percent hire someone to pose as me like that—to throw Jenny off the scent."

Jenny bumped fists with Drew.

"This is why he's the sidekick," she said. "He's exactly right. No offense."

"Uh, Maddy, you should get home, I think," said Penny. "My friends need to talk. Grown-up stuff."

"How did you get here?" Dinah asked.

"Rode my bike," said Maddy.

Her face had somehow gone even paler with the sudden appearance of the Stranger. Jenny took Lilah back, cooing to calm the baby, while Dinah rubbed Maddy's shoulders to settle her down.

"I can take her home in my Tacoma," said Drew.

"Real quick, let's do this properly," said Jack.

He took the makeshift urn from Jenny and walked them the short way to Mason's casket. With a grunt, he hefted the lid enough to slide the ashes inside and closed it again.

"There," he said. "She's with Mason now."

"May they find peace together," said Penny.

They all stood a moment in silence. As Jenny mourned her friends, an epiphany blossomed within. No longer was her heart frozen to the core—it was on fire! Ablaze with a bold new idea. Trouble would never...

But first, she needed to get poor little Maddy out of the awful story she'd found herself in. She looked reluctant to go, so Dinah offered to tag along.

"I know where she lives," Dinah said. "Come on, Maddy. Let me show you my new lipstick."

Jenny frowned as the three departed. Given her suspicions about Dinah, she didn't like the idea of Drew riding alone with her. But surely, with Maddy there and all of them witnessing their departure, she wouldn't try anything, right?

"Come right back," said Jenny. "We have much to discuss."

The other three stayed behind, avoiding conversation. Jenny was consumed with the germ of her new plan, and neither Jack nor Penny was eager to speak. They stood back and watched as Tyrone and his partner lowered the coffin into the grave and covered it up. By the time Drew and Dinah returned, it was fully dark in the cemetery, and Aunt Shelly was texting Jenny, demanding to know why she was taking so long to get to the reception.

ShellsBells: I could really use your help!

ShellsBells: You better not be up to anything!!

Jenny: We're saying goodbye in our own way.

Mason's friends, that is. Be there soon.

"Well," said Drew, walking up with Dinah. "What'd we miss?"

Penny nodded to the covered grave. "Just that."

"Is this where we all cut our palms and make a pact of revenge?" asked Jack.

Jenny held up her hand. "Before we do, we need to discuss the party at the mansion last week," she said. "None of us have been arrested, so that's something. But has anyone been cleared? What did you tell the feds?"

"I was alone in the billiards room on the second floor," Penny said, shrugging. "I'd just stepped out onto the balcony when I heard Alicia scream—and then glass breaking."

Jack hissed, and Drew shook his head.

"I was following one of those maps from the globe," said Penny. "Do those mean something? Is that why the Stranger attacked?"

"The maps don't mean anything," said Jenny. "Alicia's clue was just a pun by RJ. A red herring."

"I was out on Cellar Drive, calling the cops," said Dinah.

"We were gonna check the kitchens and then meet at the study," Drew said to Jenny. "When you didn't show, I went back upstairs to look for you. Then I heard the front door slam—and a scream. What happened to you?"

Jenny vaguely recapped running into Dinah after they split up, then finding Tori in the basement and sending Dinah for help. Jack's face turned red when she got to the part about sending Alicia into the study alone.

"You basically sent her straight to the Stranger!" he said.

"And where were you?" Jenny replied.

He hung his head in disgust. "She called me, you know? Alicia. But the signal was bad. My phone cut out immediately. I didn't think anything of it 'cause she was right downstairs. I was in my room, looking for a flashlight. And then I heard her scream."

"And Kazu?" Drew asked.

"She was injured, I think," said Jenny. "I know they found her unconscious in the study and took her to the hospital. From what I heard from Blake, it sounds like she woke up during the ambulance ride, freaked out, and jumped out the back."

"Shady," said Penny.

"I think she was probably freaked out of her mind," said Jenny. "I'm guessing she ran like hell and booked the first flight she could back to Okinawa. What about Lai and Thanh and JeRay?"

"They were all together, in the master bedroom," said Penny. "I heard from my mom. That clears them."

"Unless they're all in on it together," said Drew. "Which seems unlikely."

"So any of us could be the killer, is what I'm hearing?" said Jack.

"Well…" said Dinah.

"None of us have rock-solid alibis, at least," said Jenny. Avoiding Dinah's gaze, she pressed her palm against Mason's brand-new headstone and closed her eyes to think. Near as she could tell, none of them was lying. But she'd been fooled before. "You know, when RJ died, I stood here a long time. Swore a bunch of oaths of vengeance over his tomb. I don't think I understood what I was doing, then. But I think I get it now, and I can't play his game anymore."

"Whose game?" asked Penny. "RJ's or the Stranger's?"

"It's the same game," said Jenny. "Everything that's happened in the past year and a half tells me that right now, the four of you should be taking your GED and getting the hell out of town. The Stranger doesn't like it when I have help. It breaks canon. He killed Declan for trying to sell his heirloom. He attacked Drew for helping me. He poisoned Jack and Tori to get Alicia's key back after I bought it. And he killed Nilay for acting as Val's proxy last fall.

"So here's what we're going to do," said Jenny. She paused, taking one last moment to question her newfound intuition. Was this the right play? It wasn't what the original Trouble would do. But what about the grown-up one from *I Dream of Trouble*? "We're going to trust each other, and we're going to do exactly what he doesn't want us to do. We're going to ignore all of the risks, and we're gonna go after him together. Despite what Drew said earlier, I don't believe any of you is the Stranger," Jenny lied. "And I can't do this on my own. I need help."

Jack and Dinah furtively raised their eyebrows.

"More help than usual," said Jenny. "If I'm going to catch the Stranger, it will be because he had too many of us on his scent, not too few. The Stranger might be very smart, and the Stranger might be very meticulous, but nobody's perfect. Even the Stranger makes mistakes. With all of us working together, he's bound to make another."

She covered Lilah's ears again.

"Fuck the Unfridgeables. We're the Troublemakers. The Stranger can't keep tabs on all of us at once."

The other four all seemed to take an involuntary step back. Jenny caressed Lilah's hair, giving them time to process it.

"Truh-buh!" said Lilah.

"That's right," Jenny whispered to the baby. "Trouble. That's my name."

Penny let out a reluctant breath. "I should have done early admission to Pepperdine."

"Too late now," said Jack. "I'm an heir, Jenny, I have to be in."

"I meant what I said at the party," said Dinah. "I'm not going anywhere this time."

"No way your sidekick is ditching you now," said Drew.

"Fuck it," said Penny. "If we catch this guy, and I break the story, I won't even need Pepperdine. I'll have my own Substack, a podcast, and a guest column in the Atlantic. I could be a senator at…" She cocked her head, calculating. "Thirty-one."

"Take that, AOC," said Jack.

"Would," said Drew.

Jenny's heart swelled, and her face broke into the first genuine smile in days. In the past, they'd all seemed more like Eliza's friends than hers. Like they just tolerated her and figured some days Jenny was a bitch for no reason. But here they were, all putting their lives on the line for her. Not Lizzy, Jenny.

"Won't the Stranger come after us?" asked Penny.

"There's safety in numbers," said Jenny. "Penny, Drew, you're a team now. Attached at the hip. Same for Dinah and Jack. You don't go anywhere outside of school without each other. I wasn't just talking shit earlier. The Stranger is, at heart, a coward. He's afraid of getting caught. Book Stranger didn't have to deal with modern forensics. Our Stranger knows it's long odds to go after us and get away with it if we're ready for him."

"What about you?" asked Dinah.

"I've got the feds up my ass right now," said Jenny. "So I'll be on research, but I'll help out where I can."

What Jenny didn't say—what none of them may have figured out yet—was that if one of them were the Stranger, attacking their partner would put a big glowing neon **GUILTY** sign over their heads. They'd be forced to play along. And if the Stranger wasn't one of them, she'd have three teams hunting the bastard.

"Do we have any leads?" asked Drew.

Jenny dug her notepad out of her bag and glanced at it. "Yes, but I'm gonna keep these need to know. Penny? Drew?"

She tilted her head for them to come closer.

"Can we be Blue Team?" asked Drew.

"No, we call Blue Team," said Jack.

"Fine, we're Gold Team," Drew replied.

On the list—which she shielded from the others—Jenny had plenty of leads. But which one felt right for Penny and Drew?

Leads

- DEB high score = Dinah Eve Black??
- Yvonne's heirloom, *The Stranger of Sausalito* book
- ~~Arty's Parking Ticket~~ (Maybe where murder weapons were purchased?)
- The Hospital: site of the actual murder?
- The P.I. who worked for Stratford Photography ("Too hot!")
- ~~Eliza?~~

Really, with Penny on Gold Team, there was only one possible choice. She tucked her head in close between Penny and Drew and spoke softly so only they could hear.

"You guys are on Yvonne's heirloom," said Jenny. "The book. Penny, your mom swears it's a dead end, but I can't take her word for it. RJ apparently wrote it. We have to find out more about it. Can you do that?"

"Don't think I haven't been trying to get my hands on it for months," said Penny. "I don't know where she hid it."

"Maybe we don't need her copy," said Jenny.

"How so?" asked Drew.

"People rarely throw away books," said Jenny. "It feels philistine-ish, ya know? They donate or sell them. So I need you guys to hit up every library and used bookstore in the county. There's got to be another copy out there somewhere."

"That's a needle in a haystack," said Penny.

"I know. Which is how we're going to beat him. By doing the work no one else would," said Jenny.

"Nice. I've got some ideas, too," said Drew. "Let's get going."

The two said their goodbyes and walked to Drew's truck. Jenny consulted her Leads list, debating what to assign the former couple, Jack and Dinah. Eliza was already on the Little League photo. She couldn't exactly ask Dinah to search for people with the initials DEB, and if the fatal attack on RJ happened at the hospital, Jack would be a prime suspect, having spent so much time there at Dad's bedside. So… what to assign them?

"Eliza found another secret passage at the mansion," Jenny said, her eyes flicking unbidden to Mason's grave. "Well, Mason and Meghan found it first."

Since these two knew about her twin, she gave them a quick rundown of what really happened in the study that night, as far as they knew.

"The Stranger couldn't have left by the conservatory passage because that's how I entered. And he couldn't have used the fireplace passage without running into Lizzy. So how did he get out of there?"

"The broken window?" Jack proposed.

"Maybe. But then, shouldn't the feds have found some evidence of it? A blood trail? Something?" Jenny bit her lip. "We need to know if there are any other secret passages at the mansion that the Stranger might have used. You know, check the original blueprints, go around knocking on walls, whatever you have to do."

"Not the most adventurous of tasks," said Jack.

"We're not going to catch this guy by splitting heads, Jack," said Dinah. "Speaking of your sister, where is Eliza in all this?"

"Busy. And hiding," said Jenny. She wrinkled her nose. "I think Lilah needs a diaper change. I better get her back to her grandpap."

"My car's down the way," said Dinah.

As they walked to the cemetery gates, Jenny allowed Dinah to gain on them and signaled for Jack to hang back.

"What's up?" he asked softly.

"Have you heard from Tori?" Jenny replied.

Jack grimaced and shook his head. "She gave a vague statement to the cops and vanished. Those feds are up mine and my mom's ass about her now. Why?"

"It's nothing," said Jenny. "I need to talk to her, is all. Let me know if she surfaces?"

Jack nodded.

"Also," Jenny said, leaning closer, "there's at least a 35 percent chance that Dinah is the Stranger. Keep a close eye on her."

Her brother smirked, turning his head to Dinah ahead, and then back to Jenny.

"Are you gonna tell her the same thing about me?" he asked.

"Of course," said Jenny. "But for you, it's only 25 percent."

Chapter Nine

Hospital Blues

With Mason and Meghan laid to rest, life at Blackbird Springs Academy returned to some kind of normal. The rest of their classmates might be caught in the grip of senioritis, checking out and slacking off, but the Troublemakers had a higher purpose now, and part of that meant keeping up the appearance of good behavior for the feds.

Jenny dutifully attended her classes on time and more or less awake, though she'd already completed most of her schoolwork a month ago while serving her suspension. Shelly somehow found a way to disapprove of this new, responsible Trouble, claiming she could have been Valedictorian if she'd only applied herself like this from the start.

"Fat chance, Shells," Jenny said one night as they watched a reality TV show. "I'd never make it through Honor's Algebra II. That was Kazu's department."

Blake grumbled beside Shelly, but Baby Lilah's presence on his lap prevented another eruption.

The authorities had figured out by now that "Kazumi" was a fake identity, and that the Okinawa branch of the Onishi clan had never heard of her. Awkward for the Blackbird Springs branch. But hey, how were Jiji and Baba supposed to know the emails they got from distant relatives were phony? They were all having to play dumb about it now, and Jenny could tell Blake wasn't totally buying it.

"She can't be the Stranger," said Jenny. "Too short, for one, and she only showed up here last fall."

"I still like the undercover reporter theory," said Shelly. "That makes the most sense."

"If that's the case, then she ought to come in and clear things up," said Blake. His hand drifted to his side, where his service pistol was usually holstered. "I'd love to give her a quote."

Jenny winced inwardly. She wished there was a way to redirect his suspicions, but the girl who vanished into thin air made a more compelling suspect than the other students at the mansion that night.

By unspoken decree, Thanh, Lai, and JeRay had cut the Troublemakers loose from their friend group. Instead, those three hung out with the rest of the seniors, leaving Jenny and the others free to eat lunch at their favorite table by themselves.

Erring on the side of caution, they kept their lunch conversations strictly focused on pop culture, sports, and college plans, never once bringing up the Stranger. Each had installed Signal on their phones, and they did all their Trouble business in an encrypted group chat.

What little business of it there was. Jack and Drew were both in the thick of baseball season, and Dinah was still doggedly trying to catch up to Penny for Valedictorian. So far, there was naught to report on *The Stranger of Sausalito* or new secret passageways in Valentine Manor. As near as she could tell, based on her last Signal message, Eliza wasn't faring much better.

"It's not that I'm not making progress," said Eliza, "it's that I'm not getting results."

She was tucked into a nook at Village Pizzeria in Windsor, having a voice chat with her sister on Signal. She lost count of how many places like this in the North Bay Area she'd visited over the last week. This one was charmingly old-fashioned. Her little wood-paneled nook had an actual working payphone in it, probably installed before their late mother was born. And on the wall next to the quaint phone, she'd found a plaque commemorating the 2014 Windsor Wizards.

They were a Big League team, and the plaque included a nameplate and a team photo of a dozen or so teenage boys with acne, and two adult coaches. The photo bore the same telltale scratches as the one of Jack and Drew's team from that year. The same scratches as on the blackmail photo found in RJ's briefcase. And the same as on Jenny's heirloom photo of their parents. It was a photographic fingerprint that pointed—they were pretty sure—to the bastard who'd been spying on their mother in the days and weeks before she died.

Jenny and Eliza had strong reason to believe this person was working for Valerie Valentine, but hard proof had so far eluded them.

"How've you been?" Jenny asked. "You don't say much in your texts."

Eliza massaged a twitching nerve in her forehead. How many hundreds of miles of highway had she ridden in the past week, the double yellow divider line rushing past in a blur? She'd tracked down four other Little League team photos taken by Stratford Photography, all bearing the photographic footprint, but none of them led to a solid ID on the photographer. Progress, but not results.

"I'm okay, just tired," Eliza said on the phone. "None of the boys I've found even remember taking the photo. And of the three coaches I was able to track down, two of them only remember that it was a man—maybe—and the other guy wouldn't talk to me."

"Why not?" asked Jenny.

"I think I made him nervous," said Eliza.

Maybe she should start leaving Secret with her bike before knocking on doors.

"Don't be scary, Lizzy!" Jenny said on the line. "Holy shit!"

"What?"

"Uhhh nothing."

"*What!?*"

"Err… it's just…" Jenny stammered.

"I think I can actually hear you blushing over the phone," said Eliza.

"So, all the Troublemakers are using Signal now," said Jenny. "And

Dinah discovered the destructible message feature and has been using it to send me photos. You know…"

"Wow, that's so unlike her," said Eliza. "Unless she's a killer trying to distract you and regain your trust."

"It's working."

"Jenny, don't be stupid!"

"Hey," said a man, ducking into Eliza's nook. "You're not supposed to take those down."

He was a bulky guy in his twenties, wearing an apron dusted with flour and gesturing with a big spoon at the team photo plaque she'd pulled down to check the portrait studio print on the back.

"I gotta go," Eliza said into her phone. "Don't be stupid and horny—oh, and text me about Drew!"

She hung up and turned to the pizza man.

"Sorry! I'll put it right back." She scrambled to hang the photo back on the wall and pointed to the teens in it. "Do you know any of these kids?"

"I know that guy," he said, pointing to one of the players.

Eliza glanced at the man in the photo and gave a surprised yelp: it was him!

"Oh! That's you! Sorry, but this is important, do you remember who took this photo?!"

The man smirked. "That's not me, that's my brother," he said. "I was on the Healdsburg Hellions."

But he looked so much alike—wait! All the hair on the back of Eliza's neck stood up.

"You're twins?" she whispered.

This is a sign, right? It has to be!

"Yeah." The pizza man frowned at her, nonplussed.

"Do you remember who took your team photo?"

"Not even a little."

"What about your brother? Can you call him?" she asked.

"Nah, that's weird."

"Please?!" Eliza pleaded, batting her lashes.

"He's on a work trip," the guy said. "I'm not gonna bug him, but we're doing a fantasy draft here on Friday evening. He might talk to you then."

Hope bloomed in Eliza's heart. Maybe she was deluding herself, but this clue felt different. It felt *close.*

"I'll be there," she said.

THAT FRIDAY, JENNY CHECKED HER PHONE WHILE WALKING TO lunch and nearly tripped at the sight of the leopard-print bra Dinah was wearing underneath her conservative turtleneck.

"Goddamn, Miss Black, you're killing me here," Jenny said when the two met in the cafeteria.

They exchanged saucy smiles and got in line for lunch.

No, but seriously, this was killing Jenny. Dinah was more flirty than ever, clearly looking to pick up where they'd left off on the floor of the Valentine Manor archive room. And Jenny would love to do so, but that required trust. And trust meant finding out why Dinah's initials were left at the scene of Rob Haines's murder. And to do that, she'd have to finally confront her girlfriend, which she'd been too chickenshit to do all week—constantly making excuses in her mind about the heat from the feds being too hot to risk alienating Dinah.

As if to stress this point, a roving foot nudged Jenny's leg underneath the cafeteria table. Jenny looked up from her chicken nuggets to see Dinah smiling at her, sultry and suggestive.

"What are you doing this weekend, Valentine?" she asked.

Jenny tilted her head to her left, toward the next table over where a new girl named Zoey had been sitting for the last three days. A girl they all understood to be an undercover FBI agent.

"Dare we risk it?" Jenny asked.

"I've got a biscuit," Dinah said, almost purring.

Fuuuuuucckk. Would sleeping with the Stranger be so bad?

She was saved from her moral dilemma by a Signal notification on her watch.

AmbilynnEversong: You bitch! Are you going to come
 visit me, or what?

Oh, it's you! Perfect!

"Looks like I might be busy after school," Jenny said. "Maybe later?"

Dinah nodded with a sigh.

"Is everything okay?" she asked.

"I mean, no, but yes." Jenny reached out to place her hand atop Dinah's. "Soon, I promise. Once things get a little less crazy."

It had been over a year since Jenny visited Blackbird Springs General Hospital. She didn't much care for hospitals; they always made her antsy. Like, at any moment, someone in a white coat might prevent her from leaving. She walked down a broad hallway, stepping only on the peach linoleum tiles, passing X-ray and Nuclear Medicine on her way to Inpatient Care. The federal agents tailing her took no such care with their steps.

On your own heads be it.

After checking in with the front desk, Jenny followed another hallway until she located the room she'd been directed to.

"Fear not, AmbienEverdork, the bitch is back," Jenny said, pushing the door open.

A high-pitched squeal erupted within, and Jenny caught a brief glimpse of her brother kissing a bedridden Alicia, his hand somewhere under the covers.

"Oh god, why!" Jenny shouted and spun around, feeling her ears flush bright red.

"Trouble!" Alicia yelled.

"Can you fucking knock!?" Jack shrieked in an even higher voice than his girlfriend.

Jenny shoved her fist into her mouth to keep from gagging and/or laughing, she wasn't sure which.

"I didn't need to see that!" she shouted back. "I thought you wanted me to come see you!"

"A little warning would have been nice!" said Alicia.

The door swung open again, and one of those feds burst in, eyes darting around for signs of danger.

"What's going on in here?" the agent asked.

"Nothing!" Jack and Alicia shouted in unison.

Then the charge nurse joined them, asking, "Miss Aaron, are you all right? Your telemetry was showing some very odd readings."

Poor Alicia, bed covers pulled up to her chin, turned crimson.

"Everything is fine," Alicia told the nurse through gritted teeth.

"She's only allowed one visitor at a time," the nurse told the fed. "The rest of you need to leave."

Nobody moved.

"I guess you can catch up later, Junior," said Jenny. She turned to the fed. "Piss off, G-man. You're not on the list."

The fed glared at each of them before leaving. Alicia nodded to Jack, mouthing "sorry" to him. As he walked to the door, Jack paused to have words with Jenny.

"Be nice, and don't push her too hard," he said.

"She'll never get there if you're too gentle, Junior," Jenny replied evilly.

"What have I done to deserve a sister like you?" said Jack, scowling.

"Surely, not enough."

Once the rest of them had left, Jenny took a seat at Alicia's bedside.

"I guess I know which one you are," Alicia muttered.

Jenny held a finger to her lips. *Shush!* "Well, anyway. Hi. How are you?" she asked.

"Getting better. Slowly," said Alicia. "They let me get up to use the toilet now."

Jenny winced in sympathy. "Do you need anything? Besides a Hitachi?"

"Shut up!" Alicia said, but she was smiling.

"I'm hoping you've got some good news for me, Red," said Jenny.

Alicia frowned and shook her head. "I don't remember who it was," she said. "I don't think I saw them. It was dark, and then something punched me super hard in the stomach. It didn't feel like I thought it would at all—getting stabbed. When the railroad spike hit my leg, I went into shock. But a knife… It's not like in the books. It hurt so bad, Jenny. I think I blacked out."

Jenny glanced at the softly chirping vitals monitor next to Alicia's bed. Her heart rate was rising fast. She reached out and caressed Alicia's wrist, trying to soothe her.

"Don't think about that part," said Jenny. "You told the cops all this, right?"

"Yeah," said Alicia, calming a bit. "I didn't see poor Mason and Meghan. They asked me about that. I guess that happened after."

Jenny made a mental note. So the Stranger had been after Alicia, not Mason or Meghan. They must have walked in right after, and there could be no witnesses…

"It's my fault," Jenny said. "I'm sorry, Alicia. My heirloom was in my Coach mini bag. I think that's what the Stranger wanted. He took it before he left."

"Not just your fault," said Alicia. She leaned forward and whispered, "He took mine too. The key. I didn't tell the cops that, but it was missing, and my mom checked for my personal effects and it wasn't in there either."

"It was a copy, though," said Jenny.

Alicia cast her eyes down, staring at the medical bracelet on her wrist.

"I lied," she said. "I gave you the copy and kept the original. Somehow, the Stranger knew."

"Because he had the copy," said Jenny. She sighed. "Nice try, though."

They sat in silence for a while.

"I thought we were being so clever," Alicia said. "Unlocking that globe. It felt like I was about to win the game. Did you figure out what it led to? My key? All those maps?"

Jenny forced a smile, inwardly wincing. Alicia wasn't going to like this… She explained the red herring thing. How it was all just a pun. A dad joke. Alicia's heirloom didn't mean anything. The poor girl took it better than Jenny expected.

"At least I got some money and a book deal out of it?" She shrugged. "Thanks, RJ."

"He didn't do it for you," Jenny snapped. Alicia's face fell. "I didn't mean it like that. I meant… he wasn't considering the consequences, when he picked you."

Alicia fixed Jenny with a piercing stare that made her feel antsy again.

"Do you want to talk about that?" Alicia asked.

"No." Suddenly, it was time to go. "Anyway, duty calls. I'm glad you're doing all right."

"You can't stay longer?"

"Sorry. The game is still afoot. Take care," said Jenny, already halfway out the door.

She was not prepared to have that conversation. Let alone with Alicia fucking Aaron. Jenny put Inpatient Care behind her and traversed the peach tiles to the ER. Her watch vibrated with a message from Eliza.

> **dangergranger:** I'm meeting with a guy from a team photo tonight. At Village Pizzeria in Windsor, just in case. Got a good feeling about this one.

At least one of them was making progress. Jenny texted a quick reply and walked up to the intake nurse, a bearded male with a slight build who was ensconced behind a plexiglass shield at the front counter of the ER.

"Name and date of birth?" the nurse asked mechanically.

"Trouble, three-ten-oh-three. But I'm not here for treatment," said Jenny. "Did you work here in August of 2019?"

The nurse blinked. "What?"

"I need to talk to someone who was working in the ER on August 10th, 2019."

"Um, no, I didn't work here then," he said.

"Do you know someone who did?"

"Even if I did, they wouldn't be able to talk to you about a patient—"

"The patient is deceased," said Jenny, but she could already see the guy's walls going back up. "He was my father. Can you just point me at someone and let them make the call?"

He looked past Jenny and bit his lip. She glanced back to see Agent Tierce leaning against the wall by the ER entrance, watching her. They made eye contact and he waved. Asshole.

"I know who you are," the nurse said softly.

"Then help a girl out," Jenny said, and slid one of her precious $100 bills over to him.

He stared at the cash, stared at Trouble.

"We got a problem, Valentine?" Tierce asked, walking up behind her.

Jenny spun, using her body to block the agent's view of her cash transaction.

"Only a nosy fed salting my game," Jenny said. "Get your own leads, man."

"Hey! Tell her she can't bribe me for confidential information!" the nurse said loudly. He tossed the $100 bill back in Jenny's face. "Next patient, please."

Jenny scowled and grabbed her cash.

"You're lucky he didn't take that, or I'd have had to arrest you both," said Tierce. "Double the paperwork. I hate that."

"I thought you goons loved your paperwork," she said.

"Move it along, kid."

"Yeah yeah," Jenny said, turning to go back the way she came.

"Ah ah, exit's that way," said Tierce, jerking his thumb at the ER entrance behind him.

"My friend is here, I'm visiting her," Jenny replied and headed for Inpatient Care again.

Once she was out of the agent's sight, she uncrumpled the $100 bill in her hand to read the message the nurse had hastily scrawled on it.

Ask for Shirley on the night shift.

Progress! Perhaps Jenny had underestimated the people of Blackbird Springs. But the night shift didn't start for hours. She had some time to kill.

Returning to Alicia's room, she knocked first.

Look at you learning, Trouble!

"Are you decent?" she asked.

"Um, yes!" Alicia squeaked from within. "What happened to the game being afoot?" she asked when Jenny entered.

"Maybe we could hang out a little longer," said Jenny. "If that's all right."

Alicia grinned. "It's the least you could do, after sending Jack away!"

"Great. Now I need you to explain to me what the hell was going on in that book *Harrow the Ninth*, because I was totally lost…"

FRIDAY EVENING HAD THE PIZZERIA BUSTLING WITH FAMILIES AND beer league softball teams. The pizza guy's brother from the Windsor Wizards was here with his bros, taking over one of the party rooms to do their baseball fantasy draft. Eliza sat amongst them, trying to get the brother to talk to her.

"Sorry, it's an auction draft, so I gotta be locked in," said the brother, whose name was Travis.

"Have a drink," said the guy on her other side, pushing a sudsy pint of beer over.

"I'm good, thanks."

It was the third beer she'd turned down already tonight. Men. She should have brought Secret with her instead of leaving it with the Kawasaki.

"I just need to know if you remember who took this photo?" Eliza said, trying once more to get Travis's attention.

"Fuck it. I'm passing on Ohtani, he's injured," Travis said, finally turning to peer at the photo. "Jesus, those fucking zits, man."

"This would have been taken in Campion Park, in Blackbird Springs," said Eliza.

"Sure." Travis squinted hard at the photo, biting his lip. "Yeah, I don't know. I don't think we ever got his name or anything. They were moving us all on and off the risers pretty quick."

Eliza's spirits fell. She had such hopes for this guy. A twin and everything.

"But it was a man? You remember that?" she asked.

"I think so."

Maybe she ought to have a beer after all.

"My boyfriend would say you're crazy for passing on Ohtani," Eliza said.

"Aw, damn, see, guys!" said Travis. "Harmony's taken!"

The other dudes booed and chanted, "Dump him!" Travis winked at her and took a gigantic bite of pizza. Eliza forced a grin and picked a skinny slice of meatball and olive off the pizza pan.

"Mmmph." Travis wiped his mouth and scooted closer. "Ya know, Harm, there was one thing I do remember about the guy."

Eliza braced herself for a tacky pickup line. Ten seconds later she was scrambling for her phone.

Hours later, Jenny was pretty sure she knew what was going on in her favorite (only) lesbian necromancer fantasy series.

"So many unreliable narrators," said Jenny. "Why did she write it that way?"

"Sometimes authors must tell lies to reveal a greater truth, Trouble," Alicia replied.

Quoting RJ at her. Real cute. And again, that expectant look on Alicia's face.

We are not having this conversation, Red!

Jenny's watch tapped her on the wrist. Saved by a Signal call from Eliza! But this room was surely bugged, right?

She answered and said, "Heyyy, Dinah, what's up?"

"Why do I have to be Blondie?" It was noisy wherever her sister was. She could hear a lot of dudes laughing in the background, and rock music playing.

"Oh, no way," Jenny ad-libbed.

"Whatever. Jenny, you're not gonna believe this shit," said Eliza. "Hey, Travis, tell her what you told me."

There was a pause, and the sounds of a phone changing hands, then a man came on the line, exhaling in a half-burp.

"Okay, so the guy had a weird hat, like, you know, 'shine ya shoes, guv'nor!' That kind of hat," said Travis. "Except he didn't talk like that. He had this Eurotrash accent like he was German or something. You know, 'You zere, hold up ze baseball bat and say ze cheese, jah!' That kinda shit."

More scuffing as the phone switched back to Eliza.

"Who do you know who's a private eye, who wears a jaunty little newsboy hat, and speaks with a German accent?" Eliza asked with glee.

"Austrian…" said Jenny.

Jenny's heart froze to the core. Her mind froze with it, locked in a spiral of dread as she considered the implication. How had he come into her life? By wiretapping other P.I.s—or wiretapping her? Hadn't he given her photo samples of all the private detectives in Calistoga County? Sure, all of them, except for his own.

"Motherfucking Lambert!" said Eliza.

Chapter Ten

Three's a Crowd

Eliza stepped out into the cool autumn air, free of the noise and melted cheese fumes. She had one AirPod in while she researched on her phone.

"There's an ex-cop named Franz Lambert in Sebastopol who used to be registered as a P.I.," said Eliza. "I've got an address. Looks like a house."

"I want to come," said Jenny on the phone.

Eliza reached the Ninja bike and climbed aboard. "Are you sure that's a good idea? With the feds on your ass?"

"I'll find a way to lose them first."

"Hi Danger," said another voice.

"Oh my god! Alicia!" Eliza's heart lightened. "How are you?"

"Not dead yet," said Alicia.

"Stay that way," said Eliza. "I'm texting you the address. Meet me around the corner."

They said their goodbyes, and Eliza hung up just as Travis came out of the pizzeria looking for her.

"Ya know, you look kinda familiar, Harmony," he said, a little smirk on his lips.

"I get that a lot," Eliza said.

She pulled on the black helmet but left the visor up.

"If I'm not mistaken, you're more Trouble than Harm, aren't you?" he asked.

Eliza lifted Secret by the scabbard and slid it down the back of her ArmorGel jacket between her shoulder blades.

"I'm not her," she said. "We just look the same."

"Can I get your number?" Travis asked.

"Sorry, too dangerous."

"I'll protect you."

"Not for me, dummy." Eliza slid her visor down. "I am Danger."

She hit the throttle, and the Ninja sprang away from the parking lot, rocketing her toward the man who may have killed her mother.

Lambert. It couldn't be. Except it had to be. Jenny cursed herself for her naiveté. A private dick showed up, lurking on her phone line, and she just went with it? Even asked him for help?? Of course she did. Because she was Trouble, and wasn't that the sort of thing that just happened to Trouble?

"I need to get to Sebastopol," Jenny whispered.

"Do you even have a car?" Alicia asked.

Jenny shook her head, staring at the address in her Maps app. In the satellite view, it looked like a small Craftsman house. How nice and cozy for him, the lying bastard…

Keys jingled, and Jenny glanced up just in time to catch the keychain Alicia tossed at her.

"You can borrow mine if you promise not to crash it," Alicia said.

"Who are you talking to, Alicia?" said Jenny. "You know I can't promise you that."

"Okay, then I'll claim you stole it if you wreck it," Alicia said. She lowered her voice. "It's parked at my condo building. You'll know it when you see it. But what about your tail?"

"I didn't spend my whole childhood becoming the world's greatest Girl Detective to be foiled by some bozo in a cheap suit."

Alicia snorted. Jenny crept to the door and peeked out. Sure enough, that fed was posted at the end of the hallway. She was about to step out when her heart scolded her for her cowardice. She released the handle and pressed her forehead against the cold door.

"Alicia… I never told you why I tested your DNA," Jenny said. She swallowed hard and turned around. "I was t-terrified that you might be RJ's daughter."

The little redhead stared at her, echoes of wonder and shame passing over her face.

"I used to daydream about that," Alicia said in a small voice. "On bad days. What's it like? For it to be real?"

Jenny tried to consider the question, but even venturing near that topic in her mind threatened to pull her down into the abyss.

"It was a stupid fear," Jenny said instead. "Lizzy and I should be so lucky to call you sister."

She ruffled Alicia's hair and kissed her on the cheek. Now, she could leave.

Out in the hallway, Jenny crossed over the peach tiles to the Inpatient Care exit. The fed detached himself from the wall to follow.

"No, you stay put," Jenny said. She poked him in his chest. "Someone should be watching her 24/7, in case the Stranger tries again. Tell Agent Tierce I'll see him at the ER exit."

Before he could argue, she threw the double doors open and stomped back into the main hospital wing. Just as she'd promised, she headed straight for the ER—until a group of medics wheeling a patient on a gurney passed her, and Jenny used the cover to duck inside Nuclear Medicine. She moved from room to room, navigating the employee corridors and acting like she belonged, until she came to a laundry nook with fresh linens. Quickly, she pulled on some purple scrubs over her hoodie and jeans and produced a blonde wig from her Coach mini backpack.

A minute later, she walked past Agent Tierce on her way out of the ER exit. He didn't even glance twice at her.

It was a 10-minute walk to Alicia's condo complex. Jenny circled it twice, making sure she wasn't being followed, before finding the entrance to the parking garage underneath. She hit the Lock button on Alicia's key fob. Lights flashed and a horn honked at the far end of the garage.

Alicia's car was a crimson red convertible Ford Mustang.

"You can take a girl out of Alkali Estates…" Jenny said to herself, smiling. "But you can't take the trailer park out of the girl."

Franz Lambert's two-story Craftsman house was tucked away in a quiet bedroom community, one of a dozen identical towns littering the corridors of Highways 12 and 101. The lights were on, but no movement stirred within.

Her watch vibrated, tapping her three times on the wrist. Jenny was here.

"Nice jacket, Trinity," said Jenny.

"Is it too much?" Eliza asked.

"No, we look hot." Jenny squinted at the house. There were no streetlights in this neighborhood, leaving the front yard and porch bathed in shadow as dusk deepened to night. "Anything going on in there?"

"Quiet as a tomb," said Eliza. "Should we—wait!"

"I saw it too," said Jenny.

The light in the window flickered again, like someone walking in front of a lamp.

"Do we knock?" Jenny asked.

"Are you in a knocking mood?" Eliza replied.

Jenny shook her head. Together, they stole across the street and crept up to the porch. Eliza reached back for Secret when Jenny touched her arm.

"What do we do if we're right?" she asked. "If he really did kill Mom?"

"Fulfill our oath," said Eliza.

With a note of ringing steel, Eliza drew Secret from its sheath. Jenny pulled on black nitrile gloves and tried the door handle.

"It's unlocked," she said. "On three?"

"Three," said Eliza.

Jenny shoved the door open.

The smell hit Eliza first. Sweet and pungent and rancid with decay. They raced through a living room full of shabby furniture and stacks of newspapers toward the moving shadows in the back of the house.

"Lambert!!" they shouted in unison and charged forward into the parlor.

A fancy chandelier hung from the vaulted ceiling. Swaying from it by a noose, his face purple and swollen and very dead, was Lambert. Pinned to his chest by a letter opener was a white paper with **GUILTY** scrawled in red across it.

"What the fuck?" shouted Jenny.

Eliza lunged forward and grabbed at the dark figure trying to hide behind the far doorway. It was Tori Valentine.

"What the fuck?" echoed Eliza.

Tori gawked, her eyes darting back and forth between Eliza and Jenny. Realization dawned on her face.

"What the fuck?!"

THE PEPPER SPRAY WAS IN TORI'S HAND BEFORE JENNY COULD stutter out a half-assed explanation. Her brain was still stuck on Lambert's corpse, swinging from the chandelier.

"N-no, wait!" Jenny yelled, raising her hands.

Tori blasted Eliza in the face. Her sister managed to block her left eye in time, but the right one took a direct hit from the stream of pepper spray.

"AACCHHH!!!" Eliza yelled, dropping her sword. "FUCK! WHY!!"

"Um, uh, milk!" Jenny said, running to the kitchen. "Goddamnit, Tori!"

"Twins!" Tori shrieked. "I should have fucking known! It was you, wasn't it? You killed RJ Valentine!"

"No!" Eliza yelled. "Was in"—*cough!*—"LA!"

"Oh, I've heard that before!" said Tori.

Jenny grabbed a carton of milk and sprinted back to the parlor. Eliza was doubled over, violently coughing, snot dripping out of every orifice in her scrunched-up face.

"Let me see," said Jenny.

She tried to tilt Eliza's head back, but her sister slapped her hand away and coughed hard.

"Hold her!" she yelled at Tori.

"Fuck you, I'm calling the police!" said Tori.

Tori already had her phone out, holding off Jenny with the pepper spray in one hand while she dialed with the other.

"You do that, and you'll never know the truth!" Jenny shouted. She wasn't entirely sure what she meant by this, but it was enough to stop Tori from dialing for a moment. "If you call them, I'll say you killed Lambert. You were here first. And practically dressed as the Stranger, to boot."

Tori frowned and looked down at her attire: a fashionable black coat over black leggings.

"I'm not—"

"And using the same noose that killed Casey Klein, too," Jenny added, pointing to the rope Lambert was hanging from.

Eliza groaned and threw up her pizza dinner. Tori scowled at them, shaking her head.

"That's not the same noose," Tori said. "Don't you get it? It was her. She's the one who visited RJ the day before the attack. While you were in that psych ward in LA, this one was up here killing him."

"She wasn't, she was at the psych ward with me," said Jenny.

"Then she came back and killed him at the hospital the next day, just like we theorized," said Tori.

"Eliza wouldn't do that," said Jenny.

"How would you know? She never even told you she came to see RJ, did she?" said Tori.

The slick intuition caught Jenny short.

"That's what I thought," said Tori.

"I didn't!" Eliza said from the floor, in between coughing fits.

"Why should I believe you?" asked Tori.

Eliza managed to master her coughing and retching long enough to spit out, "Because Jenny tried to kill herself that night, and I wasn't about to drive 400 miles away and leave her alone."

It was Tori's turn to be caught short. Her eyes found Jenny's, the question unspoken. Jenny nodded.

"Right. I forgot about that."

Tori glanced between Jenny and Eliza a few more times, sighed in a great huff, and grabbed Eliza's head, forcing it back. Jenny dumped the milk all over her swollen eye. Eliza sagged on the floor, the coughing fit finally subsiding.

"Eugh!" she said and grabbed the milk carton, squinting at it with her one good eye. "Fucking Lambert, this is two weeks expired!"

Her sister scrambled off to the bathroom to wash up. Jenny's attention returned to the hanging body between her and Tori.

"Has he been dead that long?" she asked.

"Don't think so," said Tori. "His body temperature suggests a time of death in the 18–24 hour range. The letter opener must have been postmortem, or there'd be more blood."

"Look at you, Girl Detective," said Jenny, perhaps a bit snottily.

"I was doing this when you were still in diapers," said Tori. "Would you like to explain how the bloody hell you've had a secret twin all this time?"

"Not until you tell me what you were doing here in the first place," said Jenny.

Following up on Jenny's own lead, apparently. Tori hadn't forgotten about Jenny and Dinah searching the archives for records of Stratford Photography's contract employees. Once she'd given her statement to the feds and gotten them off her back, Tori had combed through the digital archives for the names of every contractor the company had ever paid. For the past week, she'd been diligently checking out every single one of them for connections to the Valentine family.

"How was Lambert connected?" Jenny asked.

"He wasn't," said Tori. "But he also wasn't answering his phone, and the fact that he used to be a policeman was a red flag. I came here hoping to feel him out. When it seemed like nobody was home, I thought I'd do some snooping and found this." She waved at the body. "How did *you* find him?"

"The hard way," said Eliza, returning from the bathroom with a towel to wipe down her face. Her right eye was swollen shut. That whole side of her face was tinted an angry red. "I'm Eliza, by the way. You bitch."

The two sized each other up.

"Well, you had a sword, you psycho," said Tori. "Are you the one who hesitated with the EpiPen when the Stranger poisoned me and Jack?"

Eliza pointed to Jenny. "That was her. I'm the one who saved your mom's life at the Crow's Nest. And I killed Campbell Batori, too."

Tori raised an eyebrow, allowing a very RJ-like mischievous smile.

"Go ahead and say it," Jenny said. "Everyone likes her more."

"Wait, you must be Kazumi!" Tori made a face. "Weren't you hooking up with my brother?"

"No! Did he tell people that!?"

"I mean, he took you to homecoming," said Tori.

"Can we focus, people?" Jenny said. She pointed to Lambert's body. "This proves it, then. This is the connection we were looking for. Valerie Valentine hired Lambert to spy on Mom and Dad. He killed her, on Val's order. And then Val killed him when we were getting too close. Probably, she noticed you looking into the records."

Tori rolled her eyes. "Wrong, and wrong. First of all, Val doesn't control the Stratford businesses, her brother does."

"So *he* hired Lambert," said Jenny.

"He doesn't do anything," said Tori. "He has a business manager who runs things. And they wouldn't be the one to hire contract photographers, either. I spoke to the shift lead at the studio, and she says they'll hire practically anyone with a professional camera come Little League season because they're swamped."

Jenny bit her lip, thinking through the angles. Eliza threw the towel down in disgust.

"So… you're saying the photographic fingerprint on the team photo is a coincidence?" Eliza asked.

"Maybe?" Tori shrugged. "I mean, this is probably still the bastard who killed your mom—unless the Stranger is trying to throw you off the scent."

"Oh, he is," said Jenny. "He's been trying to stop me from following this clue the whole time. And he definitely didn't want me asking Lambert any questions about it. Fuck! How is he always two steps ahead of me?"

"He stole the archive files, didn't he?" asked Tori.

"Right. Shit," said Jenny. "I practically led the Stranger right to him."

"Lambert must have known something," said Tori. "Something that connects to the Stranger. That suggests someone older, if this goes all the way back to your mom."

"Like the mayor," said Jenny.

"Hector?" Tori cocked her head, considering. "I wouldn't entirely put it past him."

"Guys, can we talk about the elephant in the room?" Eliza asked. "Or rather, the swinging corpse? What are we going to do? Our DNA is all over this place."

"You should start by turning yourself in," said Tori.

"She can't!" said Jenny. "I need her. I can't investigate with the feds up my ass."

"That's not my problem."

"We caught Casey's killer for you!" Jenny said. "You owe us!"

That put an affronted scowl on their stepsister's superior face.

"It's what he wanted," said Eliza, returning her sword to its sheath. "That's what RJ and I talked about. He said I should be the ace up Jenny's sleeve. Her secret helper."

Conflicting emotions warred behind Tori's eyes. "Until you age out," she muttered to herself. "Fine. But I'm not helping you with the game. I'm the executor, remember?"

"Fair enough," said Jenny. "Just don't tell anyone."

Tori nodded. They all stared up at the corpse.

"It will have to be a fire," said Tori. "I can fake an electrical one."

"Wait, shouldn't we search the place, first?" asked Eliza. "Maybe there's something here that connects Lambert to the Stranger."

"You haven't seen his den," said Tori. "It's already been ransacked."

Sure enough, it had. Drawers had been ripped out of Lambert's desk and emptied. A wall safe hung open, and the Dogs Playing Poker painting that must have covered it lay smashed on the floor. All the books on his shelf were tossed haphazardly on the floor.

"I'm guessing the evidence you're looking for was in that safe," said Tori.

Jenny stared at Lambert's little leather newsboy cap, hanging from a coat rack. She couldn't stop thinking about all the times she'd spoken to him. Stood right next to him. Never once did she catch even the slightest hint that he'd killed their mother… Could this all be a trick? Or was she not the judge of character she thought she was?

"We have to clean up," said Tori. "Put all the drawers back, rehang the painting, et cetera. This needs to look like a suicide and a house fire."

Eliza got to work while Tori readied the fire. Jenny returned to the parlor to pluck the letter opener out of Lambert's chest. Hopefully the fire would hide that wound, if the forensic pathologist didn't look too close.

A memory flashed in her mind: that drug dealer Jorge Lopez, lying dead in his bed at Alkali Estates. The Stranger had left a similar note, stuck to Jorge's chest. If the Stranger was trying to silence Lambert now, had he been trying to silence Jorge Lopez then? About what?

"We ready?" Tori asked from the kitchen.

"More or less," said Eliza. "What do you say, regroup at Mel's?"

"Are you sure you're good to drive?" Jenny asked.

"I'll manage," said Eliza.

Jenny had her doubts. Poor Lizzy's eye was still comically swollen shut.

"I don't care where you go, just leave me out of it," said Tori.

Eliza nudged Jenny and pointed to Lambert.

"I thought I'd feel something more," Eliza said. "Knowing we caught Mom's killer. But all I feel is empty."

"Sometimes, there's peace in feeling nothing at all," said Tori.

Funny, Jenny wasn't feeling very peaceful.

Tori fiddled with the toaster, pressing down on the lever. There was a loud *pop!* and all the lights went out. Jenny could smell burnt plastic. A moment later, flames licked up the side of the appliance.

"Ladies, it's been a pleasure," said Tori. "We were never here. Let me know when you need a good therapist; I can recommend a few."

The twins snuck out the front door, leaving Tori to her own getaway. Jenny agreed to meet Lizzy at Mel's and hurried back to Alicia's convertible, parked up the street. Already, she could smell smoke from the fire. The fire department would get here before it spread to other houses, right?

Fuck it, that's on Tori.

Jenny slid in behind the wheel, started the ignition, and did a double take at the seat next to her.

She'd left the top down because she couldn't find the button to close it. There in the passenger seat were a few stapled pages of letter-size paper, with a note from the Stranger on top.

YOU'RE CHASING THE WRONG CLUE.

Chapter Eleven
And Introducing...

JENNY'S SELF-CONTROL LASTED THE WHOLE DRIVE TO MEL'S IN Santa Rosa. It was dark, and Highway 101 at night was scary. As soon as she pulled into the parking lot, she took the first open space, hit the parking brake, and dove into the new manuscript pages.

Chapter 3

The best way to find a dead guy's address is to go to the county clerk's office in Town Hall and ask for his death certificate. They have to give it to you, even if you're a known scamp, because it's a public record.

Unfortunately, Town Hall is closed until Monday, and I'm impatient. To the library!

"Reading on the job? Tsk tsk," I say to the girl engrossed in her copy of *Sense and Sensibility* at the check-out desk.

Dinah glances up, notices me, and covers her mouth in surprise. Good surprise? I hope so.

"Jenny! What are you doing here? Are you all right? What did the police say?"

"I'm fine," I say, blushing a little. "I'm Trouble, remember. It's you I'm worried about. I wish you hadn't seen that guy at the theater."

"I had the most dreadful dreams last night, and you were in them," says Dinah. She puts the book down, clutching a hand to her heart. "Sorry, did you need something?"

"A girl can't make a social call?" I say with a smirk. "But sure, I need you to help me find a book."

"What book?" Dinah asks.

"It's a mystery. A real page-turner," I say. "The problem is, my father returned it before I could finish it, and it's already been checked out again. I posted in the library Facebook group and found out the guy who has it is named Eugene Hodgson. Can you give me his address so I can go pick it up from him?"

Dinah narrowed her eyes.

"Does this work on people? Be for real, Trouble."

"I was hoping it would work on you," I say, batting my eyelashes. "Plan B is to release a skunk into the building and run behind the counter when all the employees flee."

"Well, in that case." Dinah smirked. "Who is Eugene Hodgson?"

"The dead guy."

A tempest of emotion storms across her flawless face. Fear, revulsion, curiosity, and a thrill. My world frightens Dinah, but it also intrigues her.

"Do you want to come?" I ask.

"What are you expecting to find?" Dinah replies.

"I don't know yet," I say. "That's the best part."

She hesitates just long enough to make me sweat, then she slaps a **Next Window** sign in front of her.

"Let me get my purse."

#

The aforementioned dead guy lives up in the mountains that overlook Blackbird Springs. If I were alone, I'd be slinging my cherry-red Mustang convertible around each switchback like an Italian Formula 1 driver, but Dinah gets carsick, so I have to take it easy.

"What can you tell me about Mayor Villanova?" I ask.

"HUH?!!" Dinah shouts back.

I suppose driving with the top down makes having conversations a challenge, but I love feeling the wind in my hair, and the smell of the crisp alpine air. I slow down even more (a shame) and lean over to yell in her ear.

"What do you know about the mayor!? Your family is friends with him, right!?"

She scrunches her nose like a particularly cute chipmunk and shouts back.

"My mom and his wife are friends, I guess!" she says. "He's usually too busy to stop by! Why do you ask!?"

"Eugene Hodgson was his old partner on the force!" I shout.

That raises some eyebrows. Dinah checks the maps and points up ahead.

"Make a right up here!"

Hodgson lives in a ramshackle cabin at the end of a private road. Signs are warning me on the way that trespassers will be shot, but I don't need to worry about that anymore. Not since the Stranger plucked out his eyeballs and finished off what too much alcohol and red meat had already begun.

The cabin sits in the shadow of Black Rock Peak, meaning my tires are still crunching over a slurry of old snowfall as I roll to a stop in his driveway. I'm wearing a brand-new purple trench coat, just purchased this morning from Burberry, to protect from the cold. Dinah looks glamorous as always in a faux fur from Prada and a red scarf.

I didn't take Dad's fedora when I left the house. Didn't want to tip him off to what I'd be up to. This is something new for me: lying to him. Sure, I used to get into so much you-know-what, but it was always with a wink and a nod and a look the other way from Daddy. This time, he's given me an explicit order, and not just for show because Lockhart is around. He means it, and I'm still defying him. Sorry, Dad, but you should have expected this when you and Mom named me.

"We going inside, or just going to stare?" Dinah asks.

"Of course," I say. "Let me go first, in case there are traps."

There aren't any traps. What a letdown. Hodgson's place is a sty. It smells like lumber and turpentine and something else I can't place—but it's vaguely familiar. This is an old-school log cabin, bare wood walls, but fairly cozy. There's only a kitchen and living room, with an office in the back and a bedroom loft above it.

Dinah and I agree to split up. She'll take the kitchen and living room, I'll get the office and loft. We'll look for anything out of the ordinary, or that has my name or the mayor's on it. Dinah finds rotten eggs, and milk two weeks past its due date. I find a whole crate of old VHS tapes under his ratty mattress that, going by their labels, contain vintage pornography.

I don't watch them on Hodgson's ancient VCR to confirm.

"He must have drank like a fish," Dinah says, coming in from the back door. "I found three trash bags full of these next to the woodpile."

She shows me a brown bottle of Dillion's Reserve whiskey. I can't claim to know much about spirits, but I'm pretty sure that brand counts as "the good stuff." Interesting.

We've been here an hour now and still racking up

zeros. I can tell Dinah is over it, but she won't say so. She'll let me call it a day. So studious and proper. God, I want her to like me. Who would have ever guessed that Trouble would fall for Blackbird Springs' most well-behaved blue blood?

I knock on every log, testing for hollow cavities. Check for false bottoms in every drawer. I even cut open Hodgson's disgusting mattress. There's nothing inside but rusty springs and foam that's starting to go moldy. The only interesting detail is his file cabinet: it's totally empty.

Dinah figures out why.

"Looks like a receipt from the old body shop," Dinah says.

She's found a pile of fresh ashes in the wood stove, and a couple scraps of paper that didn't entirely burn up. From what I can tell, it's the fragment of a work order from a car mechanic's shop in town. That place went out of business years ago. It's almost worth ignoring, except for the date.

"Weird," I say.

"What is it?" Dinah asks.

"This is dated a week after my mom died," I say.

"And she died in a car accident, right?"

"Huh? No, she had a brain aneurysm."

Subconsciously, my hand goes to my temple, like it always does when I think about that day. I was so young I barely remember it anymore. Just Daddy taking me out of kindergarten early. We went to the mall and he let me ride the merry-go-round, but even at that age, I could tell there was something wrong. After I got off the ride, he told me. It's still the only time I've ever seen him cry.

"What's the significance, then?" Dinah asks, examining the burnt piece of the body shop receipt.

"I don't know. But it's a piece of the puzzle. And there's no such thing as an extra puzzle piece."

I kneel to examine another scrap of paper that escaped the flames. Looks like the corner of a manila envelope…

Eureka! I didn't even think of it until now.

"The mail!" I say, leaping up.

It's the oldest move in the book: if you need to hide something for a few days, mail it to yourself!

Dinah waits by the door while I troop across the packed snow to Hodgson's mailbox at the end of the driveway. Sure enough, under a pile of junk mail is a bulky envelope addressed to Hodgson. Lots of stamps on it, but no return address. It rattles a little when I shake it. Whatever is inside feels no bigger than a matchbox.

I tear the envelope open. Technically this is a federal offense. Don't tell.

Inside I find a mini cassette, like the kind you would use in an answering machine—or a hidden recording device. It's unlabeled.

"What could be in here?" I ask myself.

"Jenny!" Dinah shouts from the cabin.

I look back and wave. "I think I found something!"

"No! Look out!"

She points in horror! I spin around just in time to see a dark shadow rushing toward me amongst the winter-white landscape. A tall, dark, and Strangesome menace. Beware!

I'm too slow to react. Out of practice. The Stranger slams into me and knocks me off my feet. My hands splay open and up into the air flies the mini cassette. I can see it arcing across the cloudy mountain sky as I fall.

A black-gloved hand reaches out and snatches the cassette out of the air as I crunch into the snow. For a moment, I can't breathe. It's like the lights went out.

Then I'm sputtering for air, my face dusted with frost. Lucky. This would have hurt a lot more on asphalt, but now my whole backside is freezing.

"He's getting away!" I hear Dinah shout.

At the same time, a throaty engine roars. The Stranger has hopped on a motorcycle down the lane and started it up, about to speed away.

There's no time to think. No time to wait for Dinah to catch up. I leap to my feet and race back to my Mustang. Keys in the ignition! No time for a safety belt! Foot on the gas! I back out of there and whip the hood around, just how Daddy taught me. Then I'm away on the chase.

The Stranger has a few hundred yards on me, but I'm gaining. He's on some old dirt bike, I can see now. Mine's faster! I whip around one switchback, then another. He's headed downhill, back to the city. I'm gaining. Just a couple more turns and I'll have him—

Well, I *would* have him. If not for the milk truck that I didn't see coming around the bend!!

I jerk the wheel left to go wide, and my tires begin to fishtail. It's all I can do to avoid a crash. The milkman passes by on my right so close that I can see the fillings in his teeth as his mouth gapes wide in shock.

My car is spinning around now. Spinning. Spinning—

An awful grinding stop saves me, thank god. Something just tore up my car's undercarriage, for sure. But I've got more immediate problems! Over the hood, the view is fantastic. I can see the whole valley from up here, all those beautiful vineyards, and my lovely town in the center. The angle is all wrong, though. My rearview mirror shows nothing but that cloudy mountain sky and the tip of Black Rock Peak. It's slowly rising and falling. Or, rather, my car is.

I'm hanging off the edge of the cliff!!!

My heart freezes to the core. I'm afraid to even breathe. One false move, and I'll teeter over the edge. Stupid, Trouble! This wasn't your world anymore! Didn't Daddy tell you to leave it alone?

No! I can't! This is important, I just don't know why, yet. Trouble never gives up on a case!

I lean back as carefully as I can and shift into reverse. Hopefully my drivetrain still works. The gears grind, and the Mustang wobbles. Maybe I should try leaping out?

Crossing my fingers, I release the brakes and tap on the gas. I can feel the engine rev, I can hear the wheels spinning behind me, but nothing happens.

Oh hell! This is a rear-wheel drive vehicle, and my rear wheels are two feet in the air!

"You are well and truly screwed this time, Trouble Valentine!" I say to myself.

Maybe if I make a joke of it, I won't be so terrified. Jumping out is sounding real good now.

"Ease off a bit!" shouts a voice behind me.

A very familiar voice. I risk a glance back, but all I can see is the sky and the trunk sticking up. But then, a hand reaches up. A slender hand, with an Ace of Clubs tattooed on the wrist. It grips the rear taillight. The teetering stops and I can feel the car stabilize. My savior must be pushing down on the bumper. The horizon is returning to normal, and with it, glorious firmament once again presses against my back tires.

"Okay, real slow now," says the voice. It's a girl's voice. "Don't go too fast or you'll run me over."

Following her instructions, I gently give the Mustang a little gas. The wheels catch traction and begin the pull. There's a lot of nasty grinding under my seat. If I didn't ruin the undercarriage before, I certainly am now!

Inch by inch, my car backs away from the cliff. Then my front tires hit the edge, and after one last push, I'm over the hump and gliding back onto the shoulder of the switchback. My mysterious rescuer has jumped out of the way to let me pass. As soon as I'm sure the car is on steady ground, I kill the engine and scurry out of my seat, relieved to put my feet back on terra firma.

When I look up across the convertible to the passenger side, my own face is staring back at me.

I blink twice? Am I dreaming? Did I actually just die? How is this possible? She looks just like me!

"Hey," she says. "I'm Danger."

MEL'S DRIVE-IN WAS ONE OF THOSE RETRO '50S DINERS WITH SPARKLY red vinyl booths and old-fashioned mini jukeboxes at every table that took actual quarters to play. It was a few towns away from Blackbird Springs, so Eliza and Jenny felt comfortable coming here together. Eliza thought they would be processing what happened with Lambert, but her sister came in white as a ghost and shoved some typed pages in her face.

"Read it."

Eliza withheld a sigh and did as requested. She could feel Jenny's eyes on her the whole time, and when she got to the end, she understood why.

"Everything all right?" asked the waiter, frowning at them.

Neither had touched their fries and ranch.

"Fine, thank you," said Jenny. She waited until he left. "This is getting weird, right?"

"Are we sure RJ wrote this?" Eliza asked. "It's so… specific. The Dinah stuff especially. Maybe the Stranger *does* know about me, and this is their way of making me canon."

Jenny shook her head. "No, the Ace of Clubs tattoo."

"Wouldn't the Stranger know I have one, too?" Eliza asked.

"Even if he did, Trouble in the story doesn't have one," Jenny said.

"If the Stranger was writing this, we'd both have the tattoo. Only Dad would know that you got yours first."

Eliza wondered if RJ wrote that part about the tattoo before he met her, or after. Did he give her the tattoo to make sure she matched his idea of her, or did he add the tattoo to this manuscript afterward?

She shivered and ate a french fry. It was cold now, too.

"They know now," Eliza said. "If the Stranger is the one leaving these for you, and this is the real final manuscript, then they know about me."

"You keep saying 'they,'" said Jenny.

"Because it could very well be a woman," said Eliza. "Tori? Penny? *Dinah?*"

Jenny grimaced. "I know. I'll talk to her soon. But technically, the Stranger—male or female—knows about *Danger*, not you. Maybe they will assume it's just a corny plot twist for the book."

"Maybe."

Neither of them said anything for a minute, mulling over the possibilities. Dinah had known about Eliza for months. And here she was, suddenly prominent in the story. Could this be Blondie's work?

"No…" Eliza said to herself.

"What?"

"I was trying to imagine Dinah writing this," Eliza said. "But this still feels like a man wrote it. Honestly, it feels just like RJ."

"I agree," Jenny said.

"You're right, though. It is weird, having him write me into the story. I feel like I'm being posed like a doll. Why did this never freak you out?"

Jenny scowled. "It's not like that! At least, it wasn't." She bit her lip. "But I know what you mean. It feels different now."

"Because you're older."

"Not just that. This Trouble is different. She's too… aware. Like, the young Trouble would never talk about 'her world.' It's like—"

"It's like she knows she's in a *Trouble* book," said Eliza. She smirked at Jenny's pouty face. "It's because Dad isn't writing Book Trouble anymore. He's writing *you*."

Eliza studied her sister as Jenny chewed that one over. She could practically see in real-time as Jenny packed her confused feelings into a box and set them aside.

"Let's assume the manuscript is real." She tapped the pages. "What do we make of the implication that Hodgson killed Trouble's mom? Maybe on Mayor Villanova's order?"

"What? Since when?"

"In the manuscript," said Jenny. "The receipt they found for the body shop."

"That part was weird," said Eliza. "She *did* die of an aneurysm, right? Our book mom, that is?"

Talking about their fictional counterparts was already giving Eliza a headache.

"Yes, but our real mom didn't. I think Dad is mixing fiction and reality. He's trying to tell us something with this story. Or he's insinuating it, at least. And maybe that's why they killed him."

"They?"

"The mayor, the town elders, the Big Six wineries? Who knows, but this connects some dots," said Jenny. "Dad knew someone was trying to kill him. Maybe he wrote this book as, like, a dead man's switch. If he dies, he exposes all the dirt on Blackbird Springs's blue blood elites. It's like insurance."

"If that was his plan, he shouldn't have made solving his murder a prerequisite to getting the manuscript," said Eliza. "Broader question: why is the Stranger, whoever they are, giving you these pages? Especially after possibly stealing the evidence we needed from Lambert's safe."

"He's trying to encourage me," said Jenny. "I think he got mad when I spent so much time at Pixeldrome. He wants me to play the game. That's probably why he killed Rob. To make me move on. And to do me a solid for mom's sake, I guess."

Eliza didn't care for the way Jenny framed those events. It was almost like she appreciated the Stranger for getting her back on track. She was about to say so when Jenny grabbed her hand.

"He didn't make me, though, you did," Jenny said, her voice

cracking a little. "I haven't forgotten that."

"I know, thank you," said Eliza. "In the spirit of that, why don't you listen to your sister for once: don't get too wrapped up in *I Dream of Trouble*. I want to catch Mom's killers more than anyone, but the Stranger isn't trying to help us, they're trying to help themselves. Don't forget, they tried to stop us from even finding Lambert. Okay, the Stranger isn't trying to right some wrong here, which is why that "you're welcome" business with Rob Haines was bullshit, too. Think about it: what's the *real* reason the Stranger killed that guy?"

"Mmm, access to the VIP room?" Jenny guessed.

"He already had it, he stole Nilay's card," Eliza said, suddenly struck with that epiphany. "That's why he was rummaging in Nilay's pockets after he killed him."

"Okay, so maybe Rob was just down there in the VIP room, and the Stranger had to kill him to get the high score and leave me the pages," said Jenny.

Eliza turned the idea over.

"Maybe," she said. "Maybe we haven't been thinking about motives enough. You know, cui bono? Who benefits."

"It's funny you say that," said Jenny. "The note on Lambert got me thinking about Jorge Lopez, remember him? The drug dealer? The Stranger left a 'You're getting colder' note on his body the same way. But why? He normally doesn't leave a body with his hints. And that reporter guy, Warby Parker: the Stranger didn't leave a body for him at all."

Eliza shook her head. "That's because he's not dead. Jeffrey Jordan started tweeting again, a few months ago. I forgot to tell you because we weren't really speaking."

"For real? What does he tweet about?"

"Just stupid shit about Koreatown zoning laws. I think he moved there. He's one of those housing activist dudes now."

"Okay. I guess that's good if he's leaving me alone," said Jenny. She bit her lip. "Does that mean the Stranger let him off with a warning? Maybe we should put him and Jorge on the leads list. There's something we missed."

Eliza got out her phone to edit the list when Jenny added, "Shoot. I gotta get back home before Tierce and Steele arrest me for ditching them."

"Oh, okay," said Eliza. She wasn't expecting Jenny to wrap things up so fast, but they probably should be splitting up. Even three towns away, it was dangerous to be together like this. And not the fun kind of danger. "Say hi to Drew for me. I mean, not really, but, you know."

"I will. I'll think of something to tell him. And I'll talk to Dinah— no matter how awkward that's gonna be."

Jenny stood up, staring at Alicia's keychain.

"How did the Stranger know where we'd be to plant these pages?" she asked. "It wasn't even my car. And the only one who knew I was going there besides you was…"

Alicia. Eliza had a hard time believing Alicia was even capable of that kind of villainy. But wasn't writing her off as a suspect its own form of disrespect? Could the little wallflower girl have everyone fooled?

"The Stranger could have just followed you. Maybe check your purse for trackers," said Eliza.

"Good point, I will."

Still, her sister hesitated.

"What?" asked Eliza.

"It's probably just a coincidence that Alicia Aaron drives the same car as grown-up Trouble, right?"

"Probably," said Eliza.

Chapter Twelve

One Surprise After Another

J ENNY DIDN'T WANT TO BELIEVE ALICIA COULD BE EVIL. NOT AFTER they'd shared that special moment. They were unofficial sisters now. Alicia would have to be the best actor in the world to fake that. But then, Jenny never picked up any bad vibes from Lambert, and that son of a bitch tried to kill her. There was a good chance the Stranger was someone Jenny knew, someone she trusted, someone she'd overlooked as a suspect.

Which brought her suspicions back to her girlfriend. It was too weird that Dinah was so prominent in *I Dream of Trouble*. If they were going to be together again, they couldn't have this hanging between them, Dryden Street be damned.

But on Monday, Dinah was feeling crappy because of her period, and that seemed like the wrong time to bug her about it. On Tuesday, the undercover fed girl sat at their table and tried to make small talk about the prom. Wednesday brought the sun out, and all the Troublemakers ate in the quad because it was such a nice day. They were happy, for once, and Jenny didn't want to ruin the mood.

That night, on their Signal video call check-in, Eliza was getting impatient.

"It's all fine and good for you to take your time until the vibes feel right," Eliza said on screen. "I'm the one who has to sleep in hostels or that moth-ridden storage closet above the movie theater! Do you know how long it's been since I've had a real shower?"

"I did think you smelled a little ripe last weekend," Jenny replied. "Things are still fragile. If I push Dinah too hard, too fast, she'll just cut me off again."

Jenny was taking the call in her bedroom closet because Blake was downstairs with Shelly. He'd brought Lilah over, of course. Doing that thing men do where they pretend to be bad at something until the woman steps in to do it properly. In this case: parenting.

"Just get Blondie all lathered up and then refuse to go further until she spills," Eliza said.

"Danger, really!" Jenny whispered. "Sounds like someone's missing a woman's touch."

"Or a man's!" said Eliza. "Did you talk to Drew?"

"Uh, I told him you were fine, and back in Okinawa, but you couldn't talk because of lawyers and shit," Jenny said. A white lie; she'd told him nothing. "I'll talk to Dinah tomorrow, I promise."

"You'd better!" said Eliza. "Or else I'm gonna dye my hair purple too and do something rash!"

JENNY WAS ABOUT TO GIVE DINAH THE THIRD DEGREE ON THURSDAY (*seriously!*), but then Penny and Drew showed up at lunch with big news.

"Ask, and ye shall receive," said Penny.

She was holding out a candy bar. The kind the theater kids were selling to raise money for their play. It was cookies and cream, which Jenny hated.

Penny frowned and gave Jenny a knowing look that screamed *take it!*

"Thanks, you shouldn't have," Jenny said and accepted the candy bar.

With it came something else. Something small and plastic that Penny pressed into her palm. Jenny stole a glance at her hand. It was a flash drive.

"Oh, I just love these," she said. "But I'm allergic to gluten. What are the ingredients?"

"You're gonna shit yourself," Drew said.

A broad grin spread across Penny's face. She was positively giddy, and suddenly Jenny's heart was racing. *What is it??*

"How about some music?" Jack asked and proceeded to play some droning Montreal indie rock on his iPhone before anyone could respond. He motioned for them all to lean closer to his phone and said, "Let's hear it, Pen."

"Well, as you know, my mother refuses to talk about her heirloom book," said Penny. "Not to me or you or seemingly anyone at all."

"And we've had no luck finding it anywhere else," said Drew. "We checked like a dozen libraries."

"But when you told us RJ wrote it, it got me thinking," said Penny. "My mom is an editor, right? She runs the *Blackbird Times*. She's edited every essay I've written since freshman year. Also, she and RJ were friends from way back. Before he married Val, even, she said. Are you following me?"

"You're saying she edited the heirloom book?" Dinah asked.

She leaned forward, her hand resting on her chin in that classic coquettish pose of hers. Jenny could only guess what she was thinking behind those bright eyes.

"Hmm. There's already a lady in New York who Dad worked with since the first *Trouble* book," Jack said. "Don't think he's ever had another editor."

"Lily Castell," said Jenny. "He thanks her in the Acknowledgments of every book."

"Sure, but authors are vain," said Dinah. "RJ would have wanted as much feedback as he could get."

"Yes, and *The Stranger of Sausalito* was written before *Trouble*—if you'll let me continue!" Penny said. "I asked my mom about it, and of course, she gave me nothing. Total poker face. So I thought, what if there's a digital trail? They used email back then, didn't they?"

Jenny bit the inside of her cheek, thinking. The impression she got from Jiji was that Dad wrote this book before she was even born.

"I managed to get access to my mom's laptop the other night for a few minutes while she was in the bathroom," said Penny. "But I couldn't find a single mention of 'Sausalito' in her Gmail. Nada. Nothing."

"And then your sidekick had a brilliant idea," said Drew.

Penny smirked and gave Drew a fist bump. "You tell it," she said.

"I was just thinking Gmail didn't even exist back then," said Drew. "Everyone had weird email where you downloaded messages to your hard drive to read them. And so if Ms. Griffin emailed RJ about the book, it wouldn't be in her Gmail. It would be on her computer. Specifically, her old computer."

"My mother's fatal flaw," said Penny. "She saves every old Mac she's ever had because she's one of those weird Apple people. So Drew and I waited until she was out with friends, and then we ransacked her little shrine of old technology. You wouldn't believe how long it took to turn on."

"Like three minutes!" said Drew.

"Okay, and I take it you found something?" said Jenny. She appreciated their ingenuity, but the suspense was killing her. "What's on the flash drive?"

"The manuscript," said Penny.

Wait! Did they have a complete copy of *I Dream of Trouble*?

Jenny blinked. "The manuscript of *what?*"

"*The Stranger of* motherfucking *Sausalito*," said Drew. "Score one for Gold Team."

After school, Jenny broke into the copy room and used Aunt Shelly's copy card (which she'd stolen long ago) to print out the whole manuscript. Once she got home, she curled up in the comfy armchair in Jiji's study and read RJ Valentine's first novel.

It wasn't very good. Sorry, Dad.

Essentially, *The Stranger of Sausalito* was a cat-and-mouse crime thriller about a narcoleptic, down-on-his-luck homicide detective on the trail of a serial killer in the North Bay Area. Every other chapter, the perspective switched between the cop and the killer. The tone was arch and edgy, full of labored metaphors about sewage, roadkill, sex crimes, and any other lurid pulp clichés RJ could think up.

The detective—despite his cantankerous attitude, disheveled attire, and infrequent bathing—was absolutely swimming in babes. Gorgeous women were dying to throw it at him. Literally. They kept getting murdered by the serial killer after their liaisons with the detective (who was never named). Being charitable, Jenny interpreted the story as a surreal, impressionistic journey into the City's corrupt underbelly, reflecting the detective's loosening grip on his sanity. But RJ never quite got there.

Have you guessed the twist yet?

On a technical level, the writing was decent. Clever turns of phrase and fifty-cent words abounded. Ms. Griffin might have helped, but Dad was always a skilled writer. He just hadn't found his groove yet with this book. He was trying too hard. He wasn't interested in the characters beyond their plot utility. Everything was in service of the big reveal.

Seriously, if you didn't see it coming…

All that said, Jenny found herself comforted by its badness. This wasn't a book made with love; this was the work of a bitter, disillusioned young man. If she had her timelines right, Dad would have been writing this around the time Val was cheating on him. No wonder it was so bleak: he hadn't met Mom yet. *My Name is Trouble* had all the heart *The Stranger of Sausalito* lacked. Just thinking about the *Trouble* books now was like being enveloped by her parents in a warm, loving embrace.

"Are you crying? What's wrong?" Eliza asked over their video call.

"Nothing!" Jenny snapped, wiping her eyes. "It's just, ya know, special to read more of Dad's early work."

"Mmm."

"Whatever. The point is, we finally have Ms. Griffin's heirloom clue," said Jenny. "So what does it mean?"

While Eliza chewed that over, Jenny peeked out from her closet, where she was hiding to make the call. Blake wasn't over tonight, but better safe than sorry. She thought she'd heard footsteps in the hall, but after taking an AirPod out, the only audible noise was the quiet drone of an NPR podcast from Aunt Shelly's bathroom.

"Fuck if I know," said Eliza. "Ms. Griffin has claimed she knows what the heirloom means, and that it's a dead end. Maybe the book was based on a real serial killer case? She would probably know about something like that."

"I'm gonna have to ask her," said Jenny. "She can't dodge me now, not after I've read it."

"Read what!?"

Aunt Shelly burst into the room and threw the sliding closet door open hard enough to bounce it off the doorjamb. Jenny yelped in surprise as her aunt lunged for her iPhone and snatched it away.

"I knew it!" Shelly screamed and glared lasers at the screen. "Elizabeth Valentine, you come right home this instant! This has gone on long enough!"

Lizzy stammered in response on the other end.

"Don't you dare hang up!" Shelly yelled.

"I—I'm sorry," Eliza said. "You know I want to, Aunt Shelly. But it's not safe."

"Safe! Federal agents are hunting you! They will shoot you on sight!! How is that safe!?"

Fuck. Jenny needed to act fast. Eliza was no good at being a bad girl; adult authority always made her fold. She leaned to look past her aunt, searching for a solution. If only she had her chloroform—

"What are you doing!?"

Jenny realized belatedly that her aunt was yelling at her, not Eliza. Her gaze shifted back to Shelly and her aunt did something bizarre: she shifted her hips.

Friendly eyes and warm smiles will deceive, but the body never lies.

It was one of Book Trouble's many detective maxims, and she wasn't wrong: people with something to hide usually struggled to keep it from showing in their body language. And just then, Aunt Shelly twisted away from Jenny in a classic tell.

"What are *you* doing, Shells?" Jenny said, a sly smirk spreading on her lips. "What's that you've got behind your back."

"Nothing."

"Okay, then turn around."

"I don't have to do that," Shelly tried lamely.

"What's going on?" Eliza asked on the video call. "Is everything okay?"

"It's fine, Lizzy. Our aunt is just hiding something from me."

Jenny stood up and had the satisfaction of seeing Shelly back away. She was trying to be casual about it, but the hand without Jenny's phone in it was being held rigidly at her side, tucking some object behind her wrist.

"It's nothing, it's just personal," said Shelly.

She was blushing now.

"Oh my god, is it a—oh jeez, I can't even say it!" Eliza cackled on the phone.

"It's not *that!*" Shelly said.

"Prove it!" Jenny said. "Or I'm telling your mother!"

"Do not even think about it!" Shelly snapped.

It was more of a plea than a command. She grimaced and hung her head. Covering her face with her phone hand, she extended the other out, revealing a small, pen-shaped object.

"Oh my fucking god!!" Jenny said when she got a look at it. "You're not!!"

"Not what!? Let me see! Let me see!" Eliza shouted on the phone.

Shelly held up the object to the phone's camera and Eliza shrieked.

"Shit, I hope nobody heard that," her sister added. "Is it? Are you?"

Jenny didn't even need to see it up close to know. Her aunt's face told the whole story. The object in her hand was a pregnancy test, and Shelly had flunked it.

THIS WAS POSSIBLY THE GREATEST THING TO EVER HAPPEN. NOT just Aunt Shelly's mortified face, but the whole deal! Pregnant! Eliza was about to have another sister! Or maybe even a brother! With Lockhart?! That baby was going to be so hot!

"Are you going to keep it?" she heard Jenny ask over the video call.

"I—I don't know," said Shelly. "I just found out. Look, come here."

There was some scuffing on the mic, and the picture shifted. Shelly had set the phone on Jenny's dresser and made Jenny sit down next to her at the end of the bed so she could address them both.

"This isn't how I wanted you to find out," Shelly said.

"Are you and Blake not good?" Eliza asked.

Shelly smiled tightly. "It's complicated. He's...he's a mess right now. And he's got his hands full already. I'm not sure another baby is the best idea right now."

"But what do *you* want?" asked Jenny.

Through the tiny screen, Eliza could see Shelly wrinkle her nose and wipe her left eye.

"I...I guess I'd stopped thinking that this was something that would ever happen for me," Shelly said.

"That means yes!" said Eliza.

"All that talk about being safe!" said Jenny. "Very ironic, don't you think! Oh, how the worm has turned!"

"Jennifer, I have neither the time nor the temperament to deal with your bullshit right now," said Shelly. She leaned forward to address Eliza directly. "You need to come home."

"I'm sorry, Shells, but I can't," said Eliza. "Not yet. We're making progress. Jenny probably didn't tell you, but we found Mom's killer. He's dead now."

Shelly glanced up from her pregnancy test, horrified. "You didn't...?"

"He was dead when we found him," said Jenny. "He was a retired cop and P.I. We still think Val hired him, but he took that secret to the grave."

Shelly blinked, fighting tears.

"We're not done yet," said Eliza. "But Lala can rest a little easier now."

She'd meant it to salve Shelly's emotions, but it pushed her over the edge instead. Their aunt choked back a sob and covered her mouth.

"I'm sorry, I can't right now," Shelly said through tears and got up from the bed. "Don't tell anyone."

Jenny grimaced as Shelly left the bedroom. "Hormones, I guess," she said.

"It's not just that," Eliza said.

"I know it's not just that," Jenny replied, her voice cracking. It was hard to tell on the small screen, but her sister might be misting up again herself. She coughed and cleared her throat. "I'm gonna try to talk to Ms. Griffin tomorrow. Maybe you should lay low for the weekend."

"Yeah, sure."

"Did you find anything on Jorge Lopez?"

Eliza shook her head. "There's four people who might know about him. Or might have known. I think Mason had sold him some weed, but we can't ask him now. And Arty Porter lived in Alkali Estates, but he's gone, too."

"Alicia lived there," Jenny pointed out.

"She did," said Eliza. "And if you'll recall, Val was going to pay Jorge for an alibi, but then the Stranger killed him. Maybe that's why: it would have been cheating at the game."

"Sure, but we cheated, too," said Jenny. "Who knew about that? Val? That reporter?"

Eliza braced herself. "And Dinah. She claimed she was trying to get info on what Val was up to, right? You know, you could bring that up with her—if you ever find the nerve."

A ripple of guilt passed over Jenny's face. "She has a field trip on Saturday. To Safari West for her Zoology class. Shelly's supposed to chaperone, so I'll find a way to tag along. The feds shouldn't be there. I'll get some time alone with Dinah and ask."

Eliza chewed on her lip. Whether or not Jenny would actually confront Dinah was a dubious proposition, but it was a plan, at least. A wild idea of her own sprang into her mind.

"Thank you," she said. "Um, in that case, I'm gonna chase another lead. It might have me out of town for a while."

"Oh. How long?" asked Jenny.

"A few days, maybe."

"Do I get to know what it is?"

"Only if it pans out," said Eliza.

They said their goodbyes and signed off. Eliza lay back on the nest of old costumes she'd fashioned into a bed in the storage room above the Ryalto, and let out a lonely sigh.

She did want to go home. She wanted to be there for Shelly. She wanted to play with Baby Lilah. She wanted Blake to know she existed. She wanted them to be a happy, growing family. She wanted to kiss Drew.

Half the appeal of this new lead was giving herself an excuse not to think about any of that for a few days. But still… if she was going to be out of town, maybe there was no risk in doing the really stupid thing she was about to do.

The Troublemakers, as they called themselves, all had Signal accounts. Eliza knew that Drew's screenname was **hersidekick707**. She couldn't message him as **dangergranger**, but what about the secret account she made for Kazumi? She signed in with the other screen name and sent **hersidekick707** a message before good sense had a chance to stop her.

zumizumizoo: Guess who?

Chapter Thirteen

Tunes for Mister Valentine

Friday morning started bright and early for Jenny, awoken by Aunt Shelly retching in the bathroom. Hopefully that wasn't an omen.

"I'm so glad I'll never have to deal with this," Jenny said, passing Shelly a warm washcloth to wipe her mouth.

"Don't be so sure," Shelly said, looking a total mess as she knelt over the toilet.

"Uh, if you're hoping this is a phase, you're going to be very disappointed," said Jenny.

"I didn't mean like that," Shelly said. "Turkey basters exist."

It was Jenny's turn to retch. "Thank you for guaranteeing that I will die a childless old maid. Are you gonna be too sick to go on that Safari thing?"

"I'll manage," Shelly said.

"Good, I'm coming along," said Jenny. Her aunt narrowed her eyes. "I want to see my friends without the Men in Black crawling up my ass!"

"This is an educational trip, Jennifer."

"Sure, whatever," said Jenny. "Educate me."

In reply, Shelly whirled back to the toilet to heave up the rest of last night's dinner.

"I think I'll get my own ride to school," said Jenny.

She prepared another washcloth for Shelly and skedaddled out of there.

Class was a breeze without the stress of the Dinah situation on her mind. Jenny would handle it tomorrow, no need to worry about it today. At lunch, they canoodled at their usual table, whispering naughty ideas in each other's ears.

"What are you two laughing about?" Jack asked, sitting down with his DoorDash order.

Of course, that only made them laugh harder.

"Very mature," he said.

While Jack fussed with his order, Drew bounded up, grinning from ear to ear.

"You guys hear about Lai?" he asked.

"No, what?" Jenny replied.

"He and Zoey are dating, said Drew.

"Who?" Jenny frowned, trying to recall who Zoey was. The name was familiar...

"The new girl," said Jack.

"Oh, the fed!" said Jenny.

Drew shushed her. "Don't let her know we know!"

"I'm not sure who's getting played more," said Dinah. "Lai, or her."

"Definitely her," said Drew. "Lai's locked in."

"He's gonna be locked up if he tries getting past second base," said Penny, joining them.

"A girl should be so lucky," Dinah murmured in Jenny's ear.

Oh, to be back in the mansion's archive room again...

Please don't be evil! At least not in a bad way, where I can't ignore it!

They spent the rest of lunch scheming up cockamamie plans to exploit this new intel. Most of them ended with Lai handcuffed to the hotel bed on Prom Night.

After school, Jenny walked with Penny back to the *Blackbird Times* offices. Drew and Jack had practice, and Dinah's presence was required at a Black family function celebrating their new *Ressort Rouge* batch, so it would be just the two of them giving Yvonne Griffin the third degree. There was an extra skip in her step. She always liked hanging out with Penny.

When they reached the *Times* offices, Ms. Griffin was working at her desk.

"Penelope. Jenny. Dare I even ask what brings you two here?" Ms. Griffin asked.

"You may dare," said Jenny. "But you can't be surprised. Ms. Griffin, I'm sorry, but I'm going to have to insist that you tell me about *The Stranger of Sausalito*. No more playing dumb, it's important."

Ms. Griffin favored her with the mother of all eye rolls and blew a raspberry.

"Oh, you insist, do you?" asked Ms. Griffin. "Jennifer, I know you *think* it's important, but I can assure you: it's not. Certainly not worth the grief this game has wrought."

"Blake Lockhart didn't play, and where did that get him?" Jenny said. "You think the Stranger won't come for Penny just because you wanted to stay out of it?"

It was harsh but true.

"If he comes for my daughter, it will be because she or I stuck our nose where it didn't belong," said Ms. Griffin.

"Too late for that, then," said Penny.

Ms. Griffin frowned at her daughter.

"Can't raise a journalist and not expect her to be nosy," said Jenny.

"What did you do?" Ms. Griffin asked Penny.

Penny opened her mouth but stopped short of confessing. Some sort of psychic war was taking place between mother and daughter. Intriguing, but Jenny was impatient.

"She found a digital copy of *The Stranger of Sausalito*," said Jenny. "The one you edited for my dad. So it's no use playing dumb."

Yvonne Griffin seethed in her desk chair. Penny was so busted.

"I thought I'd deleted that."

"Not the copy in your old email," said Jenny.

"And you've read it?" Ms. Griffin asked.

"We both did," said Penny.

"Okay, then you know it doesn't have anything to do with the

Stranger," said Ms. Griffin.

"At the risk of being obtuse, Ms. Griffin, would it kill ya to elaborate a little?" Jenny asked. She took a seat at the open desk next to Penny's mom. "At least entertain the idea that if you open your kimono, it might turn out that I know something about my dad that you don't?"

Yvonne snorted. "Let me tell you a story about RJ Valentine," she said.

"WHAT THE HELL IS THIS?" YVONNE GRIFFIN ASKED, SCOWLING AT THE reggae-tinged speed punk coming out of her car speakers. Her navigator and radio operator, RJ Valentine, had just inserted a new CD into the stereo.

"Uh, only the mother of all Black hardcore bands," RJ Valentine scoffed. "You've never heard of Bad Brains?? Tsk tsk, Evie."

They were in Yvonne's trusty old Honda Accord, driving up Highway 50 on their way to Folsom State Prison.

"Oh piss off, Johnny," said Yvonne. "You've never heard of Bad Brains. Where did you get this?"

She hit the eject button and pulled out the CD. It was a jet-black CD-R, with a note scribbled on it in silver Sharpie marker.

Tunes for Mister Valentine
These songs will make you cool
—L

"Oh I see," said Yvonne. "'Mister Valentine?'"

*RJ rolled his eyes and grabbed the CD, stuffing it back into her stereo. The Bad Brains song began again. He hit the **Next Track** button, and they were treated to the opening strands of "The Killing Moon" by Echo & the Bunnymen. Fitting for this trip, but Yvonne wasn't letting RJ off that easy. She hit the pause button and shot him a glare.*

"What?" he asked, all phony innocence. "Watch the road."

"You know what?" said Yvonne. "Who's 'L'?"

"One of my TAs thought I needed to listen to better music," said RJ. He was playing it cool, but the tips of his ears were shading pink. "I didn't

want to be rude and not take it from them.”

“Male or female?”

“Female. It’s nothing, relax,” said RJ.

His face was definitely flushing now.

“Is she cute?” Yvonne asked.

“I mean…” RJ couldn’t hide it. The corners of his mouth curled up into that shit-eating grin of his. “I guess you could say so.”

“Oh, you guess?” Yvonne laughed. “Johnathan, you ignorant slut.”

“Nothing happened! She just made me a mix tape. She’s always teasing me about my music because I put on Everclear in my office one time.”

“So she’s in your office a lot, is she?”

“Only during our weekly prep meetings, and never alone,” said RJ. “Well, there was one time, but that was—”

“No need to get so defensive!” said Yvonne, laughing harder. “I believe you. But if you plan on listening to this around Val, you’d better practice not looking so guilty.”

“I’m not guilty,” he said.

Silence hung between them. Yvonne shrugged and reached for the play button.

“Yet,” he added.

“Aha! I knew it!”

“I don’t even know if it’s like that,” RJ said. “It’s just… Val’s sneaking off with that piece of shit ‘old friend’ of hers again. Meanwhile, we haven’t touched each other in months. The writing is on the wall, Evie. I realized the other day while Laura and I were grading papers that I would rather be at work with her than at home with my wife. That’s fucked up, right?”

Yvonne put her turn signal on and took the exit for Folsom Boulevard.

“Well, just remember that you’re her boss,” said Yvonne. “Be careful you’re not getting the wrong impression.”

“Yeah, I know, come on,” RJ said. “She made me the mix tape out of nowhere, okay? I didn’t ask for it. She’s…” He got lost in a reverie. He did that sometimes. Yvonne glanced over and caught a genuine smile on his face. “She reminds me of—well, she’s not like her, but the way she makes me feel reminds me of the way I felt with Mariel.”

“I’m pretty sure you said the exact same thing about me,” she said. “The

night I dumped you."

"Probably," said RJ, his ears flushing red again. "But for different reasons."

"Sure."

Breaking up with RJ after a week-long fling was the best decision Yvonne ever made. She gained a great friend and confidant, a fellow writer, and a lover of the craft. And she cut loose what was sure to be a miserable relationship with a man who would never, ever get over his first love.

"And anyway, that's what you said about Val, too," said Yvonne. "Once upon a time."

"Well, that was before she cheated on me," RJ said, an unmistakable trace of bitterness in his voice. "Which is why I need this book to kill! It's gotta cut like a razor, you know? Get it on the bestseller list so I can leave Viv without having to worry about her ogre of a father getting me shitcanned and blacklisted from every college in Northern California."

"Let's not get ahead of ourselves," said Yvonne. "We don't even know if this guy will talk to us."

"He will," said RJ. "Killers love to talk."

The "he" RJ was hoping for an audience with was Angus Andrews, a.k.a. the Jewel City Thrill Killer. The convicted murderer had fourteen strangulation counts in his jacket, with another half-dozen killings suspected—but never proven. Angus had been uniquely hard to catch during his reign of terror back in the '60s because of his day job as a Los Angeles County police detective.

RJ thought that dichotomy was perfect for the concept he'd been kicking around: a cat-and-mouse mystery about a detective hunting a serial killer, told from each of their perspectives. Yvonne was going to write the detective's POV, and RJ would write the killer's. It had been slow going so far. RJ couldn't find the right voice for his killer. Thus, this field trip to Folsom State Prison to talk to a real one.

After an hour of security pat-downs, liability waivers, and lectures from the prison guards, they were finally led to a windowless room where a weathered, white-haired septuagenarian was chained to a long metal table.

"*So you're writing a book?*" *Angus Andrews asked in a voice like limestone gravel.*

"*Trying to,*" *said RJ.*

Yvonne and RJ took their seats at the other end of the table, well out of the killer's reach.

"*I'm missing Knitting Club,*" *said the man.* "*You get three questions, so make 'em count. And hell, make 'em interesting. I'm sick of talking about goddamned Emilia Spencer.*"

Emilia Spencer was the daring meter maid who had tailed Andrews of her own accord after spotting his police cruiser too many times around the Glendale area, out of his jurisdiction. She was instrumental in his arrest.

RJ flashed a smirk at Yvonne and fixed the Jewel City Thrill Killer with his most winning smile.

"*When the police did that press conference after your fifth murder—you know, the one where they implied you were impotent? Did that get the juices flowing, or only make it worse?*" *RJ asked.*

Angus Andrews roared with laughter. Then he launched himself over the table.

"*THANKS A LOT, JOHNNY!*" *YVONNE SHOUTED, STOMPING BACK THROUGH the parking lot to her car.* "*I think I tore a seam in my jacket!*"

"*Sorry, Evie,*" *said RJ, pinching the bridge of his nose to keep it from bleeding.* "*They really need to quality check their restraints at this place. That was a nice box out on him, though.*"

"*Yeah, well I wasn't all-defense at Pepperdine for nothing,*" *said Yvonne.* "*You couldn't have led off with a less incendiary question? We just drove two hours for nothing!*"

"*Not nothing. I got what I needed,*" *said RJ.*

"*Did you?*"

They'd reached Yvonne's car.

"*Absolutely. I feel I understand him completely,*" *said RJ.* "*It's quite banal, honestly. I was thinking there must be some unknowable monster lurking under his skin, but really, he's just a pathetic loser with a broken dick.*"

"Hmm."

"That was one time, and I'd been drinking," said RJ.

Yvonne snickered and got in. She started the ignition but left it in **Park***, taking a deep breath and letting her frazzled nerves regroup.*

"I'm sorry about your jacket, really," RJ said. "And thank you, if I didn't say it before. Uh, do you have any tissue?"

"Here, lean back," said Yvonne.

She made RJ tilt his head back and shoved a tampon into his bloody nostril.

"Mind the string," she added with a laugh. "You think he meant what he said? That he'll track us down if we ever put him in the book?"

"About that," RJ said.

Something in his tone set off warning bells. "What?"

"I think I'd better write this one solo," he said, forgetting the nosebleed and staring at his feet. "Just in case."

It was like taking an elbow in the solar plexus. Yvonne hadn't even wanted to do it in the first place; she'd just agreed because it sounded like an interesting experiment! And now he was firing her?!

"What the fuck?" she said. "Don't even try to pretend this is some chivalric act to protect me. I thought you liked my pages!"

"I did! And I do!"

"Then what gives?"

He was back to staring at his shoes again, his ears turning red.

"You really want to know?"

"'Thick skin,' bitch," said Yvonne. "I know the rules."

Thick skin *was their mantra when editing each other's work at Calistoga College. Meaning: put on your thick skin and get ready to listen to the harsh, unvarnished truth. No sugarcoating, no holding back.*

"It's not that your pages are bad, okay?" RJ said. "Our tones don't match anymore. They did when we first started doing the back page column together, but now they don't. And I feel like people are gonna be able to tell. It will feel like two different books smooshed together, which isn't the concept, right?"

Yvonne bit her lip. He wasn't wrong. RJ's first stab at writing the serial killer had been rough, but in theory, meeting Angus Andrews was supposed to help with that.

"I mean, if anything, your writing has gotten better, and mine hasn't," RJ added.

"Okay, well, that's some happy bullshit, Johnny," said Yvonne.

"I just—look, I can see the future, and this ends with us having a mess of a book and a lot of fights over it, and one of us insisting they rewrite the other's part," said RJ. "And since you didn't even want to do this in the first place, I figure it's better to skip to the end now. Like a band-aid. One motion. Right off!"

It all made sense, but Yvonne was still feeling furious with him.

"See, this is why you dumped me," he said.

"Oh, eat shit!" said Yvonne.

It was petty, but she was feeling petty, so she reached over and yanked the tampon out of his nose by the string. Fresh blood gushed out of RJ's nose and spilled down one of the stupid bowling shirts he was always wearing.

"Really?" he said nasally, trying to plug up his nose with his pinkie.

"You couldn't have said something before I drove all this way up here??"

"Well, I'd been thinking about it, but getting beaten up by a serial killer has a way of sharpening you up, ya know?" said RJ.

"Oh please," said Yvonne. The anger was leaving her now, and honestly, she felt sort of relieved. Now she could focus on getting her master's without getting sidetracked writing as some clichéd hard-boiled gumshoe. "That son of a bitch has five consecutive life sentences. He's never getting out."

"Now, I know what you're thinking," said Ms. Griffin. "That the serial killer could be a suspect after all."

Actually, Jenny was still stuck on the idea of Mom making Dad a mix CD. So cute!

"But Angus Andrews died of lung cancer in prison on August 12th of last year," Ms. Griffin went on. "Two days after RJ's attack. I know. It was the first thing I checked after the will reading. Andrews had been bedridden for a month. There's no way he's the Stranger."

"Maybe he had a son? Or a daughter? Taking revenge?" Penny hazarded.

Yvonne shook her head. "He didn't."

Jenny sagged in the chair, forcing her mind back into the present. Ms. Griffin's explanation made too much sense. Dad left the book to Yvonne, knowing that she would check on the old serial killer. *Damn.* Jenny didn't realize until now how much she'd been hoping that this clue would be the one.

"Was the twist his idea?" Penny asked.

Ms. Griffin snorted. "When did you guys guess it?"

"Second chapter," said Penny.

"Second paragraph," said Jenny.

Spoiler alert: the killer and the detective in *The Stranger of Sausalito* were the same person. Like a split-personality thing.

Oooh! Big twist!

"To be fair, that was a decent twist, back then," said Penny's mom. "It hadn't been done to death, yet."

"It was so obvious!" said Penny. "I'm still cringing just thinking about it."

"I mean, it could work," said Jenny. "It's very meta."

"Johnny couldn't *bribe* an agent to read it," said Ms. Griffin. "He weaseled a few grand out of Val to print a hundred copies at the college press—to sell at the campus bookstore. He was convinced that once people started reading it, he would build some buzz. It was a total flop. They didn't sell a single book. Then your mom died, and Jack was born, and I was trying to adopt Penelope, and we kind of forgot about it.

"Months later, I was at the campus bookstore. I think Michael Lewis was there, signing copies of *Moneyball*. I made a joke to the manager about digging up *The Stranger of Sausalito* from the storeroom to get it signed—maybe then it would be worth something—and he told me they'd destroyed all the copies because they needed the space."

"Well, almost all," said Jenny. "Dad must have kept one copy, at least. To leave to you."

"I suppose he'd tucked it away somewhere and lost track of it," said Ms. Griffin. "He left me a note on the inside jacket: 'Look what I found.' Talk about a blast from the past."

"Can I see it?" Jenny asked. When Ms. Griffin hesitated, she added, "Come on, I already know all about it. What's the harm at this point?"

Ms. Griffin bit her lip again and looked at Penny.

"Lock the door, just in case," she said.

While Penny took care of that, Jenny followed Ms. Griffn into the back room, where an industrial-sized printer and some old-fashioned print shop tools lay gathering dust.

"I haven't had to paste up an issue in years," Ms. Griffin told Jenny. "But I hung on to this anyway, just in case. It's useful as hell for wrapping Christmas presents."

She was referring to an old pasteboard. It was a flat rectangle, about as thick as a pizza box, maybe four feet by five. The top was covered in semi-transparent plastic riven with grooves from thousands of pen knife slices. Ms. Griffin reached back behind it and flipped a switch.

The surface of the pasteboard flickered to life, filling the room with blinding white light from the fluorescents underneath the plastic.

"Is this like for X-rays?" Jenny asked.

"No, it's how we used to make the news," said Ms. Griffin.

"Looks like you have a bulb out," said Jenny.

She pointed to the left half of the board, where a conspicuous rectangle of light was dimmed. Ms. Griffin chuckled and fiddled with the side of the pasteboard. A little panel opened up, and she pulled out the only surviving copy of *The Stranger of Sausalito*.

The cover art was a pulpy illustration of a hard-boiled detective. There was no byline—as if RJ himself was embarrassed to be publishing it.

"He used a nom de plume on the title page," said Ms. Griffin, answering Jenny's unasked question.

She passed the book over. In Jenny's imagination, her fingers sparked when she touched it. The elusive final heirloom was in her hands at last. She turned to the cover page.

The Stranger of Sausalito
By
Reynard Fuchs

"Figures," said Jenny.

Reynard, for Dad's spirit animal, Reynard the Fox. And *Fuchs* for Mariel Fuchs, Dad's first love—the mercurial Austrian duchess who died at Schloss Schwarzwald on Y2K. Whatever his original name was, Dad hadn't treasured it.

"Men never get over the first girl to break their heart," said Ms. Griffin. She pointed to the opposite page, where someone had left a message in blocky letters. "There's the message your dad left me."

LOOK WHAT I FOUND!

"It did surprise me, your father leaving this as a clue," said Ms. Griffin. "I'd stopped thinking about Angus Andrews years and years ago. But RJ must have still been worried that he was going to break out and come after him." Ms. Griffin smiled sadly and patted Jenny on the shoulder. "I think he'd never been punched before. It stayed with him."

"Hmm," said Jenny. "Not according to his diary."

"Honestly, anticlimactic," said Penny. "This isn't winning me a Pulitzer. I'm hungry. Can we cross it off the list?"

Jenny wasn't so sure. A funny feeling grew in her stomach: her Trouble intuition saying something was wrong.

"Hold on a sec."

Jenny set the book down on the glowing pasteboard. She had a picture of it somewhere... After scrolling back a whole year in her Photos app, she found what she needed: a picture of the coaster Mr. White kept pinned to the wall behind his desk. On the back of it, Dad had left his old traveling companion a note:

KiLLROY WAS HERE
À Votre Santé! -Renny

Jenny held up her phone to the book page and pointed to the **LOOK WHAT I FOUND!** note.

"This isn't RJ's handwriting," she said.

Ms. Griffin frowned and leaned closer.

"Isn't it?" she said. "The Ls and Os and As are the same. The little loop in the A?"

"Yeah, but not the K," said Jenny.

Dad's **K** was a straight vertical stroke, with two slanted strokes meeting in the middle of it. The **K** on the book note, however, had the bottom slant branching off of the top one instead.

"Huh, you're right," Ms. Griffin said.

Jenny pulled her phone back and scrolled for another photo. This, of the note the Stranger left her at the end of the first chapter of *I Dream of Trouble*.

> **WANT TO READ MORE? START TAKING THE GAME A LITTLE MORE SERIOUSLY. YOU'RE RUNNING OUT OF TIME.**

She held up the phone again to compare, though she was already certain of what she'd find.

The **K**s matched.

"My dad didn't leave this note for you, Ms. Griffin," said Jenny. "The Stranger left it for my dad."

Chapter Fourteen
Safari West

THE *STRANGER OF SAUSALITO* WAS A LIVE CLUE, AFTER ALL! WHAT AN excellent discovery for Jenny! Not so much for Yvonne Griffin. She took the book back and kicked them out. In the group chat on Signal, Drew and Penny agreed to renew their search for the book. They had RJ's pen name now, so that might help. Jack and Dinah hadn't found any new secret passages yet, but Jack helpfully commented that he read *The Stranger of Sausalito* last night and liked it. Of course he did. Jenny kept mum about her other strategy for chasing the clue: Danger.

> **sallydraper2003:** Never mind laying low, got a new job for you. Go up to Calistoga College and snoop around. See if you can find another copy of the book, or find out how the Stranger got it, at least.

It took almost an hour for her sister to respond. Jenny was back home now, looking after Baby Lilah while Shelly and Lockhart prepared dinner. Shelly hadn't told him about her condition yet. Things were awkward and stilted between them. If Lockhart was half the detective Jenny was, he'd have to know something was up with her aunt.

> **dangergranger:** Umm. It might take me a couple of days.
>
> **sallydraper2003:** Why?
>
> **dangergranger:** Because I left town, I told you I was going to.
>
> **sallydraper2003:** Like, you took a vacation?

Her phone vibrated with an incoming Signal call.

"Come on, Lilah, let's go find that toy you wanted," Jenny said, picking Lilah up and retreating to the garage before answering. "I can't talk long. Where are you?"

"The Grapevine," said Eliza.

Goddamn, her ass was sore. She'd been riding the Ninja nonstop for hours, save for a stop to pee in Coalinga. At present, she was pulled over at the big rest stop before the Grapevine to gas up rest her poor behind. Eliza explained her situation and plan to Jenny and got the expected reaction.

"That's gonna take forever!" said Jenny over the phone.

"You know this has to be in person," said Eliza.

Jenny made a face but didn't argue because Eliza, as usual, was right. Besides, Eliza had ridden too far to turn back now. Might as well see it through; *The Stranger of Sausalito* would have to wait. Jenny caught her up on Yvonne Griffin's story, and Eliza was charmed to hear about their mom making a move on RJ with a mix CD. It made her feel slightly less guilty about texting Drew last night. Onishi girls knew what they wanted and went for it. But she didn't tell Jenny about any of that.

"I can't talk long," said Jenny. "Bring back some carne asada fries from Brick & Flour!"

Eliza ended the call and bent over, stretching her sore legs. Riding like a bat out of hell wasn't quite as much fun when you did it for four hours straight. She should get back on the road, but she had new messages from **hersidekick707** to read…

> **hersidekick707:** Not that I don't trust you, but can you send me a picture, just so I know I'm not being catfished?

Eliza bit her lip, rummaging in the only luggage she'd packed: a lightweight backpack. She did bring her makeup bag, just in case…

> **zumizumizoo:** Hold plz. A girl needs to put her face on.

"IT'S SETTLED, THEN!" SAID AUNT SHELLY AS JENNY RETURNED FROM the garage.

"Fine!" said Lockhart.

It didn't seem fine. Jenny was about to make a snide comment about not stressing Shelly *in her condition* but remembered just in time that Lockhart didn't know yet.

"What's settled?" she asked, shoving the baby back in Lockhart's arms.

"Blake will be helping chaperone the field trip tomorrow," said Shelly.

"What? Why?!"

"Because I asked him to," Shelly replied, glaring.

Wonderful. The whole point of going on this stupid field trip was to ditch her fed tail, and now a goddamned cop would be there.

"He'll also be taking me out to dinner on Sunday," Shelly added.

"And what do you get out of this?" Jenny asked Lockhart.

"Your aunt will be helping look after Lilah until I can arrange childcare," Lockhart answered stiffly.

"Okay, then who's watching her on your date?"

"You are," they answered in unison.

Son of a bitch. *There goes my whole weekend.*

It was a 45-minute ride to Safari West—one Jenny spent half-asleep, head leaning against the bus window as she drooled. The wild animal park was in unincorporated Calistoga County, where hundreds of acres of nature preserve superficially matched the Serengeti. The brochure said they had elephants, tigers, giraffes, and tons of other wild animals. Jenny was excited to see the Egyptian geese. They came highly recommended by Mr. Duck.

The tour started with an open-topped Jeep ride around the park, and Jenny got to pet a giraffe. The only bummer, besides Blake and Shelly and their bad vibes—and the impending awkward conversation with Dinah—was that Jimmy Figg was allowed to come on the trip. He was back from his suspension and still harboring very hard feelings for Jenny.

"Hey Jenny, why don't you try that tiger while you're at it!" he snarked after they met the giraffes. "You like petting pussy, don't you?"

"Why don't you suck a dick, Jimmy?" Jenny shot back.

"Enough!" Shelly yelled at them. "Both of you!"

"Now, ya tiger's a lot like a housecat when it comes to pettin'," said their tour guide, as if sensing a teaching moment. He had an Aussie accent that Jenny was pretty sure was an act. "The domesticated ones generally like to be petted, but the ones raised in the outback like our boy Stripes? You'll get a lot more than scratches if he doesn't like the smell of ya. So don't try it, mate."

"Does he let *you* pet him?" asked Drew.

"Oh sure," said their guide with a grin. "So long as he's heavily sedated. You should see those mitts of his up close. One swipe could take a man's head off!"

"Meow!" Dinah whispered in Jenny's ear.

Hey Dinah, remember when we almost did it in the archive room under Valentine Manor? How about we pick up where we left off? Also, are you the Stranger?

Jenny squeezed her girlfriend's hand. The tour was ending, and they had a free hour to roam. It was now or never.

"I gotta pee," said Dinah, hurrying to the little one-person bathroom hut.

"Meet me by the pond," Jenny said.

And if you're not the Stranger, then what are you hiding?

ELIZA COULD THANK THE STRANGER FOR ONE THING, AT LEAST: Kazumi and Drew finally had something to talk about!

Her pit stop at the Grapevine turned into a marathon three-hour video call, cut short only because her battery died. In her guise as Kazu, she chatted with Drew for hours about how crazy that night at the mansion was, how much they missed each other, and all the kinky things they would try once they could be together again. She even sent him a few nudes. He didn't ask where she was and agreed not to tell Jenny they were talking. Maybe it was a foolish risk, but Eliza needed it.

The call ran so long that she barely made it to the LA hostel before curfew. Her ass was killing her, and the ride left her grimy and gross, but all she could manage the next morning was a whore's bath in the loo. Luckily, half the clientele at her destination looked like they hadn't showered either.

The Bean was a boutique coffee shop in Silverlake with great WiFi, the go-to hangout for hipsters, writers, and digital natives with fake email jobs. Eliza bought herself an $8 mocha from a girl with bad bangs and several face piercings, then found an open stool along the wall from which she could keep an eye on the entrance.

Three hours later, she was beginning to worry she had misread her mark. But, right when she was about to give up and try another coffee shop, he finally walked in. He'd grown a scruffy beard since she'd last seen him at Valentine Manor, and ditched the chunky plastic glasses for irritating round copper frames that wrapped around his ears.

Eliza waited until he'd ordered a drink (English Breakfast tea, the wanker) and made himself comfortable at a long shared worktable, ready for a hard day of tweeting and shitposting on Reddit about zoning laws. She detached herself from her stool and walked over, mentally subsuming herself into Jenny's persona again. She was all out of Adderall; she'd just have to fake it.

"Jeffrey Jordan," she said, taking a seat across from him. "You're in big trouble."

THE GEESE WERE CAUTIOUSLY INCHING CLOSER AT JENNY'S URGING when Dinah found them.

"Have you named them yet?" Dinah asked, sidling up next to her.

"That one is Ramses," Jenny said, pointing to the one with the red masking coloration who had ventured closest. "You know, because Egypt. The others haven't inspired me yet."

"I see," said Dinah.

"How's it going on Blue Team? Any new secret passages?" Jenny asked.

"None that show on the blueprints," said Dinah.

"Got it. Keep on it," said Jenny.

It came out more dismissive than she'd intended. A pregnant pause hung in the air.

"You know, a reasonable person might assume you were giving me and Jack bullshit busy work to keep us occupied," said Dinah. "What I keep asking myself is: who don't you trust? Jack? Or me?"

"I never said I didn't trust you," Jenny replied lamely. "What are you talking about?"

Now that it came to it, she was reluctant to say anything. What if this ruined things between them forever? Jenny walked away from the pond with no destination in mind. Dinah followed.

"You know what I mean," said Dinah. "You've been weird ever since that night at the mansion. At first, I assumed it was, you know, because of all the killing and chaos. But it's still there. There's some hesitation in you that only shows when I'm around."

"How would you know it's only when you're around if you're not always around?"

"Don't you hurl tautologies at me," said Dinah. "Come on, just say it. Whatever it is. We'll get through it—or we won't. Only one way to find out."

Jenny's aimless walk had taken them to the path around the big cat cages. She stared at a leopard lounging in the sun, and metaphors about changing spots ricocheted around in her head. A quick look over her shoulder told her they were alone; the rest of the class was at the snack bar.

"After the mansion, I went to Pixeldrome to hide. That's where I found Rob Haines," she said.

"Yeah, you told us."

"Well, what I didn't tell you was that there was a *Trouble* video game in the VIP room called *Mystery Girl*," said Jenny. "And that I'd been left a tip by my dad to watch out for any new high scores on it. The arcade token heirloom was bait: to see if the Stranger would show up and try to leave their mark."

"Okay… And did they?"

"When I found Rob, there was a new high score. The initials were D-E-B."

A confused frown crossed Dinah's heart-shaped face, followed by an eye roll and a smile.

"I don't play video games, Jenny," said Dinah. "Except *Animal Crossing*, for the aesthetic."

Jenny's gaze burrowed deep into Dinah's hazel eyes, asking the question without saying a word.

"I'm not the Stranger," Dinah said.

No nervous tics, no sideways glances, no tells. Then why was Jenny still picking up deception?

"I know you're not," Jenny said.

"But?" Dinah prompted her.

She turned away from her girlfriend's fierce gaze to stare at the big cats. There was a lot of murky ground to cover between *I'm not the Stranger* and *I'm innocent…*

"Just effing say it, Jenny," said Dinah.

"Hey, Dinah?" Jenny said. "Not to change the subject, but wasn't there a tiger in this cage earlier?"

"Huh?"

Jenny pointed to the cage in front of them. It was large enough to give the tiger room to roam, but she couldn't spot Stripes anywhere. In the back, the chain-link fence gate was swinging lazily in the breeze.

"Oh dear," said Dinah.

"I WAS WARNED NOT TO TALK TO YOU," SAID JEFFREY JORDAN.

"The Stranger can't get to you here," said Eliza. "He thinks I'm still back home."

Jeffrey laughed charmlessly and leaned back, taking off his wannabe Harry Potter glasses and rubbing his scruffy beard. They had relocated to a booth in the corner for some privacy.

"You're so naive it's almost cute."

"I'm always cute. And don't patronize me," said Eliza. "Start at the beginning. What happened?"

Jeffrey took a sip of his drink, and his eyes went unfocused as he forced himself to return to that fateful night when he disappeared at their front gate.

"That post you did on Instagram," Jeffrey began. "Accusing me of blackmailing you. I was getting massive impressions. All those dumb little stans trying to cancel me. I thought I might be able to parlay it into something bigger if I kept it going. I had information that might interest you, so I went to the mansion to make a deal. And that's when he found me."

"You should have listened to my sis—my warning about getting out of town," said Eliza.

Jeffrey let out another one of his bitter chuckles and went on. "He must have parked down the road so I wouldn't hear him coming. I was waiting at the gate when he jumped me. Put me in some kind of choke hold and knocked me out. When I came to, we were somewhere up in the hills, miles from town. He woke me up and told me who he was. And then he beat the shit out of me. He beat me until I was coughing up blood, and then he told me to leave town and never come back, or the next time he'd bring a shovel."

All things considered, it seemed almost generous of the Stranger. Nilay should have been so lucky.

"Did you recognize his voice?" she asked.

"Oh yeah," said Jeffrey. "His face, too. He made sure I'd remember him."

Eliza's heart froze to the core. *Had he? Could it be? Could Warby fucking Parker identify the Stranger?*

"Who?"

"That ape of a sheriff," he said with a scowl.

"Wait. Blake? Blake Lockhart?" Eliza asked, bewildered.

"That's the one. Bastard."

Jenny and Dinah stared at the empty tiger cage, too tense to move, when Aunt Shelly came stomping up behind them.

"Hey! Don't wander off, you two," said her aunt. "Lunch is served."

"In a second," said Jenny. "Um, where's Mopey?"

"Who?"

"Your sad bastard boyfriend," said Jenny.

"Bathroom, I think," said Shelly.

"Did he happen to bring his service revolver?"

"I should hope not! What are you looking at?" asked Shelly.

"The tiger is gone," said Dinah.

Shelly shielded her eyes from the sun and peered inside the cage, frowning.

"Maybe that gate leads to a feeding area?" Shelly offered.

A low, guttural growl on their left disabused Shelly of that notion. They all spun and saw a hulking Bengal tiger stepping around the corner of the cages. Stripes, the guide had called him. Stripes was nearly as tall as Jenny and over ten feet long, at a guess. He growled at them again and took another stride forward, his massive paws sinking into the grass with each step.

"What do we do?" asked Dinah, clutching Jenny's arm.

Now would be an acceptable time to panic so, naturally, her anxiety abandoned her. Jenny locked eyes with the tiger, mentally turning down the volume of her pounding heartbeat, and thought back to the morning's safari tour. What was it the guide had said?

"Don't move," said Jenny. "Try to be tall."

"I wore flats," said Dinah.

"We're Japanese," said Shelly.

"Hush!" said Jenny. "He's already agitated, look at his ears. If he crouches, that means run."

"Run where??" hissed Shelly.

"Maybe *into* the cage?" Dinah suggested.

"Let's try taking a slow step back," said Jenny.

Without turning, Jenny carefully lifted her foot and took a step backward. The tiger responded with a terrifying, full-throated growl.

"Stop stop stop!" Shelly whispered.

A tremor of flexing muscle rippled over the tiger's massive orange-and-black flank.

"He didn't like that," said Dinah.

The tiger leaned back, falling into a crouch. Oh, fuck.

"Shelly!! DON'T MOVE!!" Lockhart shouted from behind them.

Jenny's pulse was throbbing in her throat now. Never before had she felt like such a helpless tasty morsel. *The throat. That's where he'll bite first when he pounces.* At the edge of her vision, she could sense movement.

"Hey! Hey! Over here! Look at me, you bastard!!"

Lockhart was trying to draw the tiger's attention away. And it was working. Stripes let out another growl and turned his head to consider this new distraction. Jenny risked a glance and saw Lockhart ducking down on all fours, mimicking helpless prey. She'd hoped to see a pistol in his shooting hand, but it was empty.

"Yeah! Come on! Follow me!" Lockhart shouted and began to retreat.

The tiger obliged and trotted his way. Shelly screamed, blasting out Jenny's eardrum.

It all happened in a blur. Blake leaped to his feet and sprinted away. Stripes pounced after him with lethal speed. Cries rang out from the other students at the snack bar as they witnessed the disaster unfold. Blake was making fast for the bathroom hut. The building was all cinderblocks and cement—if he made it, he'd be safe. But what about the rest of them??

They'd never know.

Blake was still meters away from the hut when the door to the men's room swung wide and out stepped Jimmy Figg, still drying his hands on a paper towel.

"What's all the shouting?" Jimmy asked.

"Kid! No!" Blake shouted.

He peeled away from the bathroom and waved his arms wildly, gesturing for Jimmy to get back inside—only, Jimmy hadn't spotted the tiger! He frowned at Lockhart, stupefied. Stripes abandoned his chase with Lockhart and gathered up his legs to pounce on Jimmy.

"Jimmy! Look out!" Jenny shouted.

"Hey, what the?" Jimmy said, finally noticing his oncoming doom. SNAP!

Just as Stripes leaped, something whistled and the tiger let out a pained yelp. Jimmy froze in panic as the massive bulk of the animal flew through the air. Jenny winced, unable to look away—

The tiger slammed into the cinderblock wall, only inches from the little nerd, twitched, and went still. His striped flank had sprouted a metal cylinder as big as a Red Bull can with a wispy tuft of fiber for a tail.

"Right then," said their guide, lowering a long-barreled tranq rifle and walking forward carefully, his eyes never leaving the tiger. "You shoulda worn your brown pants, mate."

Jenny didn't understand the guide's meaning until Jimmy turned and waddled back into the bathroom hut, a dark stain on the seat of his jeans.

"Why does this keep happening to me?!" came his plaintive moan as the door slammed shut.

Chapter Fifteen

Jumping to Conclusions

IT WAS ALMOST AS GOOD AS JIMMY BEING EATEN BY A TIGER, AND, IN Jenny's opinion, grounds for celebration. But instead, Aunt Shelly was sprinting at Lockhart, hurling curse words at him the whole way.

"What the hell is wrong with you!?" Shelly screamed. "You could have been killed! I won't be with someone who has a death wish! I can't!"

Blake had been trying to get a word in the whole time as the other students came up to peep the tiger.

"I know it's not important," said Jack, who jogged over with Drew, both housing corn dogs. "But if Jimmy just shit his pants upon *exiting* the bathroom, then what was he doing *in* the bathroom in the first place?"

Penny made a jerk-off motion with her hand, thought better of it, and made the gesture with two fingers instead. Drew nodded sagely.

"I mean, I'm not gonna lie, Jenny," Drew said. "Your aunt in that sundress would have awoken things in me at Jimmy's age."

"He's like two years younger than you!" said Penny.

Speaking of her aunt (*Ew! Gross, Drew!*), Blake had finally managed to shut Shelly up with an emphatic shout of "I don't want to die! Not now!"

Shelly's schoolmarm suspicion kicked in, and she demanded to know what that was supposed to mean.

"Because you're—you know!" He nodded to her belly. "I want to live! What kinda deadbeat do you think I am? I want to be there for that! For him. Or her."

"No shot?!" Penny said, beaming.

Shelly gasped. "How did you know?"

"Oh my god! Really!" Dinah grinned and clutched Jenny's arm.

I guess we're cool again?

"What are they going on about?" Jack asked Drew, clueless.

"I *am* a detective," said Blake. He nodded to Jenny. "She's not the only one who can read a clue or two."

That was all Shelly needed to hear. She flung herself into his arms and the face-sucking began. Disgusting. The boys watched for a moment, dazzled, before turning away with pink cheeks.

"No one will ever have better sex than the sex those two have tonight," said Penny.

Jenny plugged her ears and marched over to the safari guide, who was tending to the unconscious tiger.

"How did he get out?" she asked.

The guide grimaced and wiped his brow. "Helluva thing. Some right, dirty business, I'll warrant. I checked those cage locks myself this morning. I don't know, maybe the feeder cocked it up."

"I doubt it," said Jenny. "Do you have cameras on the grounds?"

"That's the bugger," said the guide. "They've been on the fritz all morning."

"What a coincidence." Jenny spun and jogged back to the tiger cage.

She could feel the others on her heels as she followed Stripes's massive pawprints in reverse and came to the open chain-link gate. The evidence was clear as day: a discarded padlock lying in a bare patch of soil, the shackle neatly snipped in two.

"Do you think this is about us reading the heirloom book?" Penny asked.

"What do you mean?" asked Drew.

"We learn about *The Stranger of Sausalito,* and then the Stranger unleashes a tiger on the field trip all the Troublemakers attend, when no feds are present," said Penny. "Maybe he's sending us a message."

"If he is, he's slipping," said Jenny. "That tiger could have eaten Jimmy just as much as one of us."

"Maybe the Stranger wants to cause chaos," said Dinah. "Muddy the waters, and get us chasing a red herring."

"What red herring?" asked Jack.

"That it has to be someone on the field trip, right?" Dinah said. "Isn't that what the evidence suggests?"

Before Jenny could offer an answer, her watch tapped her on the wrist.

> **dangergranger:** Keep Blake away from Shelly.
> Jeffrey Jordan just identified
> him as the Stranger.

Jenny was all out of adrenaline, too numb to be shocked. The void in her soul grew a little larger. Lockhart? Seriously!? She gazed across the field at the lovestruck couple. How the hell was she supposed to keep them apart now?

ELIZA PUT HER PHONE AWAY AND ASKED JEFFREY TO CONTINUE, afraid of what else she might hear.

"And that's when you skipped town and moved down here?" she asked. "Was part of his demands that you not tell anyone where you were going?"

Jeffrey shook his head. "No no, we're not done with that pisshole town yet," he said. "The sheriff was just the opening act. He tossed a water bottle at me, told me which way was south, and drove off. Cocksucker."

Eliza frowned. It was hard to square this version of Blake with the one Shelly loved, but he did always have a darkness to him…

"I walked along the fire trail for maybe a mile when I heard a car engine," said Jeffrey. "At first, I thought I was in luck, but then I spotted the car in the moonlight. Its lights were off, and it was headed straight for me."

Eliza leaned forward, intrigued.

"And then?"

"And then I went over the fucking hood, man!" said Jeffrey.

He had a shrill way about him that was attracting frowns from the other hipsters at Bean.

"Chill out!" she hissed. "You lived, don't be such a dramatic bitch."

"They had to remove my spleen!"

"Oh, your spleen. What else? Did you see the driver?"

Jeffrey shivered. "Yeah. He stopped and got out. He was tall. Covered all in black, with a dark trench coat. He must have had some kind of mask on because I couldn't see his face, no matter which way the moonlight fell."

Beware!

"He told me he would kill me if he ever saw me in town again, or if I ever contacted you. He said he'd know if I did, and that he'd be keeping tabs on me." Jeffrey reflexively looked over his shoulder. "I figured I'd be good if I just stayed away. But then, last fall, I was on my way home from a DSA meeting—"

"Hold on." Eliza got her phone out and checked Signal.

sallydraper2003: wtf??? Is this for real???

dangergranger: Sorry, false alarm. But there's more darkness in Blake than I thought. Don't leave him and Shells alone.

"Anyway, I was on my way home when someone grabbed me and pulled me into an alley," said Jeffrey. "It was him!"

Eliza might not have lie detector skills as honed as her sister's, but she was pretty sure this guy was telling the truth. He seemed too spooked for it to be an act.

"The point is, the Stranger is always watching," said Jeffrey. "I'm not safe anywhere, so if you don't mind, can you please get fucking lost and leave me alone?"

"Soon, but I have two—no, three more questions," said Eliza.

"First: was that all the Stranger did? Pull you into an alley and scare you?"

"Oh, right," said Jeffrey. "He'd shipped something to my address and needed me to get it out of the package box in my apartment's lobby."

"What was in the package?"

"He didn't open it in front of me, but I recognized the logo on the box: Bronze Age Tactical."

"Never heard of it," said Eliza.

"They make body armor," said Jeffrey. "I know, I started wearing some."

He pulled down the collar of his wrinkled henley shirt to reveal a thin black vest underneath.

"I see. Good to know." Eliza bit her lip. "Second question: Jorge Lopez. You and Val tried to make some deal with him, right? So he'd give Val an alibi? Did anyone else know about that?"

"Jeez, that asshole," Jeffrey said. He shook his head. "That was a bluff, the son of a bitch wanted too much, and Val wouldn't pay."

"Okay, but did anyone else know about it?"

"Not on our end," said Jeffrey. "But Jorge was working for someone else, too. When I made the offer, he said, 'I just got paid double that for another job, and I didn't have to testify in front of any judge, either.' So, who knows?"

"Interesting." Eliza wasn't sure what to make of that, but she took down the quote in her Notes app. "Last question: what was the dirt you had on RJ?"

"Tsk tsk, that information was contingent on a deal, Trouble. Don't go asking for freebies."

Eliza got her phone out and dismissed a panicked message from Jenny.

"The deal is you tell me, or I give you all those impressions you wanted on Instagram again," she said.

"Don't even joke, you psycho!" he hissed. "Look, you don't want to know, ok? Trust me."

"Wish I could say I was in a trusting mood, Jeffrey," said Eliza.

A staring contest ensued. Jeffrey lost. Unhappily, he wrote something down on a torn-off corner of his notepad and slid the scrap of paper over to her. On it was a peculiar name.

Ivy Manson

He rose to his feet, packing up his things.

"Wait, who is she?"

"Don't shoot the messenger," he said. "And don't come looking for me again."

"I'll do as I please. Good luck with your communism or whatever."

"I'm not a communist, I'm a Marxist," he replied.

"I don't care."

Eliza returned to the alley around the corner where she'd stashed Secret and her bike. Swinging her leg over the Ninja's seat, she considered her options. Head home now? Or chill out for a while and ride home tomorrow? Her ass was already sore again, just thinking about the long trek up the 5. She'd learned some useful information about Blake, maybe. Enough to give her second thoughts about Shelly having his baby. And Ivy Manson? Who even knew?

Fuck it, she wanted some carne asada fries. The ones in NorCal just didn't hit the same. And maybe Kazu would have another chat with Drew. Then she'd ride home.

Jenny watched the Safari West work crew move the tiger with a forklift, feeling increasingly panicked about Shelly's proximity to Lockhart when her sister replied on Signal to clarify.

> **dangergranger:** Sorry, false alarm. But there's darkness in Blake I didn't know about. Don't leave him and Shells alone.

What the fuck am I supposed to do with this info, Lizzy?

She tried texting her sister, but Eliza wasn't returning her messages. Hopefully she was on the road back. Jenny needed her here.

"Everything all right?" Dinah asked her.

"I don't even know anymore," she replied.

Dinah squeezed her hand. *Fuck it.* Jenny silenced her mistrust and leaned her body into Dinah's. Whatever was going on with her girlfriend, she wasn't the Stranger, at least. Right?

"The bus is going to take us back early," Dinah said.

"Thank god," said Jenny. "I have decided that the wild Serengeti is not for Trouble. She's a city girl."

"I'll get you camping one of these days."

Because you want me alone? Or because you want me alone?

A short time later, the class filed onto the rental bus. Jenny returned to her spot in the rear by the window and found a large manila envelope waiting for her on the leather seat.

"What's that?" Dinah asked.

"It's uh… it's for me," said Jenny.

Inside was another chapter of the *I Dream of Trouble* manuscript, and a note from old Killroy.

ALMOST GOT YOU.

Chapter 4

I have a sister! A twin sister! It sounds crazy, but when Danger explains it, it all kind of makes sense. A mix-up at the nursery, a kidnapping, and a stillborn birth passed off in her place. Mommy and Daddy were told the twin didn't make it, and a barren nurse took Danger home for herself.

Danger, whose first name is Elizabeth, grew up three towns over, never knowing about me—or even her real middle name! It was only when the nurse died a few months back of an opioid overdose that Eliza found her real birth certificate hidden at the bottom of an old file box.

"That's crazy!" I say.

Dinah makes a noise like she wants to say something

and squeezes my hand under the table, but she bites her tongue. I can tell she doesn't trust the situation—doesn't trust Eliza—but the truth of my twin's story is written on her identical face. How else could you explain her? A clone?

We're back at Hodgson's place. It's not my preferred destination; I'd rather be at Rosie's diner with a hot butterscotch sundae. But Danger thinks it's best if her existence remains a mystery. She says she'll be the ace up my sleeve, pointing to her tattoo.

"Once I found out who my real mom was, I started investigating how she died," Danger says.

"The aneurysm?" I ask.

"No." Danger frowns. "It was a car accident."

"Wait!" It's my turn to be suspicious now. "That's what you said earlier, Dinah! How did you know?!"

Dinah winces, holding up her hands in surrender. "It's what I heard. Back when it happened," she says.

"Why would Daddy tell me it was an aneurysm?"

"Because he didn't want you looking into it, is my guess," Danger says. "Because I don't think it was an accident. Someone—some evil bastard—was sending Dad a message by running Mom off the road. He told you it was an aneurysm so you wouldn't go asking questions. So you'd be safe."

"What makes you think that?" I ask.

This is all so crazy. Daddy would never lie to me like that, would he?

"Because two days after I started asking around about the accident, the guy who used to live here tried to kill me," says Danger.

Whoa.

"Eugene Hodgson?" Dinah asks.

"The same," says Danger. "I barely made it out alive, and it's taken me weeks to track him down. I finally thought I had him cornered at the theater last night, but then I saw who he was sitting next to. You. It was a warning. He was letting me know how easy it was for him to get to you—if he wanted to."

"Why didn't you say something?" I ask.

"There were too many people around," Danger says. "And Hodgson was still lurking somewhere, waiting for me, so I slipped out the emergency exit."

"Then, you didn't kill him?" Dinah asks, her fingernails digging into my hand.

Is that what she's been worried about? Oh, Dinah, you're too pure for this business.

"No," says Danger. "I got out of there and only heard about the murder later. I wish I'd stayed. I might have seen who did it."

"It was the Stranger," Jenny says. "My nemesis. The guy I was chasing when I almost drove off that cliff. Eugene Hodgson coming out of retirement must have brought him out, too." I turn to face my sister. "Hodgson mailed himself a piece of evidence. A mini cassette. I bet he thought it was insurance. Damn! I had it in my hands, and the Stranger stole it from me!"

"You've run into this Stranger before?" Danger asks.

"Loads," I say. "He's the only one I could never catch. Always a step ahead of me. But before last night, I hadn't heard from him in six years. Right before the mayor was elected, come to think of it."

I close my eyes, seeing the puzzle in my head, testing each piece to see which ones snap together.

"Dad was scared last night. It's the only time he's ever asked me not to take a case. Hodgson was the mayor's old partner when he was in Vice, and Daddy says the mayor isn't the kind of guy you want to cross. I think the mayor's up to something dirty, and he killed our mom to scare Dad off the case. In fact, I'll bet good money the mayor is the Stranger himself."

"We need to warn Dad," says Danger. "Also, I—I'd like
to meet him."

"You will," I say. "But that's where the Stranger
assumes we'll go, isn't it? I say we flip the script and
go where he least expects."

Danger raises a questioning eyebrow.

"City Hall," I say. "I think it's time I did a
citizen's audit of Mayor Villanova's records."

IN JENNY'S PROFESSIONAL OPINION, HER FICTIONAL ALTER EGO MIGHT
be skipping steps in her deductive reasoning. It took a lot of leaps to
get to Villanova as the Stranger. Still, Dad did this sometimes in the
books. You kind of had to hold young readers' hands when it came
to mysteries. If Trouble had a theory, she was usually going to be at
least half-right. Which meant it probably wasn't the mayor, but maybe
someone connected to him. Could it be Lockhart, after all?

Needless to say, the near-death experience and baby news ended
any potential "situationship" status between Blake and Shelly. Her
aunt packed a suitcase and left to spend the night at his place. You'd
need a crowbar to keep them apart, and Jenny wasn't going to force
the issue until Eliza called her back and explained herself. When she
finally did, late that night, she was still in LA.

"Quite the little vacation for you," Jenny said with maybe too much
bitterness, eyeing the Brick & Flour bag on Eliza's hostel bed.

"You had me riding all over the North Bay for days!" Eliza shot
back.

"All right, all right. Thank you for all you do," Jenny said. "Warby
freakin' Parker. He couldn't have told us this shit a year ago?" Jenny
asked.

"He legit seemed pretty scared at the sight of me," said Eliza. "What
do we do about Blake and Shelly?"

"Honestly, you're taking this way harder than I am," said Jenny.
"I always knew he was a prick, but roughing up that stupid reporter

might be the nicest thing he's ever done for me."

"I just think we need to be sure if he's going to be part of our family."

"Okay, I'll talk to him." Jenny bit her lip. She had plenty more on her mind. "So, Jorge had to be working for the Stranger, right? That would explain why the Stranger killed him. Not because he was messing with the game, but to keep him quiet."

"Maybe. What would he be doing for the Stranger?" Eliza asked.

There was a detail tickling the edge of Jenny's mental Big Board, but she couldn't nail it down.

"I don't know. Any chance he drove a brown sedan—like that one at Mason's funeral?"

Eliza shook her head. "I think he drove a truck. Hey, my battery's dying. What do you want me on when I get back?"

Jenny got out her notepad.

Leads

- ~~DEB high score = Dinah Eve Black??~~
- Yvonne's heirloom, *The Stranger of Sausalito* book — Sent by the Stranger!
- ~~Arty's Parking Ticket~~
- The Hospital: site of the actual murder?
- ~~The P.I. who worked for Stratford Photography ("Too hot!")~~ — It was Lambert. DEAD
- ~~Eliza?~~
- ~~Jeffrey Jordan~~
- ~~Jorge Lopez~~ (Killed because he worked for the Stranger?)
- ~~Sheriff Blake Lockhart?~~ (Need to have a chat about his intentions toward Shells)
- Ivy Manson

The book, the hospital… and Ivy Manson. When Eliza gave her the name, Jenny said it didn't ring a bell. But it did. Ivy Manson was the girl who'd been stalking RJ. The one he got a restraining order against. The one who killed herself a few months before Jenny arrived in Blackbird Springs. Jenny wasn't sure she wanted to know what dirt Warby Parker dug up about her and RJ. Ivy wasn't the Stranger, obviously. Did some scandal between her and Dad really matter now?

Yes. Yes, it still does, Trouble.

Jenny sighed. Trouble never gave up on a lead, no matter where it led.

"I'll research Ivy," said Jenny. "I need you at the college. See if some of those copies of *The Stranger of Sausalito* weren't destroyed after all. Maybe there's still a copy at the library or the print shop."

"Hmm. Okay." Eliza didn't seem too happy. "I'll do that as soon as I'm back tomorrow—well, Monday, probably."

Did Jenny suspect? LA to Blackbird Springs was doable by tomorrow afternoon, but not if Eliza wanted some quality FaceTime with her boyfriend. She glanced at the message he sent her during the call.

hersidekick707: I almost got eaten by a tiger today! I need to see your pretty face.

The door to the unisex bathroom at the hostel opened. Eliza swooped past the objections of a vagrant who'd been waiting and texted Drew back.

zumizumizoo: Give me a half-hour? Finishing up dinner.

That should give her enough time to do her makeup.

Chapter Sixteen

Fan Fiction

IVY MANSON'S OBITUARY SAID SHE WAS SURVIVED BY A BROTHER, BUT it didn't give his name, and Jenny couldn't find any other references to him. Jenny was beginning to suspect that Ivy Manson wasn't her real name.

Undaunted, she tried a different tactic. Eliza had found Jenny by trolling *Trouble* message boards, hadn't she? And surely Ivy was a fan, too, right?

That sent her to r/TroubleNovels on Reddit, a place she'd sworn off years ago after some dickhead mod banned her for "Violating the community's rules on respectful conversation." Eventually, Jenny found an old poster named **MansonGirl707** who fit the profile of a too-obsessed fan. It was past midnight now, but Jenny couldn't resist diving in to read every single one of MansonGirl707's comments, starting from the beginning eight years ago.

If this was the real Ivy, her digital footprint was at turns insightful, mundane, and depressing. Aside from the *Trouble* subreddit, she posted a ton in writing forums, offering boundless advice on mystery storytelling, often mentioning that she was "friends with a well-known mystery author" to back up her assertions. Was that true, or just her delusion?

Ivy's last posts came about two years ago, in early March. She got

178

into a flame war, arguing about the ending of *Trouble Eight Days a Week*. Her final post was deleted by a moderator, and then nothing.

"Well, that was depressing," Jenny said to herself and let out a loud, unladylike yawn.

In all those posts, she hadn't come across anything that hinted at the Stranger, just a sad girl without any IRL friends, and now the night was getting lighter outside her window. Fuck. It would be dawn soon.

Jenny lay back on her pillow and yawned again, only to be awoken what felt like seconds later by a notification on her watch. Bleary-eyed, she squinted at her wrist, slowly taking in the confusing details. It was just after 8:00 AM, and she had a private message from Jack.

> **hisboyelroy:** Can you come over to the hospital?
>
> **sallydraper2003:** Sure, when?
>
> **hisboyelroy:** Now. Meet me in Alicia's room.

Jenny parked her bike by the ER and made her trek through the labyrinthine hallways to Inpatient Care. Jack was waiting in front of Alicia's room, dressed sharply for the weekend in a tie and blazer.

"What's up?" Jenny asked.

Rather than answer, Jack opened the door and waved Jenny inside. Alicia's room was empty, the bed neatly made and awaiting a new patient.

"Where's Alicia?"

"She's gone," said Jack. "Didn't give me so much as a warning. Just left this."

He passed her a small card with a note written in bubbly penmanship.

> Jack,
>
> Trouble is right. I'm getting out while the getting's good. This isn't forever. Wait for me? I love you so much.
>
> —XOXO Alicia

If the flaring nostrils and V-shaped brows were anything to go by, Jack considered this all Jenny's fault.

"What did you tell her?" he demanded.

"I don't know! That getting the hell out of town while the Stranger is loose might not be a bad idea?! And it's not!" said Jenny. "Of course, hiding now might also be the move of a guilty party…"

"She's not guilty, she got stabbed in the guts!"

"Be honest, she's enough of a maniac to do it to herself, Jack. Did she tell you about her father?"

Jack's scowl told Jenny the answer was yes. Honestly, Jenny found it sweet. Alicia was already so head over heels for Jack that she'd confessed a murder to him. If only Dinah loved her like that.

"She could have given me some warning," he said.

"What about the feds?" Jenny asked. "Weren't they watching her? I don't like it."

"Neither do I." Jack climbed onto the hospital bed and lay despondently, an arm stretched back behind his head. "She was the only one who remembered my birthday, you know? My actual birthday. This semester has been so ass."

He pouted and hurled a tongue depressor at the ceiling, where it stuck into the styrofoam drop panel.

"Budge over," Jenny said.

She pushed him to one side and joined him on the hospital bed. It was a tight fit, but Jenny was small enough to squeeze between the bedrail and her brother's right flank, tucking in under his arm.

"Not exactly built for two," she said.

"You'd be surprised," Jack said, that signature Valentine shit-eating grin stretching across his profile.

"Ew, don't ruin the moment."

"Who says we're having a moment?" he said.

Jenny wriggled her phone out of her back pocket. With a few taps, she had some music playing. She cranked it, filling the room with lesbian dance pop.

"Were you ever in the room when your mom was trying to cut a deal with that reporter and Jorge Lopez?" she asked.

Jack raised an eyebrow. "Only enough to get a look at him—the reporter, that is. Jorge was never there. Why do you ask?"

"We think Jorge might have been working with the Stranger," said Jenny.

"Does that matter now?"

"Not sure. Maybe." Jenny laughed. "Jeez, it took three people beating the shit out of that prick before he finally left town for good."

She briefly told him about Blake and the Stranger both taking their cracks at Warby Parker.

"I feel like I should be insulted," said Jack. "I barely phased him."

"We never really talked about that," Jenny said. "I didn't realize you could be so violent."

"I'm not, normally," said Jack. "I could just tell he was bad news for my mom."

"You're protective of those you love," said Jenny. "I respect that. It's why you won't tell me the truth about what happened the night Dad was attacked."

He turned his head to face her, his big eyebrows furrowed in consternation.

"You've got to stop covering for Dinah, Jack. She's my responsibility now."

"It's not a story you'll want to hear," he said. "And it won't help you catch the Stranger."

"I can't know that for sure unless you tell me," she said.

Jack shifted, rolling over to face her without craning his neck. On her phone, the song changed to one of those plaintive Canadian indie rock ballads Dinah had introduced her to. How appropriate.

"Fine," he said, and a savage smile spread across his lips. "Only on the condition that you never tell Dinah I told you. And Jennifer? Don't forget: you asked for this."

It's lower than you think.

The fanfic Jack read online always drilled this point home. Now, with the moment finally upon him, he knew exactly what he was doing. He thrust forward, sheathing his—

"Ow—stop! Stop!" said Dinah underneath him.

There were tears in her eyes. And not the good kind, he didn't think. His ego wasn't that big.

"Sorry!" Jack said, pulling away. "Did I, um, miss?"

"No, it's just—I can't. My body is like, you know." Dinah made a gesture, tenting her fingertips together. "Closed for business. Sorry."

Jack rolled off of her and settled onto the King-size mattress—

"Okay, I didn't need to hear about that, Jack! You fucking fuck!"

Jenny rolled off the hospital bed, eager to put some distance between herself and her brother.

Dryden Street. Dryden Street. Dryden Street!

"You said you wanted to know!" Jack shouted, mock-outraged. "Don't ask questions you don't want to know the answer to, Trouble!"

"You could have simply said you were making out!" Jenny yelled back.

Her skin itched—like spiders and insects were crawling all over it. She was disgusted. Repulsed. It felt like a violation. Maybe Jack hadn't done anything wrong, but it sure felt like he had.

"We were doing more than that. And it's important to the story," said Jack. "You need to know my state of mind. To understand why I did what I did."

"Your state of mind? What? Horny?" Jenny asked, not wanting an answer.

"I was embarrassed," said Jack.

"Oh, I'm sure your ego was totally bruised," said Jenny.

"I mean, yeah?" Jack said, pouting. "I'm a human being; I have emotions. Sometimes. It was my first time, too."

"Can we just skip past that part?"

"Fine. The point is…"

FOR JACK, IT WAS SUPPOSED TO BE THE CULMINATION OF A PERFECT SUMMER. Days of scheming had been building up to this moment. Subtly incepting his mother into holding the annual Valentine Foundation Gala on a Saturday—when Dinah's parents would be out of town. Making up a whole fake summer reading assignment that Jack insisted he needed to stay home and work on. Sneaking Dinah onto the grounds through the east gate and into the conservatory where no one would see. Confidently purchasing a package of prophylactics from the lady at the mini-mart. No self-checkout for Jack Valentine, he was a man's man! Or he was about to be one!

Dad almost foiled him by refusing to go to the gala, but he was locked away in the study in the west wing, writing (a.k.a. drinking). Jack knew from experience that the odds of him interrupting things after a few glasses of scotch would be slim to none. All systems were go.

But now, rather than celebrating in Dinah's tight embrace, he was lying on top of the covers, with Dinah curled up and weeping underneath the comforter next to him. The only tight embrace came from his boxer briefs, making the strange ache in his sub-abdomen feel even worse. Honestly, he might be dying.

"What did I do wrong?" he asked.

"Nothing, Jack," said Dinah. "You've never done anything wrong."

"You say it like that and I feel like you mean the opposite."

"All right, that was cunty of me." Dinah rolled over to face him and wiped her nose. "It's not your fault, it's mine. I tried to be what you wanted, but I—I'm not that girl, Jack."

Jack swallowed, and the ache deepened. "Will…will you ever be that girl?"

She sniffled. "I don't know."

"Would you be that girl for some other guy, but not me?"

"That's not what this is about, Jack."

"Then what is it about?!" He hadn't meant to shout, and now she was cross. "I'm sorry, I just—I don't know what I'm supposed to do," he said.

"You don't need to do anything," said Dinah. "You're respecting my boundaries, and I appreciate that."

She could put it however she wanted to; Jack was no fool. He could read the writing on the wall.

"Do you want to break up?" he asked.

"I didn't say that," Dinah said.

"Okay, fine. What do you want, Dinah?"

Dinah buried her head, her voice muffled by Jack's ethically sourced goose down pillow. "Let's just rest," she said.

Jack sighed, forcing his preconceived notion of the night out of his mind. Like the Oakland A's, this just wasn't his year. He rolled over, stretched his arm across the Dinah-shaped lump under the covers, and they lay together in silence.

Soon, she was snoring softly.

Oh, to be capable of such bliss. Jack was seriously dying here. His whole body felt inflamed—like he'd caught a fever or fallen ill. The ache in his groin was spreading. It felt like a 20-pound weight dragging him down. All he wanted… well, what he wanted was no longer on the night's menu. What he needed could be handled, but it would be very poor form on his part if Dinah were to wake up and catch him doing it here.

Carefully so as not to disturb his love, Jack rolled away and slipped off the bed. Pulling on his gym shorts didn't help the situation, but he didn't want to run into Mrs. Rivas like this. He grabbed his Kindle and snuck out of his bedroom.

The hallway was empty. The faint hum of a vacuum reached his ears from somewhere in the west wing. Perfect, the housekeeper would be busy cleaning the common areas for a while. There was a guest room downstairs that would serve his purposes—

"WHAT THE HELL ARE YOU EVEN TALKING ABOUT?" JENNY ASKED.

"You said you didn't want all the details," Jack replied, his ears turning pink.

"Okay, but we're talking about a key moment during the night Dad was attacked. One that completely contradicts your official story! You're saying you were in pain like you were dying? And what was the Kindle for?"

Jack blanched. "Reading! Look. Sometimes, when a man is… when he's been *encouraged*, but unable to… achieve jubilation, it hurts. You know? Or I guess you don't."

Understanding blossomed in Jenny's mind, and she cackled.

"That's not real!" she said, slugging Jack lightly on the shoulder. "That's just something dudes make up to get handjobs. We learned all their excuses from those videos we watched in Health class."

"Oh, perfect. You're right, Jenny. What was I even thinking?"

She searched for the lie on his face, waiting for him to admit what he was *really* up to. It didn't come.

Wait. Really?

"Really?"

"Yeah, really!" Jack said. "Believe me, I didn't think it was real, either, until it happened."

"That's crazy," said Jenny. "I'm so glad I'm a woman."

"Yeah, so is Dinah," Jack said bitterly.

"So, wait. So you went off to, uh, achieve jubilation, and then what? You're telling me neither of you guys have an alibi?"

Technically, none of them did. Besides Eliza, only Dinah and Tori knew about RJ's insane plan with the sedatives. And neither of them knew what Jenny had learned from the paramedic: that RJ's vitals had been normal when they found him in the study. The real attack had come later.

"I would have heard Dinah in the hallway if she was anywhere near Dad," said Jack. He smirked. "Dudes gain, like, superhuman hearing in certain… times of need."

"Jesus. Okay, great, so you handled your business, and then what?" Jenny asked.

ONCE RELEASE HAD BEEN ACHIEVED, JACK PROCESSED THE INEVITABLE GUILT and shame that always followed. Maybe he'd pushed Dinah too hard. The signs were there, but he hadn't wanted to see them. She was already under a lot of pressure trying to be Valedictorian. He just needed to ease off and let her set the pace. He was a good boyfriend. He wouldn't let this one get away.

Back in his bedroom, Dinah was still asleep under the covers. He slipped out of his clothes and eased himself back onto the bed next to her. Gently, he reached his arm around her again. Pressed so close, he could feel her kind heart beating like a rabbit. Beating with love, he still hoped, for him.

This was good. This was enough for now.

She stirred and twisted around to face him.

"Hey," said Dinah, yawning. "I should probably go."

"Sure," said Jack.

"Um, do you mind if I shower first?"

"No, of course not," said Jack. Did he dare hope?

"I meant, you know, with some privacy," Dinah said.

"Right." Damn! "Of course. Just let me…"

Jack got out of bed and dressed in a fitted Tom Ford shirt, his 501s, and a pair of Moncler trainers. An idea was forming in his head: maybe he could look in on his old man and ask for some advice. Nothing that would give away what he'd been up to, but Dad was always good for an entertaining yarn, though he rarely featured in any of them himself. It was always about a friend or a guy he heard about in the next town over.

He jogged back down the stairs and headed for the study. On the way, he swung by the kitchen to grab the turkey sandwich he'd ordered earlier. It was supposed to be a victory sandwich. Now, it was more of an "Almost! Next time!" sandwich. He took a hearty bite and flexed in the mirrored refrigerator door.

"I'm the best!"

He almost believed himself. Dad's study door was closed, like always, so he gave it a hearty three-note knock.

"Hey Dad, you got a minute?" he called.

Jack took another bite and chewed, waiting. There was no response. He tried the handle, but it was locked. Frowning, he located the intercom button on the wall and pressed the talk button.

"Come on, Mom's not here; you can come out of hiding."

Still nothing. There should have been an intercom button on Dad's desk that he could use to reply. Maybe he'd gone to the gala after all? More likely, he had his headphones on and couldn't hear anything.

Jack sighed and returned the way he'd come. In the kitchen, he wrapped up the remaining half of his turkey sandwich, stashed it in the fridge, and called his mother.

"Jack?" she answered loudly. He could hear the buzz of the gala in the background. "What is it?"

Mom sounded stressed. She was forever trying to impress those awful friends of hers with these galas. The Big Six wives resented the hell out of Valerie Valentine, née Stratford, because she married better than all of them combined. Of course, none of them thought so at the time. Jack got the impression that Dad was seen as something of a rake back in the day. But then his books took off, and suddenly, owning a famous winery was nothing compared to authoring the books their daughters were obsessed with.

"Is Dad with you?" Jack asked.

"No! Would you tell him to get down here? He's not answering his phone!" replied his mother.

"I tried his study, but it's locked," said Jack. "I think he might have his headphones on."

"Go around and get his attention!" his mother said. "He needs to get down here and make an appearance. The mayor is giving me the stink eye. He promised a bunch of donors that RJ would be here."

Jack left through the east door and stepped into the conservatory, taking care to stay on the path so that his Monclers wouldn't be soiled with red dirt.

"What does Hector care?" asked Jack. "Everyone's getting free paperweights, aren't they? Mr. Webb says those will be instant collector's items."

He exited the conservatory and turned left, circling the greenhouse and walking back toward Dad's study.

"Some people like to get a photo," said his mother. "It's worth more than a trinket or autograph. It's proof that they met."

That was the last exchange Jack remembered. He must have reached the tall bay windows into the study right after. Then, it all became a blur.

Dad's feet sticking out from behind the desk, the empty tumbler beside his shoes. Jack pounding on the window and getting no response. Racing back to the study and kicking the door down. Dad lying face up on the carpet. Feeling for a pulse, and his hand coming away wet with blood. Screaming for his mother to call 9-1-1.

All his worry about punching his V-card washed over him in bitter shame. The police and ambulance were on their way. They couldn't know what Jack had been up to. Couldn't know he'd been so busy trying to get it wet that he hadn't even realized his dad was injured—maybe dying—only a few dozen yards away.

"Jack, what's wrong?" Dinah asked when he burst into his bedroom. She was dressed again, drying her hair with a towel.

"Um. Accident!" It was all he could manage. "Dinah, you have to get out of here."

He grabbed her backpack and thrust it into her hands.

"Are you mad at me?" Dinah asked, frowning.

"No! Sorry! It's not that," said Jack. "My Dad. He might have hurt himself. You can't be here. Sorry, it's just—I was supposed to be alone."

"Oh my god!" Dinah covered her mouth in shock. "Is he okay?"

"I think so. He's breathing. Come on."

He hustled her to the bedroom door. She was still confused but seemed to sense this was not the time for questions. They took the stairs together, and he pointed her to the conservatory door exit.

"I'll explain later," Jack said. "Just go out the east gate like before. If anyone asks, you were home all evening."

"Okay…" Dinah said, still confused and concerned.

"The ambulance will be here soon. I'll call you. Everything's fine. It's gonna be fine. You'd better hurry."

He didn't shove her out, but he may as well have, from the cross look on her face. There was no time to apologize; he was already sprinting back to the study, frantically dialing Tori, leaving smears of Dad's blood on his phone screen.

It was just a concussion, probably. He'd be fine. He'd be fine. He'd be fine…

Chapter Seventeen
Vital Signs

"**Y**OU START TO BARGAIN WITH YOURSELF," JACK SAID. "FIRST, IT'S just a concussion. Then, okay, maybe it's a skull fracture, too, but only a minor one. The medics would be more frantic if it were serious, right? The surgeon will patch him up. The coma is just until the swelling goes down. Head injuries are tricky, but people come back from them all the time. Maybe he's got a little brain damage— but the fun kind, like he hates bananas now and can't remember our old dog's name. There's a doctor in Chicago who's an expert on these injuries. We just need him to look at the X-rays, and he'll know what to do…"

Jack's voice got very small. "Maybe he'll wake up as soon as we turn off life support. His body just needs some encouragement."

He turned away to wipe his eyes.

"Those must have been three very hard weeks," said Jenny. "I wish I'd known. I would have tried to get up here sooner."

"But you understand why I did it, right?" Jack asked. "Why we had to lie? Everyone would have blamed me. And then they'd find out, and they'd all know that I…"

"That you were cranking it to erotic fanfic when RJ was attacked?" said Jenny. "Yeah, I'd take that one to the grave. You are the most ridiculous boy I've ever met. No wonder we're related."

"And all because I couldn't close the deal with Dinah," he added glumly.

"Well, I think we know why that is now, Jack," said Jenny. "It wasn't about you."

"Obviously," said Jack. "But then suddenly it was a murder, and lying becomes a sign of guilt. It's like a—a snowball rolling downhill. Once it gets going, you can't stop it. And it wasn't hurting the investigation. Not really. Am I wrong? Like, this didn't help you at all, right?"

Jenny furrowed her brow and chewed on the inside of her cheek. *Probably not...*

"You're sure Dinah didn't get up while you were... relieving yourself?" she asked.

"Positive," said Jack. "She was exactly how I'd left her."

"How long did you take? Downstairs?"

"Maybe half an hour?" he said with a shrug.

"*Half an hour?*"

"You don't have to rub it in."

"Sounds like you were the one rubbing it—"

"Jennifer, I swear to god," said Jack. "I feel bad enough as it is."

"Well..." Jenny hesitated. How much did she trust him? Fuck it. "The thing is... I'm pretty sure it doesn't matter. I'm pretty sure Dad was perfectly fine when you found him. I think he faked the whole thing, and the real attack didn't come until later."

Jack frowned. "What are you talking about?"

"Walk with me to the ER, and I'll tell you something you didn't know about dear old Dad."

JENNY GAVE JACK AN ABBREVIATED RUNDOWN OF DAD'S INSANE PLAN A to fake his own coma in hushed murmurs as they walked back to the ER. She also revealed what the paramedic had told her about Dad's condition at the mansion, something only Eliza had known until now: that RJ's vitals were normal when they found him.

"I can't believe Tori never told me!" Jack said, shaking his head.

"The fucking madman. If he had pulled that off, it would have been legendary."

"Yep, and instead, he's legendarily dead," said Jenny. "Shit!"

She froze, mortified.

"What?!" asked Jack, frowning.

Jenny winced, dragging her foot off the cream tile she'd accidentally stepped on.

"I might have fucked us all, there," she said.

"Oh, don't worry, I've been stepping on only the white tiles to cancel out your bad vibes," said Jack.

Jenny slugged him on the shoulder again. "Speaking of Tori, did she tell you about our encounter?"

"No, what?" Jack asked.

"Never mind, then."

"Hey, come on," said Jack. "Get me off the bench, here. I need to be doing something. There aren't any more secret passages in the house; Dinah and I checked everywhere. I need a new lead."

Jenny considered bringing up Ivy Manson but wasn't in the mood to have that conversation. Luckily, a better option was just around the corner.

"Okay, little brother, let's try to put together a timeline of when RJ *actually* got murdered."

They arrived in the ER, bustling as always with sick patients and nervous anxiety. An old man with a nasty cough passed them, hacking up a lung. Jack produced an N95 mask from somewhere and pulled it on.

"I need to see if a charge nurse named Shirley is working," Jenny told him. "She normally works graveyard shift, so she might have left already."

Jack flagged down a passing orderly and asked, "Hey man, is Shirley working?"

"I'm off!" said an older black woman behind the orderly wearing pink scrubs. "Just came back to pick up my paycheck. You're going to have to get in line like everyone else."

"Wait! Wait! Shirley!" said Jenny.

The woman was already walking out the sliding doors. Jenny grabbed Jack's hand and followed her to the covered roundabout where Shirley's Honda minivan was idling behind an ambulance. It smelled of exhaust, diesel, burnt rubber, and iodine.

"Please! Can we talk?!" Jenny called.

The nurse glanced back and frowned. "I can't help you."

"I need to know what happened the night you treated RJ Valentine!" Jenny shouted.

Shirley froze with her hand on the minivan door latch. *Yes! Yes! Take pity on me!* The woman seemed to deflate, and turned back around.

"We meet again, Miss Valentine," she said.

"I don't believe we've met before," said Jenny.

"You were unconscious," said Shirley. "This was when they found you on the side of the road with a broken arm and a concussion." An ambulance siren whooped and pulled out of the roundabout. Shirley glanced over at Jack. "You Valentines certainly have a way about you."

"Ah, right," Jenny said, remembering the incident with poor Mason's Dodge Challenger. "Only the second—no, third time the Stranger tried to kill me."

Shirley was unamused. She moved over to a cement ashtray, placed the minimum mandatory distance from the ER entrance, and produced a pack of cigarettes from her purse. Jack was on the spot with a lighter.

Why did Jack have a lighter? Oh, who knew with this boy??

Once she'd taken and released a long drag, Nurse Shirley condescended to address Jenny's question.

"I'm not sure what you want to know, but I haven't got much to tell you," said Shirley. "I've already told the police all this twice, and even sat for an interview with those agents eavesdropping on us."

She gestured with her cigarette. Jenny spun to see Agents Tierce and Steele exiting a black Chevy SUV, having just parked on the far end of the roundabout. Steele waved, and they shuffled on over in an unhurried gait.

"Quickly, tell me what you can, please?" Jenny begged.

"Your father arrived with a depressed skull fracture and suspected intracranial hematoma," said Shirley. "He was triaged by our on-staff emergency physician, rushed to radiology for imaging, and immediately sent into surgery. They did everything they could, but the trauma to the brain was too severe."

Her eyes shifted to Jack, and she grimaced. "They kept him on BLS for a few weeks, but everyone knew it was a lost cause. His brain was dying from the moment he rolled through those doors."

She gestured to the automatic glass doors they'd just come through.

"I um…" Jenny winced and coughed. Nurse Shirley's cigarette, and her clinical recounting of RJ's injury, had robbed all the moisture from her throat. "I thought his vitals were fine when the paramedics found him."

"Busy morning for you, Jennifer," Tierce said, strolling up. "No church for you?"

"They could have been," said Shirley, ignoring Tierce. "Head injuries have a way of going south in a hurry."

"Was there a lot of blood?" asked Jack.

Agent Steele made a clucking noise.

"What!?" Jack said, flashing some of that protective Valentine fury.

"You were there, weren't you, Jack?" said Steele. "According to your statement, you're the one who found him."

"Yes, thank you, I was," Jack said. "I'm asking about when he arrived at the hospital."

Jenny would have preferred Jack leave it alone with the feds listening in, but there was naught to be done about it now. Shirley stroked her chin, thinking.

"The dressing the EMTs put on was pretty well soaked through if I recall," she said.

"Now, why would you ask a question like that?" asked Agent Tierce.

"It's how I process trauma," said Jack.

"Of course," said Steele. "I *know* you wouldn't be trying to stick your nose into our investigation. We've made the consequences of obstructing a federal case quite clear, haven't we?"

"Thank you, Shirley," Tierce said with a curt nod.

It was a clear dismissal. Shirley rolled her eyes and smirked at her half-smoked cigarette. Tierce raised a hand, so she passed it to him and marched off to her car. He took a drag, and Agent Steele turned to face the two siblings.

"Miss Aaron leaving in the middle of the night without informing us of her plans has us rather concerned for her safety," he said.

"I thought your people were watching her," said Jenny.

"They were, but she wasn't a prisoner," said Steele. "She checked herself out. Do you know where she went?"

"As soon as I hear from her, you'll be the first to know, sir," said Jack, forcing himself back into his golden boy persona, the big man on campus who respected authority.

"We'd appreciate that," said Agent Steele.

The agents made to leave, but then Tierce stopped and turned back to Jack, ashing his purloined cigarette. "Come on, now. Why ask about the blood?"

Because if what Shirley said was true, then RJ Valentine was really, truly, mortally wounded when he arrived at the hospital. But if what Dalton the paramedic told her was also true, RJ *wasn't* mortally wounded when the EMTs found him at the mansion. Meaning… meaning the attack must have happened *during the ambulance ride!*

Jenny's heart was pumping so fast she almost missed Jack's cover story to the feds.

"I um—when I found him, I didn't do anything to stop the bleeding," said Jack. "I just ran to call 9-1-1. I've always been haunted by that. If I could have made a difference, you know? But it sounds like he was dead before the ship even sank."

Agent Tierce studied Jack closely, his sea-gray eyes boring into Jack's skull. Jack shrugged, unbothered. Finally, Tierce relented and leaned back, taking another drag.

"With your friend Alicia discharged, it seems like you no longer have a reason to be here," he said and blew smoke in their faces.

"So it does," said Jenny. "I'll call you later, Jack."

Her brother nodded to her, his face an unreadable mask, and Jenny walked away toward the bike racks. This was something. This was progress. They were narrowing the window of attack. Now she desperately needed to talk to Dalton. But how to do that without Tierce and Steele up her ass?

AFTER CONSIDERING EVERY ANGLE FOR AN HOUR, JENNY ARRIVED at the disappointing conclusion that she was better off waiting to contact Dalton. She didn't even have his number, and besides, she had to babysit.

Lockhart lived on the north side, where the land began its gradual upward slope toward the mountains. No, wait—there were no mountains north of town. That was only in the last *Trouble* manuscript. Jenny cracked her neck to clear her head as she rolled her bike to a stop in front of a ranch-style home with burnt-orange stucco walls and a tile roof.

Something was off. It was too homey. She'd always pictured Lockhart living inside a brutalist cement compound with a bench press for a couch...

"What are you looking at?" Blake asked.

Mason's jeep in the driveway.

"Nothing," said Jenny. "I can't believe I'm babysitting for you."

"Neither can I, kiddo," said Blake. He got out his wallet and offered a $20 bill. "Will this cover it?"

"Be serious," said Jenny. "And send it to my phone so I can order DoorDash."

Blake muttered curses under his breath while taking *forever* to send a whole $40 to her. Then he insisted on giving her the full rundown of Lilah's dietary preferences, her bedtime, and where all the emergency numbers could be located.

Jenny dutifully wrote his instructions down in her notepad. When she was done, she couldn't help flipping back to her list of leads.

"What?" Blake asked, sensing her hesitation.

She tapped her pen against the paper. "I might have something for you. But I'm not sure if I can trust you."

"Oh yeah?" He glanced at his watch—a gold one that Shelly had given him for Christmas. "Is this urgent?"

Only Jack knows about the paramedic's story. And I didn't tell him Dalton's name.

"No. But we should talk soon."

"At your service, Jennifer," he said with enough condescension to make sure they weren't getting too chummy. Gotta keep the canon intact, after all.

Once he and Shelly left, Jenny spent the afternoon playing blocks with Lilah, trying to teach her funny words, and feeding her lots of applesauce. Blake texted no less than twenty times to check in. Jenny wanted to tell him to chill, but she knew why. The last time he'd gone on a date with Shelly, he came back to find his son murdered.

At 7:00 PM, Jenny put the little one to bed, ordered pork dumplings from a new Chinese fusion place, and picked the lock to Blake's bedroom door. She wasn't looking for anything in particular, but a little snooping couldn't hurt.

It became immediately clear that Blake was a psychotic neat freak. His shoes were organized by color and utility in little cubbies. Freshly pressed uniforms hung on fancy wooden hangers in his closet. He had a gun safe with a ballistic glass door, full of an alarming amount of firepower, locked behind biometric sensors she couldn't get past. Jenny found a single book on his nightstand: a huge doorstopper a thousand pages thick about World War II code breakers. He even ironed his sheets.

Aunt Shelly was doing her best to break him. It was like her suitcase had exploded, erupting blouses and pants and bras all over her side of the bed. In the bathroom, the countertops were completely covered with Shelly's various haircare, skincare, and makeup products. If Blake hadn't murdered her yet, maybe it *was* love.

Dinah texted, but Jenny didn't have the strength to face that whole situation right now. How was she even supposed to talk to her after hearing Jack's story?

Am I being unfair? Maybe? It was easier when it was just Dryden Street—

Loud pounding sounded down the hall. Someone knocking on the door!

Jenny's heart froze to the core until she remembered she'd ordered food. Thank god, she was starving! She locked up Blake's room and tiptoed back to check the peephole. Good. The delivery guy was gone, and her food was on the doormat.

Grabbing the bag, she retreated to the kitchen and shoved a whole dumpling into her mouth, chasing it with a squirt of sriracha from Blake's fridge.

Delicious! She devoured two more before she noticed something odd about her delivery. Below the copious napkins, there was something else at the bottom of the bag. Reaching in, her fingers found smooth-textured paper, several pages of it, folded up.

Jenny frowned and pulled the papers out. Unfolded, it was a dozen pages of letter-size white paper, covered in Courier New. The Stranger had delivered another chapter of the manuscript.

Chapter Eighteen
Déjà Vu

JENNY RACED OUT ONTO LOCKHART'S FRONT PORCH, POINTING A borrowed chef's knife in front of her for anyone who dared. She scanned every shadow for a sign of the Stranger, but the night was dark and the street was as quiet as a cemetery.

"Coward!" she yelled and went back inside.

Quick as a fox, she locked all the doors and closed all the drapes. Should she call Lockhart? No, the Stranger didn't want to fight, he wanted her to read, right? Jenny settled into the rocking chair in Lilah's room to keep watch, just in case. Then she allowed herself to take a look at the manuscript.

Chapter 5

I talk Dinah into splitting up. Her job is to go to my father's office and warn him about the mayor. She doesn't like it, but seeing the Stranger in the flesh is a lot different than hearing about him in rumors and old stories. She gets it now. This is real. This is my life. Until I put an end to him, that is.

Before we begin, Danger and I make a quick detour to my bedroom for a costume change. When she's in my spare purple trench coat, you can't tell us apart. That's the plan, anyway.

City Hall sits right in the middle of Town Square, surrounded by the park. Convenient, since there's always an excuse to be milling around, but also tricky because security can see you coming from every direction. I've always wanted to try breaking in but never had a good reason before tonight.

A good reason… memories are flooding back now. Little details and comments from Daddy that I never put together… The way he'd often lament that he missed our old mayor, Mr. Alger. How we never went to any of Mayor Villanova's fundraisers or election parties. Even the time I told him that he should run for mayor in the next election, and he replied, "They don't let guys like your old man become mayor."

What had he known?

"Are you sure you don't want to try a smoke bomb or something?" Danger asks me.

We're just around the corner from Town Square, lurking in the alley.

"I think that would tip them off," I say. "If we do it this way, they'll think they've got eyes on me. They won't suspect."

"Okay, let's do it!" she says. "Trouble and Danger against the world!"

We high-five, and she steps out of the alley and heads straight for City Hall. I watch from the corner, waiting for my cue.

I can see it all happening from my spot across the park. Danger goes inside, and through the window, I can see her at the front desk, bouncing on her heels. Mrs. Green, the mayor's receptionist with the cat-eye glasses and beehive hairdo, points her to the bathroom on the west side of the building.

My turn.

I retrace Danger's steps exactly, jogging up to the front entrance and entering with the same frantic "I need to pee" energy.

"Mrs. Green! Can I use the ladies'?? The bathroom in the park is so grody!" I say.

It was the exact same thing Danger said to her. I know, because we rehearsed it. Mrs. Green frowns, her jaw hanging slack as the hamster upstairs tries to put two and two together.

Kids, don't try this one at home. This only works if you have an identical twin, and your mayor's receptionist likes to imbibe from a bottle of peppermint schnapps in her desk drawer.

"Oh um, why sure, darling," says Mrs. Green. "Heavens, I just had the most powerful déjà vu! It's down the hall there on your right."

I hurry off to the ladies' while Mrs. Green is either swearing off drinking for a while or taking another nip as soon as I'm out of sight. When I enter the bathroom, Danger is waiting for me by the last stall.

"Did it work?" she asks.

"Like gangbusters!" I say. "Boost me up."

There's an air vent above the toilet in the last stall. Danger stands on the seat and helps lift me so I can open the grate. Then I'm climbing onto her shoulders and pulling myself up inside the metal shaft.

"You got it?" she asks.

"Solid!" I say. "Now go be conspicuous by the window in front of Mrs. Green's desk."

Danger gives me a salute, and she's off. As far as Mrs. Green will know, I came into the bathroom to pee, and now I'm leaving.

Except the real me is just getting started. One of the advantages of being a pint-sized Girl Detective is that moving through these air ducts is a cinch! Or at least, it was when I was eleven. Were these shafts always so tight? Did they replace them with smaller ones?

No matter, I make it where I want to go without causing too much of a ruckus. One right turn and two lefts, and I'm staring into the City Hall Library. Not a real library like the one Dinah volunteers at; each new mayor adds his selections to the official mayoral collection. It's supposed to be a distinguished business, and Daddy was awfully put out when Mayor Villanova added a bunch of James Patterson books. At the time, I thought he was peeved that none of *his* books were selected, but now I'm sensing that Daddy just hates the mayor.

The library is two stories tall, so this air vent is looking out from behind a row of books about halfway up the stacks. I'm in the John Irving section, I see, once I get the vent open and push some of them aside. Probably added before I was born. I peek my head out to get my bearings, and I'm in luck! The rolling ladder to access the upper stacks is only a couple of feet to my left!

It takes a hell of a stretch, but I just manage to grasp a rung on the ladder before the rest of my body falls out of the vent, through the bookshelf, and into thin air! I swing freely, using the rung as a fulcrum, and the momentum sends the ladder racing along its track. Wheee!

I glide to the east wall of the library and zip around north as the track curves with the architecture. By now, I've gotten a foot onto a rung below, and hang on for dear life as the ladder comes to a jarring stop at the end of the line. And a good thing, too! If I hadn't secured myself, the inertia would have shot me straight through one of the library's tall windows!

The ladder has taken me right where I need to go. Up on the ceiling, just above the ladder track, is another air vent.

This takes me straight through to an office on the third floor, and I can leave these grimy vents behind. After a good patting down to brush off the dust, I peek out into the hallway. There's only one security guard up here. He's sitting on a chair in front of the double doors facing the stairwell. The mayor's office.

I check my watch. Any second now…

POP! POPPOPPOPPOPPOP!!!!

A series of small explosions go off somewhere outside. The guard leaps to his feet, knocking over his chair. To him, those pops will sound disturbingly like the rat-a-tat of a tommy gun. He doesn't know, like I do, that they're merely a handful of firecrackers set off inside a metal trash can by my brand-new sister!

The distraction works perfectly. The guard hurries down the stairs to get a better look at the commotion, and I'm out of this office, down the hall, and through those double doors before anyone's the wiser.

Now, to the real challenge. Somewhere in Mayor Villanova's office, there's evidence that links him to Eugene Hodgson. To Mom's death. I know it! That mini cassette! If I'm right, and Villanova is the Stranger, he'll have stashed it here for safekeeping. Scum like these guys, they never destroy their evidence. They always want to save it for leverage.

The mayor's desk is massive. They must have killed a whole sequoia to make this thing. The huge top is held up by pillars two feet thick on either side, each containing rows of drawers. The top one is locked, but that's never stopped Trouble before. It's a matter of a moment to jimmy that sucker open, and I'm in.

What have we here? A pistol? Loaded, even. For shame,

Mayor Villanova. There's a bottle of Macallan 18-Year-Old Scotch in the bottom drawer on the right, and some dirty polaroids of widowed Mrs. Bishop in the top drawer on the left. Gross!

The center drawer is stuck when I pull it open. Not locked—something is blocking it. I get my little fingers in there and find the culprit: a rolled-up document is catching at the top of the drawer. I push it down and slide the drawer open. It's a blueprint! Curiosity gets the better of me, and I unroll the plans onto the huge desk.

It's a map of downtown Blackbird Springs, that much is obvious. But there's something strange about it. This map doesn't line up with reality; it's some future version of the town. A version with a casino where the town rec center sits now. Half the park turned into a parking garage. The Poison Pen replaced with luxury condos. And at all these sites, a small notation: Campion Construction.

Campion. Hector Villanova is a Campion through marriage. Got himself hitched to the heir of the Campion fortune. And now he's scheming to expand those coffers…

"You son of a—"

Rough, callused hands cut me off, covering my mouth before I can scream.

A surly voice with booze on his breath grunts in my ear. "Boss wants a word with you."

I bite down hard on a finger, and he yelps. I don't even want to think about the taste. His hand pulls back, and I make a run for it—but my foot catches. I fall sprawling onto the carpet. Before I can move, a bag is thrown over my head. Something pinches a nerve in my neck, and all goes black.

203

THE DUMPLINGS WENT COLD WHILE JENNY WAS READING—AND RE-reading—the new pages of *I Dream of Trouble*. Honestly, all the stuff about crawling through air ducts and swinging around the library was more Danger-coded than something Jenny would do. Maybe RJ was reluctant to do a full POV shift to his new character. Maybe if he'd gotten to know Eliza more, he would have.

Or if he'd gotten to know me at all…

Jenny sighed and refolded the pages, tucking them into her pocket. No, that was her frustration talking. Every time the Stranger gave her one of these secret chapters of *Trouble* lore, it felt like Dad was about to provide her with the missing link to his case. But inevitably, she ended each chapter with more questions and no answers.

What's up with the Campions? Didn't Dinah say something about one of them recently? Is Mrs. Green a real person, too?

She rubbed her temples and rummaged in Blake's cupboards, searching for some cooking oil and a skillet to reheat her dinner.

"Does she have to keep saying 'Daddy'?" Jenny said aloud. "Come on, RJ, she's supposed to be seventeen."

She wanted to ask Dinah about the Campions, but she'd been ignoring her girlfriend's texts all day. What else did she do with Jack? Was she scared of not fitting in?

Stop it! That's not fair, and you know it!

Yeah, texting Dinah now would end in disaster, so Jenny spent the rest of her babysitting shift Googling the Campions instead. They were one of the Big Six wineries in Blackbird Springs, and the most profitable now that Pinehall was kaput and the Carnegies got decimated by the *Ressort Rouge* scam. The elder Campions only had one child: Betty Campion, married to Hector Villanova, the mayor.

Looking up "**Campion Casino**" produced no hits. Maybe RJ just had beef with Hector and wanted to stick it to him, knowing he'd be dead if the manuscript ever got out, and the mayor wouldn't be able to fire back.

Lockhart returned at 10:00 PM with Aunt Shelly. Her aunt barely said hello, making a beeline for the bedroom to change. Definitely some chilly vibes there. Interesting. Lockhart played things cool while

Jenny debriefed him on his granddaughter.

"She was an angel, so I gave her an extra applesauce," she said. "What's up with you and Shells? You better be treating her right!"

"We're fine. Not that it's any of your business," said Lockhart.

"I mean, it is a little," said Jenny. "Especially given your violent tendencies. That's right, I've been in touch with Jeffrey Jordan. How can I trust you with my aunt when you might fly off the handle?"

His eyes widened at the news. "I did that to protect your aunt," he said through gritted teeth. "And you. I would never lay a finger on her. I don't hit women."

"There are other kinds of abuse. Why is she mad at you?"

"She's not mad at me," said Lockhart. He rolled his eyes and pushed past Jenny to fish a Gatorade out of the fridge. "We had a run-in with Betty Campion at the restaurant."

All the hair on the back of Jenny's neck stood up. Déjà vu.

"What about?" Jenny asked.

She reached out to grip his forearm, which only made him laugh.

"It—it's not important," he said. "They've hated each other since high school. Women, right?"

"Mister, you are on thin ice with me already!" Jenny said, but she released his arm. "Seriously, though, the Campions have been popping up in my investigations. Was there anything between RJ and them?"

"I mean…" He shrugged. "Everybody hates the Campions. It wasn't just RJ. Tell me more about these investigations. You said you might have something for me earlier."

"I'm still not sure if I can trust you," said Jenny. "When are you going to make an honest woman out of Shelly?"

His lip twitched, and Jenny thought she saw his hand unconsciously move toward his chest before stopping. Beneath his shirt, Jenny could make out the outline of the ring he wore on a chain. His late wife's wedding ring.

"Not a good time for that," he said. "Don't change the subject."

Jenny chewed on the inside of her cheek. Should she tell him about Dalton?

No.

"You know that stalker my dad had?" Jenny asked instead. "I think she had a brother. Maybe he was angry at RJ and blamed him?"

"She did, and I already cleared him," said Lockhart. "First thing I did after Johnny's stupid will reading. His alibi checked out."

"Okay, well, I haven't cleared him," said Jenny. "And people's alibis might, um… they might not be as solid as you think."

"Meaning what?" he asked, suspicious.

Before she could answer, Shelly returned from the bedroom in pajamas.

"What are you two conspiring about in here?" Shelly asked.

"Tell me about Betty Campion!" said Jenny.

"Fuck that whore," said Shelly.

"Oh, it's like that," said Jenny. "Story time?"

"No," said Shelly. "Bedtime. Blake will drive you home."

Another mystery to add to the list. Jenny peeked at her notebook while Lockhart retrieved his keys and added some notes.

Leads

- ~~DEB high score = Dinah Eve Black??~~
- Yvonne's heirloom, *The Stranger of Sausalito* book — Sent by the Stranger!
- ~~Arty's Parking Ticket~~
- The Hospital: site of the actual murder?
- ~~The P.I. who worked for Stratford Photography ("Too hot!")~~ — It was Lambert. DEAD
- ~~Eliza?~~
- ~~Jeffrey Jordan~~
- ~~Jorge Lopez~~ (Killed because he worked for the Stranger?)
- ~~Sheriff Blake Lockhart?~~ (Need to have a chat about his intentions toward Shells)
- Ivy Manson — Next of kin?
- Betty Campion

They were walking to the front door when the bell rang, making Jenny yelp with a start.

"Jumpy, are we?" Lockhart said and answered the door.

Jenny winced. What if it was the Stranger?

It wasn't. It was Agents Tierce and Steele.

"Evening, Sheriff," said Steele in that raspy voice of his. He nodded at Jenny. "Got some questions for this one."

"Sure, now you show up!" said Jenny.

"Fellas, it's a school night," said Lockhart. "Can we do this later?"

"Kazumi Onishi was spotted in Los Angeles this morning," said Tierce. Jenny sensed Lockhart tensing up next to her. "You used to live there, didn't you?"

Oh fuck! Dammit, Lizzy! Wait—why did they say Kazumi? Wouldn't they have thought it was Jenny?

"We lived in Glendale," Shelly said. "LA's a big place."

"Any family there she might be staying with?" asked Tierce. "According to our research, your great-grandparents grew up in Pasadena."

"Yes, and then they were relocated to Manzanar," Shelly said quietly.

Tierce's smug grin froze on his face. Jenny swallowed hard and squeezed her aunt's hand.

"They weren't much for the desert after that," Shelly said. "All the Onishis are up here now, or in Okinawa. I was the only one who lived in Glendale, and that's because I went to college there."

"Right. Sorry," said Tierce.

"Then why did this one lock up and panic when we mentioned her 'cousin' down there?" asked Steele, pointing to Jenny.

"Fellas, you've stuck your foot in it enough for one night," said Lockhart. "You know you're not supposed to be talking to her without her lawyer."

"And *you're* not supposed to be bird-dogging all your former officers, asking for info about our case," said Tierce. "Some people might call that obstruction."

"Some people would be idiots, then, not to utilize my experience," Lockhart replied.

"It surprised me, is all," said Jenny, not wanting Lockhart to do anything stupid for her sake. "I thought Kazu was back in Japan."

"Anything else you're thinking that you might be wrong about?" asked Tierce.

"What a question!" said Jenny.

"Gentleman, it's past her bedtime, and she needs to be getting home," said Shelly. "Talk to our lawyer if you have more questions."

Agent Tierce's hand reached behind his back, and for a moment, Jenny thought he might move to arrest her. But then Agent Steele patted him on the shoulder and said, "We'll be sure to do that."

The ride home with Lockhart was an awkward one. He made her sit in the back seat like a perp, saying nothing the whole drive, and when they got back to Jiji and Baba's house, he parked the car on the curb but kept the back doors locked.

"Those guys are assholes," he said apologetically.

"I know, thank you."

"What aren't you telling them about Kazumi Onishi?" he asked, his eyes boring into her through the rearview mirror.

"Lockhart, you know how there's all this circumstantial evidence that points to you and Alicia being the Stranger?" Jenny said. "Your alibis stink. You helped her cover up a murder once before. The Stranger conveniently forgot to kill her, she conveniently can't recall who attacked her, and now she's conveniently disappeared. You've got a documented history of violent outbursts. Et cetera, et cetera. And yet I ignore it all and still trust you with my aunt. Because I know you would never, ever, do anything to hurt Mason."

Lockhart's lip curled into a snarl at the mention of his son.

"Well, I'm gonna have to ask you to extend Kazu the same courtesy," she said. "She had nothing to do with Mason's death. You're just going to have to trust me on that. Don't forget I outed Drew's dad. It's not like I pull punches if someone is guilty."

He turned around to get a better look at her. After a moment, some internal debate was decided, and he gave her a slight nod.

"I'll get you an address for Ivy's brother," he said.

With a click, the back door unlocked. She hurried inside before he changed his mind.

What a day. All Jenny wanted to do was sleep until noon, but school was stupidly scheduled for tomorrow morning. She schlepped upstairs to her room and flopped onto her bed.

"Did Shelly come home with you?" Eliza whispered in her ear.

Chapter Nineteen

An Honest Woman

WAS IT DANGEROUS, SNEAKING INTO JIJI AND BABA'S HOUSE LIKE this, with the feds watching Jenny all day and night? Sure. But what was her goddamned middle name for, anyway? Honestly, Eliza was sick of the road life. Sick of her butt being sore from the motorcycle. Sick of smelling funky under her ArmorGel jacket. She missed Aunt Shelly. Missed Jenny. Missed being a teenage girl. It was time she came in from the cold.

Jenny reacted about like she expected.

"What the shit!" her sister shrieked and leaped out of bed, grabbing at her sides for a non-existent weapon.

"It's just me!" Eliza hissed. "Keep it down!"

"Are you crazy!? What are you—you're gonna get us both caught!"

Eliza scowled and snapped her finger at Jenny's little portable Pokémon speaker. Jenny mastered herself and turned it on to play a little night music. For all they knew, the feds had bugged the place.

"It's fine," Eliza said when they had some audio cover. "I snuck in through the neighbor's yard behind us. They didn't see me."

"They were seeing you in LA, *Kazumi*!" Jenny snapped.

"Who was?"

"Tierce and Steele! The feds! Why are they seeing Kazumi in LA?! I thought she was dead?"

Eliza felt her ears warm. How the fuck had they seen her?

"I— When was this? When did they say?" she asked.

Jenny recounted her visit from the feds at Blake's and reiterated her question: why were they seeing Kazumi and not Jenny?

"I…I had to put the makeup on to prove to Drew that I was the one texting him on Signal," she said.

Jenny's eyebrows shot through the roof. "You're still talking to Drew!!"

"Only a little! Look, I was fucking lonely, okay. And Drew's cool, he won't tell anyone."

"This is very risky of you, Elizabeth," said Jenny.

"Well, Danger is my middle name."

Hah! Take that!

Eliza was expecting more of the third degree, but then RJ's little mischievous grin curled at the corners of Jenny's mouth. She was still Trouble, after all. They took turns in the shower and curled up in Jenny's bed after, giving each other a full accounting of all they'd done since they'd last chatted in person. Had it really been all the way back at Mel's?

"You can't let Drew know you're in town," Jenny said after Eliza finished reading the latest manuscript pages. "Tierce and Steele are going to be extra paranoid after you popped up in LA."

"It must have been when I went on the Warner Brothers studio tour," Eliza said with a grimace.

"You went on the— I thought we were almost broke!"

"We are, which is why I came home. I need food. We're running low, and eating out is expensive," said Eliza. "And Drew bought the tour ticket for me, so crawl out of my asshole! I was FaceTiming with him right before and didn't change until I hit the road."

Jenny's lips compressed into a judgmental frown.

"They have a Harry Potter museum there," Eliza added meekly. "The Sorting Hat called me a Hufflepuff, which was horseshit…"

"Jesus Christ."

"Whatever! Don't worry about Drew, he won't snitch," said Eliza. "But I'll tell him I'm headed to Tokyo or something, just in case they get his phone. What was my next lead, the campus bookstore?"

"And the printing press at the college," said Jenny. "But no, let's hold off on that a sec. We need to talk to Dalton. And Blake, too. I've been thinking…"

Jenny unfolded a new scheme. A surprising one, for her, but Eliza felt oddly okay with it. She had only one suggestion.

"Can I go to school tomorrow?" she asked. "And be you?"

"You never dyed your hair purple."

"Fine, I'll do it," said Eliza. "Please? Just for a day? I miss people."

"Okay, okay," said Jenny. "But don't wake me up in the morning. I'm sleeping in!"

Eliza had never known true, feral yearning until she was sitting next to her boyfriend at the lunch table and completely unable to do anything about it.

Drew was being polite and giving "Jenny" appropriate space, as they were purely platonic. The other Troublemakers didn't talk much, except in banalities about homework and the upcoming prom. All the real conversation, she knew, would be happening in their group chat. Maybe switching with her sister wasn't the best idea after all. Still, it felt invigorating to be around her friends, even if she wasn't allowed to jump one of them and kiss him all over. She rapped her fingers on the table to distract herself.

"I love your nails, Jenny," said Penny, noticing Eliza's fidgeting. "What color is that?"

Eliza glanced at her electric blue fingernails, courtesy of some gel tips she snagged at a boutique in Hollywood. "It's called Blue Ruin."

Penny grinned and said, "Nice."

They bantered about movies until the bell rang.

"Hey, Jenny, hold up?" Dinah asked.

The others shuffled off to class. Eliza lingered to see what Dinah wanted.

"I figured it out, you know," Dinah said. "Why you're avoiding me. I had to beat it out of Jack. I can't believe he told you that."

"Right…" said Eliza.

Dinah frowned and cocked an eye at her. "Oh fuck me! Are you serious!"

"I missed you too, Blondie," said Eliza. "What did Jack tell her?"

"Nothing. It's personal," said Dinah. "Would you just tell her to call me?"

"I'll tell her," said Eliza. "Whether or not she calls… I guess it depends on what Jack told her, doesn't it?"

She gave Dinah a nasty smile and hefted her backpack, but Dinah put a hand on her arm.

"Walk with me, Jennifer. We must keep up appearances."

Eliza shrugged and awkwardly clasped hands with Dinah, and together they strolled out of the cafeteria.

"This is weird," Eliza muttered under her breath.

"Believe me, it's a lot weirder on my end," said Dinah.

When they arrived at the quad, Eliza released Dinah's hand, trying to remember her last class.

"HUM-9, that way," Dinah said, pointing to the Humanities building.

"A pleasure as always, Dinah, of the most noble house of Black," said Eliza.

Dinah rolled her eyes and leaned over to brush Eliza's cheek with a kiss, for appearance's sake.

"Can I just ask you to do one thing for me?" Eliza said suddenly. She backed away a little and held up her hand at waist level. "Kick my hand."

"Huh?"

"Just kick it."

Dinah shrugged and rotated to kick with her right leg. Standard taekwondo style, perfect form. It triggered nothing in Eliza's memory. Whatever Nilay saw in the Stranger's kick, it wasn't there in Dinah's.

"Thanks. Be seeing you," she said.

Eliza headed for the Humanities building, counting off five paces before stealing a glance behind her. Dinah was still watching, and her face was white as a sheet.

A day of sleeping in and laying around in bed was just what Jenny needed to clear her head and rethink her latest gambit. Could it go horribly wrong? Yes. Was Jenny doing this to force an outcome, exhausted by the grind? No, she didn't think so.

The fact was, there came a time in every Girl Detective's investigation when she had to make a call without perfect evidence. Read the clues, read the person, and trust in her finely honed intuition.

But she couldn't lie, the prospect was more than a little scary.

At noon, she dressed in Eliza's soiled motorcycle riding gear and snuck out the back door. The Ninja motorcycle was parked a street over. She hopped the fence and went through the yard behind her. A half-hour later, Jenny successfully climbed to the roof of the Ryalto without barfing and returned to their little hidey-hole on top of the Cinedome.

> **dangergranger:** Call Dinah. She says Jack told
> her what he told you, whatever
> that means.

The three little dots showed Eliza had more to say, but they went away without another message. Okay, be like that, Lizzy.

Now for the hard part. Jenny gritted her teeth and sent off a response to Dinah before she had time to second-guess herself.

> **sallydraper2003:** Look. I get it. You could have told
> me. I wouldn't judge. It's fine.
> It's whatever. Dryden Street. I'm
> still crazy about you.

Jenny scowled, knowing deep in her heart that she didn't totally mean that last line. Not at the moment. Hopefully she would feel that way again soon.

> **agoodyearforwhine:** Thank you. We should talk soon.
> When you and Miss Bennett
> switch back.

Miss Bennett. *Meow!* Jenny was pondering a chill reply when her phone started vibrating with a phone call. Jenny didn't recognize the number, but it had a Blackbird Springs area code.

"Hello?"

"Jenny Valentine?" asked a woman's voice. Jenny thought she might have heard it somewhere before.

"Who is this?" she asked.

"Your stepsister's fiancé," the woman replied.

Jenny had to think on that one for a second.

"Officer Peña?"

"That's right," said Darcy Peña. "Boss says he has something for you, and to meet him at a quarter to four at the place you bamboozled us all."

"Oh, okay, thanks," said Jenny. "Wait— Fiancé?! Ohmygod! When? Who asked who?"

Peña laughed. "Later, when I'm not flirting with a federal charge."

The call ended. Jenny smirked, feeling as though she deserved some credit for Tori and Darcy's engagement. She pulled up her thread with Eliza and replied.

> **sallydraper2003:** Thanks. Jenny has a meeting with Lockhart at the Bad Egg at 3:45 PM.
> **dangergranger:** In town?
> **sallydraper2003:** His suggestion. It'll work.

AFTER SCHOOL, ELIZA KILLED TIME WATCHING THE BASEBALL TEAM take batting practice. Jack was showing off his elaborate new batting stance routine to Drew and the team.

"If I'm ahead in the count, I tighten my left wrist," Jack said, demonstrating with the velcro strap on his batting glove. "If I'm behind, right wrist. Then tap the plate once for each man on base, then ease back and wait."

"You don't set your feet?" asked Drew.

"No, you let the pitch come," said Jack sagely. "It's all about relaxing your mental. I swear it's like the ball moves slower if you're chill about it."

"They're so dumb," said a girl nearby on the bleachers. "Which one's yours?"

"Oh, none of them," Eliza lied. She pointed to Drew. "That one's my sidekick."

The girl nodded to mask her confusion. "Mine's Lai. He's so funny. I'm Zoey, by the way."

"Zoey! Right! You and Lai. Love that for you," said Eliza.

"I'm glad the boys are laughing again," Zoey said. "All these murders are so crazy. Not the kind of thing you expect as the new girl, you know? Have you heard anything?"

Eliza's watch tapped her: it was 3:15 PM. Time to get going.

"I know the cops are looking for this girl who stayed with us in a foreign exchange thing," said Eliza. "But it wasn't her. Can you keep a secret?"

Zoey leaned closer, eyes widening.

"Everyone knows you're a fed," Eliza whispered. "Can you watch my bag? I gotta pee."

Zoey stammered for a response. Eliza took it as a "yes" and left her bag behind, heading to the ladies' room. It would take Zoey about ten minutes to realize Eliza wasn't coming back. And by then, she was pulling up to her destination on Jenny's bicycle.

The Bad Egg was a sleepy dive bar on the west side, known for its cheap liquor and rough clientele. As she entered, the sour stench of spilled beer and '90s complaint rock on the jukebox triggered a sense memory in Eliza of that last time she was here, doing a switcharoo with her plastered sister after Tori got Jenny drunk and called the cops. That little stunt ended up with Eliza in jail for two days.

"Hopefully not an omen," she said to herself.

"Hey! Nancy Drew!" Blake called.

He waved her over to a booth in the back of the dive bar. Eliza slid in across from Blake and smiled. It had been a while for them, too. He looked a lot less hollowed out and haggard than the last time, though an ocean of sorrow still churned behind his eyes.

"Did anyone follow you here?" she asked.

"No, I made sure not to drive a patrol vehicle," he said.

"Blake Lockhart, finally forced to join Trouble on the wrong side of the law," Eliza said.

"Sounds like bullshit your old man would have put in his last book."

"Honestly, you're barely in it so far," said Eliza. "What have you got for me?"

Blake slid a scrap of paper across the table to her, and Eliza found herself momentarily mesmerized by those coiled steel forearms of his…

"You gonna take it, or what?"

"Right, sorry," said Eliza.

The paper had a name on it: **Forrest Fowler**. And an address in Napa.

"Ivy Manson's brother," he said. "Though I don't see how it will help."

"Gotta run down every lead, Blake," said Eliza. "Only way to drive the Stranger to ground. Thank you."

She slipped the paper into her pocket.

"Uh, I was under the impression you had something for me," said Blake.

Eliza leaned back, giving him one final appraisal.

"I'm still not sure I can trust you," she said. He flared his nostrils. "What are your intentions toward my aunt?"

Lockhart hesitated a moment, swallowing his first response and taking a breath. The door to the bar opened behind him, and the silhouette of a motorcyclist strode in.

"I'll admit, I hadn't been planning on any of this," said Blake. "Sometimes, life kicks you in the teeth. And then it fucks you in the ass. And then it backs over you with a semi, just to make sure the job's done. And you keep going on like a zombie because you don't know any other way." He clenched his jaw as a wave of grief crested and rolled back. "But I don't want to be a zombie, even if it hurts. I think

I can be good for her, and no one can argue she hasn't been good for me. I'd—I'd like to start a family with your aunt. If that's all right with you."

Eliza dug her nails into her thighs under the table. "I never had a father figure growing up. Never really wanted one—"

"Come on, Jenny," he said. "I'm not trying to replace RJ. I know I could never fill those shoes."

"That's just it, Blake," she said. "I'm not Jenny."

His lips froze halfway into another protestation.

"You're— What?"

"My name is Elizabeth Danger Valentine. Eliza, for short. Loved ones call me Lizzy. You can too, if you want." Blake frowned, confused. Eliza braced herself for the worst. "But you would have known me as Kazumi Onishi."

It was like a switch flipped. A curtain of rage fell over Blake's confusion. His hand shot out from under the table in a blur of motion, clenching his service revolver.

"Easy, Lockhart," said Jenny. "It's me."

Shrouded in the motorcycle helmet, her twin swung around from the table behind and pressed a firm hand on his shoulder. Blake scowled, rotating the pistol to point at her. Jenny raised her hands in surrender and cautiously slid into the booth next to Eliza.

"Who the hell are you?" Blake hissed.

Jenny pointed to her helmet. He nodded an okay, his weapon still trained on them both. Jenny tugged the helmet off and shook her head.

"Did I stutter? My name is Trouble." She set the helmet aside. "Hate these things."

Blake gawked, his expression cycling between rage, awe, and bafflement.

"What the fuck?" he managed.

"She had nothing to do with Mason," said Jenny. "Neither did I. We can explain, but you need to put that away before the bartender notices."

It took him a moment to consider his options. Fortunately, the competent sheriff part of his brain won out, and the service revolver disappeared back under the table.

"Thank you," said Jenny. She grabbed a weathered menu. "It's a long story. We're gonna need drinks."

NOT THAT IT WAS THE MOST IMPORTANT THING RIGHT NOW, BUT Jenny was getting damn good at these reveals. Each one was a little more fun than the last.

Blake received a crash course in Danger—and all that the twins had been up to under his nose—while they sipped on virgin mai tais. He grinned proudly when they told him Mason figured it out first, and lowered his eyes when he learned that Eliza had been the one he'd interrogated after the murders at the mansion. By the end, he was bewildered and battling the urge to be impressed.

"That's how you beat the fucking breathalyzer," he said, shaking his head.

"I did tell you it was the oldest trick in the book," Eliza said.

"That was you??"

"She's the one who likes you," Jenny said. "I'm the one who's always a pain in your ass."

"Right. Uh, about that." Blake glanced at Eliza. "Our conversation earlier…"

"Like I said, you need to make Shells an honest woman," said Jenny. "We talked about it, and we agreed that you should have this."

From beneath the ArmorGel jacket, Jenny withdrew her locket on its chain, along with a red diamond engagement ring. She unclasped the chain and let the ring slide into her hand. Blake whistled at the sparkling gem, but then he scowled and shook his head.

"Girls, I can't."

"You don't want to marry Shelly?" Eliza asked.

"No, of course I do—"

"Then shut the fuck up, Blake," said Jenny. She slid the ring over to him. "That's a 2.1-carat, princess-cut red diamond. It's priceless. I helped an international eco-terrorist steal it off an albino crypto bro on a cruise ship last summer."

Next to her, Eliza whispered, "Just go with it," to him, for some reason.

"You can't use the ring on your chain," Jenny said. "That's Lilah's."

"And don't do it somewhere public," said Eliza. "Shelly'd hate that."

Blake scowled and picked up the ring. "Uh, thanks. Jesus. Two of you. And I thought I knew what I was getting into."

"You're in it now, which means you can't tell anyone," said Jenny. "Especially not the feds, they'll just arrest us, and the Stranger is still out there."

"You don't think the FBI could do a better job than a couple of teenage girls?"

"Considering that they haven't caught me yet? No," said Eliza. "Jenny will check the stalker's brother out with Dinah and Jack, and I'm going to try to track down where Yvonne Griffin's heirloom book came from. We need you to find that paramedic."

"The Stranger had to be in Dalton's ambulance when he took RJ to the hospital," said Jenny. "Or maybe the first person to help take my dad into the ER. Based on what the nurse told me, that's the only window when it could have happened."

"The name Dalton's not very common," said Blake. "Shouldn't take me long. How do I get in touch with you?"

"I set you up a Signal account," Jenny said. She tore a page out of her notebook and handed it to Blake. "Here's your login info."

"'Unemployed Wife Guy,'" Blake said, reading the screen name. "How aspirational."

"Welcome to the Troublemakers." Jenny pushed the motorcycle helmet over to Eliza. "Sorry, time to switch back."

"Yeah, yeah, meet me in the bathroom in a sec," she said.

Jenny got up to let her out of the booth.

"It's nice meeting you, Lizzy," Blake said. "Officially, I mean."

Eliza beamed. "Same!"

Gross! Too wholesome!

Once her sister was out of earshot, Jenny turned to the sheriff and raised an eyebrow. "Don't make me regret this."

"Yeah, sure," he muttered half-heartedly.

Jenny frowned. His face was twisted up in pain, his eyes glassy. "What's wrong?" she asked.

"Every time I turn around, my family gets bigger," he said with a hoarse voice. "All of a sudden there's a granddaughter, and a baby on the way, then two girls with Shells instead of one."

"You're not having second thoughts, are you?" Jenny asked.

"No! No. I—I just don't want Mason to feel like I'm forgetting about him," said Blake.

"You're not," Jenny said. She surprised herself by hugging him. "We'll make Eliza name one of her kids after him."

"You might want to run that by her, first," said Blake. "I've only just met her, but she doesn't seem like the settling down type."

"She is," said Jenny. "It's just not her time, yet."

"So, I gotta ask," said Blake. "What could I possibly have done to win you over? Don't you hate me?"

It was a good question. "Not anymore. I mean, you roughed up that reporter for me," she said. "That was nice. But honestly…that Lambert guy fucked me up. I didn't see that one coming—at all!"

"That was me and Campbell Klein," said Blake. "I never even considered that she would hurt Casey."

"Exactly! It's making me take a step back and try to view the board with new eyes, you know? And the longer I stare at it now, the more things start to come into focus. Not just things, people. Um, I know we've had our differences, but for the record, RJ was wrong about you," Jenny said. "You're a lot more than the dopey sheriff from the books."

"This must be killing you," Blake said.

"It is."

"Then, in the spirit of your compliment, I will humbly suggest this: *you're getting warmer.*"

Jenny smirked and headed for the ladies' room. She'd spend the rest of the evening trying not to let that remark come into focus.

Chapter Twenty
Calistoga College

For the first time in forever, Jenny was glad to be going to school. They'd told Blake about Danger, he hadn't turned them in, and now they had another secret weapon against the Stranger—and new leads, too.

Every silver lining must come with a cloud, though. Dinah's smile for her at lunch was somewhere between frosty and Leo at the end of *Titanic.* Then the cool seniors made a rare visit to the Troublemakers' table, and not to say hello. That undercover fed Zoey had vanished, and everyone blamed Trouble.

"Why'd you have to tell!?" Lai shouted. "You couldn't have just left it alone? Now, who am I supposed to take to prom?"

Jenny just wanted to eat her chicken nuggets with her sullen girlfriend in peace.

"For real, Jenny," said JeRay.

"She woulda let me hit, too!" said Lai.

"No, she wouldn't have," said Jenny.

"Oh, she def would have!" Lai insisted.

They were interrupted by Vice Principal Carter joining them with Agents Tierce and Steele in tow.

"Is it true, Miss Valentine?" the vice principal asked her. "Did you expose Zoey Cartright's embedded status?"

Penny smiled at Jenny and said, "Hah!"

"I mean," said Jenny.

"Because these gentlemen are saying that's enough to warrant an obstruction charge," said Mr. Carter.

"Oh, give it a rest, Dick," Dinah snapped at him. "Is it a crime to notice crow's feet? Were we supposed to ignore all her outdated slang and insipid, emoji-filled texts? *Everyone knew!*"

Jenny hid a smile, delighted to witness Dinah's secret bitchy side unleashed on somebody besides her.

"Is that true?" Mr. Carter asked the other students.

They all stared awkwardly at their feet.

"Bro, come on," said JeRay.

"It was sort of obvious, Mr. Carter," said Thanh. "I mean, she was always asking about Jenny, and what happened at the mansion. And we really did tell you everything."

Mr. Carter glowered at them all and turned to Tierce and Steele.

"Better luck next time, gentlemen," he said.

Steele grumbled and thrust out Jenny's backpack at her. "You forgot this at the bleachers," he said in his raspy voice.

"Oh, thank you," said Jenny.

The feds excused themselves, but Vice Principal Carter lingered. "I thought I heard someone mention prom," he said. "Sorry to rain on your parade, Miss Valentine, but you will not be attending. Neither will you four," he said to Jack, Drew, Dinah, and Penny.

The girls arched their brows in outrage but managed to bite their tongues.

"For the record, this is bullshit," said Drew, who could not.

"Language, Mr. Porter," said the vice principal.

"Drew was still hoping he could take Kazu as his date," said Penny, smiling at Jenny again.

Great. Am I missing some inside joke between her and Lizzy?

Jack shrugged. "Whatevs. I'll still win Prom King," he said. "Watch me."

"Good fuckin' luck with that shit, bro," said Lai. "Oh, sorry, Mr. Carter. Good fuckin' luck with that stuff, bro."

Mr. Carter pressed his thin lips together but declined to engage with Lai. The other seniors returned to their table, and the Troublemakers could finally dine in peace. Jenny rummaged in her backpack, checking to see if the feds planted bugs in it.

"My mother will be wroth," said Jack. "She's already cleared a space on the mantel for my Prom King crown."

"When you think about it, you're the real victim, Jack," said Dinah.

"That's not a claim I'm making," said Jack. "But I could."

Jenny finished searching her main backpack pouch. As far as she could tell, it was clean of listening devices. She moved on to checking the front pockets.

"So, given that Zoey no longer graces us with her presence, can we talk shop?" asked Drew. "Any new leads? Did you have any luck with the book? 'Cause we—"

"You mean that rare edition of *Dial T for Trouble?*" Jenny cut him off. "No luck yet!"

She shot Drew a glare and held her index finger to her lips. From the bottom of her front backpack pouch, she pulled out a circuit board the size of a quarter, trailing a wire antenna a few inches long, and showed it off to the group.

"Hold it steady," Dinah said and reached under the table.

"No more Blue Ruin?" Penny asked. She was staring at Jenny's fingers.

Fuck. Lizzy's gel tips. Sloppy.

"Nah, I took 'em off," said Jenny.

Dinah brought up her hand and smashed the bug to oblivion with a Jimmy Choo flat, narrowly missing Jenny's fingers.

"Thanks!" Jenny said to an unreadable Dinah. *Okay...* She turned to Drew, shaking her head. "OpSec, sidekick. As for our leads..." She consulted her notebook, where she'd made an updated list the night before. "Let's see."

Leads

- Yvonne's heirloom: how did the Stranger get it?
  Visit Calistoga College.

- Find Dalton!
- Ivy Manson's brother: Forrest Fowler, lives in Napa.
- What work did Jorge Lopez do for the Stranger?
- Betty Campion?

"Heirloom soon," said Jenny. "Once I figure out a way to get Tweedle Dum and Tweedle Dee off my ass. But I do have a lead on one Ivy Manson, the woman who was stalking RJ Valentine."

Jack and Dinah both scowled at the name.

"*Ivy Manson?*" said Jack. "That crazy lady?"

"Did you meet her?" Jenny asked.

"She interrupted us at the Winchester once. Total loon," he said.

Penny turned to Drew, a lightbulb turning on. "Was her handwriting in the packet of stuff from Mr. Webb that you put on the Big Board?"

"I think so," he replied.

"We should check it and compare Ks," said Penny.

"Oh, good idea," Jenny said.

"But Ivy took her own life months before the attack," said Dinah.

"I know," said Jenny. "But she had a brother, and now I've got his address."

"Score!" said Drew. "How'd you swing that?"

"The town sheriff is sleeping with my aunt." Jenny turned to Dinah and Jack. "What do you say, Blue Team? Field trip after school?"

"Won't you still need to ditch the feds for that?" asked Penny.

"Come to the mansion after school with Dinah," said Jack. "I've got a plan to deal with the feds."

Dinah and Penny made mock-impressed faces.

"Is your plan just money?" asked Drew. "Because I could do that."

"Not money. Private property," said Jack.

The lunch bell rang. Everyone rose to collect their things. Jenny frowned at her nuggets. She hadn't even touched them.

"Money, property: it's all capital," said Penny.

"Okay, Trotsky," said Jack. He loomed over Jenny and glanced at her Leads list. "Who's Dalton?"

"Someone I need to talk to," Jenny said and tucked her notepad away. "See you after school."

Calistoga College was technically outside Blackbird Springs city limits, belonging instead to one of the bedroom communities nestled on the other side of the ridge, collectively known as Moon Valley. As she walked across the campus, Eliza tried to imagine that the Stranger was caught. That this was her life now: a normal college student.

In a way, she had a leg up on her sister. Jenny would always be Trouble, the Girl Detective, but Eliza could be whoever she wanted. Was she majoring in Women's Studies with a work-study job at the Student Union Health Center? No, with this wig on (a black bob), she was more likely to be in Computer Science. Learning Game Development and playing the triangle in some upperclassman's indie rock band on the side. Or maybe she was a scamp like her mother, with her sights set on a cute lit professor?

Would Drew still go to ASU? Would he want her to follow him there?

"What are *you* doing here?"

Eliza spun, her hand reaching for Secret, only to remember she'd stashed it with her motorcycle. She tried to play it off by adjusting her hair and regarded the person who'd snuck up behind her. It was Jenny's ex-girlfriend. The toxic one from the arcade.

"Oh! Asha," said Eliza. "Um, I'm just visiting, you can ignore me."

"Hard to ignore you when you're on my campus," said Asha. "Tell me you're not thinking of attending. I still have another year before I transfer to Stanford."

"Boy, talk about irony. Guess who's a legacy admission there?"

"Oh, come on!"

Maybe it was seeing her out in natural light for once, but Asha's baseline hostility didn't seem as strong as it used to be.

"Don't worry, I'll probably be murdered or arrested before I ever have a chance to attend," said Eliza.

"I heard about that," said Asha. "I'm *so* glad I rid my life of you before all that happened."

"So am I," said Eliza.

Asha didn't seem to know whether to take that as a nicety or an insult. "Well, they haven't got you, yet," she said.

"Sorry about Rob."

"He was washed, anyway. I got out just in time."

"Did you find a new job?"

"Computer lab." Asha nodded. "It's easy. They're basically paying me to shitpost on Reddit. I'm thinking of getting into online gaming."

"That'll be good for you, I'm sure," said Eliza. "Can you point me to the print press?"

Asha pointed out a squat administration building abutting the west side of the grounds. "Just keep going that way until you walk into the ocean."

Eliza gave her a tight smile and made for the building, trying to remain hopeful. She'd already struck out twice today. Neither Reynard Fuchs nor *The Stranger of Sausalito* had a record in the library's catalog system, and combing through the mystery section of the stacks didn't turn anything up. A friendly bookseller searched in the back room of the campus bookstore for twenty minutes with no success. If the print shop didn't pan out, they were looking at a dead end on *The Stranger of Sausalito*.

The admin building Asha pointed Eliza to was a hideous cement block of brutalist architecture that felt closer to a prison than a school. Their directory system was a nightmare, and Eliza was beginning to suspect Asha had intentionally led her astray before she finally found the sign for **Campus Press**. It was in the basement, buried at the end of a hallway lit by flickering yellow fluorescents that hadn't been replaced since the Clinton administration. When she opened the door, the overpowering smell of glue and ink hit her nostrils. It was like overdosing on a library.

"Oh," said the clerk behind the front counter. "We don't get many visitors down here."

He had a pinched face, sideburns, and beady eyes that looked too far apart. For all Eliza could tell, he lived down here and had never seen natural sunlight.

"I have a strange request," Eliza said, and explained her situation.

She was a collector of all things *Trouble*. Recently, she learned through her research that RJ Valentine once had a book printed here under a pseudonym, eighteen years ago. Was there any chance they'd printed more copies since then? Or maybe they held onto some of the originals?

"I don't think we've got anything like that hanging around anymore," said the clerk. "I've only been here a few years, but I know there was a big downsizing when admissions took over one of our storage rooms. That was before my time."

"Do you know who worked here before your time?" Eliza asked.

"That'd be the guy to ask, I suppose," said the clerk, rubbing his chin. "He was a lifer, put in forty years here, so he would have been around when this book got printed."

"Oh, that's great! That's exactly who I need to talk to."

Eliza felt her pulse quicken. She waited eagerly, assuming the clerk would offer up the lifer's details, but he only stared at her as if confused that she was still there.

"Um, can you give me his name?" she asked. "The guy who ran the place before you?"

His broad face curdled. "We're not supposed to give out that kind of info."

Eliza pulled a $20 bill from her wallet and slid it across the counter. "Can you tell me now?" she asked.

"I could lose my job if someone found out."

Like anyone would! This guy probably got three visitors a week. She peered into her wallet and grimaced. She had $208 left: a $5, three $1s, and two $100 bills. Pulling back the $20 bill, she pushed forth a $100 bill in its place.

"Well," said the clerk. He checked over his shoulder and made the bill disappear. "His name was Michael Smith."

Visions of riding the Ninja to a hundred different Michael Smiths in the North Bay danced behind Eliza's weary eyes. Please, no.

"You've got to be kidding me." He wasn't. "It'd take me years to find the right one. You gotta give me an address."

The clerk held up his hand and rubbed the thumb and forefinger together.

"I just gave you a hundred!"

"You look familiar. A collector, you said?" the clerk asked with a smirk. "Yeah, I'm pretty sure I've seen your picture in the campus newspaper. They love writing about RJ Valentine. And his daughter."

Fine. Eliza held up the $20 bill. The clerk shook his head.

"I'll bet an original RJ book would go for some real cash—even under a nom de plume."

Eliza slapped the other $100 bill on the counter. "I need the rest to eat, if that's all right, you little troll!"

"Now, now, let's be polite," said the clerk. His hand swallowed up the second $100, and he retreated from his desk. "Give me a moment to check our records."

While he did, Eliza sent her sister an update. School had just let out, and Jenny was headed to Jack's place, and then to see the stalker's brother.

sallydraper2003: Find out if you're the only hound
on the scent.

Right. Good thinking. The clerk returned with a slip of paper, on which he'd jotted down an address for this Michael Smith person. Eliza snatched it away before he could extort her further.

"Thank you. Last question: has anyone else come around asking about this book?"

"Gosh, my memory sure does get fuzzy," said the clerk, rubbing his fingers together again.

"I haven't got any more," said Eliza. "This person—if they did come here—has murdered at least nine people. And they've made a habit of killing anyone who might be able to identify them. So I'd think real hard about whether or not you want to help me catch them."

The clerk's already sickly pallor turned a shade greener in the dank light.

"No! No. Just you," he said.

"Good. If I were you, I'd forget I was ever here, just in case," said Eliza.

Returning to the surface and daylight was a relief. Michael Smith. If that bastard in the print shop dungeon wasn't playing her, the retired lifer lived only a mile from Drew...

Eliza smiled to herself as an idea sprang into her head. Probably ill-advised, but fuck it. Eliza was sick of the grind. She was broke, and she was hungry. Trouble was going to succeed because of her friends, wasn't she?

DINAH WAS WAITING FOR JENNY IN THE PARKING LOT INSIDE HER Acura when class let out. They made it to the highway, silently listening to the radio, until Dinah let her have it.

"I feel like you're judging me, and I haven't done anything wrong," said Dinah. "My therapist agrees."

"Good for her," said Jenny. "Dinah, of course you've done nothing wrong. I know that, like, intellectually. It's just... Jack gave me a lot more information than I wanted to hear, and I'm trying very hard to forget all about it."

"We never actually, *you know!*"

"Oh, believe me, I know. Jack did everything but draw me a picture," said Jenny. "You were really asleep the whole time he was downstairs... taking care of himself?"

Dinah hesitated, and—thank god—her lips finally curled into that beautiful smile of hers. "I did wake up when he came back to bed. Honestly, I couldn't stop thinking about whether he'd washed his hands."

Jenny gagged. "I can't believe you guys have *still* done more than we have."

"I seem to recall us getting pretty close in the archive room." Dinah accentuated the point by reaching over the gearshift to squeeze Jenny's thigh.

Oh hello.

"So you're not mad at me?" Jenny asked.

"I can never hold a grudge," said Dinah.

"How much better would all our lives be if the Stranger had done a better job of hiding Tori's unconscious body?" Jenny asked.

Dinah slowed and turned the car onto Cellar Drive.

"Would you seriously want our first time to be like that?" she asked.

Yes!

"I don't know. Maybe?"

Her girlfriend smirked. "Maybe we can ask Lord Junior for a half-hour alone in the Red Room."

"Not that room, but yes! I'll distract him with his Kindle."

Dinah stopped at the cast iron gates with the big V for Valentine and punched in a code to let them in. Jenny leaned out the window and gave two middle fingers to Tierce and Steele in the black SUV behind them.

"Suck it, bozos! Private property!" she yelled.

"Are you sure you want to do that?" Dinah asked.

She pulled through onto the mansion grounds. Tierce and Steele could only watch as the gates closed on them.

"Just playing my part," said Jenny. "They'll get suspicious if I'm too coy."

Valentine Manor loomed ahead. The pristine green lawn. The wishing well in the middle of the roundabout. The sun-kissed stucco and Tuscany flagstone steps up to the entrance. She'd once called it home. If she could only solve this damned mystery, she would again.

Dinah drove them to the underground garage below the mansion and pressed a button on her Acura's fancy digital console. The garage door ahead rolled open.

"How is it you still have their garage door opener?" Jenny asked.

"Uh, Jack programmed it into my car a long time ago," Dinah said and stifled a yawn.

Okay, *that* was a lie.

But before Jenny could follow up on this detail, they were inside the garage, and Jack was waiting for them. Jenny hefted the backpack between her knees.

"Are we coming back here?" she asked.

"Depends on Junior's brilliant plan," said Dinah.

"Ugh, fine." Jenny grabbed her pack and hopped out. "Okay, hotshot, what's your big plan?" she asked Jack.

"Over the garden and through the woods to stalker girl's house we go," he replied.

Jenny turned to Dinah. "This is the guy you almost lost your gold star to."

"What?" asked Jack.

"Valentine, I swear to god," said Dinah.

"Hey, no flirting in front of me," said Jack. He pointed both thumbs over his shoulders and added, "Before we go, I thought we'd return to the scene of the crime."

A shiver ran down Jenny's spine. Which crime?

Jack led them upstairs, and down the west wing hallway to the study. Jenny gasped as she stepped inside. Dad's study was immaculate. Freshly vacuumed carpeting, a gleaming, pristine mahogany desk, and brand-new, sparkling bay windows. All evidence that a double murder occurred here had been scrubbed clean.

"As soon as we got the okay from the police, Mom had a crew come in and tear up the carpet," said Jack, perhaps reading Jenny's expression. "The blood had seeped into the sub-flooring, so that had to come out, too."

"What about the desk?" Jenny asked.

"They used a power washer," Jack said. "Took off the finish and a millimeter of wood underneath, then re-sanded and varnished the whole thing."

"And they didn't find any more secret passages?" Jenny asked.

"Jack and I knocked on every square foot of the wall in here ourselves," said Dinah. "According to your timeline, it seems like the only way the Stranger could have escaped was through the window."

"When the cops let us back in, I saw they'd roped off a section right outside," Jack said, pointing to the bay windows. "It was raining, but maybe they found some drops of blood."

"Makes sense," said Jenny.

But she wasn't listening to him anymore. Memories of the awful night returned unbidden. Meghan: laid out across the desk, her life spilling out the gash in her neck. Mason: sitting peacefully in Dad's chair, a knife piercing his heart. Alicia: curled up by the bookshelf in a pool of her blood. The broken bay window letting the rain blow in. The Stranger might have left that way, but how did he enter? As an interloper, or as a guest?

She closed her eyes and forced herself to remember. The front door had slammed first. Because somewhere else in the mansion, another door had been opened. Then Alicia's scream. Then the glass breaking...

"Something's different," said Dinah.

"It's the carpet." Jack brightened. "I picked it out. I thought it set off the drapes and Louis XIV chairs better."

"It's not just that," said Jenny. "It's the smell."

"Hardly smells like him at all anymore," said Tori.

She appeared at the door, carefully studying Jenny. Trying, Jenny guessed, to tell which one she was.

"It's me," said Jenny.

"What are you doing here?" Jack asked.

"Visiting our mother," said Tori. "I have something for Jennifer. A word, *Trouble*."

Tori spit the name out like a mouthful of acid. She cocked her head, indicating the west side of the study. Jenny set her backpack down and followed Tori to the reading nook by the fireplace.

"Anything new on our late photographer friend?" Jenny asked.

Tori shook her head. "I'm not sure if you knew, but Jimmy Figg has been volunteering at the Foundation Offices as punishment for breaking in last month," she said in a low voice. "He's become quite fixated on how you tricked him and set him up. Or so he claims."

"Yeah, I heard he wouldn't shut up about it when he got caught," said Jenny, smirking. "So?"

"He has a theory about Kazumi posing as you that's quite compelling," said Tori.

You're so close, Jimmy. Fuck. "I hadn't considered that," she said.

"I expected not," said Tori. "You should start."

"Right. Is that all?" Jenny asked, frowning. Something nagged at her—something to do with Jimmy Figg, but not this…

"No, let me get a pen."

Tori sauntered back to RJ's desk and made herself at home in one of the guest chairs. She grabbed a pen and a pad of Valentine stationery and wrote something down.

"Victoria?" called a voice outside. The voice's owner, Valerie Valentine, soon followed, and she wasn't happy to see them. "Junior! You shouldn't bring her here. Those agents said not to go anywhere near the crime scene."

"It's my house, they can eff right off," said Jack.

"Technically, it's the estate's house," said Tori. "They'll be leaving shortly, Val."

"We're going to Napa," said Jack.

Val wrinkled her nose. "Must you?"

"I must."

"Hey Val, was there anything going on between RJ and Betty Campion?" Jenny asked.

"Get out of my house," Val replied, snapping her finger and pointing toward the front door.

Tori tore off a page of stationery and handed it to Jenny. It was a name and an address.

Dalton Doyle
314 Janero Place

"Please tell that overgrown gorilla to stop using Darcy as a go-between," said Tori.

Jenny folded up the note when a memory struck. "Oh! Can I see the ring?"

Val narrowed her eyes. Tori smirked and held up her left ring finger. Jenny and Dinah cooed over it until Val threatened to call the FBI.

"All right, all right, we're going!" said Jack. "Come on."

But rather than exit the study, he led them to the bookshelf by the desk and triggered the latch to open the secret passage.

"What was that about with Tori?" he asked once they'd closed the

234

false door behind them.

"Something for a side project of mine," said Jenny. "Actually, can we make a stop before Napa?"

"Do I get to know what about?" asked Jack.

Jenny bit her lip. The only people who knew about Dalton were Eliza and Blake. Her intuition was telling her to keep it that way.

"Not yet," she said.

Chapter Twenty-One
Serendipity

J ACK'S PLAN TO EVADE THE FEDS WAS TO USE ONE OF VALENTINE Vineyard's silver jeeps that he'd stashed in the woods. They left the mansion through the conservatory and snuck over the grounds to the east gate. Just in case, Jenny pulled on her best wig, the chestnut one modeled after Tori's hair. To all who didn't look too closely, Jack was with his sister and Dinah.

It was only a short walk through the copse of oaks to the treehouse where the jeep was waiting. What was left of the treehouse, anyway. Where a mighty oak tree once stood supporting a deluxe, professionally made cabin, now only the charred trunk and a pile of ashes remained.

"What happened?" Dinah asked. "Electrical fire?"

"Some asshole torched it in a fit of misplaced rage," said Jenny.

"Wait. How would *you* know that?" asked Jack.

Her pained smile gave her away.

"Jenny!" said Dinah.

"I'm sorry! I was in a bad place; you know that. I'll rebuild it, once I get my inheritance back."

"I ought to leave you here," said Jack. "I made a lot of fond childhood memories in that treehouse."

"Maybe it's time we moved past our childhoods," she replied. They stared at her. "Yes, I know. Let's just do this. I've got a feeling we won't like what Ivy's brother has to say."

"What makes you say that?" Dinah asked, frowning.

"You know, Dad gave out those seven heirlooms, seven clues to people who might want him dead," said Jenny. "I never really considered it at the time. What kind of guy has at least seven different people who want to murder him?"

"That's a little unfair," said Jack.

"I'm not saying he wasn't a good guy, Jack." Jenny swung herself into the jeep's front seat. "Only that sometimes being the hero of your story means you're the villain in someone else's. 'Everyone's got their reasons.' That's Trouble herself in *Trouble Brewing.*"

"She truly is a wonder," Dinah said, taking the seat behind her.

They off-roaded to a maintenance road and drove through the vineyard's fresh crop of Riesling before turning back onto Highway 12 a mile down the road. Who knew how long the feds would stick around at the mansion, waiting for Jenny to leave? But for now, she was free to trouble the world once more.

Jenny had Jack take them to 314 Janero Place first. Dalton's neighborhood was all pre-fab houses, laid out in circles—sort of a glowed-up Alkali Estates. Jenny unbuckled and slid out.

"Just gimme a minute, okay?" she asked them.

"Careful," said Dinah, pointing to the house. "It says 'Beware of Dog.'"

Jenny nodded and approached the door. The house siding was made of metal, painted a fading shade of tan with spots of brown to make it look like stucco. This was what an EMT salary bought you in this town. She knocked on the aluminum screen door and waited.

After thirty seconds, she knocked again and called out, "Dalton?!"

Nothing. There was no car in the driveway. *Damn, he must be working.* Jenny debated leaving a note but decided against it. She didn't want to scare him off. Most EMTs worked 12-hour shifts. She'd just have to try him again in the morning or later at night. A good job for Eliza.

"I don't think he even has a dog," Jenny said, climbing back into the jeep.

"That it?" asked Jack.

"For now," she said. "Let's go pay a visit to Forrest Fowler."

"KNOCK KNOCK, BITCH! ARE YOU DECENT?" ELIZA SHOUTED, pounding on the door to Drew's Masturbatorium.

From within, she heard Drew say, "Hey Siri, unlock the door."

Eliza waited. And waited. Ten seconds later, she heard an Irish voice say, "I'm sorry, I didn't get that."

"Oh, Jesus!" someone else exclaimed.

Footsteps, and then the door was flung open by Penny Griffin.

Damn, Penny's here.

No, this is good. No temptations!

Wait, why is Penny here?!

"Penny! What are you doing here?" Eliza said, maybe more forcefully than intended.

"Uh, not *that*, be for real, Jenny." Penny rolled her eyes and ushered Eliza inside. "The Ks did not match. Drew's just downloading *Cruel Summer* for me, now."

"Is that code for something?" Eliza asked, baffled.

"It's a teen mystery show, you'd like it," said Drew. "I thought you were with Blue Team?"

"Uh, he wasn't home," Eliza said. "We'll try him a little later. In the meantime, I have this!"

She held up the scrap of paper from the Campus Press clerk and passed it to Drew.

"Michael Smith?" he asked, frowning.

"The former boss of Calistoga College's print shop," said Eliza. "He worked there when *The Stranger of Sausalito* was printed. Bonus: he only lives a mile away. Care to go on a little Gold Team mission?"

Drew was game, as always. Penny didn't reply at first, staring past Eliza like she'd just asked her the square root of 13. "Penny?"

"Oh, right, yeah," said Penny. She shook her head to clear it and grabbed a hammer from Drew's workbench. "Just in case."

"Cool. Drew, you're driving," said Eliza. She stepped back outside and called, "Shotgun! Also, not to be a broke ass bitch, but do you think Drew Inc. can make a donation to the Trouble Fund: Money for Trouble?"

Drew smirked and pulled out his chunky wallet. "I don't have much cash on me," he said, thumbing through the bills.

"That'll do," said Eliza, grabbing the whole stack and savoring the pleasant spark when their hands touched.

"Oh, you're on one today, aren't you, Jenny?" said Penny with a knowing smile.

"I've got a good feeling about this one," Eliza said. "Michael Smith might be just the guy to blow this case wide open!"

Ten minutes later, they rang Michael Smith's doorbell, but an unfamiliar woman in her forties answered instead. Oh balls, did that clerk screw her over?

"Um, hello," Eliza said. "My name is Jenny Valentine. I'm looking for…"

"Forrest Fowler?" asked Jenny.

The young man in the doorway frowned, running an eye over the three of them.

"I already donated to the school color guard," he said. "Whatever it is you're selling, I'm not interested."

"We're not here for money, sir," said Jack. "We, um, we were wondering if…"

He was having a hard time saying it, so Dinah butted in.

"We understand that Ivy Manson was your sister, Mr. Fowler," she said.

Forrest Fowler's whole demeanor changed to sorrow and then suspicion. "What about it?"

Jenny reached up and pulled off her wig. "My name is Trouble. I think you know 'what about,' don't you?"

Fowler locked eyes with her, making some mental calculation before letting out a weary sigh.

"I see it now. In the cheekbones," he said. "You must be here about the rumors."

"What rumors?" Jenny asked.

"Before she died, Ivy gave birth to a baby girl," said Fowler.

Jenny's heart froze to the core. Dinah grabbed her hand and squeezed hard.

"Are you saying…?" Dinah asked.

"That RJ Valentine was the father?" replied Fowler. He sneered, old resentments rising to the surface. "According to Ivy, he was. I think you'd better…"

"Come inside," said the woman in Michael Smith's doorway.

Eliza could feel Penny's wary side-eye beside her, but they had Drew with them; they'd be fine.

The three filed inside a nicely appointed house full of mid-century modern furniture and an excited Scottish terrier that leaped up to bounce on Eliza's thighs.

"Killroy, no!" the woman said.

The little dog ceased his bouncing and weaved between all of their legs instead, panting happily.

"You named your dog Killroy?" asked Penny.

The woman smiled and said something about getting them drinks. They all took a seat on the long green velvet couch, and Eliza allowed the dog to play with her feet.

"Anyone else have a bad feeling about this?" Drew asked once she was gone.

"I don't know what to feel anymore," said Eliza.

The woman returned and passed out glasses of lemonade. She seemed pleasant enough, but Eliza would not be letting a drop of this touch her lips.

"Michael Smith was my father," the woman said. "I'm sorry to have to tell you this, but he passed away two years ago, now."

And it's another dead end. Figures.

"Oh. Damn. I'm so sorry," said Eliza.

"So sorry!" said Penny.

"For real, we shouldn't have come," said Drew.

"Oh, I don't mind," said the woman. "I have to admit I was intrigued when the Girl Detective herself showed up at my door."

Good thing I came. Jenny would be insufferable.

"Your father was the manager at the college print shop," said Eliza. "RJ Valentine had a book printed there eighteen years ago. I know this is a long shot, but by any chance, did your dad ever bring home copies of books he printed?"

"Oh yes, he was quite the packrat," said the woman.

Wait, for real?

"Dude! Do you still have them?!" Drew asked, on the edge of his seat.

"Sadly, no. They were all sold during the estate sale."

This lady is a damned rollercoaster!

"Son of a…" said Drew. "We have the worst luck."

"I can probably tell you who bought it, though," said the woman. "I ran the sale myself. I'm a tax attorney, so I kept detailed records. Let me get…"

"…My wife," said Forrest. "She's got the baby upstairs. Wait here."

He walked to the kitchen, leaving them standing in the entryway. Jenny did a quick reconnoiter.

Fowler's house was a study in contrasts. The couch was a cheap Ikea job, the kind every college graduate bought to furnish their first studio apartment. But the coffee table was a beautiful slab of maple with a live edge river of polished resin running down the center that had to retail for ten grand, easy. Everywhere Jenny looked, the pattern repeated. Gorgeous silk drapes; plastic cat food dish. A vintage audio receiver and turntable; flatscreen TV from the low-end brand she and Shelly used to have in Glendale. When Forrest handed her something to drink, it was SunnyD in a crystal tumbler from Williams Blackbird Springs.

Jenny did the math. Forrest couldn't have been more than thirty.

He must be an orphan, like her. He inherited a nice house from wealthy parents who died young, but he wasn't pulling the kind of paycheck to keep it in fancy furniture himself. Probably had to sell a few heirlooms off when an unexpected child came into their lives, courtesy of his sister Ivy and… could it really be? RJ Valentine?

"Sweetie, can you get in here?" he called upstairs. Then, to them, "She'll be out in a minute. Take a seat."

Perhaps he meant to be hospitable, but it almost felt like an order. Now that Jenny had a better look at him, she noted his size: at least six feet and well-built. Jack shot what he probably thought was a subtle warning glance at Jenny and took the antique wooden rocking chair closest to Forrest, leaving the stiff couch to Jenny and Dinah.

"Nice table," said Jack. "Is that a Haworth?"

"I couldn't say," said Forrest.

They were spared further forced conversation by the arrival of Forrest's wife, holding a toddler in her arms.

"This is Abby," he said. "Abby, these folks are here about Ivy's baby." He nodded at Jenny. "That's you-know-who there."

Abby raised her eyebrows and said hello.

"Is it true?" Jenny asked, staring at the child. "What's her name?"

"Serendipity!" said Michael Smith's daughter, Hailey. She was holding an iPad, scrolling through her estate sale database. "*The Stranger of Sausalito*, by Reynard Fuchs."

"He had a copy!?" Eliza asked, leaping to her feet without meaning to. "You found it?!"

"He did indeed, and yes, I've found the record of sale," said Hailey.

Eliza's heart pounded in her chest. All those miles on the Ninja, sleeping in hostels and moth-ridden attics, subsisting on energy bars and fast food, her only social life a chat window with Drew, using an identity she'd already left for dead… And suddenly, when she'd least expected to catch a break: pay dirt.

"Who bought it?" Drew asked.

Hailey pursed her lips, appraising them. "Ordinarily, this isn't the sort of information I just give out."

"Ma'am, I'm so broke," said Eliza.

"Not like that, I don't want money," said Hailey. "But one usually doesn't reveal private sale records to just anyone at the drop of a hat."

"Would it help if I showed you my school press pass?" asked Penny.

"The person who purchased that book is our prime suspect for all the recent murders in town," said Eliza.

"I see. Well, that complicates things," said Hailey. "Seeing as the name of the purchaser was Reynard Fuchs himself."

"That was RJ's nom de plume," said Eliza. "I can't imagine many people knew it."

Val. Mr. White. Arty Porter, maybe. And Yvonne Griffin, too.

"Does that mean…?" Hailey hesitated to voice her question.

"No, he's very dead. We dug him up to confirm and everything," said Eliza. "Cheeky of the Stranger, to use that name. Would you have met this person during the sale?"

"It was all done on eBay," said Hailey, tapping her iPad. "They used a credit card. Probably an untraceable Visa gift card, I'm sure. That's how I'd do it. But there's a shipping address. They had to have it delivered somewhere. 1421 East MacArthur. Oh, haha." She looked up and grinned at Eliza. "Your Stranger has thought of everything."

"Why, what's at 1421 East MacArthur?" asked Penny.

"The truth?" Fowler repeated to himself. "The truth is, my sister Ivy liked to make up stories. And she had a hell of yarn about RJ Valentine. The way she told it, they met at the Poison Pen one summer. RJ complimented her on the book she was reading, and they hit it off. Soon enough, she was sending him sample pages of her short stories, which he loved, and he would complain about his wife and how he wanted to leave her—just as soon as his kids graduated."

Jack seemed dubious but said nothing. Dinah gripped Jenny's hand tighter. Serendipity bounced happily on Abby Fowler's knee, smiling and oblivious to their conversation about her.

"You can imagine where the story goes from there," said Fowler.

"When RJ said that he didn't know Ivy and called her a crazy stalker, well, that was just his cover so Valerie Valentine wouldn't suspect anything, right? She'd get these packages in the mail: jewelry and handbags. All from him, she'd swear. She'd cancel plans with friends, telling them she'd be in Blackbird Springs with her 'writer friend.' When she started showing, she wasn't shy about naming the father to anyone who asked. That's what prompted the restraining order.

"Ivy used to say, 'All my lies are only wishes.' I wish I'd put two and two together sooner." Fowler paused to sip his SunnyD and swallow a lump in his throat. "The truth is, my sister was assaulted by an ex-boyfriend. I think she couldn't process the trauma, so she gave herself a better story. Maybe she really did bump into RJ at the bookstore one time. That would have been a nice memory for her. I don't think she ever meant to bother your father like that. She just got too wrapped up in the story she was telling herself."

"I'm so sorry, Mr. Fowler," said Jenny.

She squeezed Dinah back to get her girlfriend to let up on her poor fingers.

"Sorry," Dinah whispered.

"That's awful," said Jack. "Just so we're clear, you're saying that Serendipity isn't, uh, related to me?"

"She's not," said Abby Fowler. "We had her tested after Ivy passed, just to be sure."

"The truth was in the DNA," said Fowler. "The DNA and the note Ivy left. That truth put her ex away for ten years. It's a shame Ivy wasn't around to see that."

Jenny cleared her throat and slid her notebook out of her back pocket. Her intuition told her to cross Ivy Manson off her Leads list. Forrest Fowler was never mad at RJ; he was mad at himself. But she'd come this far, so she'd best be thorough.

"I'd like to do something for Serendipity. If I ever come into my inheritance," Jenny said.

"You don't have to," said Abby Fowler.

"Honey," Forrest said, admonishing.

"I know, but I want to," said Jenny. "It's nothing to do with my dad. I know what it feels like to believe there's no way out." She tore an empty sheet from her notepad and handed it and her pen to Forrest Fowler. "If you don't mind, can you put your number down? And write 'Keep in touch with Serendipity' on it."

Fowler shrugged and wrote it down. Jenny accepted the paper and pen back and thanked him before exclaiming a new thought.

"Preschool!" said Jenny. "That's coming soon for her, isn't it? Mrs. Fowler, can you write down when you think she'll start?" She passed the paper to Abby Fowler. "Just put 'Pre-K' and your best guess at the month and year."

Abby Fowler narrowed her eyes at this request but did as told. And then it was time to go. They thanked the Fowlers, waved at little Serendipity, and got the hell out of there.

It was dark outside as they walked back to the jeep. Jenny's stomach was rumbling, but she wasn't feeling much like food at the moment.

"Jesus, that was fucking depressing," said Jack. "Are you really going to pay for their preschool or whatever?"

"She was getting their handwriting," said Dinah, her expression sour.

"But yes, I will if I have the money," said Jenny. "Are you okay?"

Dinah was looking rather wan under the yellow streetlights.

"That SunnyD didn't agree with me," said Dinah. "What's the verdict?"

A glance at the handwriting was all Jenny needed to cross Ivy Manson off for good.

"No match," Jenny said.

"And to think you had a bad feeling about this one," said Jack. "Honestly, it sounds like Dad was pretty chill about the whole thing."

"This was always a long shot, but we needed to check," said Jenny.

Her watch vibrated with a new message. Neither Jack nor Dinah reacted, so it must not have been to the group chat. She turned her wrist to check it.

> **dangergranger:** Jackpot! Maybe! Stay out of town a while longer. "Trouble" is on the hunt with Drew and Penny.

Goddamnit, Lizzy!

What had gotten into her lately? Did they need to go back to switching every day?

"Uh, it sounds like I need to…" Was Jenny imagining things, or did a passing car's headlights just— "Wait. Shit!"

Jenny grabbed Jack's shoulder and pulled him back from the jeep.

"What?!" Jack asked.

"Um. Pretend we're arguing about who gets to drive," Jenny whispered. "Dinah, three cars down on the right, this side of the curb."

"I've seen you drive, Jenny," Jack said loudly. "*My Name is Trouble?* Yeah, Trouble with merging in traffic."

"Wow, that feels personal."

"Yes, it's those agents from lunch," said Dinah. "They're watching us."

"Fine, you drive, but I'm picking dinner, then," Jenny said. "We're going to Oxbow."

Despite Jack's big plan to elude them, Tierce and Steele had somehow followed them here. And now Eliza was out and about in Blackbird Springs posing as the real Trouble at the same time!

Chapter Twenty-Two
Minutemen Mail

I421 EAST MACARTHUR WAS THE ADDRESS OF MINUTEMEN MAIL, A shipping and supply store on the east side of town. The business was in a rundown strip mall, wedged between a hydroponics wholesaler and a burger joint. Between the flashing neon signs in the window for parcel services that Eliza had never heard of and the hippie out front smoking a joint, the place practically screamed "Pick up the cocaine you ordered off the dark web here."

Drew parked in the spot at the end of the row, and they piled out.

"Explain it to me again," said Eliza.

"It's called a package receiving service," said Penny. "You have something shipped to them, and then you come in and show your ID to pick it up. That way, you don't have to have it shipped to your address."

"That's legal?" Eliza asked.

"It can be," said Penny.

Damn, she and Jenny used to have stuff shipped to a neighbor who worked in the City all week. This was way better.

"Um, I know it's a book," said Drew. "But in *Ready Player One*, the character uses a re-shipping service that accepts a package and then ships it again to obscure the real recipient. Are those real, too?"

Good thinking, Drew!

A reply from Jenny tapped her on the wrist.

sallydraper2003: Bad idea! Tierce and Steele are
on my ass. Lay low!

I'm already here! I'll just have to do this quick.

"Let's ask 'em," said Eliza.

Skinny blinds covered all the front-facing windows, including the glass door, which Eliza pulled open, clattering metal on metal and triggering an electronic alert tone. Inside, they found a brightly lit lobby with a wall of private mailboxes and a few rows of overpriced shipping supplies.

"Here comes Trouble," said the man behind the counter, looking up from his book. He nodded past Eliza at her friends. "And she brought a party with her. A cleric and a… bard? I think you need more offense."

He was short and a bit portly, with a patchy beard to give some definition to his round jawline. But where the clerk at the print shop gave her the ick, this guy felt game. Some measure of intelligence danced behind his squinty little eyes.

"Drew's plenty of offense," said Eliza, slapping her hands on the tall counter. "And you shouldn't underestimate me. I keep a sword with my other outfit."

"That doesn't sound canon to me," he said.

A quiet warning bell sounded in her mind. A stickler for the *Trouble* canon. Coincidence, or something more?

"You have me at a disadvantage," said Eliza. "You already know all about me."

"I never forget a face," he said.

"That's easy, I've been in the news."

He leaned back, casting his gaze at the ceiling. "At GolfMax last summer, you were walking past the first-floor driving bays. I remember, I was there on a Bumble date that didn't end well. She thought I was taking her to mini golf, and I'd lied on my profile and said I was five-foot-nine."

"Five-seven would be pushing it, my dude," said Penny, joining her at the counter. "You really never forget a face? That's impressive. And relevant."

Penny gave Eliza an odd smirk. Drew stayed back, examining the list of services on the wall and generally trying to appear imposing but not threatening, just like she'd coached him to do way back during their misadventure with the Fortune Teller…

She, not Jenny. Sometimes, she wished Drew would realize the difference. Would it be awkward and bad OpSec? Sure. But shouldn't he be able to tell her from the other one? At some primal level? They'd shared, well, a lot.

"What about me?" Penny asked.

"The library, dozens of times," said the guy. "You always pass up the good books for more V.C. Andrews."

"I'm not sure I like this man," said Penny.

"He's too short to be the Stranger," said Eliza. "Who are you?"

"I'm Ben," he said.

"How long have you worked here, Ben?" asked Penny.

"Jesus, too long."

"Longer than two years?" Eliza asked.

He sighed and said, "Yes."

"Have you ever given out a package to someone going by the name Reynard Fuchs?" Eliza asked.

Ben pursed his lips and shrugged, unsure.

"So not a photographic memory, then?" said Penny.

"Would I still be working here if I had one?" Ben replied. "Just faces."

"Ben, I'm going to show you some photos of people, many of whom you will no doubt recognize, but that's beside the point. I need you to tell me if they've ever used Minutemen Mail's package delivery service. Or come here to pick up a package," said Eliza.

"Now, why would I do that?" Ben asked, grinning.

Please don't ask for money!

"Because you never forget a face," said Eliza. "And I've asked you nicely. Please?"

"Well, since you said please."

Eliza started with Mayor Villanova. Ben chuckled but said, "No." Lambert? "No." Blake? "No." Calderon? "No." Betty Campion? "No." Valerie Valentine? "No." Tori? "No." Jorge Lopez? "Once, the winter before last."

Okay, interesting. But Ben didn't remember anything to do with "Reynard Fuchs" from the encounter.

Jack? "No." Dinah? "Nope." Damn. Arty Porter? "No." Declan Dillion? "No." Lai? "No." JeRay? "No." Jimmy Figg? "No." Rob Haines? "No." Mr. Webb? "Nada."

"What about her?" Eliza said, jabbing her thumb at Penny.

"Hey!" said Penny. "Don't answer that."

"No," said Ben, laughing.

"And him?"

She gestured to Drew. Ben shook his head.

Eliza turned to Penny. "Am I missing anyone?"

"RJ," she said. "And, well, if we're being thorough, my mother."

Good points, but both received a negative from Ben the shipping guy. An electronic alert tone sounded at the door, and Eliza flinched, Jenny's warning about the feds resurfacing in her mind. But it was only a long-haired man in a houndstooth jacket entering the store.

"Do you guys do re-shipping?" Drew asked, approaching the counter. "You know, like in *Ready Player One*?"

"Yeah, not usually," said Ben. "Too much paperwork and it attracts the wrong kind of attention. The owner prefers discretion without liability."

"A man going by Reynard Fuchs picked up a package from here on or around February 23rd, 2019," said Eliza. "Do you recall *anything* about that?"

"Can't say that I do," said Ben.

"Shouldn't there be records?" Penny asked.

"Deleted after the mandatory ninety days," said Ben. "Like I said, discretion without liability. But, um, you should check Fiverr."

"Fiver?"

"With two Rs. It's what someone like your Reynard would use," he said, and gestured for them to step aside for the new customer.

"What'll it be?"

"Scratchers," said the man, displaying some lottery tickets. "A hundred-twenty in wins if my maths are correct." He had a British accent. A real one.

"Are we reinvesting?" asked Ben.

"Naturally," said the man.

Eliza grimaced and motioned for Penny and Drew to follow her to the exit. The sun had long since set, and none of the streetlights in this strip mall worked. Had it been this dark in the parking lot when they arrived? Another quiet warning bell had Eliza's fingers itching for her kunai dagger as they walked back to Drew's truck.

"Fiver with two Rs," Penny said, who had walked ahead, unperturbed by the darkness. "Oh, Fiverr. Like gig work."

"What if the Stranger is hiring someone to pick up his packages for him?" Drew suggested. "We could post a fake ad for something similar? See who replies?"

"Not a bad idea, Drewboo," said Eliza.

"Oh shit. Maybe we won't need to," said Penny. "Look."

She pointed at the car next to Drew's Tacoma. In the dim light, all Eliza could tell was that it was a dark sedan.

"What is it?" Eliza asked.

"Come here," said Penny.

The tone of her voice made Eliza hurry over to the sedan. Penny held up her phone and switched on the flashlight, aiming it at the back of the car. It was a brown Honda Accord, Eliza saw now. The bumper was a lighter shade—like it had been replaced on the cheap by a mechanic. The warning bell tolled in her brain a third time. What memory was this car bumper triggering?

"This is the car from Black Rock," said Penny. "After Mason's funeral. You took a video of that, right?"

Shit. She did! Or, rather, Jenny did.

"Hold on," said Eliza.

She opened up her Photos app and tapped on her and Jenny's shared album, trying not to appear suspect while shielding her screen from their view.

"What other videos you got on there?" Drew asked, grinning.

"Really, Drew?" said Penny.

Eliza blushed fiercely.

Don't worry, you've seen them all, mister!

"None of your business. Here we go," Eliza said.

She found Jenny's blurry video of a car driving away after the Stranger—or whoever had been wearing the outfit—made an appearance after Mason and Meghan's funeral. The image was fuzzy, but this sedan's bumper sure seemed to be discolored in the same way as the one in the video.

"That's it," said Penny. "This is the same car."

A tone sounded as the door to Minutemen Mail opened, and the man in the houndstooth coat walked out. He was heading their way, clutching a new strip of lottery scratchers.

"Hey buddy, is this your car?" Drew called to the man.

He glanced up at them, and his eyes locked onto Eliza.

"Bloody hell," the man said, and took off in the other direction.

The Oxbow Public Market was a popular destination in the heart of Napa, beloved for its boutique eateries and ample parking space. That was thanks in part to the Calistoga Cabernet Express, a wine train that departed from the station on the other side of the lot.

"Maybe we can lose them on the train," Jenny suggested, picking at the Ethiopian chicken wrap Jack purchased for her.

They were sitting in the food court area of the Public Market. Those feds, Tierce and Steele, were enjoying a flight of red blends two eateries down, making no secret now of their surveillance on Jenny and company.

"Following a train isn't exactly difficult," said Jack. "They would just be waiting for us at the next stop."

"Not if we jumped off beforehand," said Jenny.

"Do you know how dangerous it is to jump off a moving train?" Jack asked.

"It doesn't matter," said Dinah. "That train only runs on weekends and Wednesdays this time of year."

"Okay. So what do we do?" asked Jack.

"What can *they* do?" said Dinah. "There's nothing illegal about eating at Oxbow. People from Blackbird Springs come here all the time."

"Do those people visit their murdered dad's stalker's brother beforehand?" asked Jack.

"All the time," said Jenny. "Maybe you're right, Dinah. We're not the problem, are we?"

She stared pointedly at her phone.

"Anything?" Dinah asked.

Jenny shook her head. She'd messaged Eliza on Signal a half-hour ago, but there'd been no response.

"I can't figure out how they followed us," said Jack. "Could they have hacked our Signal accounts or something?"

"If they did, they would have arrested me already," said Jenny.

"The blonde one seemed a bit swishy," said Dinah, staring back at the feds. "Jack, why don't you go see if you can seduce him and get his gun."

Jenny laughed as Dinah squeezed her knee under the table.

"Rather droll of you, Dinah," said Jack. "Though I am the prettiest one here."

"Feeling better?" Jenny asked her girlfriend.

"Yes. I needed this," Dinah said, taking another bite of her shawarma.

"Why don't you two just lure them into an alley, and I'll taser 'em?" Jenny suggested.

"Pretty sure that's a federal offense," said Jack.

Finally, her watch vibrated. It was Eliza.

> **dangergranger:** Huge, huge jackpot! FaceTime later. Laying low now. I'll be back at the Ryalto in 20."

"Good news?" asked Dinah.

"Seems like it," said Jenny.

> **sallydraper2003:** What jackpot? Did we identify the Stranger??
> **dangergranger:** LOL not that huge.

Dammit, Lizzy, give me some details!

"Let's get some dessert, and then we can go, I think," she said. "Be cool about it. You're just some popular, rich, bratty seniors blowing off homework for a night in Napa with their old pal Trouble."

They got up and bused their trays before strolling back to the other end of the market. Jenny made sure their path took them by the feds. She leaned over their table and stole one of Steele's fries.

"Fry inspector," she said.

"Don't push me, Valentine!" said Steele. "I have my limits."

"We're gonna get gelato and head back to Blackbird Springs," said Jenny. "See you at my place in… 45?"

"For the record," said Dinah, "getting a flight of red blends at Oxbow is like ordering a corndog at the French Laundry."

Sassy Dinah! Where has she been hiding? That must have been a hell of a shawarma.

"Dinah, these men are from Sacramento, they've never heard of the French Laundry," said Jack.

"That a fact?" said Tierce.

"It's not actually a laundromat if that's what you're thinking," said Dinah. She flagged down the waiter. "Why don't you get these gentlemen a bottle of Campion Merlot? They're on the clock; they can expense it."

I'm so turned on right now.

"What vintage?" asked the waiter.

"2003, if you have it," said Dinah. And to the agents, "That was a good year, for wine."

THE MAN IN THE HOUNDSTOOTH JACKET DIDN'T EVEN REACH THE street before Penny grabbed him. Eliza was impressed; Penny was even faster than Drew when properly motivated.

"Going somewhere?" Drew asked, catching up to restrain the man.

"Yeah, away from you tossers!" said the man. "Let me go! I'll scream!"

His voice was reedy, with an un-posh flavor of English accent that Eliza mentally associated with losers and ugly men. She took an instant dislike to him.

"Wrong neighborhood for that," said Eliza. "No one will come for you."

The man stopped struggling in Drew's half-nelson and squinted at Eliza, furrowing his brow.

"What are you playing at?" he asked. "You didn't send me anything for this."

"Why would I send you something?" Eliza asked. "We've never met."

"Right, but…" the man trailed off, and his face went white. "Oh no."

The hair on the back of Eliza's neck stood at attention.

"What the fuck is going on?" Penny asked.

Shit! Was this guy working with Jenny? Did I just fuck it up?

"Um, let's start with the basics," Eliza said. "Maybe we got our wires crossed. If we let you go, do you promise not to run?"

"Can't see why I shouldn't," he said.

"We just want to ask you some questions," said Eliza.

She nodded to Drew. He didn't seem pleased, but he released his hold on the man's head. The guy made an exaggerated job of adjusting his jacket collar and smoothing his stringy black hair.

"Right then, what of it?" he asked.

"Let's start with your name," said Eliza.

"William Cromwell."

Penny snorted. "Really? Are you sure it's not Richard Englishman? Or Henry Londonshire?"

"Fuck off, ain't like we're mates. You can call me Willie, and that's enough."

"Wait!" Penny turned to Jenny, grinning. "I know this guy—or I've heard of him, at least. You're One-Eyed Willie."

"He's got both eyes where I'm sitting," said Eliza.

"What can I say, my reputation proceeds me," said Willie, looking rather chuffed with himself.

"Oh, ew!" said Eliza, getting the nickname.

"This is the guy who keeps Harbor High kids stocked up on weed and meth," said Penny.

"Fucking Harbor High," said Drew.

"Willie, why were you at Mason Lockhart's funeral, wearing a Stranger outfit and scaring my friends?" Eliza asked.

"I meant to say because you hired me," said Willie. "Though judging by the stupefication on your face, that's not correct, innit?"

Penny raised an eyebrow. "Did you?"

"No," Eliza said.

I didn't. Jenny would have mentioned it if she did, right?

"Well you see, it's all been over email, so how was I to know?" said Willie.

"What all? Have you dressed up as the Stranger before?" Eliza asked.

"Coupla times," said Willie.

"Why don't we start from the beginning," said Eliza.

It started with a gig job Willie found on the internet two years ago. Pick up a package from Minutemen Mail and deliver it to a dead drop. It was unscrupulous and paid well, both big plusses in Willie's world. His unknown client was pleased and petitioned Willie for another job, all under the table. He was to cosplay as the villain from those *Trouble* books and drive a sports car past a girl dressed like the titular character.

"That was you!?" Eliza gasped. "You nearly killed—"

"I wasn't expecting you to step out into the lane without looking," said Willie. "Nearly shat my pants, I did."

"Where did you get the car?" asked Eliza.

"It was parked around the corner, keys in the ignition," said Willie. "Instructions were to speed past you, go a few blocks over, and park again. Leave the keys, the note said."

"And that didn't seem like a weird request to you, dude?" Drew asked.

Willie threw his hands up. "It was the day that old tosser Valentine died. Meaning no disrespect. I assumed it was a tribute, like. I thought *you* hired me," he said, pointing a finger at Eliza. "Or the publisher, at least."

"That must have been you later, then, in the park, when, uh, I saw you," said Eliza. "After the traffic light dropped."

"Right, I figured it was some sort of viral stunt," said Willie. "And right after, you announced yourself on the scene and began running around pretending to be a Girl Detective. Two and two made four, innit?"

"What else did 'I' hire you for?" Eliza asked. "Wait, did you attack me and Drew in an alley with a knife?"

Willie blanched. "Come on, now. That'd be crossing a line and a good way to get pinched. It was mostly a package pickup now and then. I dressed as the Stranger again at the last harvest festival, but I'm not sure you ever showed up."

"No, we were at your house, remember," said Drew.

Eliza didn't remember. She was at the harvest festival that night. She tried to think back. Charlie had dressed as Drusilla from *Buffy* and was flitting around speaking nonsense to all the carnies. Meghan May had a flask of something strong. As Kazumi, Eliza passed it to Drew after they skipped him in the rotation, and he smiled at her. But then he left to hang out with Jenny.

Sigh. He was smiling at her the same way now. Except he thought she was Jenny and was thinking about some Trouble shenanigans they got up to, not Eliza.

"Okay, well, I wasn't the one hiring you, obviously," said Eliza. "I'm pretty sure the person who did is the Stranger."

"Bugger all," said Willie.

"Are we sure it wasn't actually some viral stunt from the publisher?" asked Penny.

"They wouldn't have had him doing pickups and dead drops," said Eliza. "The Stranger had Jeffrey Jordan doing that, too. What kind of stuff were you picking up, Willie?"

Willie shrugged. "It was all in boxes, I couldn't say."

"Big boxes? Little boxes?" asked Drew.

"It varied," said Willie. "Nothing I couldn't lift by meself."

"None of it had labels?" Penny asked. "Seller shipping addresses?"

"I weren't paid to be nosy like that," he said, crossing his arms.

"Willie, you don't strike me as a total moron," said Eliza. "You must possess some amount of low cunning to have evaded Sheriff Lockhart for this long. So why don't you cut the bullshit, and tell me something useful, or I'll have Drew here give you a face to match your nickname."

Looming behind, Drew placed his hands on Willie's shoulders and purred into his ear, "If you've got any astigmatisms, you'd best tell me which eye is the good one now."

Okay, that was hot. Stop it, Danger!

"Oi! Relax! I'm only explaining how it was!" said Willie, shrugging himself out from under Drew's grip. "A lot of the stuff was from Amazon, so the shipping address wouldn't help you. But, uh, if I had to guess, it was electronics. Some of the boxes had those warnings about batteries on them."

Eliza bit her lip. That made sense but didn't help much.

"And the dead drops?" Penny asked. "Can you show us where?"

"It wouldn't do you no good," said Willie. "It was a different spot every time. Under a flower pot, behind a dumpster. After you inherited RJ's money, I tried watching one. Figured it might be lucrative if I had a recording of you picking it up."

"And?" Eliza asked.

"The video ate up all my phone's storage after twenty minutes, and then I got bored," said Willie.

"Damn. Okay. Okay, thank you, Willie," said Eliza. "Important question: what were you doing here tonight? Did you make another pickup for the Stranger?"

"Lottery only," Willie said, shaking his head and holding up his clutch of scratchers. "You want to scratch 'em off together?"

"Can we?" asked Drew, perking up.

"Another time. I need to get off the street," said Eliza, recalling Jenny's warning text. She got out her phone and fired off a quick reply.

<pre>
dangergranger: Huge, huge jackpot! FaceTime
                later. Laying low now. I'll be
                back at the Ryalto in 20."
</pre>

"Willie, if the Stranger contacts you for another job, I need you to let me know," said Eliza. "Do you use Signal?"

Willie shook his head.

"Damn. Um… I can't just have you call me; the feds are for sure listening."

Eliza glanced at her phone, thinking. Jenny had messaged back, thinking they'd caught the Stranger, so Eliza replied to settle her down.

"He can call our tip line," said Penny. "My mom's, for the *Blackbird Times*." She got a scrap of paper out of her purse and scribbled down a number. "Just say it's Willie and leave the drop date and location. I'll get it to Jenny and erase it before my mom hears."

Their source demurred, his lips all pouty.

"What?" asked Eliza.

"Shite ain't free," said Willie. "If I snitch on my client, he ain't likely to hire me again."

"I imagine that would be the least of your worries," said Drew.

"Right, if I'm sticking my neck out, then I deserve compensation," said Willie.

And here I am being Danger for free…

Eliza scowled and turned to Drew expectantly.

"You already took all my cash," he said.

"Motherfucker."

Eliza dug out the cash she'd borrowed, which was a mistake. Once he had eyes on it, Willie extorted all but her last $20 bill before he agreed to help them. She hoped, for her grumbling stomach's sake, that the Stranger would reach out with a new job soon.

Jenny, meanwhile, would prefer to leave the Stranger on read for the night. She had another, less dangerous game on her mind.

Jack drove them back to the mansion, but this time, Jenny rode in the back with Dinah. They kept their hands to themselves with Little Brother a few feet away, but the energy vibrating between them was palpable. Something had changed in Dinah at Oxbow, and Jenny desperately needed to get her alone to investigate further.

They said their goodbyes to Jack, and Jenny climbed into Dinah's Acura in the Valentine Manor garage. He warned them to keep an eye out for Tierce and Steele. They both nodded, all business. Dinah drove back down the driveway and through the gates. Without either of them saying anything, Dinah turned left instead of right and drove to the berm at the end of Cellar Drive. There were no streetlights here, and the cloudy sky hid the almost full moon. Once Dinah killed her headlights, the night afforded ample privacy. Wordlessly, they unbuckled their seatbelts, got out, and moved to the back seat.

And then it happened.

This was special, wasn't it? It felt like it should be special. It felt like more than a hookup. Was this love? Jenny struggled to hang on to the feeling. Like a concertgoer with her phone camera out, trying to capture the moment instead of letting it pummel her ribcage. She was thinking too much.

Don't think, just feel…

It was hard to say how much time passed. The windows were still fogged up when Jenny awoke from the afterglow in Dinah's arms.

"Hey," said Dinah.

She kissed the side of Jenny's cheek from behind, and Jenny felt a cold trickle on her face.

"You're crying," Jenny said.

"Sorry."

"Good tears?"

"Yes," Dinah replied quickly.

Jenny didn't need to feel Dinah's heart pounding against her bare back to know it was a lie. She took a heavy breath. Did she have to do this now? And ruin the moment?

Yes, you have to. She's practically begging you to, you coward.

A tap on her wrist saved her. It was Lizzy.

dangergranger: help

Chapter Twenty-Three

Blown

WHAT WAS THE SAYING? SOMETHING ABOUT REPETITION LEADING to complacency. Eliza should have known better. CONSTANT VIGILANCE! She'd taken her eye off her most important directive, and now she was screwed.

After Drew drove them back to his house, Eliza retrieved her motorcycle and Secret from where she'd stashed them around the corner and rode back to the Ryalto. She parked in her usual spot behind the dumpster in the back and climbed up the ladder to her rooftop safehouse. The fresh cigarette butts outside the roof access door should have tipped her off, but Eliza's mind was preoccupied, thinking about Drew.

She was annoyed with him and she knew it wasn't fair. He didn't know he'd been spending the evening with his girlfriend instead of Jenny, but still! And honestly, that was the problem. He was way too excited to go mystery-solving with her sister. Those smiles and bright, excited eyes should be reserved for Kazu, dammit!

Am I wrong? Am I being crazy? Don't answer that!

Ugh. Maybe she should just tell him. He wouldn't be mad, right? Not once she explained herself.

The safehouse greeted her with the usual smells of dust and mothballs. Eliza sighed and unzipped her jacket, leaning Secret against the wall. She wanted to kick off her shoes, but she needed to use the restroom first, so she grabbed a little tote of toiletries she'd collected and slipped back into the hall.

"What are you doing?"

Eliza froze. A man in a polyester Ryalto Cinedome shirt was standing at the top of the stairs at the other end of the hall, giving her a nasty sneer like he'd just found dog poop on his shoe.

"Um. Just using the washroom," she said. "I'll be down soon."

"You work here?" asked the man.

"Yeah." Eliza tried to stay calm and headed into the bathroom.

"I don't recognize you, what's your name?" he asked, trying to follow her inside.

"Bro, chill!" she said. "Nature calls, I'll tell you in a minute."

She closed the door on him and locked it. Bloody hell! Now what?

Holding her breath, she pressed her ear against the door and plugged the other one to block out the soft hum of the bathroom fan.

"Hey Jonny?" she heard the man say, muffled through the door. "Jonny?"

Whoever Jonny was didn't answer. Eliza closed her eyes, straining to hear. Was he leaving?

"Fuck it, I'll wait," she heard him say.

Shit! Shit! Shit!

She turned on the sink faucet and triggered the air dryer. Then she texted Jenny.

dangergranger:	help
dangergranger:	I'm blown and trapped in the bathroom at the Ryalto. Some dickhead is waiting for me outside.

While she waited for a reply, she took in the bathroom. There was no drop ceiling up here, just bare duct work, too small for Eliza to fit inside. A short window up high on the back wall. Maybe she could squeeze through it if she got up that high…

Her watch vibrated.

sallydraper2003: I won't make it there in time.
sallydraper2003: Start a fire.

AFTER CONSIDERING IT FROM EVERY ANGLE, JENNY SUSPECTED SHE'D do more harm than good showing up at the movie theater now. Better to get home, lay low, and find a new place for Eliza to hide. At least that was the idea—before she spotted strobing blue and red lights up ahead as they neared Jenny's house.

"Oh no," said Dinah. "What do I do? Should I go straight?"

"A bit late for that," said Jenny.

"What do you—this is not that time for sexual innuendo, Miss Valentine!"

Dinah shook her head and pulled over at the corner before the turn onto Jenny's street.

"They'll have already seen us, running only makes it look worse," said Jenny. "You're not going to jail on my account."

"I would, though."

Dinah pouted and squeezed Jenny's hand. She meant it. She really did. Jenny tried again to mentally freeze this moment in amber, but try as she might, it slipped away into the void. As if on cue, her watch tapped her on the wrist. It took her a moment to recognize the Signal screen name: it was Blake.

unemployedwifeguy: Delete Signal now.

He'd sent it to her and Eliza.

"Uh-oh, Blake just texted me to delete Signal," she said.

"Then do it!" Dinah replied and immediately got her phone out to delete the app.

Jenny sent a quick message to the group chat first.

sallydraper2003: We might be blown. Delete Signal
                  off your phone immediately.

"Screw it, I'm going to reset the whole phone," said Dinah.

"This might be it," Jenny said. "If they arrest me, try to contact—"

"They won't. You've done nothing wrong," said Dinah. "I'll vouch for you."

"Don't. Just drop me off and go home."

Dinah scowled and pulled around the corner, where the flashing lights strobed from police cruisers parked in front of Jenny's house. They eased to a stop on the other side of the street. Shelly and Blake were waiting on the doorstep with Calderon and Peña. Tierce and Steele stood nearby with that undercover fed lady from school. As Jenny got out of the car, a fire engine siren wailed in the distance.

"You're late," said Steele when she walked up to the curb.

"And your shirt's on backward," said Tierce.

Jenny's cheeks flushed. "Honestly, you're the weird one for noticing, dude."

"Jennifer, don't say a goddamned word!" said Shelly. "The lawyer is on his way."

"Oh, I'm sorry, did you think we were here for your daughter?" said Steele. "Sheriff Calderon, take Blake Lockhart into custody."

"What!?" Jenny and Shelly both shouted.

"Accessing police records to provide the address of one Forrest Fowler to a minor?" said Tierce. "That's a paddling. Feels like obstruction, doesn't it?"

"Giving privileged information to a person of interest?" asked Steele. "Yeah, I'd say so."

Calderon grimaced but had no choice but to follow orders. Jenny expected Blake to be furious, but he only smiled and held up his hands for the bracelets.

"Look after Lilah until I post bail, won't you?" he said to Shelly and leaned in for a kiss before they could take him away.

"But that's bullshit!" Jenny cried. "He didn't give me the address, I found it on my own!"

"Did you? Did you really?" Tierce said, smirking. "That's cute, but the police database logs all remote queries. We know it was Lockhart looking up Fowler's info."

"Well, that's because, uh, I stole his login info!"

"Jenny, shut the fuck up," said Blake. "It's all parallel construction, anyway."

"What's that?" she asked.

"Careful, Lockhart. We can make this a lot more uncomfortable," said Steele.

Blake smiled and let Calderon and Peña lead him to a squad car. Jenny was helpless to watch them go. She looked to Aunt Shelly, who remained rigid with a blank expression etched on her face.

Oh fuck. She's so pissed. I'm dead.

"If it's obstruction, then why aren't you arresting me?" Jenny asked.

Tierce chuckled and winked at her. "We're not here for the guppies, kid. Only the big bass."

"But as long as we're here," said Steele. "Maybe you can tell us why someone matching your description showed up at Calistoga College earlier today?"

"I've got a theory on that," said Tierce.

"Oh, look at that!" Steele pointed at his phone screen. "She's just been spotted again starting a fire at the local cineplex. You know anything about that, Valentine?"

"She's been with me all evening," said Dinah, who'd ignored Jenny's request and joined them. "I'll sign an affidavit to that effect."

"We can do that," said Agent Steele. His mouth spread into a malevolent grin. "But for now, why don't you both hand over your cell phones."

The girls both shrugged and handed them over. It only took Steele a moment to realize they'd both been wiped.

"Cute," he said.

"There was a buggy OS update," said Dinah. "It, like, totally fried us."

"Obviously, there's nothing on there," said Jenny. "Can we have them back?"

"No," said Steele.

"God, you suck," said Jenny.

"By the way, Miss Black, that bottle of wine you ordered for us cost $1,300," said Tierce.

"Oh, that's a good deal for a 2003 Campion," said Dinah. "You're welcome."

"What's this theory of yours, then?" Jenny asked Tierce.

"Kazumi Onishi," said Tierce, puffing out his chest. "Or whoever that was pretending to be your cousin. We think she's back in town. And she's been posing as Jenny Valentine."

Fuck. Fuck. Fuck! FUUUCCCCCCCKKKKKKKK!!!!!!!!

"What!? That's crazy!" said Jenny.

"I can see it," said the undercover fed lady, squinting at Jenny. "Cut her hair, a little contouring to ugly up her face, and hunch her shoulders. They kinda look alike."

"Um. Fuck you?" said Jenny. "No, we don't."

She tried not to act relieved. These morons were so close but had somehow fucked it up and peered through the wrong end of the telescope.

"What better way to blend in than as a well-known local resident?" said Tierce.

"We gotta roll," said Steele.

Tierce tossed him the car keys and leaned in close enough to smell the tannins on his breath. "It's about to be a real dangerous proposition, running around town as Jenny Valentine without an escort from Agent Cartright. We'd hate to shoot the wrong one."

Jenny needed to warn Eliza. But how?

"I'd keep your niece inside until school tomorrow, Ms. Onishi," Tierce added.

"That won't be a problem," said Shelly.

Tierce laughed and hurried to join Steele in their government-issued black rental.

"I'll pick you up at six," said the fed lady. "I have zero period FBLA, and I like to get coffee with the girlies at the Basque first."

Jenny watched them and Dinah go, standing silently next to her aunt. She had a new ring on her finger. One set with a red diamond.

"Ohmygod! He asked! You said yes!?" Jenny yelped.

Shelly smiled brightly and grabbed Jenny by the ear, dragging her inside.

THERE WASN'T MUCH IN THE WAY OF FUEL IN THE CINEDOME restroom, so Eliza made a pile of crumpled seat liners in the bathroom sink. As she lit the paper aflame with RJ's Zippo lighter, she recalled her late father's advice on getting into places where she didn't belong.

"Walk in like you're slightly annoyed and have shit to do. No one will stop you." Yeah, Dad? Well, you never met the goddamned Employee of the Month waiting outside.

The seat liners were slow to catch, so she gave the weak flames a blast of hairspray from her tote.

WHOOSH!!

That got it going! As long as she was burning things, she tossed her Harmony Valentina driver's license into the fire.

"Sorry, Harm," she said, and hit it with a sustained burst of hairspray until it melted.

The acrid smoke from the plastic was enough to trigger the smoke alarm.

BEEEEEEEEEPBEEEEEEEEEPBEEEEEEEEPBEEEEEEEEEP

Eliza winced at the shrieking alarm. Outside the bathroom, she heard curses and heavy footfalls. The dickhead was finally running away. She counted to ten, ducking low to avoid the thickening smoke, before bolting for the door.

The hallway was empty, thank god. She raced back to her little closet to grab her jacket, backpack, and Secret. The pile of old costumes she'd been using as a bed caught her eye. Could they pull DNA from it? Probably. Fuck it. Using her Zippo and the hairspray, she set the pile of clothes aflame, too. She donned her jacket and pack, affixed Secret behind her shoulders, and ran back to the roof exit.

It was locked!

That son of a bitch must have locked it! Smoke was billowing out from underneath the bathroom door now, and Eliza heard a soft roar behind her as the fire reached a rack of clothing in the closet. Well, she was certainly annoyed now, and she had important shit to do: namely, getting the fuck out of here.

"Dude, we have to evacuate!" a man shouted below as she sprinted to the stairs.

"I'm telling you, the girl who started the fire is up there! Wait! There she is!"

Eliza barreled into the men, and they all went sprawling. She was ready for it, rolling as she hit the carpet and bouncing back up again while the dudes were still flailing. Down another flight of stairs, and then another, and she joined the rush of employees and moviegoers headed for the exits.

The torrent of bodies took her out onto the sidewalk, a block south of Town Square. Where to, now? She was all out of hideouts, and her options were slim. Get to her Ninja and go a few towns over? Come clean with Drew and hope he would let her stay in the Masturbatorium?

"That's her! Stop her!" she heard the man shout behind her.

Damn, dude, chill! She raced to the street and nearly got clobbered by a car skidding to a stop next to her. The driver rolled down the passenger door window.

"Get in!" yelled Penny.

What? How?! Eliza had questions, but she'd ask them later. She dove headfirst into the car, and Penny took off, honking at fleeing pedestrians to get out of the way with Eliza's legs still sticking out of the window.

"Is anyone following?!" Penny asked.

"Let me see," said Eliza. She managed to get her feet inside and contorted her body into a proper sitting position before looking behind them. "I don't think so, no."

"Good." Penny slowed, driving more casually.

"We should probably get off the streets, though. Just to be sure," said Eliza.

"We will," said Penny. "But I need you to answer a question for me first."

Eliza's phone vibrated with a new Signal message.

unemployedwifeguy: Delete Signal now.

Blake? What the fuck?
"Uh, shoot," Eliza said.

She was distracted, searching for the Signal app on her home screen.

"Hey." Penny stopped at a light and glanced over, eyeing Eliza warily like one might a feral alley cat. "What's your name? 'Cause it sure as hell isn't Jenny Valentine."

Chapter Twenty-Four
Parallel Construction

THAT NIGHT, JENNY STAYED UP UNTIL 3:00 AM, FEARING FOR Eliza's safety and hoping she would sneak into her room to catch up. Who knew how closely the feds were watching Jenny now? But she desperately needed to warn her sister about the new status quo. And what the hell was this "jackpot" discovery Lizzy made?

They should have planned for this. Sending an email felt too risky, and Eliza was the tech expert, not her. For all Jenny knew, the FBI monitored all internet traffic from Jiji and Baba's house. No doubt, their hackles were already up because Jenny googled "Parallel Construction."

It was a legal term. Something cops and feds did when they obtained information from a source that they didn't want to reveal. Like an active wiretap or an illegal search. To not give themselves away, they would perform some other sort of investigative activity and "get lucky." Like randomly checking the police data logs to see if anyone had queried Forrest Fowler's info.

But what was their secret source? And if it was so great, why hadn't they figured out that Kazu was Eliza and arrested them both by now? She fell asleep pondering these mysteries. Three short hours later, Aunt Shelly was shaking her awake.

"What are you doing? Zoey's here!" Shelly shouted.

"Zoeycagohell!" Jenny mumbled through bleary eyes.

"You're supposed to be ready to go!" said Shelly. "Come on, I have to get to the station to bail Blake's stupid ass out—NO THANKS TO YOU!"

Shelly tore the covers off and shoved her into the shower. Twenty minutes later, yesterday's clothes hiding under the purple Burberry trench coat, her makeup a disaster, Jenny flopped into the passenger seat of Zoey's government-issue Ford shitbox and tried to go back to sleep. Zoey wouldn't let her.

"You forgot your bag," said Zoey. "Go get it. I'm not making two trips."

Jenny growled and said unkind things to the agent, hurrying back inside to get her stupid bag. And then she figured it out.

That conniving little…

When she returned with her school backpack, Zoey smiled and said, "Sounds like I'll have to get here earlier tomorrow."

"You don't have to do anything, you know," said Jenny. "You could be out searching for the real Stranger, who I promise you is not a five-foot-four Japanese exchange student who wears too much makeup."

"If she were innocent, she'd turn herself in," said Zoey. "We'll roll up Kazumi for the mansion murders soon enough, and then we'll find out just how much of a part you played in perpetuating these fictional Stranger stories. Tierce thinks it's your coping mechanism, but I'm with Steele on this: you and your 'cousin' are working together—have been ever since Arty Porter killed himself, and you didn't want to lose the attention. I've got fifty bucks on it, so don't disappoint me."

Jenny made a yap-yap gesture with her hand and buried her head in the seatback cushion. She wanted to sleep again, but Zoey's driving was very herky-jerky, and the shower had woken her up too much already. Arriving at the Basque moments later, Jenny had to appreciate the irony. Here she was, finally getting morning coffee with Thanh, JeRay, and the other cool seniors, living out the Kazu lifestyle that had made her so jealous and bitter last fall. All it required was an FBI escort.

If twin ESP was a thing, Jenny was sending out a warning with all the mental power she could marshal. Eliza getting shot by the feds because she looked too much like Jenny wasn't the sort of fate Dad would have written in a *Trouble* book. But earlier RJ? The one who wrote *The Stranger of Sausalito*? That was just the sort of through-a-looking-glass irony that he would have loved.

"Is it cool working for the FBI?" Thanh asked Zoey over matcha lattes and scones.

"Have you ever shot a dude?" asked JeRay.

"Yes, and no," said Zoey.

Talk about someone who didn't want to lose the attention... Zoey must have been a huge dork in high school, and this was her do-over. Jenny sipped her water (she was broke, and Zoey refused to buy her anything) while Zoey blathered on about how exceptional she was to have made field agent so young.

What would Jenny Valentine do differently if she got a do-over?

Plan for a contingency with Eliza in case the feds took her phone away again. Warn Mason and Meghan to stay away from Jack's birthday party. Tell Mr. Webb to take a big step to the right. Not let Nari out of her sight on the *Susanoo*. Get to Blackbird Springs before RJ was attacked. Read a different book when she was five years old...

Stop sulking, Zoey's distracted.

Jenny let out a heavy sigh and slipped her hands under the table, feeling for her backpack. A short time later, Jack and Penny strolled up to join them—but no Dinah. They never even got a chance to talk last night. It should be illegal to take away a girl's phone within forty-eight hours of sex!

Another melancholy sigh escaped her lips. Trouble was a full-time occupation these days. No time for angst. No time for ennui. Under the table, her fingers discovered a small lump behind the front pouch of her backpack.

"Have you ever thought about joining the FBI, Jenny?" Penny asked.

She took a seat next to Jenny and nodded hello. Jenny nodded back—and did a double take. Penny's eyes were bloodshot, and her lids were heavy like she'd slept even less last night than Jenny. There was an agitation in her body language; she was excited about something.

"The FBI only takes the best of the best," said Zoey.

"I'm going to Stanford," said Jenny.

"No offense, Valentine, but with your history, there isn't a law enforcement outfit in the country that would hire you," said Zoey.

"Sure, they're busy hiring wife beaters and trigger-happy idiots who shoot Black kids," said Penny. "The world's greatest Girl Detective wouldn't fit in at all."

Jenny smiled. She didn't know where this sudden hype from Penny was coming from, but she wasn't complaining.

"*See you next Tuesday*," Jenny told Zoey. "Whatever, I'd rather work in the private sector."

"You need a clean record for that," said Zoey.

Jenny slammed her fists on the table and held them out in surrender. "Go ahead, then! Charge me, bitch!"

Everyone at the table cringed. There Jenny went again, killing the vibe. In the park across the street, two unobtrusive men pretending to read newspapers flinched and jerked their heads around to look at Jenny. Good to know.

"Zoey, do you think we could get a moment with Jenny?" asked Penny. "It's just girl talk. We promise we won't let her run off."

The fed agreed a little too easily and got up to powder her nose.

"Watch my drink for me, will you, Lai?" she said and ran a playful hand over his hair.

Once she was gone, Lai cleared his throat and said, "Still would."

He and JeRay high-fived, and JeRay declared, "He's in."

Jenny got her notepad out and scribbled a message on it for Penny to read.

Can't talk. They hid another bug in my bag.
Stitched into the liner.

"So smash it," said JeRay.

Jenny glared murder at him and held a finger to her lips. Now that she knew they were listening, she wasn't about to waste the advantage.

It all made sense now. She'd been talking about getting Forrest

Fowler's info from Blake yesterday at lunch. And she'd told Jack she'd send him the address on Signal. Both details were mentioned right after the agents returned her backpack. They put the first bug in there so Jenny would find it and relax, not expecting there to be a second one. She blushed at the thought. It was a slick move, but not too slick for the world's greatest Girl Detective. She should have been hip to it.

Oh! And their theory about Kazu posing as Jenny was actually stupid Jimmy Figg's theory! Those idiots heard just enough of her conversation with Tori to draw the completely wrong conclusions.

Jimmy Figg…

"Uh, so Drew's birthday is coming up," said Jack. "What are we doing for him?"

"No offense, but you'll never catch my ass attending another party you plan again, bro," said Lai.

"Yeah, sorry, Drew, but I'm not taking my life in my hands so you can mope around missing your fake British psycho girlfriend," said Thanh.

Penny snapped out of a yawn as if struck by an idea. "Jenny! Um, we totally need to discuss the new *Doctor Who*," she said.

I'd rather die.

"Yeah, for sure," she said instead, since Penny was urging her to agree.

"Shoot, I just realized I left my homework on my desk," said Penny, suddenly standing up. "I'll catch you later at lunch, and we can chat then."

She reached over to grab the notepad and scribbled down a message, taking care to only show it to Jenny.

Eliza is safe. Will explain at lunch.

Jenny's eyes widened. Eliza?? Penny grinned, tore out the page from the notebook, and ate the paper. Lunch couldn't come soon enough.

In the end, it was the nail polish that gave Eliza away. Leave it to Penny, the ever-observant journalist, to notice that kind of thing.

A gal switching up her nails with gel caps overnight wasn't anything to wonder about. But switching them back the next day? And then going back to the same gel caps again a few hours later? No way. Gel caps were expensive. These were not the rational actions of a broke teenage girl, even one as… peculiar as Jenny Valentine.

Eliza had been flying so close to the sun for so long that she'd gotten used to the heat.

To be fair, it wasn't just the gel cap nails. Penny had never completely let go of her initial "Trouble is dissociative" theory and had been quietly cataloging Jenny's weird behavior ever since. With that, and all of the Kazu shenanigans of the last seven months, it was only a matter of time before Penny arrived at a new theory: not two personalities, two people. Doubles. Twins.

Fortunately, Penny didn't immediately assume Eliza was evil and try to kill her or turn her in. Though she did say that not telling Drew after all this time was fucked up, which—yeah, fair.

Penny had followed her to the theater last night. She couldn't figure out what the fake Jenny was up to by climbing onto the roof, but then the fire alarms went off. Penny drove around to the front and nearly ran Eliza over. After the initial shock of the twin thing wore off, Penny took them back to her place and had Eliza sneak into her room via the fire escape while her mom was in the shower.

They talked all night in hushed voices. Penny thought it was best for Eliza to lay low and hide out in her room—until she could get word to Jenny, at least. Eliza couldn't argue with that; she had nowhere else to go.

The wrinkle was Yvonne. The *Blackbird Times* office was right downstairs. There was no way Ms. Griffin wouldn't hear Eliza moving around in Penny's room. So, Ms. Griffin would need a reason to leave for a while. Like, say, getting a message on the tip line from Kazumi Onishi herself, asking to meet. Kazu had important information to share, but only if Yvonne came alone to the City and took care not to be followed. With Golden Gate traffic, that ought to tie her up until school was out, at least.

The scheme worked like clockwork. Eliza heard Ms. Griffin lock up downstairs and leave, freeing her to get up and move around. It was time for a much-needed shower and perhaps some self-reflection on the Drew situation…

The apartment door burst open and Penny called out, "Eliza?!"

"EEEEP!!" Eliza yelped, jumping half out of her skin.

Rude of you to interrupt my dirty thoughts like that!

Penny rushed into the bedroom, clueless to Eliza's embarrassment. "Jenny's bugged. I need your help."

JENNY COULD HARDLY SIT STILL BY THE TIME LUNCH FINALLY ARRIVED. She desperately needed to talk to Penny and find out what the hell was going on. Zoey was waiting for her right outside the classroom to escort her to the cafeteria. Like at breakfast, the fed lady wanted to sit with the cool seniors, where Jenny wasn't exactly wanted.

"I'll be over there," Jenny said, pointing to the Troublemakers' table. "I'm not going anywhere, relax!"

Zoey's gaze flicked to the backpack straps on Jenny's shoulders. "Okay, but I'll be watching. Don't even think about trying to leave. We have agents watching all the school exits."

Jenny rolled her eyes and took her hard-boiled egg and Diet Coke—all she could afford from the snack bar on her budget—and joined Dinah and Drew.

"Hey there," said Dinah, with a special smile for her.

"Hi," said Jenny.

A happy little flutter passed between them. She could feel her ears turning red.

"Uh, should I leave?" Drew asked.

"No! Relax, everything's fine!" Dinah said, giggling.

That set Jenny off giggling, and Drew was making third-wheel cringe noises when Penny arrived with her sack lunch.

"Drew, can I talk to you got a sec?" Penny asked.

"Yeah, yeah. Message received," said Drew.

Jenny sensed this was part of Penny's plan, whatever it was, but couldn't see how. Did Drew know about Eliza, too? It didn't seem like it, though Alicia had been correct when she predicted more people would find out soon. Honestly, it was incredible that they'd still managed to keep it a secret from him…

Jenny bit her lip, doubts nagging at her. So many secrets, and now Eliza was in danger because of them. Well, that was her thing and all, but still…

"Sister, you've officially gone too far again," said Jack. He sauntered up, carrying a cafeteria tray with a look of pure scorn on his face. "The feds are blocking deliveries, and I had my heart set on a chicken wrap from Rosie's with balsamic vinegar and organic kale."

"The hardest struggles are born in silence, Jack," said Dinah.

Drew and Penny returned shortly, and Drew didn't look happy. Without saying a word, he reached under the table and picked up Jenny's backpack, then walked to the other side of the cafeteria and sat down with the baseball team.

"Nice, but they're going to notice after a while if they don't hear me talking," said Jenny.

"That's why I recorded an hour of conversation about *Doctor Who* with Eliza this morning," Penny said.

"Wait, she knows!?" asked Jack.

Jenny shushed him and said, "Yes, but she hasn't explained how, yet. Does Drew know?"

"He does not," said Penny. "And don't tell him. Your sister wants to be able to tell him herself. When she can. Anyway, that's not important. What's important is the guy we ran into when chasing down *The Stranger of Sausalito* last night."

Penny spoke briskly, leaning close so she didn't have to raise her voice, and Jenny learned about the incredible stroke of luck they'd had, linking this Willie character to the Stranger. She couldn't believe it. She'd started to accept that seeing the Stranger in the park that first day in town was a crazed hallucination. But no, it was real. The Stranger set it all up just to fuck with her.

"All we need to do is wait for the Stranger to get another package delivered," said Penny. "He contacts Willie, Willie calls the tip line, and when the Stranger shows up at the dead drop, we pounce on the motherfucker."

"I don't know if we can wait that long," said Jenny. "You and Lizzy don't know about what happened with Blake and the feds."

She gave her own CliffsNotes recap of last night, leaving out the glorious interlude in the backseat with Dinah. Jenny couldn't go anywhere without Agent Zoey attached to her hip, and she had no way to communicate with Eliza. If the cops or feds saw her sister in public, they'd know she wasn't Jenny. They'd arrest Lizzy, or worse, they'd just shoot her.

"You've got to warn her," Jenny told Penny.

"It might be time to come clean about your sister," said Jack.

"I can't do that," said Jenny. "The feds aren't looking for the Stranger, they're looking for an easy way to wrap this thing up. And I think the Stranger knows that. If I tell them about Eliza, we'll both get arrested and charged, and the Stranger can disappear into the ether. That's how he wins."

AFTER HER SHOWER, ELIZA NAPPED ALL MORNING IN PENNY'S BED, giving her conscious mind a break so her subconscious could run free and hash out all her feelings. When she awoke again, Eliza knew what she had to do: go to Drew's Masturbatorium, wait for him to get home from school, and come clean about the whole Kazu situation. She realized that she'd been blaming him for her own guilty conscience. When it came right down to it, dating him—sleeping with him— under these false pretenses wasn't ethical. It was an RJ kinda move, wasn't it? Maybe the apple didn't fall so far from the tree after all. She was sure Drew would understand, but she still needed to tell him.

And then we can rechristen the Masturbatorium with a new name, heheheh.

Penny's clothes didn't fit her, so she had to wear yesterday's jeans and T-shirt (sorry, Drew). She zipped up her ArmorGel jacket and affixed Secret in its place between her shoulder blades. That felt better. Before she left, she dumped her pack out on Penny's bed and took inventory.

- 2 oz. chloroform
- 1 collapsible riot baton
- 16 oz. plaster of Paris
- 1 water bottle
- 2 boxes of Pocky
- 1 red-and-gold knit beanie (Gryffindor)
- 1 makeup kit
- 3 clove cigarettes
- $20 cash

All her wigs had burned up in the fire at the Cinedome, so she'd have to hide her purple hair under the beanie. Eliza repacked her supplies, opened a box of Pocky, and took the stairs down to the *Blackbird Times* office. After Blake's warning about Signal last night, she'd reluctantly destroyed her phone. But going without the internet for over twelve hours was wearing on her. She needed to check her email, at least! And socials, and stuff.

Ms. Griffin had an iMac with an old-school clicky-clacky keyboard. It wasn't hard to access the guest user, and Eliza made sure to use a proxy before checking her accounts. She'd been hoping for something from Jenny, but there was nothing. It was so tempting to download the Signal desktop app. Surely, Drew had messaged Kazumi since last night—

The phone in the office rang, startling the shit out of her.

"Hello, you've reached the *Blackbird Times* tip line," said Yvonne Griffin's voice on the answering machine. Talk about old-school. "Please leave your message after the beep. You're not required to leave a way to contact you, but I'll be a lot more likely to use your information if I can follow up on it. Thanks."

The machine beeped, and a British man with a nasal voice began to speak.

"Hey, uh, this is Willie. You said I should call if our mutual friend contacted me for another job. Well, he just did. I'm to pick up a package from Minutemen Mail and deliver it to the luggage compartment in the second car of the Calistoga Cabernet Express. The afternoon train, later on today. Right, so. Thought you'd want to know. Don't forget to erase this bollocks."

Eliza's jaw hung open. This was it. This was the chance that hours on the road, chasing failed clues and dead end after dead end had won them. For once, they had the Stranger at a disadvantage.

She pulled Secret out of its sheath, tested the edge, and grinned. He'd never see them coming.

Sorry, Drew. We'll talk tomorrow. We'll fucking celebrate.

After locating the answering machine and deleting the message, Eliza resheathed her sword and ran back upstairs to slip out down the fire escape.

Eliza had already left when the tip line phone rang a second time. She never heard Penny's frantic message.

"Eliza! Are you there?! If you're there, pick up!!" Penny shouted. "Fuck. I hope you can hear this! The feds think Kazu is posing as Jenny Valentine. They've got that Zoey lady escorting your sister everywhere. If they see quote-unquote Jenny anywhere in Blackbird Springs without Zoey, they will shoot you! Don't go *anywhere* until we figure this out!!"

Chapter Twenty-Five

Deadly Force Authorized

After lunch, Zoey insisted on attending class with Jenny instead of chilling outside. Penny's stunt with the decoy conversation might have been too cute; the feds knew she was up to something. Jenny Valentine, the world's greatest Girl Detective, would never care that much about fucking *Doctor Who.*

Mr. Graham was teaching them about Roe v. Wade when someone's cell phone chirped. It was Zoey's.

"Asshole," Jenny uttered loud enough for her to hear.

"This is Agent Cartright, go ahead," Zoey said into the receiver. A pause. Then, "Yes, I have eyes on her… No. David, she's literally two feet away… A sword?? Sounds like she poses an imminent danger. Deadly force authorized. Light her the fuck up."

Jenny's heart froze to the core. Light *who* the fuck up?!

"Something you'd like to share with the class, Miss Cartright?" asked Mr. Graham.

"Sorry," said Zoey. Her smile chilled Jenny's spine. "Good news, Jenny. It's looking like I'll be out of your hair *very* soon."

It was a bright, sunny afternoon. Eliza wore chunky black sunglasses borrowed from Penny as she crossed the park in Town

Square. Her attention was drawn to the old City Hall building in the center. It looked way too small to fit a whole library and three stories in there. RJ had taken liberties with the scale in his *I Dream of Trouble* manuscript, for sure.

Her forehead began to sweat under the knit beanie. It was warm for the last day of March. The further she walked, passing rambunctious children and old folks walking their dogs, the more paranoid she felt. Maybe wearing Secret on her back was a bad call. Reaching back, she pulled the sword out, sheath and all, and held it against her forearm, trying to hide its shape. As she neared the pond, Mr. Duck hopped up onto the grass and honked at her.

"Sorry, I'm not her," she said. "But I'll let her know you said hi."

He honked again, indignant.

"I know, I know. Here."

Eliza dug out a stick of Pocky from her jacket pocket and crouched down to feed Mr. Duck. Then the tree trunk next to her exploded.

BANG!

Her ears rang, and bits of bark stung her face, shrapnel from the bullet striking the tree. Eliza dropped to the ground and rolled away. Mr. Duck quacked furiously at the violation and flew away with the Pocky stick in his beak.

"FBI! FREEZE!!" someone shouted.

They fucking shot at me!!

If she hadn't bent over at just that moment, she'd be a chalk outline. Some nerdy corner of her brain was fascinated by the fact that she hadn't heard the gunshot until after it missed her.

BANG!

Another shot rang out. Eliza flinched, but they missed again. She craned her neck, searching for the shooter. There he was, Agent Tierce, rushing forward on the other side of the pond with his pistol out. *Freeze?* Fuck that. She hopped to her feet and took off running.

People were screaming and ducking for cover. Eliza did likewise, crossing the street and using the parked cars to shield her. Tierce had stopped firing to give chase.

"FBI! STOP!" he shouted again.

Eliza risked a look back. She was further ahead than she'd expected. The pond must have slowed Tierce down. That bought her another block—and maybe a hundred feet on Tierce—but now the street parking was clearing up. She had to lose him before he got another open shot.

At the next intersection, a boxy delivery truck was pulling out to make a turn. Eliza ran right across its path. Tires screeched, and the truck narrowly avoided running her over. *Sorry*, she mouthed to the driver as she rounded the cab, heading down the side street.

This neighborhood looked familiar. Right, she was close to the Valentine Foundation. No sooner had the thought left her mind than Valerie Valentine stepped out from the hedge that lined the front of their office, and Eliza plowed right into her.

She expected to go sprawling, but Val executed some kind of judo move, grabbing onto her and using Eliza's momentum to swing them both around before releasing Eliza to do a header into the inner side of the hedge.

"Stay down!" Val hissed. Then, much louder, "That way! That way!"

Tierce's heavy footfalls raced closer.

"You saw her!?" he shouted.

He couldn't see her behind the hedge, but if he stopped for even a second to look—

"Yes! She went down Broadway! Hurry!" Val yelled.

Tierce's footsteps pounded right past the hedge and kept going. Eliza couldn't believe her luck. She tilted her head up and whispered, "Thank you."

Her earnest relief was greeted by a pocket-sized pistol in her face.

"Which one are you?" Val asked, a cold menace in her voice.

"What?"

"I mean, are you Jenny? Or are you Eliza?"

Four… five…

Zoey's cell phone rang again, interrupting Mr. Graham's lecture and also Jenny's deepening panic attack. She couldn't breathe. Her whole body clenched, bracing for the worst.

"What!?" Zoey shouted. "What do you mean you lost her!?"

"YESSSSS! In your fucking face!!!" Jenny said, leaping out of her chair to shout at Zoey.

"Ladies, please! Take it outside!" Mr. Graham snapped at them.

Zoey yanked Jenny out into the hallway and slammed the door in disgust.

"Where is she going?" she demanded.

"Fuck if I know!"

I really don't!

"I knew it. You are working together!"

"No, I just want you to lose," said Jenny.

"You don't want us to catch your friends' killer?"

"SHE'S NOT THE KILLER! YOU THICK-HEADED, TRY HARD, UGLY BANGS, PICK-ME MORON!!!!"

Zoey's face contorted into a wounded sneer. Maybe the bangs comment was too far. "I'm bringing you in," she said.

Jenny wasn't prepared for it. Zoey shoved her against the wall, wrenched her arms back, and handcuffed her.

"Jenny Valentine, you are under arrest," Zoey said. "God, that feels good to finally say."

She marched Jenny down the hallway, reciting her Miranda rights. Other students rushed to the windows to gawk as she passed by.

"Yeah, go ahead, get your pictures!" Jenny shouted at them.

"You had to know it was always going to end this way," said Zoey.

"No offense, Zoey," said Jenny. "But if anyone ever does take Trouble down, it sure hell won't be you."

She put on a cocky smile, but deep down, she knew she was fucked. Trouble never had to deal with the FBI in the books. Not even in RJ's latest. How the hell was she supposed to get out of this one?

"H-how do you know?" Eliza stammered.

"Get in the car," Val said, gesturing to a nearby parked Mercedes.

Eliza wasn't sure if escaping a trigger-happy FBI agent to be kidnapped by Valerie Valentine was an upgrade, but she didn't have much choice in the matter. She scrambled around to the passenger side and got in. Val got behind the wheel, still training the pistol on her, and drove them north.

Once they were clear of the downtown area, Val reached inside her coat and pulled out some rolled-up papers. She tossed them in Eliza's lap and re-aimed the little holdout gun at Eliza's forehead.

Eliza glanced down and spotted the familiar double-spaced Courier font. These were pages from RJ's final manuscript.

"What the fuck? Are you—are you the Stranger?"

"No, you nitwit," said Val. "That's how I know you're a twin. I found those pages at Dalton Doyle's place. He's dead, by the way. You didn't answer my question: which one are you?"

"Are you going to shoot me if I say Jenny?" Eliza asked. "Or if I don't?"

"So Eliza, then."

Val's finger pulled on the trigger. Eliza winced. A gold-and-blue flame shot out from the tip of the barrel, and Val grinned.

"You bitch! I nearly pissed my pants!" Eliza shouted at her.

"I need a cigarette," Val replied. "I know you little gremlins are always hiding them. Be a doll."

Eliza pouted and got out two of her three remaining cloves. After using her stupid gun lighter to light her own, Val lit one for Eliza and rolled down the windows.

"Where are we going?" Eliza asked.

"The geysers," said Val. "Be quiet. I need to think."

She took them up Highway 12 and turned off at the exit for the Minutemen Hot Springs, where Arty Porter had met his demise. Not a great omen. They got out and walked to the split rail fence that surrounded the geysers. Heavy mist and a strong scent like rotten eggs hung in the air. Val was silent, enjoying Eliza's clove cigarette.

"What are we doing here, Valerie?" Eliza asked after a while.

"Roger proposed to me right over there," Val said, pointing to a spot by the geysers a few yards away. "My first husband. I like to come here sometimes when I have a lot on my mind."

Eliza wasn't sure how to reply, so she bit her tongue.

"It's funny that you asked about Betty Campion yesterday," Val said. "She and Roger dated in high school." She took another drag and turned to face Eliza. "I don't think that agent will suspect that I helped you. But if he does, you threatened me at sword point and made me lie to him. I feared for my life."

"I see," said Eliza. "Why *are* you helping me, Val? Shouldn't you be thinking *I'm* the Stranger?"

"Once I knew there was a twin, it was simple to figure out that I was dealing with *you* at the Crow's Nest when Nilay was killed, not Jenny," said Val. "That's why I smelled Kazu's perfume on you. I was right the first time; I should have trusted my instincts. Anyway, I've seen you and the Stranger in the same place, at the same time; ergo, you are not the Stranger."

"As to your first question: why am I helping you instead of turning you in?" Val took a last drag and flicked the cigarette butt into a trash can. "I don't know. It was a split-second decision. Probably a poor one. You did, I suppose, save my life. Consider us even."

"I wanted to let you die," Eliza said. "Multiple times. I even fantasized about killing you myself."

"Am I hearing an apology?"

"No. I've h-hated you for so long." Eliza couldn't stop her voice from shaking.

"Because of your mother."

It was more a statement than a question. Eliza nodded, her heart a whirlwind of conflicting emotions. The adrenaline comedown from being nearly shot was making her jittery.

"F-Franz Lambert," Eliza said. "Does that name mean anything to you?"

"Yes, Victoria mentioned him," said Val. "I had nothing to do with hiring him to take Little League photos or whatever it was."

"And what about before?" Eliza asked. "What about when he killed my mom?"

Val rolled her eyes. "I'd never even heard the name Lambert before Victoria asked me about him."

"A non-denial denial!" said Eliza.

"Oh please," said Val. "You said he was a private investigator? Don't you know who keeps those on retainer?"

Eliza furrowed her brow. "Who?"

"Law firms," said Val. "Like your grandfather's."

"My Jiji didn't hire Lambert to kill his daughter," said Eliza.

"That's not what I meant. That *woman*…" Val forced her features to soften. "Your mother basically admitted to the blackmail scheme. She couldn't have taken the photos herself. I'll wager she hired this Lambert fellow to do it. Maybe she met him through your grandfather."

"And then Lambert kills her? Why? For what?"

"I guess we'll never know," Val said.

She smiled, and Eliza wanted to throttle her. But there were more pressing matters than Mom right now.

"Can we circle back to the 'Dalton's dead' thing?" Eliza asked. "How do you know about Dalton?"

"You got any more of these?" Val asked, nodding to the last of Eliza's clove.

"Only one. My last."

"Give it here."

Eliza grumbled and fished her only remaining cig out of the pack. Val lit up again and explained the Dalton situation.

She'd seen Tori write something down for Jenny on a stationery pad and became suspicious. So she pulled the oldest detective trick in the book: she shaded over the empty page to figure out what Tori had written down, and it turned out to be Dalton's address.

Val went to visit him by herself this morning. Instead of finding a live paramedic, she found a dead body and some manuscript pages from RJ's last, lost *Trouble* novel, courtesy of the Stranger.

"I'm no expert," said Val, "but that wasn't the first body I've found, unfortunately. Dalton was still stiff. I'd wager he'd been killed recently. Maybe last night."

A shrieking steam whistle heralded the arrival of a geyser field eruption in sixty seconds. Eliza tried to think like her sister.

"Fingerprints?"

"I'm not Victoria."

"Murder weapon?"

"They used a plastic bag," said Val. "Suffocated him. He was lying on his bed with those pages and a note that read 'Hotter than the surface of the sun!'"

"Hmm. Plastic bag. That's new for him," said Eliza. "Dalton might have been able to identify the Stranger. We believe RJ didn't receive his mortal wound at the mansion; it happened in the ambulance on the ride to the hospital."

A hint of concern flickered across Val's features. No, not concern: fear. She turned around and leaned against the split rail fence, facing the geyser field.

"There's another reason I'm helping you, Eliza," said Val. "The truth is, I'm not sure who else I can trust."

Chapter Twenty-Six

This Thing Might Go All the Way to the Top!

THE GEYSERS EXPLODED IN A CACOPHONY OF SUPERHEATED STEAM, forcing a pause in the conversation. Rancid sulfur assaulted Eliza's nose. Val was unfazed, a creepily genuine smile on her face as she watched the eruption subside. When she finally turned back to Eliza, it was with sincerity and grave concern.

"It may be that this goes further back. To Roger," she said. "And to this Lambert fellow and your mother too… It may all be connected. It may be that, well…" She nodded to the manuscript pages, which Eliza was still holding. "Read that, and you'll understand."

Chapter 6

The first thing I notice is the smell. It's sweet and
foul and coming from the burlap bag thrown over my head.
Whatever I've been dosed with is wearing off, and my
head is pounding. I try to get up and discover I've been
bound to the arms of this chair. The twine is digging
into my wrists. The reek in this bag, that sickly decay…
it's going to make me puke. I throw my head forward and

sneeze.

"Ah, look who's awake," says a male voice, rich like honeyed ham.

He pulls the sack off my head, and I can finally breathe without gagging. The smell lingers. It wasn't coming from the sack; it's wafting off this man.

He's thick and broad-shouldered, with a ruddy complexion and silver hair streaking back from his temples. Age has taken its toll on his craggy face, but he must have been an ox of a man in his youth. I'm no fashionista, but I know enough to recognize that his white suit is made of fine wool, freshly pressed, with real gold cufflinks that would pay our mortgage for three months. His dark eyes twinkle, and he smiles at me, all malice. I've seen him somewhere before.

"You're not a Campion," I say, recalling now those plans for a casino I'd discovered just before they caught me.

"No, I am not," he says, folding his hands over his ample belly.

"Not a Carnegie, either," I say, running through the Big Six founding families of Blackbird Springs in my head. "You don't look anything like the mayor. The Martins are all dead. So is Dinah's grandfather. I know the Woodhalls and none of them keep their hair past forty. So that must mean you're…"

"Killian Rosewood, at your service," says the man, bowing.

Killian Rosewood… Kill Rose… Killroy?

"Are you the S-Stranger?" I ask, unable to keep my voice from shaking.

"You foolish child." He sneers at me. "Haven't you figured it out? You're not eleven years old anymore, Trouble. There is no Santa Claus. No Easter Bunny."

"What are you saying?"

"There is no Stranger!" he shouts.

The comment hits like a lash to my face. "Yes there is, I've seen him!"

Rosewood chuckles unkindly. He circles behind me, grips the back of my chair, and drags me across the room.

The room. I finally take in my surroundings. They've taken me up into the hills, to the Rosewood Winery Villa. A long wooden bar hugs one side with dozens of wine barrels ornamentally stacked here and there, and plenty of open space for mingling. I'm being pulled away from the bar, my chair squeaking across the hardwood floor.

"Take a look!" Rosewood says.

With one last yank, he spins me around and tips me half over. My wrists scream with pain. The twine around them is the only thing keeping me from tumbling out of the chair—and right out the window! Rosewood has taken me to the edge of the Villa's tasting room, where floor-to-ceiling windows slide aside to showcase the view of the town below. If Rosewood lets me go, I'll be falling for a while before I hit the granite cliffside below.

"You see them down there?" Rosewood asks. "All those little ants going about their day? When you look, you see your friends, your classmates, your teachers, your neighbors. You know what I see? A big, fat piggy bank! Every little ant down there puts money in my pocket every day, whether they know it or not. There is a river in this town, and it flows in one direction: to the Big Six. It never flows backward!"

"Congratulations, you're loaded!" I say, trying to find purchase on something with my dangling feet. "What's your point? What does this have to do with the Stranger?"

"Do you really think we'd let some asshole in a

black coat and hat run around down there without our permission?" asks Rosewood. "Running scams with local hoodlums? Killing our little ants? Taking from our coffers? The Stranger is nothing more than a fiction, a story your do-gooder father invented to shield you from the evil men do. You never saw the Stranger. You imagined him, encouraged by your dad, so you wouldn't go digging deeper and force us to send him another message."

"That's not true!" I say, but I've lost my conviction.

It can't be true. All those times I saw him. The tall, dark, and strangesome menace. Always in the shadows, the one that got away, the one I could never catch…

"We may have tolerated your flights of fancy when you were younger," says Rosewood. "But we have our limits. Every little ant: the sheriff, the mayor, your father, Dinah Black—even you, Trouble—you all play a part. And right now, your part is to be a dumb bitch teenager. Go obsess over clothes and music and dates, and keep your nose out of the mayor's business. He's our concern, not yours."

But wait! Didn't I see the Stranger just this afternoon? Who the heck was that, then? I touched him. He was real. I didn't imagine that! Dinah saw him, too!

I want to point this out, but it might not be the best idea to piss off a murderous wine magnate while hanging over the edge of a deadly fall.

No! Don't let him scare you like that! Your name is Trouble! Pissing off criminals is your damn job!

"I know what you're doing!" I say. "You're trying to frighten me. To shut me up. And you know what that tells me? That you're the one who's scared! Scared of me! Because I'm the one who's gonna take you all down, and the Stranger, too!"

He roars and yanks me back. How sweet it is to feel

all four chair legs on the floor.

"Perhaps I haven't been clear!" he shouts, but then he's cut off by a piercing siren.

BEEEEEEEEEPPPPBEEEEEEEEEEEPPPBEEEEEEEEEEPPP

It's the fire alarm! I can smell the smoke now! Rosewood curses and hightails it out of the tasting room.

"Hey! What about me?!" I shout.

That bastard! Fine. Does he think this is the first chair I've been tied to? I wrench my body to the side, knocking myself over and putting all my weight onto the chair arm as I fall.

SNAP!

The impact hurts like hell. I'll have bruises down my whole side for a week. But the chair arm broke off, and now my hand is free. In an instant, I've got my trusty pocket knife in hand. Those idiots didn't even search me! I cut myself free as the first signs of smoke billow into the testing room. I don't stick around to wait for the fire.

The front door is hanging wide open, so I race for it. I'm expecting Rosewood and his goons to grab me at any moment as I sprint across the grass that fronts the winery, but they never do.

Someone shouts in the distance. I look back at the wrong time and suddenly my foot's touching air. I ran past the edge of the lawn! With a yelp, I find myself tumbling ass over teakettle down a hill. Ouch! Ouch! Ouch! I roll and flail until the earth rushes up and flattens out into smooth asphalt.

No sooner do I realize that I've rolled onto the switchbacking road that leads up to the villa than I hear the high-pitched whine of an oncoming car engine! Bright headlines come around the bend, zooming straight at me. Talk about out of the frying pan and into the fire!

But wait! I know the sound of that engine! It's mine!

The headlights swerve to the side, and the car skids to a stop right beside me. Sure enough, it's my cherry-red Mustang, and my identical twin Eliza is driving.

"Get in!" she yells.

At the end of the chapter, the Stranger had once again left a note in his blocky handwriting.

WE'RE GETTING CLOSE TO THE END, TROUBLE. HAVE YOU FIGURED IT OUT YET? HAHAHAHA.

Eliza scowled. "So, what, you think this is all some big conspiracy?" she asked.

"What else do you think Johnny is suggesting there?" said Val. "Admittedly, there is no Killian Rosewood. I'm not sure what he meant by that. Maybe he was trying to avoid a lawsuit."

"He'd be dead, what would he care?"

"Perhaps my late first husband got mixed up with the wrong drug dealer," said Val. "Perhaps your mother tried to run a blackmail scheme with the wrong private eye. Perhaps Johnny got what was coming to him from a crazed, jealous fan. Or maybe that's just what the Powers That Be want us to think. The Big Six never liked us, you know? Once those books took off, and we were making more than all of them combined? They took that personally."

"You're starting to sound like Jenny, that can't be a good thing," said Eliza.

Val wrinkled her nose and glanced at her phone. Her eyes widened.

"Speak of the she-devil."

"What is it?"

"According to Victoria, who got it from her friend, your sister was just arrested by the FBI," said Val.

"No! Crap!" said Eliza. "I totally forgot, I was on my way to get her! We just got our first real lead on the Stranger. He's going to be on the afternoon Cabernet Express from Napa!"

"The wine train? How tacky," said Val.

Eliza gripped the fence rail, trying to see a way past this roadblock. One dose of chloroform, an 18-inch ninjatō, and a riot baton against the tall, dark, and strangesome menace? "Fuck it," she said. "You're going to have to come with me."

"Absolutely not!" said Val.

"It can't just be me! I need backup! Wait! If you call Jack, it won't look suspicious. Tell him to bring Drew and come pick me up."

"Again, absolutely not! And the boys couldn't help you regardless; they have a baseball game in Petaluma after school."

"Is there any chance Tori can get Darcy to spring Jenny when they're not looking?"

"Be serious. Hold on." Val tapped on her phone, texting. Several seconds later, she got a reply. "Oh, she says they're not booking her at the station. They're taking her to the agents' suite at the Crow's Nest."

It was all slipping away. Right when they finally caught a break in the case, the feds screwed everything up. Eliza was flirting with despair until a new idea kindled in her skull. A very Trouble idea.

"Hold up, the Crow's Nest?" she said. "Aren't you the one who brags about all the power you command there? Concierges eating out of your hand?"

"Well, yes, but—"

"I need one more favor from you, Valerie," said Eliza. "This will prove to me that you didn't kill my mother. Then, I'll call us even."

BY A WEIRD TWIST OF FATE, AGENT ZOEY'S ROOM AT THE CROW'S Nest was the same one that Jenny had lived in for a time last spring when she ran away from home. From home, from Aunt Shelly, from Eliza, and from Trouble. She'd enjoyed a lot of hours in the suite's soaking tub, hiding from her problems underwater. Now here she was again in the fancy, black and white tiled bathroom, except the tub was empty, and her wrist was handcuffed to the brass pipe coming out of the wall.

"So you see," said Zoey, sitting on the sink counter, "there is no 'time off for good behavior' when you catch a federal charge. You're doing 85 percent of the time, no matter what."

"No, that's not true," said Jenny.

"Girl, I work for them," said Zoey.

"Congratulations. It's still not 'no matter what,'" said Jenny. "I could get pardoned."

Zoey laughed. "I wouldn't count on that. The trick is to not eat the charge. Play whatever card you're holding before it's too late. Where can we find Kazumi?"

"Bend over and I'll show you," said Jenny.

"How did the idiot cops in this town not arrest you sooner?" Zoey asked, rubbing her temples.

"They did, multiple times, but they had a hard time making anything stick." Jenny smirked. "Don't be so hard on Sheriff Lockhart. I am, after all, the world's greatest Girl Detective."

Zoey was unimpressed. "You're going to be the world's *oldest* Girl Detective by the time you're eligible for parole."

"I'm hungry, I thought you ordered room service."

There was a sharp rap at the door.

"Room service!" called a woman's voice.

Jenny raised an eyebrow, taking credit for this coincidence. Zoey shook her head and hopped off the counter. Jenny could hear her padding across the suite carpet, could picture Zoey in her mind's eye, leaning against the door to peer out the peephole.

She heard some clattering as Zoey undid the chain lock and opened the door. The wheels of the room service cart squeaked as the room attendant rolled it in. Stainless steel rang when the attendant lifted the cloche thing off the dish.

"Where's the food?" Zoey asked. "Wait!"

A muffled cry, then a crash of dishes, and footsteps.

"There you are!" said Eliza, strolling into the bathroom. "Come on, we gotta hurry!"

She was wearing a Crow's Nest uniform, with shiny black micro-braids under a little bellhop cap. Her braids were strategically positioned to cover one eye, and contour makeup gave her a long nose. It wasn't much, but enough to fool Zoey through the peephole.

"Are you wearing a mop on your head?" Jenny asked.

"And shoe polish," said Eliza. "I'm out of wigs, so I had to improvise. Come on!"

"I'm cuffed. Get her keys," said Jenny.

Eliza cursed and ran back into the main room.

"What's the rush?" Jenny asked. "Are the cops on their way?"

"No," said Eliza, returning and tossing Jenny the keys. "Willie called. He's making a drop for the Stranger. We have to be on the Calistoga Cabernet Express in… twenty-four minutes!"

"Twenty-four minutes?!" Jenny had the cuffs off in a flash. "How did you even know where to find me?"

"From Val, of all people," said Eliza. "She knows about me."

"What!?"

Eliza hastily explained the situation while changing out of the bellhop outfit with clothes from the backpack she'd hidden underneath the room service cart.

"He's supposed to leave the package in the luggage rack of the second train car. Also, there's new manuscript pages," Eliza said, tossing away the mophead wig. Her hair was all shiny black from the shoe polish. "Uh, there's a Killian Rosewood of the Rosewood Winery—who isn't a real person, according to Val—and he threatens Trouble and says there is no Stranger and implies some sort of conspiracy amongst the Big Six to rule the town or something. But then Trouble escapes before she can learn more. Val thinks it means Mom and RJ and her first husband's deaths are all connected. Like, this thing might go all the way to the top. And she didn't know anything about Lambert."

There was a groan from the floor, and Agent Zoey's eyes flickered open.

"Wha? Lambert?" Zoey asked in a daze.

Eliza cursed and lunged for her discarded chloroform rag, sending Zoey back to sleep before she knew what was happening.

"Motherfucker," said Eliza, staring at the rag. "Does this stuff lose its potency after a while?"

"Maybe?" said Jenny. "Should we cuff her? Otherwise, she'll sound the alarm as soon as she's awake again."

"No, we might need those, bring 'em!" Eliza checked her watch. "Damnit! We gotta run."

They exited the hotel suite, and Eliza led them to a service elevator while pulling on her motorcycle jacket. During the short ride down, Jenny struggled to process so much new information. Was Dad trying to tell her the Stranger was part of some larger town-wide conspiracy? If so, who were they about to ambush on the train? Just another patsy? Or, was that all a red herring? If she didn't want to serve 85 percent of a federal sentence, it had better be the latter.

Come on, RJ, you've got to give me a villain I can beat.

"How did Trouble escape?" Jenny asked as the elevator reached the basement. "In the manuscript, I mean?"

"Danger sets off the fire alarm and rescues her."

Eliza winked and pulled the nearest fire alarm.

BEEEEEEEPPPBEEEEEEPPPPBEEEEEEEPPPPBEEEEEEPPP!

They laughed as they ran down the service corridor, ignoring the stunned hotel workers and bursting out into the parking garage. The Kawasaki Ninja was waiting. Eliza stashed her backpack behind a dumpster, pulled on their only motorcycle helmet, and fitted her little sword into her jacket. Jenny hopped on behind her and clutched her arms tightly around her sister's waist.

"Go!" she shouted.

Eliza hit the accelerator, and Jenny nearly fell off as the bike exploded out of the garage. Eliza cut across traffic, turned onto Broadway, and raced east toward Napa.

THEY NEEDED TO MAKE IT TO THE OXBOW PUBLIC MARKET STATION within nineteen minutes. Eliza rode like an absolute maniac, and Jenny was sure they would die several times. They made it in twenty-two. Just in time to see the caboose of the Calistoga Cabernet Express pulling away from the end of the station platform.

Jenny cursed. "We missed it!"

"No, we didn't!" shouted Eliza.

Eliza revved the Ninja's engine, circled back to the railroad crossing on First Street, and turned onto the tracks.

"Are you crazy?!"

"That thing only goes like thirty miles per hour, tops!" said Eliza. "We can do this!"

She hit the gas and shot along the dirt path to the left of the tracks. They flew after the wine train, gaining quickly on the slower vehicle.

"But how are we going to get on?" she shouted.

The caboose was fast approaching.

"Handles!" Eliza shouted, pointing.

The train had an old-fashioned steam engine, retrofitted to run on diesel, and some classic 19th-century passenger cars and caboose. Just like in those old movies, there were handles and a short stair at the end of the caboose, where passengers pulled themselves up onto the short ledge behind the back door.

The Ninja sped ahead, pulling even with the back of the caboose, then passing it.

"You're gonna have to grab on and jump!" Eliza shouted.

Pacing the train now, Eliza eased up on the throttle until they were even with the handles on the back stair. Jenny's stomach was in her throat. The caboose inched closer. Only four feet away. Then three. She reached out with her right hand—

The bike hit the loose gravel next to the rail ties, and the ride got much bumpier. Jenny shrieked and pulled her hand back, clutching Eliza's waist. The handle and steps pulled ahead several feet.

"Almost got there! Go again!" Eliza shouted.

"Lizzy!! The bridge! Look out!" Jenny screamed.

Up ahead and rapidly approaching was a small bridge over a bend in the Napa River. It was built wide enough to fit the wine train—and not a foot wider.

Eliza shouted something and sped up again. Jenny's teeth rattled as they rode over the gravel. The back of the caboose was three feet ahead, then two, then one.

The bridge zoomed toward them, half a football field away.

Jenny winced and reached out her hand. She missed the first time—and then she had it! The handle was in her grasp!

"Got it!"

Eliza turned the bike into a skid, and Jenny was lifted right off of it. With one hand clutching the handle, she kicked her feet until they found the stairs beneath her.

Jenny pulled herself up onto the back of the caboose and looked back in panic.

There was Eliza, safely stopped at the edge of the riverbank, thank god. She shouted something, but Jenny couldn't hear it. Then she pointed to the west and turned the bike around, riding back the way they'd come.

Whatever her sister was thinking, it didn't matter now. Jenny was on the train alone, and if that Willie guy was right, so was the Stranger. This was it. No more games. No more clues. No more pages. She had one shot to take that bastard Killroy by surprise and end this tonight.

Chapter Twenty-Seven
The Wine Train

"**P**HEW! TRAFFIC'S A BITCH," JENNY SAID AS SHE ENTERED THE caboose. A bewildered waiter looked up from his workstation, where he was slicing a wheel of Vella cheese. She was in a small kitchen area. This must be where they did food prep for the wine tours. "This is neat. How many cars are on this train?"

"Um, f-five," said the waiter. "But—"

"Including the caboose?"

"No, five and the caboose," he said.

"Thanks." She pointed at his little cheese knife. "Do you got another one of those I could borrow?"

He shook his head slowly. "Sorry. Who are you?"

"My name is Trouble. Duh."

Jenny pushed open the swinging door at the other end of the small kitchen and found herself in a swanky lounge. The rest of the caboose was given over to a full bar. There were stools, bistro tables, and sumptuous linen tablecloths. Smooth jazz tinkled on the speakers while the bartender polished a crystal wine goblet with a gleaming white dish towel. Half a dozen patrons had come down to the caboose to imbibe on Calistoga County's bounty, and they all took turns gawking at her.

"What'll it be?" asked the bartender.

"By any chance, do you guys have *Ressort Rouge?*" she asked.

He snorted and shook his head.

"You know, I find once you've had it, it's hard to drink anything else," she said.

"You've never had *Ressort Rouge!*" the passenger a stool over said.

"Dude, I've had so much I used it in a red sauce." She turned back to the bartender. "What about an empty bottle?"

The bartender shrugged and pulled a green bottle from under the counter. "Can I interest you in a 2019 Rosewood Pinot?"

"That was a good year, for wine," said Jenny. "I'll trade you."

She placed a battered box of Pocky on the bar and took the bottle. At the front of the caboose, she pressed the **Open** button on the door and it slid aside. Wind rushed in. This wasn't like changing cars on the LA Metro or BART. The gap between train cars was open to the air. A two-foot-wide retractable plank and thin brass chains on either side were all that prevented a passenger from falling under the wheels.

"Close it!" a passenger yelled behind her.

Jenny steeled herself and stepped quickly to the next car. It was a relief to get inside and shut out the wind. This was Car 5. She'd have to do that three more times.

The passenger cars, too, were decorated like an expensive restaurant, with booths on either side of the aisle, lots of wood paneling, and little brass wall sconces holding real, lit candles. Outside the arched windows, Jenny could see rolling hills of green vineyards, perfectly lit in the afternoon light. Not for long, though. Dark clouds were descending from the Calistoga foothills to the north, and the train was headed right for them.

"Can I help you?" asked a waitress serving a taster's flight.

"Just passing through," Jenny said.

She moved past the drink station and small bathroom at the back of the car and walked down the aisle. At the front, the booths gave way to boarding doors and a luggage rack.

Jenny opened the forward door and braved another crossing to Car 4. Two to go. This car was identical to the last, though it contained a large and boisterous party of middle-aged women in business attire. She was studying every face she passed, searching for one she recognized, but nothing so far. Surely, the Stranger would not be an actual stranger. She felt she must know the guy, after all they'd been through together.

Car 3 was much the same. Good. If they were all like this, she knew just where she'd sit to ambush her prey. On the way down the aisle, she swiped a morsel of Vella jack cheese from the charcuterie board. Still no sign of a familiar face.

She left the car and let the door close behind her, hesitating before crossing. It wasn't so scary anymore; she was a pro at this now. But she might be about to walk smack into her arch-nemesis.

Nothing ventured, nothing gained, Trouble.

Munching on her cheese, she clutched the bottle of Rosewood in her right hand and stepped across.

The door to Car 2 wouldn't budge.

"Fuck!"

She tried the **Open** button again, but it wouldn't slide open. All of a sudden, she wasn't feeling like such a pro anymore. In a panic, she punched the button full-on with her left fist.

Success! The door slid aside and Jenny slipped through. It closed with a squeal behind her.

"I think that one could use some WD-40," she said.

There wasn't any waitress in this car to hear her. The number of patrons had been dwindling as she moved forward from the caboose, and now she was alone in the car, save a shabby-looking man with long, stringy hair. He was seated just ahead of the drink station in the first booth on the right, zoned out with headphones on. When they made eye contact, his expression twisted into alarm.

"Oi, what the bloody hell?" he said, yanking out his AirPods.

"Willie?" she guessed, based on Penny's description.

"SHHH!!!!" he hissed at her. "I can't be seen with you!"

Jenny scowled and took the booth in front of his. Without turning her head, she spoke loud enough for him to hear, but no louder.

"What are you doing here?" she asked. "I thought you would just do the drop and scram?"

"Instructions are to ride until the next stop at Calistoga Lake and get off. My payment will be waiting under a bench at the station."

The Stranger's plan unfolded in her head.

He plants the money under the bench at the station. When the train arrives, he waits to make sure Willie gets off, then boards himself— probably in a separate car. Then the Stranger crosses to Car 2, retrieves his package, and... probably rides to the next stop and gets off?

"Got it," said Jenny.

She stood up and walked to the front of the car. There was a handwritten sign on the door to Car 1.

CAR 1 IS CLOSED FOR UPKEEP
APOLOGIES FOR THE INCONVENIENCE

Perfect. The front of the car was a dead end. If she was right about the Stranger not wanting to board Car 2 directly, he'd enter from the back, via Car 3. Her ambush spot would be perfect—except that Willie guy was sitting in it.

"Hey," she said, walking back down the car. "You need to switch seats with me. Go sit at the other end."

"Like hell, I will," said Willie. "I'm sitting as far away from that package as I can."

"Okay, but he's probably not going to board from that side, it'll be behind you," said Jenny. "I can hide in the corner under the table, and he'll walk right past me. I silently follow him to the package and: BAM!" She pantomimed bashing the Stranger over the head with her empty bottle of pinot noir. "The Stranger is caught, the town is saved, and I'm rich."

"You can have it when I get off," said Willie. He nodded behind him. "Hide in the loo for now if you must."

He put his AirPods back in. Jenny checked the bathroom at the back of the car and found another note from the staff.

BATHROOM IS CLOSED FOR UPKEEP
APOLOGIES FOR THE INCONVENIENCE

"It's out of order," she told him, reading the posted sign. "Lotta upkeep around here."

Just in case, she tried the handle, but it was locked. Damn. There was always the drink station, but a waiter might find her and raise a ruckus. She was half expecting to get kicked off the train and arrested at the next stop as it was.

Willie was unconcerned with her plight and shooed her away again. Strolling back to the front of the car, she glanced at the luggage rack. The lone item on it was the package Willie brought on board: a cardboard box the size of a shoebox. She picked it up and shook it a little. It was lighter than expected, and the way the weight shifted, she pictured a compact object within.

Hmm.

Something was nagging at her. She spun slowly, taking in the train car again with soft eyes. Outside, the first errant raindrops streaked across the arched windows. Her gaze passed over the sign on the door to Car 1, and she paused.

The **K** in **UPKEEP** was written with the bottom leg coming out of the top leg rather than meeting in the middle. A horrible chill gripped her heart. Upkeep. The sign on the bathroom door had been written the same way, hadn't it? With that same K…

Something chimed next to her, and she jumped with a start. It was a phone ringtone. An older one she remembered from her childhood, when Aunt Shelly was never without one of those indestructible Nokia phones holstered on her hip. The sound was coming from the cardboard box on the luggage rack.

Oh fuck! Is that a bomb!?

Jenny grabbed the package and tore it open. Inside were a few stapled letter-size pages: the latest chapter of *I Dream of Trouble.* She shoved them into her coat pocket to get at what was below.

It wasn't a bomb, thank god, just a cheap cell phone. With mounting horror, she flipped it open and held it to her ear.

"Hello?" she said.

"Tracking the heirloom book to that shipping service was smart," said a distorted voice over the line. "But I'll always be smarter, Trouble."

At the back of the car, the bathroom door slid open, and a tall, dark, and Strangesome menace stepped out. Maybe it was the low train ceiling, maybe it was fear, but he seemed bigger than ever. In his left hand, he closed the flip phone he was calling from. In his right, he raised a vicious bowie knife. With his headphones in, Willie didn't even hear him coming.

"WILLIE LOOK OUT!!" Jenny screamed.

"Huh?" Willie replied, baffled by her outburst.

The Stranger made quick work of his accomplice. Lightning fast, he grabbed Willie by his stringy hair and plunged the Bowie knife into the nape of Willie's neck. An awful gurgle escaped from Willie's mouth, and blood poured out in a torrent. Jenny could only stare in shock, eyes locked with the befuddled, twitching Willie as his life poured out of him.

The Stranger yanked the knife out and wagged the bloody blade at her.

"Your friends are next if they keep playing our game," he said in that creepy electronic voice.

"The g-game's over," Jenny said, unable to mask the fear in her voice. "I'm right here."

"Not yet." His head turned slowly from side to side. "We need an audience before we can dance. See you soon, Trouble."

He turned and retreated to the back of the car, mashing on the door's **Open** button.

Nothing happened. Uttering a distorted curse, he pressed the button again. The door wouldn't budge. The Stranger tried using both hands to yank the door open, grunting at the effort.

"Sorry, Killroy, I think I broke it on the way in," Jenny said.

While the Stranger struggled with the door, she raced forward, her footsteps muffled by the hum of the train. He looked back just in time to receive the full weight of an empty Rosewood 750ml bottle to the back of his masked head.

Shattered glass flew everywhere, and a sting in Jenny's hand told her she'd cut her palm. The Stranger collapsed to his knees with a groan and clutched at his head.

Jenny dropped the broken bottle and pulled Agent Zoey's handcuffs from her pocket. Already, her right palm was slippery with blood. She'd never felt more terror in her life as she fumbled to close one cuff around the brass handhold next to the door. And then, too fast for him to react, she slapped the other around the Stranger's wrist.

Holy shit! I did it!

Jenny leaped back out of knife range and pumped her fist.

"YESSSSSS!!! I got you! I caught you!" she yelled. "Eat shit!"

Her whole body shook. Some alchemical process in her body took hold, the adrenaline in her veins transforming her fear into excitement. "Who's the smart guy now, asshole!? Trouble always gets her man!!"

Jolts of joy rippled up her spine, and another jubilant idea struck her.

"So, who are you, anyway? The mayor? Dinah? RJ's evil twin?"

She darted forward to yank off his mask.

The Stranger leaped to his feet, whirling around. His free hand swung around in a fist and caught Jenny full-on across her left eye. Something popped—maybe her orbital bone—and stars exploded in her vision. Moments later, he struck her on the other side, and she gasped in pain. No, wait, he didn't hit her, the floor did. She'd dropped like a ton of bricks.

Above her, the Stranger rose to his feet and muttered, "Test, test," to himself in that distorted voice. Jenny's face throbbed, and opening her eyes made her want to vomit. With a whimper, she forced herself to roll out of the Stranger's reach and push herself up onto her knees. The Stranger stared down at her, implacable behind his black mask and fedora.

"I guess it's your turn after all," he said.

His left arm was still manacled to the handhold by the rear door. Not for long. Jenny watched helplessly as he twisted his body back, winding up torque, and then exploded around in a powerful left hook that yanked the door handhold right off the wall! She had the small satisfaction of seeing him shake his hand and rub his left wrist.

"I hope you fucking broke it," Jenny said.

He disentangled the broken handhold from the cuff and tossed it aside. Then he advanced on Jenny.

She managed to pull herself to her feet without blacking out. The Stranger's bulk took up the whole aisle. There was no chance of slipping past him, and that door was jammed anyway. Where could she go?

Behind her, the way to Car 1 was locked, which meant the passenger door at the front of Car 2 was her only option. Using the booth tables for support, she retreated to the boarding entrance. Jenny grabbed the red **Emergency Only** lever fixed to the middle of it and pushed it sideways.

The wind rushed in, and her face was pelted with raindrops. It was almost soothing. The sun in the west dipped below the ominous cloud line, bathing the wine country in beautiful golden light.

The view directly below her was not so pretty. On this side, the track ran along an elevated embankment of steep, pitiless concrete. How fast did Eliza say the train ran? Thirty miles per hour? It sure felt like they were going faster. If she jumped, Jenny had no doubt she would perish on impact.

She glanced back at the Stranger, and he might have smiled under his mask. He knew he'd trapped her.

"What's wrong, Trouble?" he asked. "All out of your smart ideas?"

She grasped a handhold and leaned out of the car to look ahead. Maybe they'd drive by some soft grass soon? Nope, Jenny wasn't that lucky. But she did see something that gave her a new, terrible idea.

"You know me," Jenny said. "It's always gotta get ten times worse before it gets better."

And with that, she stepped out of the train car.

"Wat!?" she heard the Stranger exclaim from within before the rushing wind overtook her.

These were old-fashioned rail cars, complete with ladder handholds that ran up the side. Jenny had swung out onto one of the rungs, hanging on for dear life. Her bleeding palm almost slipped, but somehow, she held on.

Thunder rumbled as she climbed the rungs. She was nearly to the roof when the Stranger leaned out and spotted her. His long arm gripped her right sneaker, trying to pull her back inside. Jenny tore her foot free, leaving the shoe behind, and crawled onto the roof.

The bare metal was slick with rainwater, and the wind whipped all around Jenny. She flattened herself onto the wet surface; if a gust caught her trench coat the wrong way, she feared it might lift her right off the train. She didn't know what she was doing. Only that there was no other direction to run. Maybe she could reach Car 3 and climb down? The Stranger wouldn't risk a move with all those people around, would he?

Jenny retreated carefully toward the back of the car on her hands and knees. A horrifying thought struck her, and she spun around to face forward.

No, you're not about to enter a tunnel or get hit by one of those random things that hang over trains in movies.

That was nice. But her glance ahead revealed an unfortunate development: the Stranger was following her up the ladder to the roof. She thought back to the first time a crazed psycho wouldn't stop chasing her. That stupid Undertaker. What was his name? Chuck something. What a creep. She'd had Dinah to help, then. She was glad Dinah wasn't here now.

Unless she is?

What had her mantra been, then?

Keep him talking.

The Stranger pulled himself onto the roof and crawled toward her.

"Shouldn't you have a monologue prepared for this, Killroy?!" she shouted. "Go on, dazzle me with how you did it! How you were always two steps ahead!"

"That's your job!" the Stranger shouted back. "You still haven't figured it out yet, have you?!"

Just to prove what a badass he was, the Stranger stood up, stretching as close to his full height as he could in the wind.

"Maybe I have!" she yelled back.

The gauntlet was laid down, so Jenny unsteadily rose to her feet, too. It felt like the train might have slowed down a little. She could just make out a short bridge over another bend in the Napa River a mile or two ahead.

"You know what, man, you're right!" Jenny shouted at him. "We can't do this without an audience! What do you say we shake on it and live to fight another day!?"

"Fuck that!" shouted a voice behind her, giving Jenny such a start that she nearly fell off the train roof right then and there. She went down on one knee and gawked at the sight behind her.

A figure in a motorcycle helmet clambered up onto the roof at the rear of the car. Jenny knew they were the same size, but her sister looked so much taller at the moment. Eliza pulled off the helmet and tossed it over the side of the train.

"Hi, Trouble!" Eliza said. "Sorry I'm late. Can Danger play, too?"

THE STRANGEST FEELING CAME OVER ELIZA THEN, PERCHED ATOP A speeding train and facing down a hulking psycho with a knife.

This is where I belong.

Ever since Jenny learned to read, Eliza knew her sister went around all day with an orchestra in her head, playing her personal theme song. But today, the orchestra played for Danger.

Reaching back, she drew Secret from her sheath. The Stranger cocked his head and looked back and forth between the two sisters. Eliza got the impression he was smirking behind his mask.

"Yeah, that's right, twins," she said. "You knew it all along, didn't you?"

"Lizzy, how did you get here?" Jenny asked.

A detour across the river, a lot of traffic violations, an incredibly dangerous leap onto the train from the motorcycle…

"Long story! Get behind me!" Eliza said. She stepped past her sister and raised the sword. "Looks like you brought a knife to a sword fight, fucko!"

In truth, the 18-inch blade of her ninjatō wasn't feeling quite so impressive at the moment. The Stranger's blade was a foot long, at least.

He must have sensed her hesitation because he chose that time to strike. Darting forward, he slashed at her with the Bowie knife. Eliza blocked with Secret—and nearly dropped her weapon from the shock of the impact. The Stranger was so strong.

She pivoted to the side and let his momentum carry him past, pirouetting on the spot to deliver a roundhouse kick to his backside. Jenny shrieked and rolled to the side—perilously close to the edge— as the Stranger slid past. Maybe they'd get lucky, and he'd fall off and go under the tracks.

They weren't so lucky. But he did drop his knife.

Jenny lunged for it. So did the Stranger. They collided and sent the knife skittering off the side of the roof, lost forever.

"Jenny! Get back!" Eliza shouted.

She hurried forward and stabbed down with Secret. The blade impacted in the center of the Stranger's chest—but it didn't go in. She had to leap back to dodge his powerful kick.

Right. Body armor. The stuff he made Jeffrey Jordan purchase for him.

"That's cheating," she said.

The Stranger levered himself up onto his feet, rubbed both wrists and planted his back foot. A memory clicked. She'd seen him do this once before, right before he killed Nilay.

You've seen it somewhere else, too, Danger! Think!

"What about me gave you the impression that I fought fair?!" shouted the Stranger. "Don't you read the books?!"

"Lizzy! Bridge!" Jenny shouted from behind.

Eliza risked a glance back to see that they were getting close to a small bridge over the river. Time to press the advantage. She moved on the Stranger with a flurry of slashes and moulinets to confuse him, then slashed down hard with a backhand swing. Somehow, the bastard caught her blow on two steel handcuffs wrapped around his left wrist.

She swung Secret again to take his head off. He ducked in time to save it, but not his hat. It flew off into the wind, floating over the trailing railcars.

The wild slash was a mistake. It left her wide open to a counter-attack. The Stranger lunged to tackle her, and Eliza winced, expecting to be bowled over. But his black-booted foot slipped on the wet metal roof, and he fell on his face instead. She recovered from her overswing and stepped up to stab him through the neck.

Before she could strike, he pulled something from his coat pocket and thrust his hand at her.

Eliza only hesitated for a moment, but it was her undoing. Just as her brain recognized the device as a camera flash, the thing went off in her face.

Blinding light seared her retinas. Secret struck wide, plunging into the metal roof of the train car and getting stuck. The Stranger grabbed her by the throat and Eliza felt herself being lifted.

Up onto her tiptoes, and then up, up, up still. Her feet dangled in the rushing wind, and she gasped for breath.

Jenny screamed.

Eliza beat feebly at his arm.

"Now then," said the Stranger. "How about we make it easier to tell you two apart."

Through her bleary vision, the Stranger's gloved free hand reached for her face. With monstrous strength, he jammed his thumb into her left eye.

Eliza shrieked in agony and felt a tug, then an awful tearing, and half her world was suddenly gone. Ripped away.

With a grunt, the Stranger shoved her and let go. The orchestra soared to its crescendo. Eliza could finally breathe again, and she was falling, falling.

Her last thought, before the rest of the world went away, too, was annoyance.

Oh! That's what Nilay meant! Why didn't he just say—

Chapter Twenty-Eight

You Come in Bruised

Jenny watched in horror from her knees as the Stranger ripped out Lizzy's eye and tossed her over the side of the train. She scrambled to the edge just in time to see Eliza fall into the river—they'd just rolled over the bridge. She stared and stared at the spot where her sister went in, waiting for her to resurface.

Lizzy never did. The train pulled further and further away, and then the river was gone from view.

She had to come back! She had to! Lizzy was a strong swimmer. Nurse Bennett made her take lessons! She told me so!

"How was that for an audience?" asked the Stranger.

He didn't have to shout anymore. The train was slowing. They were pulling into the next station at Calistoga Lake.

"The next murder I solve will be your own," said Jenny. "It won't be much of a mystery."

"Thrilling!" said the Stranger. "But you'll have to catch me, first!"

Lightning flashed. He took two steps and leaped off the train—only to land on the roof of another train passing by, going the other direction.

Thunder rumbled above, and hatred kindled in Jenny's heart. He couldn't get away with this! She sprang to her feet, ready to leap after him, but the last car in the passing train was already slipping away.

Jenny ran to the back of Car 2, awkwardly stepping with one unshod foot. Without hesitation, she leaped to Car 3. If she could go fast enough, she could jump over to his train.

It felt like using one of those moving walkways at the airport. Car 3 glided by underneath. Jumping to Car 4 was almost nothing. Dammit! Why wasn't she gaining on him!? She was full-on sprinting now, heedless of the danger.

Oh, Danger…

She leaped to Car 5, and then the caboose, but it was hopeless. The Stranger easily outpaced her. He stared back and waved as his train carried him away.

"Till next time, Trouble!" His distorted voice carried over the wind.

Jenny collapsed at the edge of the caboose. This wasn't just ten times worse—it was a million times worse. This was unthinkable. They'd done everything right, followed every clue. Eliza had been a demon with that sword, and where had it gotten them?

A belated alarm sounded in her mind. If the wait staff hadn't found Willie yet, they would momentarily. They were easing into the station, which meant it was time for Jenny to go. She climbed down the caboose ladder and gently dropped onto the tracks.

OW!

Even at this low speed, she tumbled and scratched up her knees and elbows. Without a shoe, she was in no condition to run, but run she did, back down the tracks to the bridge. She had to find Lizzy.

Ten minutes later, she stood over Napa River on the bridge, staring down at a swift-flowing current, and empty shores on either side. Eliza would be carried all the way down to the sloughs if she couldn't make it to shore.

"Eliza!?" she called out. "Eliza!?"

She counted to ten, hoping for a reply.

"ELIZA!!!"

There was no response; only the lap of the river and blackbirds chirping. Maybe Lizzy couldn't get out until a ways downstream. Or maybe… An intrusive thought whispered in her ear.

Might as well jump in and join her.

No! Eliza would be so pissed at her if she did that. No! Jenny had business to settle with Mr. Killroy. She wouldn't rest—she wouldn't grieve until she did.

Okay, do that, and then join her.

Deal.

A chill crept up her spine. She shoved her freezing hands into her coat pockets for warmth. The left one brushed against folded papers and something small and plastic: the flip phone from the package. The decoy package.

What a bitter pill to swallow. The Stranger had outsmarted them—had been two steps ahead the whole time. But maybe, in his moment of triumph, the Stranger fucked up, too.

Jenny flipped open the phone and checked the tiny screen. It was still working; she had a signal. This was good. She could use this. But who could she call? She barely remembered her own phone number…

Wait! 707-555-3739! Whose number is that?

A memory flashed in her mind: buying hair dye and supplies… That's right, she used it at Target by mistake. It was Asha's or Drew's, probably. Fuck it, she punched it in and hit **Call**. The line rang until it went to voicemail.

"Hi, this is Drew, you can leave a message—or better yet, just text me," came Drew's voice over the line.

Thank god it wasn't Asha! Drew was probably at his baseball game right now, but the players always had their phones in the dugout. Jenny walked to the far bank and waited a minute before calling again. This time, he picked up.

"Hello?" he asked, wary. "Who's this?"

Oh, right, he doesn't know the number.

"Drew? It's me!" said Jenny.

There was a pause on the line. In the background, she could hear the knock of a baseball bat and the quiet buzz of voices. She pictured him in the dugout at Santa Rosa High School or wherever they were playing.

"Dude, am I your one phone call?" he asked. "I heard you got arrested."

"What? No, I got away. I need your help!"

"Porter! Hey, Porter! You're up!" someone shouted in the background.

"Shit! I'm on deck, I'll call you back," he said and hung up before she could reply.

Fine, Jenny wasn't going anywhere. Her bare foot stung from walking on gravel and wooden rail ties, so she pressed it into the wet dirt on the riverbank, savoring the cool sand between her toes. A minute later, her phone rang.

"Drew?"

"Hey, sorry," he said. He'd moved somewhere quieter.

"It's fine," said Jenny. She contemplated where to begin and stifled a sob. "Shit is fucked. Can you help me?"

"Yes, of course," he said. "Where are you?"

"Um… near the train station at Calistoga Lake," she said. "I'm on the south side of the bridge if you follow the train tracks."

"What the hell are you doing out there?"

"I—not now. I tried something, and I failed, Drewboo," Jenny said.

"Okay. Okay, forget I asked, we'll worry about that later," Drew said. "Um, what'd you say, the south side of the river?"

"Near the bridge before Calistoga Lake station," said Jenny.

Drew told her to hold on. Probably looking at a map. She moved to do the same and remembered she was on a flip phone.

"All right, I see the bridge," said Drew. "Um, do you see some buildings to the west? Like, west-south-west?"

Jenny shaded her eyes, staring into the last sliver of sunlight on the horizon. She could just make out the silhouette of a barn in that direction.

"Yeah, I see one."

"It looks like that's Ravenhart Winery," said Drew. "There's a road to it. I can meet you there."

"Oh, thank god," said Jenny.

"I'm in Petaluma, so it's gonna take me a while," he said. "Will you be okay?"

"I think so, yeah. As long as the feds aren't listening in. If they are:

fuck you, Tierce!" said Jenny. "I'll start walking over there now."

"Cool, uh, I'll tell Coach my mom is sick, or something," said Drew.

"Hey, how'd you call back so fast?" Jenny asked. "Did you strike out on purpose for me?"

"Of course not," Drew said. "I hit a home run."

It was almost enough to make Jenny smile. She thanked him again and hung up. If the feds had listened to all that with a wiretap and got here first? Well, fine. Good job, assholes. Great work catching the wrong person.

Jenny limped in the direction of the winery. As she drew closer to it, she spied a gardening shack a short distance from the road. It was unoccupied, and more importantly, dry inside. Jenny collapsed onto a stack of fertilizer bags and tried to think about anything but Lizzy. The way she'd plummeted into the water and disappeared…

Reaching into her pocket, she withdrew the other item she'd taken from the train: new pages from the *I Dream of Trouble* manuscript. The thought of reading them no longer sparked any joy in her soul, but she had time to kill, and maybe RJ would give her a useful hint. More useful than that stupid *The Stranger of Sausalito* book!

She unfolded the damp pages and began to read.

Chapter 7

"Where are we going?" Danger asks.

Once we got away from Rosewood, we switched places, and I've been meandering through the hills for half an hour to throw off the scent.

"Somewhere safe," I tell Danger. "I know just the place."

The Valentine family cabin. It's in the foothills to the northwest. I avoid cutting through town, sketching a broad arc around the northern border of Blackbird Springs. After what Killian Rosewood told me, I'm not sure who we can trust anymore.

By the time I turn down the gravel driveway to our cabin, it's past 9:00 PM. Daddy has been calling me incessantly. He wants to know why Dinah Black is at his door, warning him about the mayor. I tell him it might have been a false alarm and not to worry; I'm sleeping over at Penny's tonight. I can tell he knows I'm lying, and he knows that I know, but by unspoken agreement, we're letting that slide. Who knows who might be listening in, after all?

At least, that's my excuse for not telling Daddy about Danger. I don't know why I'm lying. Maybe because it feels wrong to tell him something like that over the phone. She deserves to break the news to him in person. And he deserves a chance to be sitting down when he hears it. I remember how shocked he was when he found out about Jack.

"When's the last time you guys were up here?" Danger asks as we get out of the car.

Our family cabin is modest by Blackbird Springs standards. Two bedrooms plus a loft. I love the loft; it's my favorite place in the whole cabin, and I would live there all the time if I could. I like being up high and able to look down on everything below. Daddy is always saying I was a cat in a former life.

"It's been a few years, I think," I say. "Dad comes up here for fishing trips sometimes."

"He doesn't bring you with him?" Danger asks.

I wrinkle my nose. "He used to, till I begged off. I hate the smell, and I was never very good at baiting a hook."

The door is locked, but I know where the hidden key under the fake rock can be found. We let ourselves inside, and I head to the basement to start the generator. There are some dry goods in the pantry, and Danger volunteers to cook dinner. It's only when my stomach rumbles at the smell of the spam she's frying up that I realize how damn hungry I am. Hungry enough to eat spam!

While she cooks, I tell her all about the encounter with Rosewood and his claims about the Stranger.

"But you *saw* the Stranger this afternoon, didn't you?" Danger asks.

"Yes, and so did Dinah," I say. "Even if I accept that all the times I thought I saw him as a child, I was actually imagining him—which I do not!—that still doesn't explain the guy who attacked me today and stole that mini cassette."

"So, according to this Killian guy, Dad encouraged your Stranger obsession to stop you from poking your nose into their business," Danger says. "But what if this is just more of the same? Telling you there's *no* Stranger now, to accomplish the same thing. They're scared of you, Trouble. Scared of us both."

"I'll drink to that," I say.

I get a bottle of Pinefall Merlot from the wine closet to pair with the spam and black beans. Danger serves up dinner on Formica plates from the cabinet. We sit to eat, and my twin sheds herself of my purple trench coat. She's wearing a white tank top and has a barbed wire armband tattoo and—if I'm not mistaken—pierced nips.

She's so cool. I get giddy every time I remember I have a sister now.

"Oh wow, this is salty!" Danger says when she digs in.

If anything, she's underselling it. The meat is so overloaded with sodium that it would probably kill that Rosewood guy on the spot. I devour it.

Something is nagging at the door of my subconscious. There's a clue I'm forgetting. I can feel it. Whenever this happens, the only thing to do is entertain all the theories you've already rejected.

"Maybe both things are true," I say. "Maybe there never was a single person who acted as the Stranger. Maybe the black trench coat and fedora are like a shield the criminals use. The way Rosewood tells it, there's some cabal of town elders running the show. Maybe the Stranger was never a criminal mastermind, just a hired thug of the Powers That Be, who they would dispatch to throw me off the scent whenever I was getting too close to uncovering the real corruption in Blackbird Springs."

"That would explain why you could never catch him," says Danger. "He only existed when they needed him to."

"But then, why did it all stop?" I ask.

"They must have threatened Dad," says Danger. "And not for the first time. We've already linked Mom's murder to the mayor. That might have been warning number one— because Dad was getting too close. And then, years pass, and now *you're* the one who's getting too close. So they threaten Dad again: rein in Trouble, or we do to her what we did to your wife."

"It's weird," I say. "I remember after the Stranger threatened me, I got chicken pox and had to stay home for a couple weeks. And then, when the blisters scabbed and fell off, and I was finally free to sleuth again, it was as though all the mystery in town had dried up. Sometimes, I'd think I was onto a clue, only to follow it to a dead end."

"I'm thinking Dad was running all over town, burying leads before you could find them," said Danger. "He didn't want you to catch a whiff of mystery. And you didn't. Not until I showed up, hunting a mystery of my own. What if—what if Hodgson wasn't trying to hurt you? What if he was trying to warn you, and the cabal got to him first?"

"It's as good a theory as any," I say. "But I need proof, not theories. We have to go back to the mayor's office. I need photos of those redevelopment plans. We can take it to the *Blackbird Times* and blow up their whole scheme."

I shove a last bite of spam into my mouth and stand up from the kitchen table.

"What? Now?!" Danger asks, surprised.

"Why not? Town Hall is closed, and town elders will have all their thugs out searching for me. They'll never expect me to come back there—and this time, there'll be two of me!"

"Screw it, let's do it!" says Danger. "Trouble on my left side!"

"Danger on my right!" I say, and we high-five.

"It'll take more than a switcharoo to get us into the mayor's office this time," Danger says, pulling the trench coat back on. "And we can't just bust in and set off the alarms. I'm betting there's more to find than just those plans in Villanova's office. We're gonna want some time to fish."

A fabulous idea sparks in my mind.

"Fishing! That's it. You're brilliant, Danger."

I hurry up to the loft, and I'm in luck! My tackle box is in the closet up here, along with my old fishing pole and photo albums of Mom that I liked to page through in bed. I grab the handle on the tackle box and turn back to the loft ladder—

CRASH!

I must have forgotten to close the latch on my tackle box. All my hooks and lures and bobbers spill all over the loft floor. I kneel to clean them up when there's a knock at the front door.

My heart freezes to the core. Who?! At this hour!?

Then I glance down, and another shock takes my breath away.

"Danger!" I shout.

WELL, IT FINALLY HAPPENED. EVEN THE *TROUBLE* BOOKS WEREN'T safe anymore. Jenny couldn't go a page in the latest manuscript without being reminded of her sister, and wanting to die.

Also, ew, Dad! Did you have to mention her nipple piercings in a Trouble *book? She doesn't even have them IRL.*

Jenny was still waiting for Drew in the garden shed. Every few seconds, her mental defenses slackened, and horrible memories from the wine train came rushing back. Willie's face and the way his body twitched as blood poured out of his mouth. The backhanded punch from the Stranger that nearly broke Jenny's face. Eliza's eye ripped from its socket. Watching her twin fall into the Napa River, maybe never to return…

Don't even think it!

The soft rumble of an approaching vehicle grew louder. Jenny peeked out the door. It was dark now, but that looked like Drew's truck. Finally! It had taken him over an hour to get here. Jenny folded up the pages and returned them to her coat pocket. Just in case, she broke the flip phone in two and buried the pieces in the mud behind the shed before waving Drew down.

He was still in his baseball uniform, eye black and all. Brave of him, considering the last time he'd worn it on Trouble business, he ended up with a knife in the shoulder.

Eliza never got a chance to apologize to you for that. I'm sorry, Drew.

"I'm muddy," she said when he leaned over and opened the door for her.

"Holy shit, what happened to you!?" he said.

"What?" Jenny asked. She leaned over to check her reflection in the sideview mirror. All the skin around her left eye was swollen black and blue. "Oh. Sorry."

"Um… this is where you're supposed to say, 'You should see the other guy.'" He forced a smile.

Jenny shook her head, and his smile faded.

"What can I do?" he asked.

She pulled herself into the truck and sagged against the seat. "Take me somewhere safe."

A chill ran down her spine as she said it. This was all too eerily similar to that last *I Dream of Trouble* chapter, except Danger wasn't with her, and the real RJ didn't have a cabin in the woods.

But the Lockhart family did.

"Did Mason ever take you to his cabin?" Jenny asked.

Drew shook his head. "Didn't know he had one."

"Good. We'll go there."

Drew pulled back onto the road, and they drove in silence. Five minutes later, once she was sure they'd gotten away, Jenny broke down sobbing.

In front of my sidekick, how embarrassing!

But she couldn't stop herself anymore. Drew hesitantly reached over and put his arm around her. Jenny melted into his shoulder, crying into the polyester of his baseball jersey. They rode that way a while until Jenny pulled herself together.

"Thanks," she said, wiping her eyes.

"No problem," he said.

His voice was stony, and Jenny noticed now, to her embarrassment, that Drew was pale-faced and anxious too.

"What's wrong?"

"Um. I have a confession to make," said Drew. He swallowed a lump in his throat. "I've been talking to Kazumi online. On Signal. She asked me not to tell you. We were trying to keep everything on the DL."

"Drew, that's okay, she told me," said Jenny.

"Oh. Good. Well, um, does… this"—he waved his hand at Jenny's whole situation—"have anything to do with Kazu? Because I haven't heard from her since last night, and I'm starting to get worried. Not that she has to or anything, but she usually replies right away."

Jenny winced and nodded. "We were on the train, and she fell off. Into the river. It was the Stranger. He attacked us. By the time I got back to the bridge, I couldn't find her."

Drew slammed on the brakes, and they nearly fishtailed right off the one-lane highway.

"Are you serious!" he yelled. "We gotta go back there!"

Shame curdled Jenny's guts. Should they? Was Jenny being a coward by not staying to search longer, afraid of what she'd find?

"The current is fast in that part of the river," she said. "She could be miles downstream, and I'm the last person who can go searching for her. I had to escape from Agent Zoey. The whole damned FBI is after me now."

Drew itched his hair under his hat, mulling it over. After a good ten seconds, he scowled and pulled back onto the road.

"Okay, I'll drop you off, and then I'm headed for the sloughs," he said. "They can't arrest *me*, right?"

It was hard to say what the feds would do now, but Jenny didn't argue. At least one of them would be searching for Lizzy.

Drew abandoned the speed limit, hurtling them recklessly toward Lockhart's cabin and making full use of his truck's four-wheel drive when they reached the last gravel roads. The cabin was dark, lit only by the moonlight when they arrived.

"Are you gonna be able to get in?" he asked.

"I'll find a way," Jenny said. "I had to ditch that phone I called you from, so you'll have to come back here to talk."

She got out of the truck, her bare foot grateful that Drew had parked on the concrete slab.

"I was right!" Drew said from the cab. "I knew Kazu wasn't the Stranger!"

"No, she wasn't."

"I'll find her, and then we'll come back with supplies," he said from the cab.

I really, really hope you do.

"Thank you," she said.

"Hold on." Drew leaned over and rummaged in his glove box. "Take this. Just in case."

He held out a sleek, silver pistol.

"Drew!" she said, far more shrilly than intended.

"It's my mom's," he said. "I borrowed it."

"It's not canon," said Jenny.

That got a manic laugh out of Drew. He tipped his cap and said, "Neither am I."

Jenny accepted the weapon, though she had no desire to use it. It was only after he'd driven away that she realized she'd never told him that Kazu was actually Eliza.

Will I ever?

No, it was fine. Eliza would tell him herself when he found her. She tucked the weapon into her coat pocket and walked to the cabin door. It was locked, but she knew where Mason hid a spare key.

Inside, she flicked the light switch, and nothing happened. Shoot. Maybe in all the chaos, Blake had forgotten to pay the energy bill for this place. The cabin still smelled faintly of baby powder and something else, something familiar...

"Stop right there!" came a whispered voice.

There was someone in the kitchen. A shadow deeper than the darkness. It glided closer, and moonlight from the window reflected off a lethal chef's knife. Jenny left the gun in her pocket and raised her hands in plaintive surrender.

"It's okay, it's just me," Jenny said. "What the hell are you doing here?"

The shadow stepped forward into the moonlight.

"It's a long story," said Dinah Black.

IN THE IMMEDIATE SENSE, DINAH WAS HERE BECAUSE OF BLAKE Lockhart. The feds had poked the hornet's nest by arresting him on trumped-up bullshit last night. As soon as Shelly bailed him out earlier today, Calderon and the rest of the local police staged a silent coup and reinstated him as sheriff behind the mayor's back. Which meant Blake knew all about Jenny getting arrested after lunch. And when the order came down from Tierce and Steele to arrest Dinah, he got there first, pretending to be her father and pulling her out of class before the feds arrived.

Blake had driven her to the cabin and stashed her up here until he could figure out what to do next. Jenny didn't mention to Dinah that he might have done this so he could exact his own justice—if it turned out she was involved in Mason's death after all.

"Why were the feds going to arrest you?" Jenny asked.

"They found traces of my DNA in RJ's study," said Dinah. "Hold still."

They'd moved to the bathroom, where Dinah was helping wash and bandage Jenny's poor foot. The power was on again—Dinah had tripped the master fuse when she heard a car coming up the gravel road.

"Sorry. But that's stupid, they already knew you were in there," said Jenny. "From when we raided the liquor cabinet."

Dinah nodded. "I guess they think you and I and 'Kazumi' have all been working together. Sure, why not, right?"

"Yeah..." said Jenny.

She scoffed and tried to ignore her inner doubt. No. She couldn't. Not anymore, not after what happened to Eliza. She reached down and touched Dinah's chin, pulling her face up to look at her.

"Why don't you tell me about the *other* time you were in RJ's study? On August 10th, 2019, while Jack was downstairs, taking care of his... carnal urges."

Dinah smiled, even as tears ran down her cheeks.

"Jenny..."

"I'm sorry, Dinah, but you can't dodge this anymore," said Jenny. "That thing with Willie was a setup. The Stranger attacked us on the train. He ripped Lizzy's eye out and threw her into the river. For all I know, she's dead. I'm wanted by the federal government. I'm all out of options. I can no longer let this slide. There's something you know about that night that Jack doesn't. I have to know."

"Can't you just please let this be?" Dinah asked. She sniffled and wiped her nose. "You won't like what I have to say."

"There's nothing you can say that would be worse than staying silent and letting this secret eat away at you," Jenny said. "There'll be nothing left of us if you won't tell."

"There'll be nothing left of us if I do."

"Dinah, the truth will never hurt me as much as you lying to me again."

"The truth?" Dinah let out a mirthless chuckle, and her face twisted in pain. "Fine! It was me, Jenny! Are you happy now!? I killed RJ Valentine!"

Chapter Twenty-Nine
Teacher's Pet

*S*HE WAS THE PERFECT BLONDE. SIXTEEN YEARS OLD. BEAUTIFUL. THE *Homecoming Queen. Head Cheerleader. A black belt in taekwondo. Number 1 in her class. She had a brand-new Acura ILX parked out front, and she was dating Jack Valentine, whom all the girls agreed was the cutest—and richest—boy in school.*

Naturally, Dinah Black was depressed.

Not that she could say anything about it. Everyone would hate her! What right did she have to complain? She had everything a girl could want—except the space to be anything less than flawless.

Things were so much simpler a few years ago. Then puberty came, and attention from the opposite sex, and the realization that she wanted nothing to do with any of the boys in school, not even the cutest one, no matter how rich he was. This required further research. No worry, Dinah could out-study the best of them. She discovered feminism, and critical theory, and Tumblr. But the more she read, the more she scrolled, the more humanity revealed itself to be a terrible mistake. What was a future prom queen to do?

Say "yes" when Jack asked her out, apparently. He'd caught her by surprise in front of Meghan May and Shani Wolf, and he was so smooth and polite about it. Sure, she wasn't into him, but it would have been so much more awkward and rude to reject him, and Dinah Black was never awkward, never rude.

Jack wasn't the worst guy to spend time with. He was wry and well-spoken and occasionally even interesting when he let the mask slip to reveal his eccentricities. And he had excellent taste in music. Like her, he was hiding all the cool parts of himself under layers of rehearsed emotion. Maybe he was gay, too? Nah, he spent far too much brainpower devising new schemes to get under her sweater for that.

It was one such scheme that sent her to the Valentine Manor study for the first time. They were on Christmas break, and Jack had found a silly hat with a little wobbly spring on top that dangled mistletoe out in front of him. She informed Jack there would be no kissing until he finished his winter reading, and removed herself from his presence so he wouldn't be distracted.

Jack's dad was supposed to be in New York for some book thing, so Dinah retreated into his study. She liked the smell in there—all that leather and ink. She helped herself to a club soda from the minibar and curled up on the fainting couch with a refugee memoir that everyone on Book Twitter agreed was an essential read for "doing the work." The exact "work" remained elusive, but as a perfect blonde, Dinah had a lot of it to do.

"Can I ask you a question?"

Dinah snapped awake, fumbling with the book on her chest. She'd only dozed off for a moment, and Jack's dad had somehow materialized right in front of her. How embarrassing! He looked a lot like Jack, except he wore a tweed blazer instead of athletic hoodies, and a shit-eating grin instead of Jack's sulky pout.

"I'm sorry, I can go!" she said.

She leaped to her feet and knocked over her glass of club soda on the carpet.

"Oh! Shoot! Sorry!"

She was mortified, but Mr. Valentine just laughed. "Better put some club soda on that," he said.

"Um, it is club soda, Mr. Valentine," said Dinah.

"I know, that's the joke," he said. "Don't worry about it, we have a maid."

Mr. Valentine had an odd quirk of moving his lips after he spoke, like he was talking to himself. He did that now as he grabbed a dish towel from the minibar to throw over the club soda. Dinah inched toward the door, looking for a suitable opening to leave.

"I'll go find her," she said.

"Ah ah ah!" he said. "You haven't answered my question."

Dinah blinked, running back the conversation, and replied, "Yes, but only one."

He nodded to the book in her hand. "Do you enjoy *reading books like that?" he asked.*

"Enjoy isn't the word I'd use," said Dinah. "They can be enriching. You learn something new about the world. Gain other perspectives."

"Hmm. I'm going to overstep my mandate if you'll allow it, and ask one more question," said Mr. Valentine. "What's the last book you read for fun?"

"Fun?" Dinah repeated. "I um... Why?"

"Every time I see you with Jack, you've got this bright smile plastered on your face, and then I read your eyes, and they say you're fucking miserable. No offense. So I was curious if girls like you ever read for fun. I'm hoping you do because I'm trying to move some Trouble *books."*

Girls like you... If he was implying something, he didn't show it. He was doing that thing with his mouth again, staring past Dinah.

"I've read the Trouble *books," said Dinah.*

"Oh yeah? Who's the Stranger?"

"You," said Dinah. "Er, Trouble's father, I mean."

He rolled his eyes, annoyed, and mumbled something about a "baseless theory with no evidence."

"It's just that there's no other interesting option," said Dinah. "There aren't enough recurring characters from book to book, so who else would it be? Lockhart? The evil heiress?"

"I see," said Mr. Valentine. His lips moved under his breath again.

"Pride and Prejudice," said Dinah. "I read that every year because I like it."

She was expecting another eye roll. Instead, Mr. Valentine smiled.

"Well, you're not hopeless, at least. You're welcome to stay. I was just

looking for a pen." He grabbed a Montblanc from the pen holder on his desk. *"But, if I could be so bold as to offer some unsolicited advice: life is short, read for fun more often."*

"What's fun to you, besides Trouble?"

He pointed with the pen to the bookcase in the corner behind her. "Fourth shelf from the bottom, on the right side. Orange-and-black spine."

Dinah was intrigued to see what bigshot author RJ Valentine considered a fun read. Watch it be, like, Fight Club. *She walked to the bookcase and searched for the book with the orange-and-black spine.*

The Robber Bride
By Margaret Atwood

"Oh, I've wanted to read this," said Dinah. "But they never test for Canadian literature, only British and American…"

She looked back to see his reaction and gasped. The room was empty.

WHEN DINAH RETURNED TO VALENTINE MANOR A WEEK LATER, SHE'D *convinced herself she imagined the whole conversation. It was New Year's Eve, and she wore her favorite navy blue evening dress to watch Jack and Mason play* Dance Dance Revolution *in the game room. They were getting quite competitive and appeared to have forgotten all about their dates.*

"What do you say, D?" Charlie Zaleska asked, nudging her with an elbow. "Should we show the boys how a body's supposed to move?"

Dinah fought the urge to blush. How was she not *supposed to stare at those crimson lips? Charlie flicked her tongue out, licking a drop of fruit punch from the corner of her mouth. Was she flirting…? No, Dinah was imagining things. Charlie had come as Mason's date. Granted, Mason only asked her hoping she'd bring Meghan May (she had not), but still.*

"In this dress? No way," said Dinah. "Actually, I need some air."

She got up from the couch and slipped into the hall. Muffled sounds of old rock music spilled out from the ballroom next door. The adult party was happening in there. Curious, Dinah peeked in to check it out. As the Blackthorn heir, she was used to mixing with her elders and wouldn't stand out like the other teens would.

"Dinah! Had enough of the kids' table?" a tipsy Valerie Valentine asked.

"Jack's having fun," said Dinah.

Val gave her a knowing smile and pushed a glass of sparkling wine into her hand.

"Oh, I shouldn't," said Dinah.

"Please," said Val. "I had to buy three cases of this swill off of Horace Carnegie to assuage his wounded pride after my husband teased him for calling it champagne. One glass won't hurt anything except your tastebuds."

Dinah thanked her and took a sip. It tasted like corked pinot gris mixed with Sprite.

"Oh, god."

"Right?" said Val. "Are you coming over tomorrow for the Christmas tree bonfire?"

"Jack hadn't mentioned it," said Dinah.

"Nonsense, you don't need an invite," said Val. "And I need help with our thank-you cards. God knows Johnny won't lend a hand."

"Where is Mr. Valentine?" Dinah asked, looking past her at the other adults in the ballroom.

Val rolled her eyes. "Sulking in his study because Declan brought Rob Haines with him." Val pursed her lips, and a little sympathy leached into her cheeks. "Also, he's not the biggest fan of New Year's Eve. Can you go grab him? Tell him we'd love it if he joined us."

Before she could protest, Val had pressed another glass of Carnegie sparkling wine into Dinah's free hand and sent her off down the hall. She found RJ's study door closed and Declan Dillion fiddling with the intercom.

"Come on, Johnny," Declan said into the little box on the wall. "It's five grand; that's like pocket change to you."

"So ask Val, then," came Mr. Valentine's voice over the intercom.

*"I did, she said to ask you," said Declan. He let go of the **Talk** button and did that thing all men do where their eyes traversed Dinah's body and did a mental calculation. For some reason, the answer their little hamster*

wheels spit out was always: neg her. "What happened, you get bored of pretending to care about Junior?"

Even if I were straight, I'd still never date your scrawny ginger ass.

"I'm not pretending," said Dinah.

"Okay, then no," said Mr. Valentine over the intercom. "Leave me alone, I'm writing."

"Sure you're not," said Declan. He scowled at the intercom and gave it the finger before turning to Dinah. "What's the score with you and Jack? Think you could get him to loan me five grand? Or would that require breaking your famous vow of chastity?"

"You're such an ass, Declan."

"A shame they don't have a daughter your age," said Declan. "The things we do to save our family businesses."

He made a gesture with his thumb and forefinger.

"I don't know what you're talking about," said Dinah. "But I'm not dating Jack for his money. My family is doing fine, thank you."

"But not Valentine fine," said Declan. "You know the best thing about money? Having more of it."

"I'm not asking Jack for five grand for you."

Declan leaned closer and spoke softly. "You're not the only one like you in Blackbird Springs. Just because we don't advertise it doesn't mean we don't exist. I'm sure Jack's a nice boy, but he's not your tribe. I can show you a whole new world if you help a guy out."

How did Declan know? Was she broadcasting something? Were there cute girls in this tribe?

The door to the study swung open before Dinah could even formulate a response.

"Piss off, Declan, she's only fifteen," said Mr. Valentine in the doorway.

"I'm sixteen," said Dinah.

"Ah hell, that means Jack's about to be sixteen. And—" Mr. Valentine paused. "Yeah."

He mouthed a word under his breath: Trouble.

"Think about it, Johnny," said Declan, walking away. "You too, Miss Black."

Jack's dad left the door hanging open and retreated into his study.

Dinah, still holding two glasses of sparkling wine, shrugged and followed him inside.

"What did he want five grand for?" Dinah asked.

"To stake him in some poker tournament," said Mr. Valentine. "He can't even beat me. I'd have better odds putting it all on black. No pun intended."

"Haha. Mrs. Valentine would like you to come join the party," said Dinah. "But I hear New Year's isn't your favorite?"

"Not since my twenties." He took both champagne flutes from her. "You don't want this; it will give you a headache."

Dinah stole a glance at the laptop on Mr. Valentine's desk while he disposed of the sparkling wine and got to work mixing something else at the minibar. A Google search page was up with results for: **popular cars for teenagers**.

"How would you characterize the severity of Val's request?" he asked over his shoulder. "Am I going to be in trouble, hehe, if I don't go make an appearance?"

"I think she'd appreciate it," said Dinah. "So Trouble's turning sixteen, then? Is that why you're taking so long on the next book, Mr. Valentine?"

"Can you please call me RJ or something?" he asked. "It's not even my real name, so you don't have to feel weird. Nobody calls me Mr. Valentine except the The New York Times."

"Avoiding the question," Dinah replied.

"I'm under NDA."

"You own the publishing company."

He turned around from the minibar with two tumblers of something pale and yellow, garnished with a slice of grapefruit.

"Tell me what you thought of your reading assignment, and maybe I'll spill," he said, handing one of the glasses over to her.

"Oh, um."

"You did read it, didn't you?"

"Yes, but…" She tried to collect her thoughts on the book and found her mind had gone blank. "I think I'm still processing. What is this?" she asked, pointing to her drink.

"A paloma."

Dinah took a sip, and her mouth puckered. "This is grapefruit juice."

"Yeah."

"Well, what's in yours?"

"Tequila," said RJ. "You thought you were getting hard liquor? You're fifteen, kid."

"Sixteen. And I'm not a kid."

Dinah glared at him. A flicker of concern crossed his face.

"You know what, I better go make an appearance," RJ said, plastering on his usual smirk and ushering them both to the door. "Don't want Val starting the year pissed at me. Why don't you give me five hundred words on The Robber Bride *the next time you're over here."*

"Like a book report?" Dinah asked.

"Writing helps you process your thoughts," he said. "Jack says you want to get into Brown, right?"

She nodded.

"Then five hundred. No quotes to pad it out."

AND OKAY, GOING STRAIGHT HOME AFTER THE BALL DROPPED AND STAYING *up till 4:00 AM to write the essay was a little Type A. But Dinah had always been a people pleaser. And she had an Adderall scrip.*

She slept all morning, plagued by dreams where Declan introduced her to the illicit Blackbird Springs underworld and everyone called her a poser and a bore. Then it was back to the mansion. She and Jack spent the afternoon helping Val write thank-you cards and pack up ornaments before the bonfire.

The Valentines had a tradition of burning their Christmas tree in the courtyard every New Year, and given that the tree was fifteen feet tall, it made for quite an alarming conflagration. Beautiful, though. With the red flames and the golden hour sunset, she got some great pics with Jack for Insta. Hashtag 2019aGoodYearForDinah.

The tree went quickly, and they retired to Jack's bedroom for the usual makeout session. Dinah let it go on for twelve minutes before making her excuses to leave. But rather than head to the roundabout driveway where her Acura was waiting, Dinah kept walking through the grand foyer until she reached the door to RJ's study. She smoothed her hair, doing her best to look like she hadn't just been kissing a boy, and knocked.

"Come in, Dinah," came RJ's voice from within.

"How'd you know it was me?" she asked as she entered.

He was at his desk, his laptop open, staring at his crystal bishop paperweight.

"Val would never knock, and Jack has not yet mastered the art of stepping softly," said RJ, without looking up.

"Impressive."

"No, I was guessing," he said. "Trouble's second maxim: bad liars will tell you five pointless details. True artists only need a single good one."

"What are you doing?" Dinah asked.

"Writing," said RJ. His fingers did not move on the keyboard. "What's another word for distraction?"

"Diversion," said Dinah. "You're being facetious, never mind."

Before she could leave, he snapped his fingers and beckoned her over. Dinah pouted and slapped her work on his desk. Two pages, double-spaced, in Times New Roman.

"You should try Palatino," he said. From his desk drawer, he withdrew a pair of reading glasses and a cheap purple gel pen. "Take a seat, this will be a few minutes."

Dinah drifted toward the minibar. "Okay if I get a drink?"

"Sure."

"I'm adding tequila this time."

"No, you're not."

Dinah couldn't hide her smile. RJ had a certain rakish charisma to his credit. The kind that a quarter of a billion dollars in Fuck You money bought you. It was hard not to feel special to have earned his spiky banter instead of the usual PR-trained platitudes. She made herself an Italian soda and waited patiently for him to finish.

When he slid the pages back over, they were covered in purple marks. Dinah's heart sank. She'd never had a paper come back so thoroughly eviscerated. Like, ever.

"Thick skin," said RJ. "It's never personal. Try those changes out and see how they feel. You don't need to bring me another revision, I trust you."

There was a dismissal in there. She rose from her chair.

"Thank you."

"You want another one?" he asked.

She managed to keep her expression neutral this time. "Why don't you tell me what you *were reading for fun at my age, because I know it wasn't Margaret Atwood."*

RJ smirked and got up to select a book.

A STRANGE ROUTINE TOOK SHAPE. DINAH WOULD VISIT JACK AFTER SCHOOL, when he didn't have practice or a game, and spend her time with him. They'd do their homework and watch a movie and sometimes she'd give him a pity handjob. Then she'd head downstairs for her sessions with RJ.

At first, their meetings were brief: a quick edit and a few exchanges about that week's book. But as January turned to February, their talks grew longer. One night, she was shocked to discover they'd been discussing The Diamond Age *for so long that her mother called. She'd missed her curfew. Dinah didn't even know she had a curfew. Her parents had never needed to set one.*

"Shoot, I gotta go."

Grabbing her new book assignment, she hopped to her feet and turned to the study door.

"Uh, you might have trouble that way," he said. "Val will have set the alarm."

"So give me the code," Dinah said.

"I'll do you one better," said RJ.

He ushered her over to the corner next to his desk and gestured at the bookshelf.

"Let's see how much you've learned," he said. "Pick the right book."

He loved these cryptic games. When this had first started, Dinah wondered why he bothered to spend time with her. By now, she'd realized that the answer was simple: to be an author was a solitary activity. It helped him to have Dinah around. The reason he liked explaining writing techniques to her was because he was really explaining them to himself. She was just there to prompt him. In exchange, she got free lessons from a world-famous writer. Fair trade.

"That's not much of a hint," she said.

"You'll know it when you see it. What's the one book on this shelf that no one is ever going to want to pull off and read?"

Tough question. Dinah would give any book a try if the spine grabbed her. She scanned the book titles, looking for an outlier. The only kinds of books he didn't like were romance and non-fiction.

"Oh, very funny," said Dinah.

At shoulder level was a familiar title: that refuge memoir she'd been reading in here before New Year's. He nodded, inviting her to take it off the shelf. When she pulled on the spine, it would only tilt, like it was stuck. She pulled harder. With a distinct thunk! *the whole bookcase swung out from the wall to reveal a hidden passage.*

"So that's how you do your disappearing act!" she said.

"It will take you to the conservatory, which is past the alarm on the east entrance," said RJ. "But keep this a secret, will ya? Even Jack doesn't know."

*F*OR *V*ALENTINE'S *D*AY, *D*INAH *DYED THE FRONT TENDRILS OF HER HAIR NEON blue; her secret tribute to Léa Seydoux in* Blue is the Warmest Color. *She was a perfect blonde no longer. Jack thought it was for him. Hah!*

She started coming to Valentine Manor when Jack was at practice or out with the boys. RJ gave her the gate and alarm codes and installed the garage door app on her phone so she could park underground. He let her use his office when he wasn't there; she could sneak in via the secret passage, and no one was the wiser.

Deep down, in the back of her mind, Dinah knew this was suspect behavior. But whatever. She was already hiding her sexuality; what was one more deception?

It's not like she was doing anything wrong, and RJ was never weird about it. They hadn't discussed it, but he seemed to understand that she wasn't into guys. From the way he talked about the romance parts of the books they read, she got the impression that he had loved a girl once, long ago, and it didn't end well. That part of life no longer interested him. He had his hands full with crazy fans sending him love letters stapled to their underwear, anyway.

In March, there was an awkward moment when Tori came into the study unexpectedly, but RJ played it off like he was surprised to see Dinah. It turned out Tori was on her way to rehab anyway, so there was nothing to worry about.

At least, Dinah didn't think so. But ever since that day, something in RJ changed. He seemed more edgy and paranoid, though he was adamant it had nothing to do with her. He'd have to kick her out occasionally to meet with his lawyer, a hawk-nosed man with horn-rimmed glasses who made Dinah nervous for no reason she could put her finger on.

"Do you ever use Signal?" RJ asked her one day.

Dinah took a sip of her virgin paloma and frowned. "Is that the app where your texts delete after you read them?" she asked.

"It's supposed to be totally secure."

"Can't say that I have," said Dinah.

RJ scribbled something on his stationery and tore off the corner to hand her.

RJ — Signal
ReynarddeFuchs

"Just in case," he said.

"In case of what?"

"I'm worried someone's trying to hack my messages," he said. "Maybe that crazy woman who thinks she's having my baby. I might have to go off the grid."

"Just get a restraining order already," said Dinah.

She tucked the scrap of paper into her school copy of The Catcher in the Rye *and promptly forgot about it.*

"I could also send you chapters of the book that way," he said.

"I told you, I'm not reading it till it's done," said Dinah. "I hate reading little pieces, and you'll go back and change everything anyway."

"Fine," said RJ. He nodded to her book. "What do you think so far?"

"This feels very much like a boy book," said Dinah.

"You're such a Sally Hayes," said RJ.

339

Spring turned to summer. Dinah went on college trips to visit Brown and Yale, so she wasn't around as often, but RJ always had a mischievous smile for her when she returned. He was up to something. He must be getting close to finishing the new book. The lawyer, Mr. Webb, came around often now. Dinah would have to go wait in the secret passage while they conspired in low voices about some ambitious new project. From what Dinah could make out, they were planning some sort of game. A big marketing stunt for Trouble 13, *she guessed.*

"The hardest thing to do as a writer is keep a secret," he told her one evening over mocktails. "You're going to want so badly to tell, to talk about your work and your craft. Don't. It's a trap. Nobody cares except for the weirdos, and you don't want them to know, the internet makes them too clever…"

He trailed off, his mouth still moving as he rehearsed versions of the dialogue in his head.

Jack texted her.

> **The Boy:** How do you feel about a romantic dinner?
>
> **Dinah:** I'd love it. With who?
>
> **The Boy:** Very funny, I'll send the driver over.

Awkward, she was sixty feet away in the same building.

> **Dinah:** No need, I'll be there in an hour. Can we do Mexican?

Jack might explode from horny soon. They were juniors now, and their anniversary was coming up. Hadn't they waited long enough? Mason and Meghan were definitely doing it, according to Jack (true). And if Drew Porter ever got up the courage to ask out Penny Griffin or Lily Geist, they would be, too (LOL, fat chance).

Dinah probably should have broken up with Jack, but she'd been too careless with his heart. Despite her mild interest, he'd become besotted with her. Maybe it wouldn't be so bad. She'd let him return the favor now and then, and occasionally she felt something. What if she was bi? Dinah made a silent deal with herself: try it with Jack, and then you'll know for sure. And if it's not for you, you're allowed to come out.

Once she gave Jack the green light, he devoted himself to making things perfect. The night of the Valentine Foundation Gala was coming up, which would get Val and RJ out of the mansion. Dinah's parents would be out of town, and Jack invented a fake summer reading assignment that he needed to stay home from the gala to work on.

As the big event drew closer, Dinah's stomach tightened, and she could hardly eat. It was just nerves, she told herself.

Her boyfriend, meanwhile, was becoming as paranoid as RJ. Tori came back from rehab, and Jack declared all his plans were in shambles. No, wait! She wasn't staying at the mansion. False alarm! Then, the day before the gala, RJ kicked everyone out of the mansion, and Jack was convinced his parents were onto him.

"*Well, what'd he say?*" *asked Dinah.*

They were getting fro-yo at Mystery Flavors. Dinah guessed right: it was blueberry.

"*He said he was meeting with a VIP, and that they demanded total secrecy,*" *said Jack.* "*He's acting super weird. I wonder if he found the box of condoms I bought.*"

Inwardly, Dinah's guts churned. She set her fro-yo aside, no longer hungry.

"*I'm sure it has nothing to do with you,*" *said Dinah.* "*Relax, or I'm calling it off.*"

You should call it off anyway.

RJ hadn't mentioned anything about a VIP, though…

No worry, the night of the gala arrived without further incident. Dinah did as Jack instructed and drove to the end of Cellar Drive to park, then hiked back to enter through the conservatory. The hidden entrance to the secret passage called to her. She wanted to go see RJ—if he hadn't left yet—and find out what was troubling him. He'd become a friend, and she was concerned.

Instead, she entered the mansion and went up to see Jack. He was mildly freaking out because RJ was, in fact, still at home. Holed up in his study, writing.

"No offense, Jack, but I don't think he cares," said Dinah. *"You can't hear anything from the east wing in the study, anyway."*

Jack's libido won out, and they got down to business. Dinah really did try, but the body said no. The door was shut. No boys allowed.

You have to tell him. It's not fair to him either, you know.

Dinah knew, but it was hard. He'd be heartbroken. He'd be convinced he'd done something wrong.

It truly isn't you, Jack. It's me.

She pretended to fall asleep but was inwardly cringing at his arm draped across her. Now that she knew for sure, she didn't want to be touched by a man ever again. The very idea of it was making her itch all over, and she was close to screaming when Jack finally pulled his arm away and left to take care of himself. Dinah waited thirty seconds before throwing on her clothes and sneaking downstairs to the conservatory. RJ was at his desk when she stepped out from the secret passage, his feet kicked up on the calendar blotter. He was holding a framed photo.

"How's Jack's reading assignment?" he asked, smirking that smirk of his.

Dinah shaded crimson. Oh god, did he know?

"Not to the boy's liking, I'm afraid." She was mortified. *"Can I have a real paloma, just this once?"*

"Well, okay," RJ said, pulling his feet off the desk. *"Since it's a special occasion."*

While he mixed drinks, she peeked at the photo. It was a much younger RJ and a cute Asian woman in a halter top standing in front of the old Poison Pen.

"Let me guess," Dinah said, holding up the photo frame. *"Was she The One?"*

"One of them," RJ said. He returned with the drinks. *"I only put a single shot in there. À votre santé!"*

They clinked glasses, and she took a sip. Ugh! Maybe tequila was not her thing. RJ chuckled at her face and put the framed photo back in his desk drawer.

"So what's the occasion, anyway?" she asked.

"Oh, right, right, you don't know," he said with another smirk that

seemed to suggest she did *know.* "It's okay. I think we can move past that now."

He got up and came around in front of his desk.

"Yeah, sure," Dinah said, baffled.

He rolled his eyes, like Dinah was being silly. Then he leaned in to kiss her.

It happened on instinct. Years of taekwondo for self-defense took over. Before his lips were close enough to touch, her palm shot forward in an open-palm strike to push him back, followed by a roundhouse kick that sent him stumbling backward—

"Hey!" he exclaimed.

—right onto the edge of his giant desk.

Crack! *The back of his head hit the corner. His body crumpled and hit the carpet, the paloma spilling out next to him.*

"Oh my god! Oh, no! I didn't mean to!"

He wasn't moving. Dinah rushed over and shook him.

"RJ, come on! I'm sorry, it's just—"

He didn't respond. She tried to turn his head, and it just flopped over, limp.

"Oh no no no! Why did you do that? I'm so sorry!"

She felt for the wound, and her fingers came away wet. Blood.

It couldn't be. It shouldn't be. It absolutely wasn't! Except it was. Dinah had just killed RJ Valentine.

Chapter Thirty

Paintball

"You didn't kill RJ," said Jenny. With a sigh, she stood up and tested her sore foot in an old pair of shoes Dinah found in the closet. Every step was pain. "Believe me, it would be so much easier if you did. You didn't know, but in the medical report, he had two head injuries from that night. The first one, from you, would have given him a concussion. Nothing more. The killing blow came after, in the ambulance. This doesn't solve anything."

"I see," said Dinah. Her eyes were lost in a thousand-yard stare. "How did you…?"

"That trailer park house I made Jack take us to. That was the EMT who drove RJ to the hospital," said Jenny. She ground her sore heel on the carpet, forcing herself to bear it. "Dalton would have been able to identify whoever rode in the back with RJ, but it doesn't matter now because Dalton's dead. Just another dead end, courtesy of the Stranger."

Dinah sniffled. "You're angry."

Jenny's whole fucking body was on fire.

"Not at you."

"This is why I didn't want to tell."

"People need to stop fucking walking on eggshells with me!" Jenny shouted. "I get it! He sucked. You and Lizzy and Shelly were all right about him, and I'm the idiot! Is that what I'm supposed to say?"

Jenny flopped back into the rocking chair and buried her face in her hands.

"You don't know how many times I've replayed that moment in my mind," Dinah said. "What if he wasn't trying to kiss me? Could he have meant to whisper something in my ear? Did I overreact because of what happened with Jack? I have tried to gaslight myself on it over and over again, but no, Jenny! It *did* happen that way. He *was* trying to kiss me. I know I didn't imagine it."

"I believe you, Dinah." The words burned like acid as they came out of Jenny's mouth. "I wish I didn't. But I do."

Dinah came over and clutched her hand, fresh tears on her cheeks. "Thank you," she tried to say, though no sound left her lips.

"I-I think I understand what was happening there," said Jenny. "He thought he'd been talking to you on Signal. But it doesn't excuse him. You did nothing wrong."

Dinah wrapped her arms around Jenny's quivering body and squeezed tight. Jenny let her. In a way, it felt like surrender. But it also felt good.

"So, what'd you do next?" Jenny asked. "After you thought you'd killed him. They only found the one glass next to RJ."

"I had to clean up," said Dinah. "I washed the blood off my fingers at the minibar, and washed my paloma glass, too. I wiped everywhere I had touched with a napkin, except I forgot about the framed photo. I was so paranoid you would dust it for prints and find out."

"Hah," said Jenny. "A real detective would have done that. I'm just a fucking moron with daddy issues. God, that's why he made Trouble a lesbian. Not because he'd been checking in on me or whatever. He just wanted his self-insert to flirt with you. I might throw up."

"Jenny, you're one of the smartest people I know," said Dinah. "And I'm smarter than you, so that's a compliment. You just have certain blinders on. We all do. Look at me, never once guessing at RJ's intention with all those private lessons."

Sure, whatever. Jenny was in no mood for compliments. The void in her soul had grown so large that she felt little more than a bag of skin stretched taut over a terrible abyss.

"I can already feel myself rationalizing for him," said Jenny. "I'm so fucking toxic."

"Girl, you think I don't?" said Dinah.

Jenny shook her head, disgusted with herself. "Wouldn't people have seen your footprints?" she asked. "That carpet is so thick; everything shows on it."

"I used the edge of a book spine, dragging it behind me as I left," said Dinah. "When I went back through the passageway, I nearly ran into Valerie Valentine. She was just chilling there in the conservatory. Thank god I thought to check the peephole first."

"What'd she do?"

"Nothing. She stood there looking at her phone for ten minutes," said Dinah. "I was losing my shit. I knew I had to get upstairs before Jack got back. Anyway, Val finally left. I snuck back into the east entrance and ran upstairs. I'd barely pulled my clothes off and dove under the covers when Jack came in. And I think you know the rest."

All the clues had been there. The way Dinah had easily found and used the secret passage when Jenny described it over the phone. The way she knew about RJ's purple pens. The way she knew—not suspected, *knew*—that Jenny had framed Val for RJ's murder. The way she always begged Jenny to drop it when asked about August 10th—even if it broke them up...

Jenny's brain had noted them all yet steadfastly refused to connect the dots. What else was she subconsciously refusing to connect because she might not like the answer?

"Why did you sleep with me last night?" she asked.

"I wanted—I needed to feel something different," said Dinah. "I wanted to feel in control."

"Did it help?"

"A little."

her groggy brain struggled to come back online and locate the threat.

She pawed for a weapon, but the bed was empty save for Dinah, whose arm was draped around from behind, holding Jenny's heart in her hand.

"What is it?" Dinah breathed in her ear.

The shrieking noise morphed and shifted in her head. It wasn't quite a scream anymore. Now it sounded more like a crowing rooster.

"Nothing. Sorry."

Gray light filtered in through the curtains. It was early morning. Jenny reluctantly wriggled out of Dinah's embrace, kissed her on the mouth, and told her not to worry. Dinah was fast asleep again in moments.

Jenny eased herself out of the bed they'd colonized in the back room and got dressed. She'd slept like death—at least until the horrible dreams began. Visions of the Stranger killing Willie. Eliza getting her eye torn out. Her father leaning in to kiss Dinah... And Jimmy Figg for some reason.

Her subconscious was trying to tell her something. Jenny couldn't fathom what, but now she was wide awake and full of antsy energy.

A heavy object bumped her hip when she pulled on her purple Burberry trench coat. She reached into her coat pocket, and her fingers touched cold steel. Right. Mirai's pistol. It was breaking RJ's canon, but who was he to be lecturing anyone about playing by the rules at this point?

Speaking of Mirai, where was her son? Jenny peeked into the room across the hall. The sheets on the empty twin-size bed were rumpled from use. She had a vague memory of Drew's truck crunching over the gravel outside, well past midnight. He must have returned alone, which could only mean...

No! It's not over till they find a body. She made it. She has to.

In the kitchen, Jenny found a note that solved Drew's absence.

> **Trouble,**
> **No luck last night. Too dark. I'm headed out at first**
> **light. ~~I'll bring back supplies~~ WE will bring back supplies**
> **after I find Kaz.**
> **— Your sidekick, Drew**

She found a ballpoint pen and left a response.

> **Drew,**
> **We'll find her. Don't lose hope.**
>
> **Dinah,**
> **I'm going for a walk, trying to jolt loose a thought. If I'm not back by noon, it means it worked.**
> **— Trouble**

Outside the cabin, the forest was covered in thick mist. Her scavenged shoes made scant sound on the gravel as she headed down the long driveway from Lockhart's cabin. A walk was no small task with her sore foot, but a night's rest and an extra sock did a lot to ease her pain. By her rough estimate, she was eight miles from town. She could cover that in three hours, maybe, if her foot cooperated.

What would she do when she got there, dressed like Trouble, a gun in her pocket, wanted by the FBI? Well, she had three hours to figure that out.

It only took two.

The forest gave way to the rolling, golden-green hills of Calistoga County Wine Country. Jenny was walking in the soft soil between rows of chardonnay grapevines to avoid Highway 12. She'd been ruminating on all the contradictory clues—excerpts from *I Dream of Trouble*, witness accounts, unverified alibis—and arrived at three mutually exclusive theories.

Theory No. 1: The Stranger was RJ Valentine/RJ's evil twin. The man in the tomb was the other twin, which was why the DNA test didn't give him away. Maybe the good RJ loved her mother, and the bad twin tried to groom Dinah... This theory was the least plausible.

Theory No. 2: There was no Stranger. Old Killroy was just a spooky story that the wealthy elite of Blackbird Springs hid behind to do their evil deeds. He was Arty Porter, Jeffrey Jordan, One-eyed Willie, and Jorge Lopez, too. RJ had been trying to expose them in the pages of *I Dream of Trouble* (when not writing creepy fanfic scenes starring his latest ingenue pupil—Jesus Christ, Dad!) and so they had him killed. This one Jenny liked the best.

Theory No. 3: The Stranger was someone very, very close to Jenny. Someone she knew well, considered a friend or mentor, and trusted implicitly. Someone she wore blinders for. Their motive would be multifarious, dependent on the culprit. RJ Valentine, with his charm, his wealth, his misanthropy, his weak morals, and his venomous opportunism, had done a masterful job of seeding love and enmity in all his acquaintances. When Jenny inherited her framed photo, she also inherited this ardent antagonism from his arch-nemesis, too. This theory scared Jenny the most and was, therefore, correct.

Up ahead, the edge of the vineyard property loomed, hemmed in by a loose barbed wire fence. Jenny ducked underneath it and crossed into undeveloped land. She climbed the golden grass to the top of a short ridge and found a basin of California poppies sloping down the other side. Highway 12 was near at hand on her right, and beyond the poppy field stood a grove of oak trees and tall redwoods. Indistinct shouts and electronic beeps carried to her on the breeze from the pocket forest beyond the poppies.

Jenny walked through the flowers, curious, seeking the source of the noise. As she grew nearer, she could make out a chain-link fence surrounding the wooded area, disguised with camo netting. A dirt parking lot had been cleared next to the highway, and a squat, square building stood nearby. More shouts reached her, excited and urgent, interspersed with hissing snaps, all coming from the enclosed trees.

Jimmy Figg's face swam up from her unconscious again. This noise, these snaps; they reminded her of him.

There was a gap in the fence where it had made room for a protected live oak, and this pint-sized Girl Detective was still small enough to squeeze through. What she found on the other side was an arena. The forest floor was covered in cedar chips, and bales of hay were scattered amongst the trees for cover. A recorded voice on a loudspeaker announced something about the next round.

All over the tree trunks and hay bales were splatters of paint in every shade of neon.

"Hey! What are you doing?"

Jenny turned toward the male voice, and a pudgy man covered head to toe in military camouflage stepped out from behind a redwood. He was holding an oddly shaped carbine rifle with a wide barrel and a bulbous cartridge attached over the trigger mechanism.

"Oh!" said Jenny. "Paintball!"

The man had on a wraparound half-helmet with a transparent visor of ballistic plastic. He frowned behind it and asked another question, but Jenny didn't hear him. She was no longer in the arena.

*S*HE WAS A FEW MILES AWAY, STANDING ON THE SIDEWALK OUTSIDE THE *Crow's Nest hotel. It was nighttime.*

Jimmy Figg skidded to a stop on his bicycle, wearing a ski mask. He raised his paintball gun at her, emptied his hopper, and missed every shot.

Jenny turned around to admire the paint splatter on the Crow's Nest doors—and RJ Valentine stepped out of the hotel.

"What the hell was that?" he asked, favoring her with his trademark mischievous grin.

"Jimmy fucking Figg," Jenny said. "But I won't figure that out till later."

"Waaayyy later. That was a big miss on your part," the RJ in her mind replied.

Jenny was in no mood for a lecture from this motherfucker. "How could you? How could you do that to Dinah? To me?"

"Come on, what have I ever done to you?" he replied.

"Exactly!" Jenny shouted. "You never visited! Not even once! Are you going to tell me that was because of some bullshit with the Campions and Villanova? That you were protecting me?"

"It's a good theory," said RJ. "It would explain a lot."

"It doesn't explain what you did to Dinah."

"I mean"—RJ shrugged—"maybe I was going to whisper something in her ear."

"You weren't."

"Maybe I was about to share some secret with her," RJ said. "Oh! What if I had just discovered who the Stranger was?! And I was about to tell her! Yes, what if, right on the very night I was going to fake my coma, I learned

the truth about the Stranger? But then, when I tried to share it with Dinah, she kicked me into the desk and knocked me unconscious anyway. Don't you love the dramatic irony! It adds a certain tragic grandeur to the whole affair, don't you think?"

"You can't gaslight me, you're my subconscious," said Jenny.

"Don't use therapy speak on me, we're not like them," said RJ.

"I don't know who I am anymore. Or who you were."

RJ shrugged and spread his hands out in surrender. "What do you want me to say? I screwed up."

"How can you be so glib?" Jenny asked, disgusted.

"This is your daydream, Trouble, not mine," said RJ. "I wish I hadn't done it, if that's what you're asking. There's a lot I wish I hadn't done. I got those Signal messages and let my lesser angels start to believe in a different storyline, because I was sick of the one I was in."

He took a step forward and gestured for Jenny to follow his gaze. Jimmy Figg was still there on his bike, still aiming the paintball gun at her, like he'd been frozen in time.

"People like you and I, we're the easiest marks," RJ said. "We're so paranoid, and we don't trust anybody. But when we do, when we finally let a person inside our armor, and it's the wrong person? There's no telling how much we'll miss before we finally realize we've been had."

A chill took hold at the root of Jenny's spine. "Is that a hint?" she asked.

"I liked your second theory," said RJ. "The whole town being in on it. Very Murder on the Orient Express.*"*

"But it's not the right one," said Jenny.

"No, it's not."

RJ put a hand on her shoulder, and Jenny tried her hardest to imagine she could feel him. But he wasn't really there.

"What did I miss? Something with Jimmy and paintball?" Jenny asked.

"Think back. What else do you remember about this night?" RJ said, nodding to Jimmy.

"I'd been trying to get info from Jack about Alicia Aaron."

"You were wasting time at that stupid arcade and trying to stick it to Alicia Aaron because you thought she might be my secret bastard daughter."

"*Maybe I should have suspected she was your secret girlfriend!*" said Jenny.

"*It wasn't like that,*" said RJ, annoyed. "*Dinah was... a surprise. And we're not talking about me, we're talking about you, and how you took your eye off the ball, and got two of your friends killed.*"

Ouch. His words stung because they were true. Jenny glanced down, fighting back tears. "*I was in a bad place, and Lizzy wasn't speaking with me.*"

The chill climbed further up her spine, branching out to her arms and legs.

"*Maybe this will help.*" RJ pulled a smartphone from his pocket and snapped a photo of Jenny.

"*Hey! Delete that! I wasn't ready!*" said Jenny.

RJ smirked, turning his phone around to show her. Jenny got a good look at the girl in the picture, and the chill gripped her heart, freezing it to the core.

"*Oh my god,*" she whispered.

"*You're on your own now, kid,*" said RJ. "*You'd better hurry.*"

"Hello? Earth to Trouble? Jeez, this bitch is cooked."

Jenny blinked, coming out of her reverie to find the paintball man waving his hand in her face.

"Rude!" said Jenny. "I am perfectly sane and well-adjusted, buddy."

"Aren't you wanted for murder?" he asked.

"I'm wanted for *questioning* about a murder. Big difference," said Jenny. "Did you drive here?"

"Uh, yeah."

Jenny pulled out the little silver pistol from her coat pocket and stuck it in the guy's face.

"I'm gonna need to borrow your car," she said.

Paintball guy drove a big Ford pickup truck. Jenny drove recklessly, fishtailing all over the soft gravel at every turn and kicking up a massive dust cloud behind her. When she reached the cabin, she slammed on the brakes, skidding to a stop in the empty driveway.

"Dinah!!!" Jenny called out, sprinting to the cabin door. "Drew!!???"

There was no response. Cold terror churned in her stomach. She raced down the hall to the back room where she'd left Dinah. It was empty, the bed unmade.

No! No! No!

She ran back to the kitchen. Her note was still on the counter. She dove for it, hoping to find a reply from Dinah.

KiLLROY WAS HERE

And a doodle of the little man in the hat, peeking over. Jenny's stomach plummeted into the abyss. Beneath the drawing was a final threat from You-Know-Who.

VALENTINE MANOR. SATURDAY AT NOON.
YOU BRING THE TROUBLE, I'LL SUPPLY THE AUDIENCE
TELL NO ONE, OR I'LL KILL EVERYONE YOU LOVE

Jenny read the note twice. Saturday at noon. Her brain was mush. It took way too much effort to recall that today was only Thursday, April 1st. April Fool's Day... Wait! Could this all be a prank? No, Dinah would never do that, and Jenny wasn't laughing.

Why not tomorrow, Killroy? Why make me suffer through two days of anxiety?

Jenny studied the note in despair, racking her brain for some cockamamie scheme she could cook up against the Stranger in the next forty-eight hours. Minutes passed, but nothing came to mind. She needed Lizzy, but Lizzy was gone... In the distance, the soft hum of the forest was getting louder. Was it the wind?

Goosebumps on her arms said otherwise. Jenny rushed to the window and cracked it open. No, that wasn't the wind, that was a vehicle—someone was coming up the gravel road! Could it be Drew? Or the feds tracking her stolen truck??

Jenny couldn't risk waiting to find out. Scrambling back to the kitchen, she grabbed a rucksack and stuffed it with some dry goods and bottled water from the pantry. Thank god there was a second exit in the rear of the cabin. Jenny left through the back door, hopped off the deck, and rolled down the incline to the gully below.

Once she had her feet back underneath her, she didn't look back. Shouldering the rucksack, she ran headlong into the thickest part of the forest. Forty-eight hours. She had forty-eight hours to get back to the mansion. She was only eight-ish miles outside of town. It was doable, but her foot was already hurting again.

Jenny smiled despite herself, recalling a conversation she'd had with Lizzy once. Her dorky sister claimed that the *Trouble* books didn't count as true epic storytelling because Trouble never went camping. That, according to Eliza, was the sign of a real classic: Girl against Nature, and all that.

Are you happy now, Lizzy? You'd better be. You'd better be doing the same as me right now: hiking back to town. You'd better be planning your rematch with the Stranger.

You'd better be alive…

You have to be!

Chapter Thirty-One
A Wolf in Sheep's Clothing

There was a front-page story by Yvonne Griffin in the Friday morning edition of the *Blackbird Times* that had the whole town abuzz.

Murder Suspect's Body Found in Slough?

BLACKBIRD SPRINGS — The reign of terror that has claimed the lives of several residents and sparked a federal investigation may have come to an unexpected end. A local fisherman discovered a body in a slough south of town, which police believe to be that of Kazumi Onishi, the suspect wanted for the murders of local teens Meghan May and Mason Lockhart.

"We haven't yet officially identified the body, but we're confident this is the Onishi girl," said Acting Sheriff Miguel Calderon. "We have reason to believe this is connected to the incident on the Calistoga Express. It looks like she fell into the river and drowned trying to escape."

If true, this would conclude a manhunt that has gripped the town in fear for weeks. The discovery also casts doubt on the FBI's strategy of centering its investigation on local hero Jenny Valentine, the Girl Named Trouble. Valentine, who remains at large, is notorious for her exploits catching serial killer Campbell Batori, a.k.a. the Mistress of Metal; exposing a wine forgery of the famed *Ressort Rouge*; and discovering the identity of the Senior Trip Massacre killer.

Onishi's body was found in the north slough, not far from Sandpiper Point. Local Fisherman John Allendorf made the grim discovery when checking traps in the early morning hours.

According to an FBI spokesperson, federal agents are confident that the gruesome find will close the chapter on the murders that occurred at Valentine Manor on March 10, provided the ID of the body is confirmed. It may have also closed the book on the mysterious death of famed novelist RJ Valentine. In a statement to the *Times*, the executor of the Valentine estate has declared the eccentric game outlined in RJ Valentine's will to be concluded.

"None of the heirs have ever suggested, let alone proven, that Kazumi Onishi killed my father," said Tori Valentine. "As it appears now that she did, the game is over. You all lost. On behalf of my father, I'm extremely disappointed in the lot of you. The Valentine estate will go to charity—to the Valentine Foundation, as it always should have."

With both investigations potentially concluded, residents are left to ponder two questions. First, why did Mayor Hector Villanova intervene and suspend Sheriff Blake Lockhart, potentially delaying the capture of Onishi? And second, where in Calistoga County is Jennifer "Trouble" Valentine?

VALENTINE MANOR LOOMED PROUDLY ON THE LOW SHOULDER OF the hill, a crown atop the head of Blackbird Springs—a crown waiting to be claimed by Jenny.

Do you even want to win anymore?

What other choice did Jenny have? Winning was all she had left.

But what about Lizzy? What would she want?

With all Jenny had learned, her sister would probably prefer burning the mansion to the ground. But come on, Lizzy, if Jenny made it out of this alive, she'd need a hell of a legal fund.

At the moment, Jenny had $2.57 to her name, plus an unopened can of Chef Boyardee, two granola bars, and Mirai Porter's pistol.

Her foot was killing her. Both of her feet were, after two days in the woods. Fuck camping. Trouble was a Girl Detective, not a damned hobbit. Thursday night, she slept terribly under her Burberry trench coat, nestled against a log. Friday, against an oak tree, wasn't any better. In the rare moments when her body succumbed to exhaustion and let her sleep, the Stranger was waiting in her dreams to taunt her with all the clues she'd missed. Early this morning, she snuck into town, seeking news, and found that damned newspaper article.

Is it ten times worse now? Did I fuck up enough? What else do you want from me?

She was thinking of her father, but this wasn't his fault. Plenty was, but not this. Jenny had engineered this disaster all on her own. She was eighteen now. A young woman. She couldn't let a series of junior readers' books run her life forever.

But her friends needed her help, so Jenny kept limping along, a zombie on her feet, drawn back to the mansion by inertia and dogged, slavish devotion to those stupid books. The Stranger needed Trouble for his grand finale, and goddamnit, Jenny was a stickler for canon, too.

Cellar Drive took her to the mansion's long driveway. Jenny paused at the gate to punch in the security code. RJ's giant iron Vs parted to let her in. The weather was unseasonably warm for Blackbird Springs in April, warm enough to ditch her purple Burberry trench coat and let the damp air from the hot springs cool her bare arms.

The earthy scent of freshly cut grass greeted her nostrils as she reached the manicured lawn that fronted the mansion. Grass, cabernet grapes, a sharp whiff of asphalt: the smells returned to her like old friends. She'd been so fucking happy the first time she came here. Jenny inhaled deeply to cover up a sniffle. These were good smells. Worthy ones, if they had to be her last.

With every step, panic threatened to overtake her. She'd always felt so protected before—like nothing could truly touch her when she had plenty of story left to tell. But now her story was rushing toward the final page, and as the article in the *Blackbird Times* so painfully demonstrated, real life didn't always have a happy ending.

She reached the roundabout and passed the fake wishing well. Briefly, she pictured herself sneaking down to the garage via the secret entrance inside the well. Maybe she could surprise the Stranger.

Jenny took two steps toward the wishing well, and out popped Drew.

"Jesus fuck!" Jenny yelped, leaping back.

"Sorry!" Drew said.

He winced and glanced around in concern, as if someone might hear. He was still in his baseball jersey and hat. Had he not been able to change in the past two days?

"What are you *doing* in there!?"

"Waiting for you! Quiet!" Drew said, lowering his voice to a whisper. "I found the note from the Stranger when I got back to the cabin. Where've you been?!"

"Uhh…" Jenny wasn't sure how to reply. "Here and there."

"I looked everywhere; a bunch of people have gone missing!" said Drew. "I had to hide out. I figured my best shot was waiting here like the note said to see if you showed."

A fresh bout of sadness washed over Jenny. "Did you see the paper?"

Drew paled. "I don't believe it! I can't. Kazu said she was a good swimmer. There has to be a mistake." He straightened his shoulders. "So what's the plan?"

"I was thinking I'd go in there and die," said Jenny.

"Oh."

"But maybe with my sidekick, I've still got a chance?"

Drew grinned. "That's what I'm fucking talking about. Let's get this asshole, once and for all."

Together, they strode up the flagstone steps, and Jenny pressed the doorbell.

Something whirred, and the door swung open. Inside, the great hall with its fabulous double-staircase balustrade was eerily quiet. Jenny looked behind the door, but there was no one there.

"Must have done it by remote," Drew commented. "Where to?"

"The study," said Jenny. "That's where the Stranger will want this to end."

In silence, they made their way down the east wing. Jenny hardly noticed her surroundings, all her thoughts bent on her sister. She paused outside the study door and took a heavy breath.

I hope you're watching, Lizzy.

Drew reached for the door handle.

"Wait." Jenny pulled her trench coat back on. "Gotta look the part."

Then she opened the door. It was pitch black inside the study. The bay window drapes were pulled closed, and only a narrow spotlight over the desk shone down, bathing the massive mahogany surface in a warm glow. Sitting in RJ's high-backed chair was the Stranger.

"Shut the door, and take a seat," said that awful electronic voice.

Jenny declined the request and considered her nemesis: the dark trench coat, the black fedora, the inky nylon mask that obscured all features. Along the front of the desk, where RJ's paper weight and lamp would normally sit, were the seven heirlooms. The Bottle, the Tarot Card, the Noose, the Book, the Blackbird Statue, the Key, and the Photo Frame. Looking closer, there was the golden Pixeldrome Token, too, along with other stolen trinkets, such as Jenny's original purple trench coat and the signed first edition of *My Name is Trouble* her father had given her.

Of course. A collector. She should have seen it so much sooner. It was all so perfectly posed, but the Stranger couldn't quite hide those dainty hands and slender shoulders.

"Hey, Drew?" she said, turning to her trusty sidekick, still hanging back by the door. "Do you remember that night at the Crow's Nest when Jimmy Figg tried to shoot me with a paintball gun?"

"Yeah, that was crazy," said Drew. He smirked at her.

"It's funny, I didn't realize it, didn't even remember it until a couple days ago, but I was dressed up like Kazumi," said Jenny. "I'd just come from talking to Jack while posing as Kazu. Because I couldn't get into the hotel as Jenny."

"Sneaky," said Drew. "How'd that go?"

"Poorly. My accent was shite, as they say. That performance was what led to us having to tell Jack about Eliza."

"Who's Eliza?" Drew asked. He still had that big smirk on his face.

"Oh, oops! Spoiler," said Jenny. "Somehow you're the only one who hasn't figured it out yet."

"That's weird, right?" said Drew. "I was the keeper of the Big Boards. I figured out that Alicia and Sheriff Lockhart were in cahoots the night of RJ's attack. I tracked down a digital copy of *The Stranger of Sausalito*. But I didn't figure *that* out?"

Jenny's breath froze in her throat. "I forgot I was dressed as Kazu," she whispered. "I was talking to you as Jenny."

"No accent, talking Trouble business," said Drew. "Tsk tsk."

"You didn't say anything," said Jenny.

Drew shrugged. "You caught me flat-footed. I wasn't sure which way to respond. So I just pretended not to notice."

"That would only make sense if... You knew it all along. Didn't you?"

"Either that or I'm a moron," said Drew.

"But if you already knew I had a twin, why were you pretending not to?"

"Ya know, Jenny, I'm sure if we stood here long enough, we could come up with a perfectly innocuous reason for it," said Drew. He laughed and fixed her with a crooked smile. "But if we're being honest with ourselves, there's really only one explanation that fits."

Jenny stepped forward and pulled off Drew's hat. He winced and turned his head, revealing a nasty purple and yellow bruise on the back of his head, visible underneath his buzz cut. Courtesy of the empty bottle of Rosewood she'd smashed into it on the train yesterday.

"It's because you're the Stranger, aren't you?" said Jenny.

"Good guess."

Jenny pulled out Mirai's pistol and fired three shots into Drew's chest.

He didn't topple back or scream in pain; he only brought his hand up, holding some sort of bulky remote device, and shook his head.

"You bitch," he said.

"Aww, did I ruin your big moment?" asked Jenny.

"Yes! Do you have any idea how long this took to set up?!"

Drew cracked his neck and pressed a button on the remote. Light bloomed to Jenny's left, illuminating the study's reading area. The couches and Louis XIV chairs had been cleared away, replaced by several metal chairs arranged in a broad arc. Blindfolded and gagged, arms tied behind them, were several of her friends—and a few of her enemies: Val, Jack, Alicia, Jimmy Figg, Yvonne Griffin, Blake, and Shelly.

Each captive was wearing a strange headband, trailing a wire. Alicia was missing her prosthetic leg. Drew's Big Board was set up behind them, next to the fireplace.

"I had a whole cool deathtrap game planned," said Drew. "Did you even know there were blanks in that gun?"

Jenny shrugged. "I was testing a hypothesis: that even the Stranger would never have risked handing me a loaded gun."

"What if you were wrong!?" Drew said. "You would have shot your best friend!"

"Oh, I'm sorry. Did you think you were dealing with Nancy Drew? My name is Trouble, asshole! And I've got no more patience for your bullshit. You took everything from me! You're lucky I didn't swap out the blanks for real bullets!"

Drew smirked again, and Jenny's stomach turned over. How many times had they shared grins, in on some secret Trouble joke? There was no camaraderie behind his eyes now, only malice and lust.

"You wouldn't, though," said Drew. "Trouble doesn't shoot people. And besides, you can't kill me, not before you've heard my story."

"Like I give a fuck," said Jenny. She tucked the pistol back into her coat pocket and scanned the room, searching for an advantage. "I'm just here for my friends. Where's Dinah!?"

"Yeah, about her," said Drew.

A Bowie knife materialized in his other hand. Keeping it pointed at Jenny, he walked around behind RJ's desk and pulled the fedora off of the "Stranger" in the chair. Underneath the nylon mask was a girl with blonde hair tendrils and a heart-shaped face: Dinah. She, too, was gagged, and she appeared to be asleep.

Drew held something under her nose, and Dinah's eyes shot open in panic, finding Jenny's immediately and screaming behind her gag.

"Easy, easy," said Drew, pressing the knife to her throat. "We've got big plans for you, Miss Black."

He placed the black fedora on his own head and practically groaned in ecstasy.

"I had a whole recorded sequence for her, you know?" he said. "You didn't get to hear the ground rules. If you misbehave, it's not you who's gonna suffer; it's them."

Drew sheathed the knife and gestured menacingly with his remote instead. He strode over to Jimmy Figg and yanked the gag out of Jimmy's mouth.

"Blech! What the fuck, man? Why am I even here?" Jimmy asked.

"Relax, Jimmy," said Drew. "You're here to prove I'm not bluffing."

Drew pressed another button on the device. Something sparked in the center of the headband strapped to Jimmy's head. Poor Jimmy barely had time to say "Wh-what?" before a geyser of white-hot flame erupted over his head. Jimmy's confused stutter rocketed several octaves higher into a horrible scream.

"AAAAAAAIIIIIIIIIEEEEEEEEEEEEHHHHHHHH!!!!!!!!"

Jenny couldn't watch. Literally, the fire burned too bright to view head-on, like that magnesium experiment in Mr. Stephenson's Physics class. Even shielding her gaze, the gout of flame and sparks had already burned into her retinas. Mercifully, the scream died out within a few seconds, and Jimmy's head slumped forward in the chair.

Jenny blinked her smarting eyes and reluctantly peeked through her fingers. A charred hole smoked at the top of Jimmy's head. The fire had burned straight through his greasy hair and into his skull, cooking his prodigy brain.

"Holy shit!" said Drew, gawking at Jimmy's head. "A dollop of thermite goes a long way. You could fit a Red Bull in there!"

That visual, plus the stench of burnt flesh reaching Jenny's nose, was enough to get her puking up her breakfast. Half-digested bits of Clif Bar and Beefaroni barely made it into the trash can under Dad's desk.

"Now you know!" Drew shouted at her. On the Big Board, he marked a big red **X** over Jimmy's photo and waved his little device at her. "I'm setting this to Val next, and we'll work our way up to Dinah from there. It was gonna be your sister, but she caught an early train outta this story, heh. So, whatever control you thought you had over this situation, forget it. You don't."

"I don't understand," said Jenny, wiping her mouth. "How could you do that to Lizzy?"

Drew grinned again. "To be fair, she lied to me," he said. "Kinda messed up when you think about it. I was taken advantage of. I consented to fuck Kazu with the 32-Ds, not Eliza in a push-up bra."

"Bullshit! You knew!"

"Okay, guilty as charged," said Drew. "It was the next best thing since you're only for girls. But still, Trouble's twin giving it up to the Stranger isn't quite as poetic as Trouble herself, don't you think?"

She could almost vomit again. Jenny swallowed hard, her throat burning.

"She liked you. Liked you a ton, and you killed her."

"Ehh, that's her fault for never coming clean with me," Drew said. As he spoke, he paraded past the other hostages, pulling off their blindfolds so they could watch. Jenny's gaze found Shelly and Dinah, psychically willing them to hang in there. "It's not like I didn't give her plenty of chances. But if you really want to know *how* I could do that to Eliza? Well, it was sort of like picking an unripe grape off the vine; you just gotta pull a little harder."

He pantomimed plucking an eye out—using Dinah as his prop!—and laughed again. Drew had never been so exuberant as he was right now. As if reading her mind, he said. "God, this feels good. Do you know how hard it's been? To keep this a secret? All that time, pretending to be your cucked little sidekick?"

"Trouble doesn't have a sidekick," said Jenny.

"Exactly!" Drew snapped his fingers. "That was the first clue you missed! Whew! Right over your head. God, there were times when I fuckin' despaired. I had to stage that whole damned intervention with you, just to get you to stop obsessing about Alicia!"

He paused in front of the little redhead to caress her cheek. Alicia snarled under her gag.

"I suppose we're all guilty of distractions. But damn, Jenny, I gave you so many clues!" He was bouncing on his toes, a giddy little fanboy. "Do you want to know what my favorite clue was?"

"Not especially," said Jenny.

"Last Halloween! My costume!" said Drew. "A wolfman, wearing a Rams jersey? Get it? A ram, a.k.a. a *sheep*? A wolf in sheep's clothing! Hahaha!"

The son of a bitch was slapping his knee. Jenny was crestfallen anew that there weren't any real bullets in her gun.

"I worried it was a little too on the nose," said Drew. "But nope. It was almost as if some part of you, deep down, sensed what was going on, but you refused to see it. You do that a lot, you know? Not a great trait in a Girl Detective."

"That whole thing cracking your dad's phone passcode? And the letter?" asked Jenny. "You made all that up?"

"Of course! Oh! Here's another one: the initials I left at Pixeldrome. D-E-B."

"For Dinah Eve Black, trying to fool me," said Jenny. "But I never totally believed it."

"Wrong again, Trouble," said Drew. "I didn't realize it until later, but my mom almost blew my cover. She told you I was named after her uncle. If you'd bothered to follow up on that, you would have discovered his full name: Andrew Esteban Bolívar."

"D-E-B," said Jenny, grimacing. She'd even asked Mirai about Drew's middle name… "Your mother would be ashamed of you."

"Only if she finds out," said Drew. "Which she won't. Anyway, Drew Esteban Bolívar is what I've been calling myself in my head for years. I just wanted to leave my mark on the *Mystery Girl* game. I had no idea it was a honeypot. Tricky, Tricky, RJ! He almost got me with that one, but you missed it again."

"So, you must have *despised* your dad, huh?" Jenny asked.

"That guy was such a prick," Drew said with a sneer. "You only saw the stick-up-his-ass public facade. You weren't privy to his belt, and his temper, and his constant cheating on my mom. He got what he deserved—right after I made him break all the morals he claimed to hold dear."

Drew brandished his Bowie knife, fingering the edge of the blade, his face twisted in rage and pain.

"Fuck him," he said. "You know, that was the only killing that was ever personal. Well, that and Declan. I didn't like the way he looked at my mom."

"Are you serious?!" asked Jenny. "I'm pretty sure Declan was gay!"

Dinah nodded behind her gag.

"Oh shit, am I canceled?" asked Drew, aghast. Then he laughed again. "Fuck it, he was breaking the rules of the game."

Lightning sparked in Jenny's mind as she made another fruitless connection.

"Jorge Lopez," she said. "You hired him to attack us in the alley."

"Well done," said Drew, nodding. "I needed to make sure my innocence was unimpeachable. I wasn't expecting your sister to throw a knife at me. She even kissed the scar later, you know? Who says romance is dead?"

"When did you know?" Jenny asked. "About Eliza?"

"That she existed? Before you even came to town," he said. "That you guys were doing the old switcharoo? Probably a few weeks into junior year. I couldn't figure out how you could be a dyke one day, and making eyes at me the next. I'm embarrassed to say I thought I was just that powerful. But then I realized, oh, duh, it's the other one. I am sorry I had to do her like that. We never even got to hook up a second time."

Jenny growled, but inwardly, a spark of hope kindled. He was so eager to tell her everything, so desperate for an audience. And that was going to be his undoing.

"Tori should be here," Jenny said.

"I know, I couldn't find her in time," said Drew.

Jenny glanced at the captives, Jack and Val, especially. "Let the record show I did solve it. I knew it was Drew before he confessed."

"Sort of. When did *you* know?" he asked. "Was it the bruise?" He rubbed his skull under his fedora. "That's what tipped your girl off."

Dinah snarled under her gag.

"Maybe my subconscious noticed," said Jenny. "It was too easy, now that I think about it, the way you came and picked me up after the wine train. And it had been raining, but you claimed to have come from your baseball game." She looked at Jack. "You guys were rained out on Wednesday, weren't you?"

Jack nodded, his eyes full of hatred for Drew.

"Shit was getting out of hand," said Drew. "And the FBI screwed up my timetable. I never got to leave you the last chapter of *I Dream of Trouble*. Speaking of which."

He charged at Jenny, too fast to react. In the space of a heartbeat, the blade of his knife was an inch from her carotid artery. This close, she could smell the reek of Jimmy on him. Drew's hot breath on her ear almost made her puke again.

"Why haven't you asked me the question you want to ask?" he hissed.

Jenny retreated until her back was pressed against the bookcases along the wall.

"What question is that? Your motive?" she asked.

Drew shook his head. "We'll get to that later." He closed the gap between them again but spoke loudly for the whole room to hear. "There's another whodunit in this case, isn't there? The one I've been doggedly keeping you from solving this whole time?"

It took Jenny a moment to get it. "My mom?" she asked.

"Bingo."

"You didn't kill my mom," said Jenny. "You couldn't have—were you even born, then?"

"Correctamundo, Trouble!" Drew yelled. "Have you figured it out yet? Who hired Lambert?"

Jenny glanced at the captives, all watching anxiously as the drama played out before them. She found Val's pinched face amongst them, staring right at her.

"Val says she didn't," said Jenny.

"She's telling the truth," said Drew.

"The mayor?"

"Nope."

"Betty Campion?" she tried.

"Ehrn! Wrong!" Drew yelled, grinning madly now.

"Tori?"

"She was like seven!"

"Rob Haines?"

"As if!"

"Aunt Shelly??" Even as Jenny asked, she knew it was absurd.

"Come on, Trouble!" Drew shouted. "You're the greatest Girl Detective the world has ever seen!"

"Then who!?" she shouted back. "Who else would have wanted my mom dead?!"

"RJ did!"

Chapter Thirty-Two

The Rake's Song

JENNY FINALLY BROKE COMPLETELY. FOR WEEKS NOW, A DARK VOID had been seeping into her soul from a thousand psychic paper cuts. Her once bright spirit had been battered and bloodied and left for dead. And right when she thought there was nothing left to lose, here came a leviathan to swallow her whole.

"It isn't true," she told Drew, even as the truth streamed down her cheeks.

"You're the human lie detector," said Drew. He used the edge of his Bowie knife to wipe away her tears. "Tell me, am I making it up?"

He held her in his gaze, and she was surprised to see tenderness behind his gray irises.

"You've lied to me before," she said, shoving him away. "Fuck you. How dare you!"

"Stop it. You're better than this," said Drew.

"No, I'm not," said Jenny.

Drew said something else, but Jenny didn't hear him. She was staring at her heirloom photo on RJ's desk. *Dad's desk.* The way Mom smiled at him. He would never. He *could* never.

"Hey!" said Drew. He shoved some typed pages in her face. "It's all right here. Read it!"

"You probably wrote that yourself," said Jenny. "Your own fanfic, where you get to be the hero."

"I'm not even in it!"

Drew grabbed her by the wrist and dragged her over to the desk. He threw her down in one of her father's guest chairs and slapped the pages in front of her.

"Go on, read it!"

"No."

"I'll kill everyone you love."

"No, you won't," she said. "You need an audience."

Jenny leaned forward, rested her head on the desk, and sobbed. *RJ did!* Drew's words echoed in her mind. *RJ did!* Each time, she felt clobbered again, harder than before.

But what about—RJ did!

He wrote the books for me—RJ did!

In her head, she tried to marshal arguments against the idea. But for every flimsy rationalization she could muster, the ugly, obvious truth slapped her in the face. This was worse than getting rejected by that girl at her old school. Worse than Penny outing her for spending time in the psych ward. Worse than her rift with Lizzy before Mel's. Jenny thought she knew her floor. Knew where absolute rock bottom waited for her. Now, she was crashing through the firmament, free-falling into oblivion.

"Fine," said Drew. He cleared his throat. "I'll read it myself."

Chapter 8

I'm staring in disbelief at the object in my hand. It's a mini cassette, like the ones they use in answering machines—or voice recorders. It's the same cassette I briefly held earlier today when I opened that package in Hodgson's mail. The one the Stranger took from me. Why the hell is it in my old tackle box?

"Jenny?!" says an anxious voice down below. It's my father.

"Uhhh," I hear Danger say.

"Daddy, wait!" I say.

My father is standing in the doorway. At my appearance, his eyes shift back and forth between me and Danger. His face is white as a sheet, like he's just seen a ghost. It's not far from the truth.

"You—" He gasps, staring at Danger. "You're—you're alive?"

There's a smile on his face I'm not sure I can trust. How can I, after what I've just found? As I scramble down the loft steps, I hear him saying, "But this is incredible! A miracle!"

"Is it!?" I shout as I reach the wooden floor.

"Trouble, it's okay," says Danger.

"No, it isn't!"

"Well, pumpkin," says my father. "I know your old man's got some explaining to do, but—"

"Yeah?" I say. "Explain this!"

I hold up the cassette, and, if possible, his face goes even paler.

"How did you?" his voice trails off.

"You weren't even expecting to find me here, were you?" I say. "You came here for this."

"Please, it's not what you think," Daddy says.

"You know what? Why don't we let the tape do the talking?"

I snap the mini cassette into my trusty little recorder, dreading what I might hear, and hit the play button.

It's so much worse than I could ever have imagined.

> *Static on the line, then a heavy*
> *thud, like a door shutting. A man*
> *with a strange accent speaks. This*
> *must be Hodgson.*
> **Hodgson:** Why ze fuck did you bring

her here?

A *woman speaks. It's—it's my mother!*

Mom: Why shouldn't I be here? I'm part of this, too! I used my last savings so Johnny could hire your worthless ass!

Hodgson: This is not what I am agreeing to!

Dad: Relax, Hodgson.

Hodgson: You told her my name!?

Mom: I couldn't care less about your name, buddy.

Dad: Yeah, I told her your name: Eugene Hodgson, a.k.a. Franz Lambert. And I'm RJ Valentine. And you know who she is, so we're all in this together now.

Hodgson: Not your real name, Reynold Jenkins.

Mom: Reynold??

Dad: It's RJ, now.

Mom: Oh, who cares! You said she'd pay! She just came to the hotel room and kicked me out! Johnny, she's gonna kill me!

Dad: No, she won't. Val's about to have her hands full with an infant.

Mom: Another minor detail you failed to mention!

Hodgson: If you two want to argue, why am I being here?

Dad: We're not arguing, we're taking stock of your fuckup. You're the one who said we should play it soft with an anonymous letter. It didn't work!

Hodgson: I said to go soft because
you didn't have stomach to go
harder.
Mom: Wait, what are you talking
about? What does going "harder"
mean?
Hodgson: There are ways—
Dad: We're not doing that! It's fine,
Laura, he's just trying to scare
you.
Mom: I'm pretty dang scared right
now, Johnny! You didn't see the look
in Val's eye. I think she'd really
do it! Or hire someone to do it.
Like with her first husband!
Hodgson: *(Laughter)*
Dad: That's just a vicious rumor,
pumpkin.
Mom: What are we going to do? We
needed that money, Johnny! My
parents took me off their insurance,
and this baby is due any day now!
Dad: I thought you said Val wrote
you a check.
Mom: Yeah, and I tore it up. I'm not
taking a handout from that woman
like some whore.
Hodgson: Jesus Christ! Now you have
morals.
Mom: She said I could never see
Johnny again.
Dad: See, that's true love, Hodgson.
(Kissing noises) I'm touched.
Seriously. But you should be
resting. Let me worry about this.

Once Val has the kid, she'll feel
extra protective, and that's when we
hit her with another demand. She'll
pay, trust me.
Mom: Okay, but what am I supposed to
do in the meantime? The Crow's Nest
kicked me out.
Shuffling feet on the recording.
Dad: Take this. Sorry, it's all I've
got. There's a Motel 6 near the
hospital in Santa Rosa. It should be
enough to tide you over until the
girls come.
Mom: Okay. Okay. Thank you. (More
kissing noises) Call me as soon as
you can.
*There's a creak as the door opens
and slams shut. Silence follows for
several seconds.*
Hodgson: It will not work.
Daddy sighs on the recording.
Dad: I know.
Hodgson: You have two options. One:
Run away with girl and be a broke
author. Be despised by everyone in
town with money. Two: Ditch girl
and raise son in lap of luxury with
Valerie. Easy choice, to me.
Dad: But I don't love Val.
Hodgson: No, you love money.
Dad: I'd be a pariah, regardless.
Hodgson: Maybe, but a wealthy
pariah. People would understand.
There's a loud bang!
Dad: Fuck!

Hodgson: Why you punch wall? Wall did nothing to you.

Dad: Laura would never let me live it down. She'd tell. Oh, she definitely would.

Hodgson: Yes, and now you have implicated me too, you fool! We tried your way. Val didn't take bait. We do things my way now?

Dad: Absolutely not.

Hodgson: If you don't get rid of her, your writing career—bah, your whole life—is over.

Dad: I'm gonna be sick. I couldn't live with myself!

There is silence again on the tape, save for someone's heavy breathing.

Hodgson: What are you…? Ah, zis again. You are not made for zis life. Let me help.

Dad: One…

Hodgson: You don't have to do anything.

Dad: Two…

Hodgson: All you need is to go about your day and secure good alibi.

Dad: Three… Four…

Hodgson: Of course, after it is done, you keep me in thoughts and prayers when rich wife needs work done on the side.

Dad: Five…

Hodgson: My rate is a bit higher than market, but it comes with ironclad NDA clause, if you know what I am saying.

Dad: Six… But I always wanted a daughter.

Hodgson: Val has a daughter. You get to skip diapers with her.

Dad: Seven… Eight…

Hodgson: I need you to say ze word, Reynold Jenkins.

Dad: Nine… Are you recording this?

Hodgson: Of course I am, for both our protection. I make you a copy.

Dad: Ten…

Hodgson: I trust I don't need to say what happens if you try selling me out.

Daddy lets out another sigh of despair.

Dad: No.

Hodgson: Enough of dramatics. You knew what you were doing when you brought her here.

Dad: Just… Just make it quick. And painless.

# # #

I pause the tape, beyond horrified. How could he do that to Mom? How could he do that to me?!

"You monster," I whisper.

"I should have known," says Danger next to me.

We've moved to the kitchen. A cozy little table for three, where he betrays everything I ever held dear. I can barely look at him. Daddy's face is twisted up in grief like he's the one who just had his heart ripped out.

"I was a coward!" he shouts. "Seventeen years ago, I

took the coward's way out. Because Hodgson scared me, sure. But because I was a venal and weak man, too. And I've been living in fear and shame that this day would come ever since."

"I used to dream about meeting you," says Danger. "What fools you've made of us."

Daddy keeps going—like he can explain his way out of this. Typical writer! Always thinking some magical sequence of words will save him!

"When I heard you survived the crash, I thought I could atone," he says. "I could give you the life you always deserved in your mom's stories." He turns to Danger in desperation. "I didn't even know you survived until very recently—"

Danger spits on him and says, "Thank god for that! I don't need your damned atonement!"

Amid my shock and horror and revulsion, the old Girl Detective intuition raps on the door to my devastated brain.

"So all the stuff with the Campions and the Mayor…" I say.

"No good mystery is completed without one," Daddy says, and has the gall to smile.

"A red herring," I say, feeling nauseous. "It's you, then. There is no secret cabal of city elders pulling the strings. I'll bet you hired those goons to kidnap me earlier. Killian Rosewood probably doesn't even exist. *You're the Stranger!*"

He grimaces and gives me a reluctant nod of confirmation.

"Your mother had these characters she dreamed up," he says. "She was always doodling them. The Girl Detective, and the Punk Daredevil, and the Tall, Dark, and Strangesome Menace. Beware. She never had much of a story for them, so that's where I came in."

Daddy smiles to himself, a gleam in his eye, and despite my revulsion, my heart breaks all over again. They were happy, once. Why did he have to be so weak?

"Bastard!" I say.

"You need to know!" he says. "I-I used to make up these little stories for her while she lounged in my office, her bare feet up on my desk. That purple nail polish she loved… After she was gone, I wanted that feeling again. I thought it would be a fun way to connect with you. To maybe bridge some gap back to the sweet hereafter between you and your mom.

"And it was fun, wasn't it? All those mysteries we solved together? The Stranger needed you as much as you needed him." Daddy slumps, the momentary spark in his eyes fading again. "But then you started getting too close, too many times. I knew we had to stop. Better to let Trouble have a normal teenage life, right? Everything was fine." He turns to Danger. "Until Elizabeth discovered she had a twin and started hunting Hodgson."

"Oh, so this is my fault?" says Danger.

"No," says Daddy. "It's mine. All mine."

"You're going to jail," I say. "I hope you know that."

"Of course I do," he says. "I thought I could win back my soul by being a good father, but that was always a fool's errand. I understand that now. I must pay for my crimes."

He pauses, and a creepy smile spreads across his face.

"Or…" he says. "Or Trouble and Danger can make this all so much easier and pay me back now."

He removes a revolver from his pocket and slides it across the table to us. I stare at the gun, and all my heartache, grief, and rage go to war in my heart.

"I won't do it," I say at last. "You taught me too well, you son of a bitch. Morals you gave me—when you didn't even abide by them yourself! I won't take the law into my own hands. And I don't use guns!"

"But I do," says Danger.

She picks up the gun.

"Thank you," says RJ. "I'm so sorry."

Danger shoots him in the head.

The End

Chapter Thirty-Three
Killroy Is Here

"**J**ESUS CHRIST, RIGHT?" SAID DREW. HE DROPPED THE MANUSCRIPT pages like they were covered in shit. "Can you believe that guy? Just doing a drive-by on the whole *Trouble* lore, and then backing over it again to make sure the books were dead."

Jenny pressed her forehead onto RJ's calendar blotter, hands over her ears.

"He even forgets mid-chapter that in the books, Trouble's mom dies when she's a child, not an infant," said Drew. "We're just breaking canon all over the place so he can work out his 'poor me' confession. Shit is unbecoming, man. He didn't even put any effort into it!

"Obviously, as soon as I read it, I knew I had to do something," said Drew. "I couldn't let him ruin the whole franchise like that. They'd have pulled his books from the shelves. You'd get canceled for even saying you still liked *Trouble*, and we'd all have to pretend we cared so much about some dead lady no one had ever even heard of before."

"I'd heard of her," Jenny muttered without looking up.

"I'm sorry, Jenny, but in the grand scheme of things, that's not important," said Drew. "You know, sometimes authors need to have their IP taken away before they have a chance to fuck it up. There should be a rule. Like, after a franchise has been going for ten years, you have to run any new stuff by a council of superfans, just to make sure it doesn't totally suck ass."

Jenny lifted her head, and her face was wet with tears. She didn't bother to wipe them away, just stared at Drew in disgust.

"And you think that'd be you?" she asked. "Drew the superfan? You weren't even the target demographic."

"It's ironic, right?" he said, laughing. "All that time, I was trying to find my way into the series. I loved it so much, but there was no place for me. I could never be Trouble, and Trouble didn't have a sidekick. How was I supposed to be the hero? And then it finally clicked one day: maybe I was supposed to be the villain?"

"Congratulations, you're the guy who loses at the end," said Jenny.

She lay back down on the blotter and covered her head with her arms. Typical melodramatic Trouble. At least she was holding his attention.

"Not this time," Drew said. "But first, we're not done with my backstory yet. Come on, ask me more!"

"I don't care," Jenny mumbled.

Drew let out an exaggerated sigh. "Daddy issues, am I right? You and I, we're not so different, haha!" He grabbed Jenny's short hair and lifted her head. *"But Drew, how did you ever get your hands on the manuscript in the first place?"* he said in a mock Trouble voice.

"Oh, thank you for asking! Well, as you know, I was so obsessed with the books. I read them cover to cover, three times a year, easy. But where was book 13?? I'd been waiting years for my next *Trouble* fix. I was on every message board, I hunted down every cheesy merchandise tie-in, looking for clues. I scoured the web for any mention of RJ Valentine. Maybe there was some detail in his real-life history that would hint at where the next book was headed.

"Eventually, I had the bright idea of requesting the plans for the mansion from the city planning office. They're public, you know. And that's how I discovered the secret passages. It was perfect. My mom and dad always worked past midnight anyway, so I had plenty of time on my own to go exploring. I'd wait until everyone in the mansion was asleep and then sneak inside. I'd read an interview once where RJ mentioned loving those classic old gags like hollowed-out books with secrets inside, so I spent weeks carefully checking every single book in this study in the middle of the night until I found the one he hid his drafts in."

Drew leaped onto the bookcase ladder, rolling along on the rail until he came to a stop at one of the shelves near the study door. Reaching up, he withdrew a thick, hardcover book bound in green canvas.

"*Unfinished Tales*, by J.R.R. Tolkien," he said. "Very cheeky."

Drew opened the book to show Jenny that all the pages inside had been cut away to create a hollow. There was a pack of clove cigarettes inside.

"My little tribute. RIP Kazu," he said. "You want one?"

Yes.

"No," said Jenny.

"Suit yourself." Drew lit up, coughed like an amateur, and returned to the desk. "Anyway, before the manuscript, I was mostly just sending fun little notes and stuff to RJ—ya know, trying to do the proper Stranger thing. But then I read that total hackwork final book and knew I had to take my villainy up a notch."

Drew blew out a stream of smoke and coughed again. "No offense to your sister, but I fucking hated that character. *Danger?* Are you shitting me? It was so hacky! Why not give her a British accent while you're at it, RJ? Yeah, I know, ironic, right? Also! Also! Trouble's dad as the Stranger is such a lame cop-out ending! It's like the most boring fan theory ever. I know you hated that, too!"

"Yeah, that was the part I hated," said Jenny.

At least she's still got jokes.

"And then, out of nowhere, a stroke of dumb luck!" Drew pointed over at Dinah, squirming in her chair. "My copy of *Catcher in the Rye* had a big ink stain on one page, which gave me an excuse to ask the hot blonde chick to borrow hers. And what do I find tucked into a random page? A little slip of paper with RJ's Signal username on it. Naughty, naughty, RJ!"

He grabbed Jenny by the hair again and spoke for her.

"*Wow, was that weird for you, Drew? Pretending to be a girl and carrying on a whole online relationship with RJ Valentine?"* Drew said in his Jenny voice. "Yeah, it was! It's a good thing I'm so well-adjusted and secure in my sexuality, 'cause otherwise, that could have seriously fucked me up."

Is… is he being sarcastic?

"RJ would tell me *anything!*" said Drew. "Even told me his real name, and all that crazy shit that happened in Austria. Not to throw stones in glass houses, but I don't think it's appropriate to tell a 16-year-old girl about your Y2K castle fuckfest. And sure, I encouraged it a little; I even deep-faked some saucy pics of Dinah to send to him. But still, he was an adult! I was a child! He took advantage of me!

"Of course, my rule was always that this relationship was only allowed online, and if he ever brought it up to me, a.k.a. Dinah, in person, I'd act like he was crazy. We had whole plans for a vacation in Paris once he caught his weird stalker. Hah! What a sucker! Men are so stupid sometimes. Seriously, if anything, that shit made me a feminist. Hashtag HeForShe."

Jenny tried to reach for Dinah's hand, but Drew swatted it away.

"See, this is my problem now," he said. "I was gonna make it look like Dinah did it. Kill off everyone else and have only us miraculously survive. The feds would like that. Very tidy. The mystery is, quote-unquote, solved, you win all the money, and we get to keep on doing this as long as we want. Trouble and the Stranger! I set up a new mystery, and you knock it down!"

Drew was really feeling himself now, pacing like the overstimulated teenager that he, at the end of the day, still was.

"We could even publish new *Trouble* books!" Drew said. "Better ones! I have this whole idea for a *Trouble*-verse. We could have, like, a Black Trouble, a Latinx Trouble, a Trans Trouble, a Boy Trouble, like, an Eskimo Trouble. All by Own Voices writers, you know, to keep it authentic? And they could cross over, like the Avengers!"

Of all things, this was what finally broke through Jenny's stupor. She forced herself upright and glared at Drew through bloodshot eyes.

"I'd be lying if I didn't admit how clever you've been, Drew," she said. "How you fooled us all. How I never gave you proper credit for your intellect. That is, until right now, when you just said the dumbest fucking shit I've heard in my entire life. In fact, I hope you kill me soon, because I can't handle living with the secondhand embarrassment for much longer."

Dinah snickered behind her gag. Drew's face went stony.

"Look, you haven't even given the idea a chance," he said. "It could work. Stop being so selfish about your character."

"It's not selfish, Drew," said Jenny. "Okay, Trouble isn't some idea that lives in all our hearts if we only believe hard enough. She's not a hashtag or a T-shirt or a Snapchat filter. Whether I like it or not, there's only one Trouble, and she's me!"

Chills, Jenny!

"Eh, there could be another," said Drew. "Look how well I did bringing you along. You'd never be the Girl Detective you are today without the Stranger pushing you, molding you to be better. I could do it again with some new chick if I had to."

Jenny shook her head sadly. "It wouldn't be canon."

"Okay, well, the point is: the money!" Drew shouted. "We could do all that, or whatever else you wanted—but only if you agree to go along with it," said Drew. He placed a hand on Dinah's neck, and Jenny snarled. "And that means saying goodbye to this one. I'm not sure you're ready to do that."

"You're so stupid," said Jenny. "How were we friends for this long, and you never understood me? I would never trade a life for the money. Not Dinah's, not Jimmy's—hell, not even Val's."

Val squeaked indignantly.

"Hmm. I suppose it was always Eliza who hated Val more," said Drew.

"I did, but we're cool now," said Eliza.

She stepped out from the fireplace passageway, finally revealing herself, and placed a reassuring hand on Aunt Shelly's shoulder. The stun-locked expression on Drew's face almost made the last three days worth it. Almost.

"What's wrong, Drew?" Eliza asked in her Kazumi accent. "You look like you've just seen a ghost."

69 hours earlier

Eliza's body plunged into the river, swallowed up by the swift current. For a terrifying moment, her heart stopped as the freezing water gripped her lungs.

It's Drew! It's Drew! It's Drew!

How had she missed it before? Touching both wrists, then double-tapping his back foot: it was Drew's batting routine. He was always messing with his stupid batting gloves. He did it every time he took a pitch. Did it so many times that he probably didn't even realize when his muscle memory took over in the middle of a fight. That's what Nilay had noticed—right before the Stranger killed him.And now Eliza spotted it, too. Only he hadn't killed her. Not entirely.

Eliza clutched at her chest, spots forming in what was left of her vision. It couldn't end like this. She had to warn Jenny. She had to take her revenge. She had to track down Charlie in Paris and kiss her one more time…

Thud!

Her knee bashed against a submerged rock, and Eliza expelled the last of her oxygen in a silent shriek of pain.

That did the trick. Like in those old movies, when Han Solo had to bang on the *Falcon* to make her engines start, Eliza's heart turned over and beat like a hummingbird. She kicked out with her other leg, found the riverbed, and propelled herself toward the gray light above.

She broke the surface and sucked in a huge gulp of life-saving oxygen. Then the wind brushed against her eye, and she immediately regretted it.

No, not her eye anymore, just an empty socket! She dove under the water again, preferring the icy numbness in her skull to the livewire shock she got on the surface.

For a while, Eliza drifted like that, coming up only briefly for air, crippled by the pain and betrayal. A minute or an hour passed. The swift current pushed her into the overhanging eaves of a willow tree as the river rounded a bend. Eliza thought of Aunt Shelly and her mom, and a train whistled in the distance.

Covering her empty socket, she rolled over and lifted her head. The tracks were on her left side now. Through her bleary remaining eye, she could see the dwindling silhouette of a southbound train. With her other hand, Eliza grabbed at the willow fronds to arrest her drift and kicked her way to the muddy bank.

She didn't have any clear idea in her head except to get back to the tracks. Crawling at first, then back on her feet when she reached the top of the bank, Eliza pointed herself toward the setting sun and stumbled onward. Her eye socket was throbbing. How clean was that river? She shuddered and tried not to think about it.

Three meters from the tracks, trudging through the tall grass, she tripped on a slippery rock and nearly face-planted.

"Ow fuck!" she shouted, looking back at the thing that had nearly done her in.

It wasn't a rock. It was a matte black orb made of carbon fiber and ballistic plastic: her motorcycle helmet.

How confident she'd been, tossing it aside. It already felt like hours ago. The fall from the roof of Calistoga Cabernet Express hadn't marred the helmet in the slightest. Say what you will about Arty Porter, the guy knew his gear.

Eliza pulled the helmet on, whimpering as she forced her wounded face to squeeze inside the foam. She nearly passed out from the effort, but once her eye socket was shielded from the elements, her pain became manageable. This was good. This was an improvement. What else might she find along these tracks?

Twenty minutes later, she came across the Ninja motorbike beside the tracks—where she'd ditched it to leap onto the train. With some effort, she got it upright and hit the starter. It thrummed to life.

Okay, Danger. You're wanted by the feds, hunted by the Stranger, and bleeding slowly from the hole in your skull where your eyeball used to sit. Where can you go?

Safety first. She couldn't take revenge on her ex-lover if she keeled over and died of sepsis beforehand. But how would she get treatment?

She'd get spotted and arrested at any ER, wouldn't she?

Eliza checked her jacket pockets. She had her backup kunai dagger, a soggy box of Pocky, and a mostly empty bottle of weak chloroform. Kidnapping an EMT was probably out of the question, but there was one doctor in the North Bay who might still do her a favor…

The drive took an hour and a half. Riding a motorcycle on the freeway with only one eye was terrifying. She couldn't trust her depth perception, so she had to stay well back of every other vehicle on the road. Somehow, Eliza made it without dying, running on fumes both figurative and literal as she wheeled into the parking lot of Santa Rosa Memorial Hospital.

"Where all my troubles began," she said to herself, and managed a feeble smile.

If Jenny were here, she'd have laughed. The doctor didn't laugh so much when she surprised him in his office.

"Dr. Singh?" Eliza said to the silver-haired obstetrician. "Sorry for the helmet. My name is Eliza Valentine, but you might know me better as Nurse Bennett's girl. You um… I think you delivered me."

Annoyingly, she began to cry. The tears burned in her empty socket.

"I remember," said Dr. Singh, once he'd recovered his wits. "You're the one your mother called 'Danger.'"

"She—she was onto something," Eliza said, catching her breath.

Wincing in pain, she removed her helmet and gave him a look at her condition.

"I can get you treatment if that's what you need," he said.

"That would be fucking dynamite," said Eliza. "But I need something else, too. You killed me once, eighteen years ago. I need you to do it again."

THE CONSPIRACY GREW IN THE TELLING.

After suturing her socket, pumping her full of antibiotics, and sending her into a dreamless sleep for the night in a spare bed in Long-Term Care, Dr. Singh got to work on Eliza's second disappearing act.

He could provide convincing medical documents, but he couldn't make the police believe them. Not without a body. That meant Eliza needed a cop on her side, and Blake had vanished. She risked it and called Tori Valentine. Good thing, too; she learned that Jack and Val were missing as well. Tori didn't need any convincing to bring in Darcy Peña, who then recruited Deputy Calderon.

Their pitch was simple. Want to catch the Stranger? Make him think he's gotten away with it.

Eliza didn't name Drew. Not yet. She didn't want to spook him without proof. Proof that she knew, finally, how to obtain.

Calderon's bogus police report would keep Tierce and Steele busy for a day or two while they got the runaround trying to get possession of a non-existent body, but how to get the word out to the Stranger himself? Talking Yvonne Griffin into printing a fake news story was going to be a hard sell, but then it became academic when Eliza learned from Penny that Ms. Griffin had gone missing, too.

No worry, Penny had been watching her mom get the *Blackbird Times* to press for years. They put in a coded message to Jenny, in case she'd escaped the Stranger on the train. Eliza felt certain she had. And if she was right, she needed her sister to keep the faith.

Don't give up, Jenny. I'm still your ace in the hole.

"What'll it be?" Dr. Singh asked after changing her dressing. "Flesh tone? Or black?"

He held out two eye patches, but for Danger, the choice was a no-brainer.

"Black," said Eliza.

She spent Saturday morning recruiting her witnesses. On the drive back from Guerneville, her new burner phone started to vibrate.

"What's up?" Eliza answered.

"Someone just opened the gate at Valentine Manor," said Tori on the line. "I got the notification on my phone."

"Jenny?"

"Or the Stranger," said Tori.

Damn. Eliza had intended to give her big presentation at the police station. Calderon had summoned the feds there for a briefing at 1:00.

"Change of plans," said Eliza. "We're doing this at the mansion."

Chapter Thirty-Four

Goodbye Stranger

Eliza stepped out from the shadows of the fireplace passage. She wore her motorcycle jacket unbuttoned over purple hospital scrubs. A black eye patch covered her missing eye, and—if Jenny's watering eyes weren't mistaken—a new katana sword was strapped to her back.

"But... *how?*" asked Drew, bewildered. "You're dead. The paper said so. So did the cops! I even heard it on the police scanner!"

"The Stranger works hard, Drew, but Trouble and Danger work harder," said Eliza.

Jenny beamed through her tears. Thirty seconds ago, she was sure she'd never smile again. Now, she was grinning so hard her cheeks hurt.

"Did you get my message?" Eliza asked her.

"I thought I hallucinated it; I was too scared to believe," said Jenny. "Did you hear that last chapter?"

"The end of it," said Eliza.

Jenny's smile faltered.

"Don't blame yourself; he had me fooled, too," said Eliza. "And I never even liked the asshole to begin with. I just never thought..."

"I'm sorry, not to interrupt the fucking *Parent Trap* reunion here, but didn't I say there were ground rules?" said Drew. "Rules and consequences. Bye-bye, Valerie Valentine."

He mashed a button on his remote. Val squealed and squirmed in her chair.

Nothing happened.

"Seriously, Drew? Did you honestly think I'd reveal myself before disabling your stupid traps?" asked Lizzy. "I'm beginning to get the feeling that you never respected Kazumi for her intellect."

"True," said Drew, shrugging. "It was mostly physical."

He lunged for Jenny before she had a chance to duck.

"But you had to know I'd do this," he said, holding Jenny close and pressing his Bowie knife to her neck.

"Of course she knew," said Jenny, speaking from the back of her throat to avoid flexing her vocal cords against said knife. "Don't you get it, Drew? We planned for everything. We beat you!"

You did plan for this, right, Lizzy?

"You didn't beat me from where I'm standing," said Drew.

"That's true," said Eliza. "To do this properly and win the game, we have to prove motive, means, and opportunity."

"To who?!" asked Drew.

"To me," came Tori's voice behind them.

Drew spun around in a panic to see the bookshelf swinging open and Tori Valentine stepping out from the secret passage with Penny Griffin in tow. The two crossed their arms, blocking that potential escape route and causing Drew to retreat with Jenny to the center of the study.

"Are you kidding me?" he said. "No guns? No cops? These are just more bodies for me to drop."

"But you won't," said Jenny. "Not yet. This is your favorite part."

He chuckled in her ear. "That's true. All right, let's hear it, then."

"Just a minute," said Eliza, hastily removing the thermite headbands and gags from the captives.

"What's there to prove?!" shouted Val. "He already confessed!"

"Did I?" asked Drew. "Did I really? Did Tori hear any of it?"

"You seriously didn't bring any police with you?" Shelly asked. "Eliza, I swear to god!"

"We had to make a last-minute venue change," said Eliza. "I wasn't expecting all this."

"Just cut me loose, Lizzy, and I'll handle the motherfucker myself," said Blake.

"Not if I get to him first," said Jack.

"I knew there was a reason I didn't want to sleep with you," said Alicia.

"Girl, same," said Penny.

"Penelope Griffin!" yelled Yvonne. "What do you think you're doing?"

"Securing the book deal of a lifetime, ma," said Penny.

"For the record, I would have just shot him," said Dinah when Penny removed her gag. "Who cares about RJ's stupid canon?"

"No! No no no!" said Drew, and Jenny hissed as she felt the sting of his knife drawing blood. "If we're gonna do this, we're gonna do it proper. Go on, Trouble. Solve the mystery. But Kazu, if you untie even one of those people, I'll slit your sister from ear to ear. I ain't playing."

Eliza backed away from the captives, holding up her hands.

"Great. Let's start with motive," said Jenny. "For those who didn't hear it, Drew was just explaining that all this happened because he couldn't find a way into the female character's perspective when he read the *Trouble* books."

"It was more than that!" said Drew.

"Yes, and also because he read the final *Trouble* manuscript and discovered it was little more than a dressed-up confession from RJ Valentine to the murder of Laura Onishi," said Jenny. "It's right there if you want to read it, Tori."

She pointed to the desk, where Drew had tossed the final pages. Tori grimaced, disgusted.

"I heard enough," said Tori. "The motive is solid."

"Wonderful. Means is simple enough," said Jenny. "Drew's a big guy. Fills out the Stranger outfit. More than strong enough to overpower RJ Valentine and crack his skull with a weapon."

"I'm not hearing a lot of hard evidence here," said Drew. "This is all circumstantial."

"Doesn't matter, you're in California," said Yvonne.

"The point is taken, though. I'd like to call our first witness," said Eliza. She ducked her head back into the fireplace passage and called out, "Hey, surplus guy, it's your turn!"

Moments later, a bearded dude climbed out of the fireplace. Eliza produced a slip of paper from her jacket.

"Behold: a parking ticket for Arty Porter from the city of Guerneville, dated a few days before the class trip last summer," she said. "Except Arty didn't get this ticket, Drew did, when he rode Arty's motorcycle to Guerneville to buy supplies from the surplus store. Do you recognize that guy?" Eliza asked the bearded guy.

"I do," the man said in a gruff voice, eyeballing them all with suspicion.

"And do you remember what he purchased from your store?" she asked.

Damn, good job going back for this guy, sis.

"Yeah, because I remember it was odd," the man said. "He bought a single 45-pound weight plate and a knife. I can't be certain from this distance, but I reckon it's the same one he's got pressed to your sister's gullet."

"Damning!" said Jenny. "So there's your giant 'coin' that killed Mr. Webb, too. How's that for hard evidence?"

"Eh, you're getting warmer," said Drew.

"I recognize the knife, too," said Val. "He nearly killed me with it."

"That's right," said Eliza. "That's also where Drew got hold of my kunai, which he used to murder Mason and Meghan."

"In the dark, like a coward," said Blake, fists clenched in fury.

"All so he could steal Jenny and Alicia's heirloom clues," Eliza said, shaking her head. "And not because they would lead to him; he just wanted them for his little collection. Gawd, what a loser."

"Yeah, yeah, here it comes," said Drew. "Now you have to pretend that you never really liked me. I suppose you'll impugn my cocksmanship next?"

"Bro, that's my sister," said Jack.

"You're lucky I never had a good moment alone with *you*, Junior," said Drew. "You had it coming after stealing Alicia from me."

"You want a moment?" asked Jack. "Untie me, and we can do the man dance right here."

"This is so sexual," said Penny. The boys glared at her. "Sorry."

"Thirty seconds!" Eliza said under the guise of a cough.

"Don't lie, it was thirty-five!" said Drew.

"Can I go?" asked the guy from the surplus store.

Eliza waved at the fireplace passage, and he departed, muttering, "You people are fuckin' weirdos."

"Opportunity!" said Jenny, breaking the awkward silence. "This is where it gets tricky. If you'll recall, RJ had not one but two head wounds in almost the same spot. The first would not have been fatal; the second is what ultimately did him in. For a long time, I thought this was because RJ *did* fall and hit his head climbing the stepladder, and then the Stranger got him right after. And I was sort of right. Dinah, can you explain how RJ got the first injury?"

"Uhh," said Dinah, her cheeks flushing.

"You don't have to go into all the details," said Jenny. "Suffice it to say, RJ had been tutoring Dinah in secret, and along the way got himself the foolish, inappropriate notion that it meant something more."

Dinah briefly recounted her tale of that night: leaving Jack's bed, seeking a drink with RJ, and getting more than she wanted from him, resulting in a roundhouse kick and RJ bashing his head on the corner of his desk.

"That's interesting," said Drew, slackening his grip on Jenny. "I never knew the Dinah part of that. Jesus, he would have been like double-canceled if I hadn't acted. Allegedly. But you're welcome, *Blondie*."

"All that time, I thought you were sneaking in to see Jack," Val said to Dinah.

"And you didn't say anything?" Jack asked, his voice cracking.

"Were you expecting a high-five?" Alicia Aaron snapped at him.

"I need a drink," said Eliza.

Her sister moved to the minibar and pulled out a bottle of something clear.

Vodka? No, Everclear.

"The point is!" Jenny said, pulling the attention back to her. "RJ was injured, but not mortally so. As you know, Tori, he'd been planning to fake a coma that night anyway. This worked just as well."

"Would have been nice to know!" Tori said, frowning at Dinah.

"If she'd told me sooner, I might have never checked with the charge nurse at the ER," said Jenny. "Which I did. According to the nurse, RJ's vitals were plummeting when he got there, but they were stable when the EMTs checked him at the mansion. Which means the killing blow must have come during the ambulance ride, and Drew, you've never had an alibi for that night. Both your parents worked late at the Winchester. You were alone."

"That's speculation, not proof," said Drew. "If I were in the ambulance, wouldn't the other EMT remember me?"

"We can check that," said Blake. He kept tugging at his restraints, his wrists going white with the strain.

"Dalton probably did remember you, which is why you killed him," said Jenny. "Once you realized I was looking for him. The other day, at school, Jack noticed his name on my list of leads and asked about it. You heard him and immediately took care of that loose end."

Drew shrugged, hiding a grin.

"To be honest, sounds like you don't have much of a case," he said. "No witness, no murder weapon?"

"Hate to say it, but he's not wrong," said Tori.

Jenny ground her teeth. If only she'd gotten to Dalton sooner. This was the one part of the case she couldn't prove. Even if she could nail Drew for all the other murders, she still needed to pin RJ's on him if she wanted to win the game.

"Ah ah, not so fast!" said Eliza, gesturing with her tumbler glass full of Everclear. "We *do* have a witness." She ducked her head into the fireplace. "Hey Ben, it's your turn!"

"You had time for all these people and not the police?" asked Shelly.

A stocky dude about Blake's age emerged from the secret passage, blinking in the harsh overhead lighting.

"This is Ben; he works at Minutemen Mail," said Eliza. She turned to Drew, pure scorn on her lips. "He's the witness you never knew you needed to kill, you fucking asshole."

"Now wait, I never went to Minutemen myself," said Drew. "Not until I went there with you and Penny."

"Yep, and that's where you fucked up," said Eliza. "You were hanging back, but when I walked up to Ben at the counter, he referred to you and Penny as, quote, a cleric and a bard."

"Gay," said Drew.

"It flew right over my head, never gave it a second thought," said Eliza. "Not until I was floating in the Napa River, bleeding out of my eye socket. I had a lot of time to think, and I started wondering: *why did the guy at the shipping place call you that?* Which one of you was the cleric, and who was the bard? And what *was* an effing cleric, anyway?"

"It's a healer class," said Ben from Minutemen Mail.

A shiver ran up Jenny's spine.

She's doing it. I've made a proper Girl Detective out of her after all.

"I reasoned that Penny must be the bard," said Eliza. "Closest thing to a journalist in D&D terms, right? So tell me, Ben, why did you call Drew a cleric?"

"Well, like I told you," said Ben, "I never forget a face. And I'd seen him once before, at the ER, on August 10th, 2019." His face paled. "I remember because it was the night I had a cardiac event."

"Are you all right?" Eliza asked, frowning.

"Yeah. Yeah, it was just a panic attack," said Ben, brightening. "Made me stop drinking Red Bull and start riding a bike now and then, though."

"You should be lifting, too," said Blake.

"I know, I'm trying to," said Ben. "Anyway, there I was, walking out of the ER with a prescription for Lexapro, when I pass an EMT pulling off his surgical mask. I remember thinking he looked so young, but maybe I was just getting old. And yeah, it was him."

He pointed at Drew.

"You're sure?" Jenny asked.

"Positive," said Ben. "I never forget a face."

"Yeah? When's the last time you saw me?" asked Tori.

"Couple weeks ago," said Ben. "You were in a car on Second Street with that hot cop with the pixie hair."

Tori raised an eyebrow. "She's taken."

Drew let out an irritated sigh and lowered his knife, though he still kept one of his muscular arms wrapped tight around Jenny's torso.

"The World's Greatest Consulting Criminal, undone by some dork with high blood pressure and hypochondria," he said. "What about the murder weapon?"

"That part was easy," said Jenny. She craned her neck to look up at him. She deserved his full attention. "You got off on it, didn't you? Leaving it around your Masturbatorium? Letting me hold it and play with it? You must have loved that. The key to the mystery was right under my nose that whole time."

Drew snickered. Jenny turned to Tori.

"He used a spring-loaded center punch," said Jenny. "Like they use in woodworking. Modified, I think, with a stronger spring for more power. It's the same thing he used to break that window after attacking Alicia in here."

She pointed to the bay window the Stranger had broken on that terrible birthday night a month ago.

"What happened there, with Meghan and Mason?" Eliza asked Drew. "You owe Blake that much."

"I owe him a lot more," said Blake, still straining in vain to free his hands.

Drew rested his chin on top of Jenny's head. Though she couldn't see his face, she could sense his malevolence warring with his need to explain his genius. In the end, it wasn't Dinah or Tori, but Drew who became RJ's true protégé; the one who took up his mantle to keep the story going. And killing, like writing, was lonely work.

"I think it was Penny who saved your life, Alicia," he said after a moment.

"How so?" asked Penny.

"I was coming out of the secret passageway." Drew pointed at the bookcase behind Penny and Tori. "Alicia didn't even see me coming. But then the front door to the mansion slammed shut. Because Penny had just opened the door to the balcony from the billiards room upstairs."

"That's right. I did," said Penny. "And I heard Alicia scream right after."

"She spun around all of a sudden," said Drew. "I'm embarrassed to say it freaked me out. I stabbed out with the kunai dagger on instinct. She screamed and dropped like a sack of potatoes. Anyway, it was dark, and I was looking for the key and photo heirlooms." He leaned away to look at Jenny. "I'd spotted the photo earlier in your bag, and then saw you giving the bag to Alicia in the conservatory. Two heirlooms in one shot, and getting a little payback on my ex, too? It was too tempting to pass up. I'd already gotten the Lambert file from the archives and chloroformed Tori. I guess I was feeling myself, you know? And I had Eliza's dagger on me, so why not, right?"

"All so you could complete your stupid collection," said Blake. He'd stopped straining, but his eyes burned with cold fury.

"Didn't Eliza chloroform you?" Jenny asked. "How'd you wake up from that so quickly?"

"Because he stole most of mine and diluted it with water," said Eliza. "That's why Agent Zoey was barely out a few minutes when I used it on her."

"A little bit of switcharoo while everyone else was watching JeRay lick Penny's knee," Drew said with a smirk.

"Excuse me?" said Yvonne.

"Truth or dare, it's—relax," said Penny.

"What next?" asked Blake.

"I knew I didn't have much time," said Drew. "Jenny was right outside, calling for Alicia. So I broke the window and pulled off my nylon mask to see better. I'd just grabbed the photo when I heard Mason behind me. I wasn't expecting them to come through the fireplace passage. I tried to play it off, pretended I'd just found Alicia like that. But Mace was always sharper than I gave him credit for. I could see it on his face: he didn't believe me."

"So you slit Meghan May's throat and stabbed my son through the heart," said Blake.

Drew shrugged. "Basically."

"How did you hide your clothes?" Blake asked. "Wouldn't you have been covered in blood?"

"I was," said Drew. "But it was dark. I waited around the corner for the cops to break the door down and ran in with them. I went straight to Alicia and made sure to get plenty of blood on me. It was easy. Jack was there too, just as bloody as I was, so it didn't seem suspicious at all."

Blake cursed under his breath. In the distance, Jenny thought she could hear the high-pitched whine of a siren.

"Sounds like they're playing our song, Trouble," Drew whispered in her ear. "Don't you want to know? Before you die?"

"Know what?" Jenny asked.

"How your father died."

For Drew, it was the culmination of a perfect summer. Months of scheming had been building up to this moment. He would finally become the man he was born to be—and he could finally stop pretending to flirt with RJ Valentine over Signal, thank god! Because that was starting to get too weird.

9:05 PM. Any minute now.

His only regret was not wearing the outfit. He'd tried it on in his room, and in his opinion, he cut quite the tall, dark, and strangesome figure dressed all in black. Beware! But the plan called for a disguise, so he wore an EMT's uniform instead. If RJ stuck to the timeline he'd foolishly divulged over Signal, he'd have sedated himself already. All Drew needed now was for the maid to find him and call 9-1-1.

9:07 PM. Come on, RJ, hurry up. Drew was getting a muscle cramp.

He was crouching inside the fake wishing well in the center of the roundabout outside Valentine Manor. He could have taken the secret passageway underneath him to get inside, but that wouldn't be necessary. RJ would come to him.

9:12 PM. Sirens. Finally.

Drew tensed. More than a little of his plan relied on multiple ambulances showing up. Everything suggested they would. Firefighters loved tagging along for free overtime.

The sirens rose to a crescendo as they got closer, then went silent. In their place, he could hear the heavy tires of several vehicles coming up the driveway from Cellar Drive. Once they'd parked, he risked a peek with a little pen-sized periscope he'd ordered online. Perfect! A fire engine and two ambulances had come. A dozen first responders swarmed the front door of Valentine Manor.

Once Jack let them inside, Drew hopped out of the wishing well and strode quickly to the fire engine. His black latex gloves would leave no prints, and he wore a surgical mask to partially obscure his face. Acting like he belonged there, Drew grabbed a medic's bag from one of the truck's storage compartments and walked to the mansion entrance. For five nerve-wracking minutes, he milled around by the door, waiting.

9:21 PM. RJ emerged on a gurney. He looked smaller in the flesh.

Drew fell in with the other medics and helped them negotiate the stairs with the gurney. As they approached the ambulance, Drew maneuvered himself to the front of the operation. The other medics fell away, except for the driver and his partner. Together, the three of them lifted RJ into the back of the ambulance, and the driver moved around to the cab.

"I got this," Drew said to the driver's partner. He nodded to the fire engine. "My driver engineer wants to sync up. Meet you there?"

It was the riskiest, ballsiest, most reckless part of his plan. But hey, nothing ventured, nothing gained, right?

"Sure, man," said the other paramedic.

He passed Drew the IV bag he was holding up, and Drew climbed into the back with RJ. The medic closed the door and gave it a hearty slap to see them off. The ambulance driver pulled out and triggered the siren once they were through the gate.

With the driver focused on Cellar Drive and the unprotected left turn onto Highway 12, he never even clocked that it wasn't his usual partner in the back with the patient. Drew leaned over RJ, studying him. With the oxygen tubes running into his nose, the famous author seemed so pathetic, so unimpressive. Drew pulled a black nylon stocking over his face. There. Now, he was in character.

"Hey," the Stranger whispered. "Wake up."

He pulled the oxygen tubes away from RJ's nose. The author's eyes flickered open, and he peered up in confusion.

"Hello, Reynold," said the Stranger.

"I always hated that name," said RJ. "Are you going to kill me?"

"Don't worry," said the Stranger. "Even after you're gone, the Stranger lives on."

RJ frowned, like he was disappointed. Lightning quick, the Stranger yanked his head forward, positioned the special center punch he'd prepared over the existing wound, and pressed hard. The spring retracted until it reached critical depth. The hidden trigger released and shot the tip of the punch into RJ's skull with a satisfying crunch!

The Stranger released RJ's head, and he flopped back onto the gurney. As Drew replaced his black mask with the surgical one and wiped off the tip of the center punch, RJ's eyes rolled back, and the pulse oximeter attached to his hand began to complain.

The ambulance arrived at Blackbird Springs General Hospital. Drew helped the driver roll RJ into the ER, where the nurses took over. Only then did the driver, whose name tag read **Dalton***, take notice of Drew and frown.*

"We had to swap," Drew said, jabbing a thumb behind him. "He wanted to chat with BSFD. He'll be along with them in a bit. Nice driving, man."

Dalton nodded, and they bumped fists. Drew walked to the ER exit and pulled off his surgical mask, fighting the urge to grin. He'd pulled off the perfect murder, and the fun was only just beginning...

Eliza strode toward Jenny and Drew, disgusted that she'd once simpered and fawned over this creep.

"You thought you'd planned it all so perfectly," she said and pretended to sip from her tumbler. "And then you took your surgical mask off thirty seconds too soon. Moron."

"Careful, *Lizzy*, or I'll save you for last and make you watch," said Drew.

Only my loved ones are allowed to call me that, you monster.

The tumbler of Everclear was heavy in her hand. Her fingers itched to use it. She tapped her pinky ring three times against the side of the glass.

Come on, Trouble, this is your cue.

"It probably helped that he'd already been injured," said Jenny, twisting around to look at Drew. "And that's a soft part of the skull, isn't it? Do you think it would have worked on his forehead?"

"I don't know, maybe?" said Drew.

"Let's find out."

Jenny pulled something small and brass from her pocket and jabbed it back behind her, nailing Drew right between the eyes.

Crunch!

"Ow! Bitch!" Drew snarled.

He tried to slice with his knife, but Jenny had already spun out of his grasp. Drew stamped his foot, grimacing, and clutched at his forehead.

"Drew, I think we should see other people," said Eliza.

She tossed the Everclear in his face, like any good breakup demanded. He sputtered and coughed, slashing around blindly for them. Jenny brought out Mirai Porter's pistol from her coat and flicked off the safety.

"Are you gonna come peacefully or not, sidekick?" Jenny asked.

"Not," said Drew, blinking at her, his face red with rage. "Those are blanks, remember?"

"Yeah, but they still make a muzzle flash," said Jenny.

She ducked and fired the gun into the carpet in front of Drew.

Bang!

Sparks erupted from the barrel, and the puddle of Everclear in front of Drew whooshed up in flames. In the blink of an eye, the fire raced up Drew's legs and enveloped his face.

Drew roared and dove for the carpet, trying to put it out. It was too grisly; Eliza had to look away. Jenny didn't. She stared at him as he howled in pain and thrashed around.

"Goddamnit, Valentine, just cut me loose next time!" Blake shouted.

Eliza looked back to see that Blake had broken free of his bindings. Deep red marks scored both wrists.

"Pardon me, sweetie," Blake said to Aunt Shelly, and reached under her long skirt.

"Dude," said Eliza.

Blake pulled his hand back—he was holding a little revolver now!

"That idiot didn't even search me," said Shelly with maximum derision.

The screaming had stopped, but Eliza could still hear Drew's loud wheezing. She risked a peek.

Drew's face was a mess of red welts and blackened skin, but the fire was out. At least, on his body, it was. In his thrashing, he'd set the bay window drapes ablaze. That might be a problem.

"I'll come back," Drew said, panting. "No cell can hold me. And right when you least expect it—"

"Hey, Drew!" said Blake. "You forgot something."

"What?" Drew asked.

"I'm canon, too," said Blake.

He raised Shelly's revolver. Drew's cracked lips spread into a feral grin.

"Yeah, but Lockhart never shoots to kill," said Drew.

"I know," said Blake.

Bang!

Bang!

Bang! Bang!

Bang! Bang!

True to his word, Blake fired one round into each of Drew's kneecaps. Another two shots completely blew off Drew's right hand at the wrist, and the final two went straight into Drew's crotch.

"Enjoy prison, dickless," said Blake.

"Blake! Would you fucking untie us?!" Shelly screamed.

"The fire!" shouted Dinah.

Yeah, that fire was a problem. Penny and Tori helped Eliza and Blake untie the others. The fire had reached the ceiling now and was fanning out in all directions. The smoke alarm was shrieking. Jack had to carry Alicia, and it was honestly so romantic to watch.

"Is there a fire extinguisher?" asked Ben from Minutemen Mail.

"Don't bother," said Val, coughing. "It's too big now."

Jenny freed Dinah and ushered her to the door, but didn't follow. Neither did Eliza. Soon, they were alone in the burning study. Only Drew's limp body remained.

"What do you think?" Jenny asked, turning to her. "Perfect time to fake your death. You wouldn't have to be Danger anymore. You could be whoever you wanted."

Eliza couldn't lie. The idea was seductive. No more living in Trouble's shadow. No more gross connection to that son of a bitch RJ Valentine. No more swords and motorcycles. No more Kazu, no more Danger, no more Eliza. She could invent a whole new persona. New hair, new style, new friends…

But what about little Lilah? And Shelly's baby on the way? And Penny and Jack and Alicia?

"It's tempting," said Eliza. "But the only girl I want to be is your sister."

"Awww, thanks!" Jenny smiled. "Sorry about your eye. I guess we're not quite twins anymore."

"Of course we are," said Eliza. She drew the short katana from her back (picked up from the surplus store, but as of yet still nameless) and leveled it at Jenny's face. "Hold still."

"Very funny. I was expecting you to do something cool with that."

Eliza smirked. "I think I discovered I'm more of a cosplayer than a fighter."

A burning bookcase collapsed nearby. Drew groaned at their feet. Jenny put a hand on her hip and fixed Eliza with a very Shelly-esque expression of reproach.

"Do we have to?" Eliza asked.

"It's what Book Trouble would do," said Jenny.

"Fuck the books."

"I know. But it's what I'd do, too. And so would you."

"Fine," said Eliza.

They each got a leg and dragged Drew's mangled ass out of there. Goddamn he weighed a ton. Thank god, Blake returned to help them. They made it to the entrance and down the Tuscany flagstone steps to the roundabout, where a ton of cops and firefighters finally took over.

Then the FBI arrested them both.

Epilogue

About the Author

So, I won the game. Yay. You might think I'd do the noble thing and say I didn't want the money. But I fucking deserve it, don't I?

The bitch of it is… well, I'm getting ahead of myself. Someone at the FBI—Agent Zoey, I just know it!—leaked the last *Trouble* manuscript online. It's been downloaded over 200 million times so far. All the bookstores and libraries pulled the *Trouble* books from the shelves within a week. Tori had been close to securing a TV deal with HBO, too. Not anymore. I inherited a piece of intellectual property so toxic that not even those weird right-wing grifters who make fake movies with Scott Baio will touch it. But at least I inherited the rest of the Valentine fortune again too, right? Happily ever after?

Shelly and Blake got married. City Hall-type deal, Calderon officiated. Blake quit the police to work private security at the Crow's Nest, and Shelly says his blood pressure has gone way down. Baby Lilah is doing well, and she's got a little uncle on the way.

Tori and Darcy haven't set a date yet, but they finally got a dog. A little Scottish terrier named MacBark. He's very cute. Val's the same old cunt as always. Jack is putting off college to run away with Alicia on her book tour, and somehow, that's my fault, according to her. I guess because I made that deal to publish *Hands of Adamant*.

Poor Mirai is soldiering on. She writes me all the time. I guess we both know what it's like to have our hearts ripped out by men we thought we could trust. Blake pulled some strings and got her hired on as the Crow's Nest sommelier. Maybe he's not such a chode after all, but I'm still never calling him dad. I'm never calling anyone dad, ever again.

Penny secured Valedictorian and co-wrote another bombshell story with Yvonne about the whole Stranger affair. HBO optioned *that!* She felt guilty, but I told her not to worry. Get the check, and have fun at Pepperdine.

Am I forgetting anyone? Right, Dinah.

This one hurts. We decided, given the circumstances, it wouldn't be fair to keep things going. She's off to Brown and fancy university life. I hope she doesn't come back with an MRS degree, but that's her business now.

Why break up? Well, see… apparently, Valentine Manor had some faulty sprinkler plumbing. And it was windy that day. The fire spread from the mansion to the grapevines and the patch of oak trees where the treehouse used to be. And then it kept spreading.

Look, gimme a break. Nobody died, and only a few people's homes were destroyed, for which they were compensated handsomely by the Valentine estate! But the fire burned a lot of land north of Blackbird Springs. And some of that land was federal land. What I'm trying to say is, they took the rest of my inheritance to cover the damages and hit me with a federal arson charge. I don't think Tierce and Steele liked me showing them up like that, so they really dropped the hammer. Total bullshit.

Stupid feds and their stupid "protected" "national" "forest." I was able to plead that down, but there was also the whole "attacking a federal agent" thing, too. Technically, that was Eliza, but I wasn't about to let them ruin my sister's life when she was finally free to be herself. I claimed that all the illegal shit was me posing as her, and they couldn't very well prove it wasn't. Twins!

In the end, all Lizzy got was a few months' probation and a shitload of community service. If I know her, she's somewhere in the south of France, eating olives and drinking pinot grigio with Charlie Zaleska—wearing plenty of sunscreen, of course. Good for her, she deserves a break from all my nonsense for a while.

They gave me eight years. It's federal, so I have to serve at least six and a half.

Don't feel too bad for me. I'm at FCI Altamont, only 75 miles away in the East Bay. Talk about Club Fed—they don't even have fences! But you get in trouble if you leave. Heheh. There's a library, and a soccer field, and exciting opportunities in textile manufacturing, like making parachutes for the army.

They even let me work it out with Stanford so I can take classes remotely. It's like college, except with more lesbians, and I have to stay on campus all the time.

Last I heard, Drew is only a few hours away, but in a maximum security joint. No badminton and movie night for him. He's got himself a different kind of Masturbatorium now—and nothing to crank it with, if the rumors are true. I hope he lives a long and painful life with no one watching to appreciate his clever little brain.

The one thing they didn't take from me was *Trouble*. They didn't see any value in it, so I got to keep the book rights and the brand. I thought a lot about making it public domain or selling it for a penny to whoever wanted it or something. But that would just be avoiding the issue.

The truth is, Trouble is a part of me, whether I like it or not. She was given to me by my mother just as much as RJ. I can't pretend I'm someone else. My name is Jenny Valentine. My name is Kohari Onishi. My name is Trouble. I'm all those girls and more. And it's time I started writing my own story.

The End

ACKNOWLEDGEMENTS

I told you it wouldn't take two years! It's done. Jenny Valentine's story is told. The mystery has been solved and the killer revealed (did you guess right?). My horcrux is complete. Trouble is out there in the world now, and nothing can stop her. That's immortality, my darlings.

What started as a way to kill time on a road trip became a project, then a passion, then an all-consuming life's work. I've begun a few other ambitious storytelling endeavors over the years, but this is the first one I saw all the way through to the finish, and it feels great to tie it all up in a bow. I owe a huge thank you to my partner in crime and co-creator Marco for sticking it out with me through moves up and down the state of California, Covid brainstorms outdoors in the cold winter night, and creating Jenny's ex Asha.

Roughly eight years ago we began the process of turning our *Trouble* TV pilot into a novel. We would hole up in a conference room at the local library and draw our own Big Board with dry erase markers, mapping out the general idea of the story. The wine bottle heirloom would be first—something to do with smugglers, because it was always smugglers in the *Hardy Boys* books. Then the noose, which would be connected to a serial killer. Jack's clue would take Trouble to Europe, because we loved the idea of a haunted castle vacation murder mystery. Alicia's skeleton key was always conceived as a joke. A pun. A "red hair-ing." Yvonne's book heirloom was the real clue, and originally, Jenny's own heirloom didn't have any larger mystery connected it. Declan wasn't even an heir, then. He got promoted from his local sleaze bag role when I wanted an extra heirloom to burn for a James Bond-style opening to Book 2.

At some point in that brainstorming session, we took a break, and a moment of intuition struck. I said to Marco, "hey, [REDACTED] is the killer, right?" And he didn't even need to think about, he instantly agreed, like it was always going to be that way, we just hadn't realized it yet. And so, the story grew in the telling. Some 550,000 words, when it was all said an done.

Thank you to Norman Buckley for encouraging us to give our idea a serious shot, to Joseph Dougherty for recommending we write it as a book. To my friend and artist Michael Manuel, who's brought Trouble to life on all five covers, plus the secret sixth one for *Trouble Takes a Holiday pt. 2: Trouble in Paradise*. To Shawn Decker, for providing an art concept and a watercolor version of the cover for *Trouble to the Last Drop*. To our beta readers, Ally and Kayla, who gave us tons of detailed feedback on the early drafts, letting us know where the mystery was hitting, and where it wasn't. To Kaitlin for being RJ Valentine's number one hater, and making us realize we needed to do more with his character. To Alex, for reading the very first pilot script and introducing me to the Alex Drake cocktail. To our first editor Karen Crain, and the wonderful work Lily Omidi of Ello Editorial has done copyediting Books 4 and 5. Lily's editing has immensely improved my writing, I'd highly recommend her to anyone who needs an Editor. To our family and loved ones for supporting us (Hi, Krystal). And most importantly, to all of you, who made it this far, because you had to know how it would all come out.

This is the end of Jenny Valentine's heirloom mystery series. But is it the end of Trouble? Who can say. With good behavior, she'll be out in 2027. The next thing I write will definitely not be a *Trouble* book, but there's always the chance of a new mystery down the line. There are, after all, so many good *Trouble* titles we never got to use. And we never did time travel! Until then, it's been a pleasure. Happy sleuthing, troublemakers.

ABOUT THE AUTHORS

James Taylor is a writer, podcaster, and retired video game player. He's written five Trouble novels and is hard at work on something new that won't star your favorite Girl Detective. When he's not writing or wasting time on the internet, he enjoys reading speculative fiction and cheesy YA novels, perfecting the perfect Top Ramen meal, hiking with his girlfriend, and playing with his cat Trudy Campbell. James holds many strong opinions about adapting beloved genre fiction to the screen, and dreams of one day writing a Star War. He lives in the Golden State.

Marco Sparks is a writer living in California. He's suspiciously tall. His fiction and non-fiction can be found in various dark corners of the internet. He is the co-host of several podcasts, particularly focused on teen murder shows. Also, he has the kind of cats where, when he suddenly ends up dead, no matter how much it looks like it was an accident, they were behind it.